# OF HUMAN MISERY

# OF HUMAN MISERY

Tammy Andrews

| Library of Congress Number: | | 2005910678 |
| --- | --- | --- |
| ISBN 10: | Hardcover | 1-4257-0445-X |
| | Softcover | 1-4257-0444-1 |
| | | |
| ISBN 13: | Hardcover | 978-1-4257-0445-2 |
| | Softcover | 978-1-4257-0444-5 |

This book was printed in the United States of America.

**To order additional copies of this book, contact:**
Xlibris Corporation
1-888-795-4274
www.Xlibris.com
Orders@Xlibris.com
30941

# Accreditation

When I was a student in junior high school, my teacher, Mrs. Cosey introduced us to a poem that greatly influenced my life. It still is one of my favorite pieces of poetic work and I have chosen to use certain phrases within as titles for my books.

I hope you enjoy!
Tammy Andrews

# DOVER BEACH

*The sea is calm tonight.*
*The tide is full, the moon lies fair.*

Upon the straits-on the French coast the light
Gleams and is gone; *the cliffs of England* stand,
Glimmering and vast, out in the tranquil bay.
Come to the window, sweet is the night air!
Only, from the long line of spray
Where the sea meets the moon-blanched land,
Listen! You can hear the grating roar
Of pebbles which the waves draw back, and fling,
At their return, up the high strand,
Begin, and cease, and then again begin,
The eternal note of sadness in.

Sophocles long ago
Heard it on the Aegean, and brought
Into his mind the turbid ebb and flow
*Of Human Misery,* we
Find also in the sound a thought,
Hearing it by this distant northern sea.

*The Sea of Faith*
Was once, too, at the full, and round earth's shore
Lay like the folds of a bright girdle furled.
But now I only hear
Its melancholy, long, withdrawing roar,
Retreating, to the breath
*Of the night wind,* down the vast edges drear
And naked shingles of the world.

Ah, *love let us be true,*
To one another! For the world, which seems
To lie before us like a *land of dreams,*
So various, so beautiful, so new,
Hath really neither joy, nor love, nor light,
Nor certitude, nor peace, nor help for pain;
And we are here as on a darkling plain
Swept with confused alarms of struggle and flight,
Where ignorant armies clash by night.

# PROLOGUE

Erich Shandon stood naked in the steamy shower as hot bullets of water beat angrily into his chest. Maybe, he thought, if he stood there long enough, they would wash away the pain that lingered there. The past twelve years had been wonderful, hadn't they? Sure, there had been climaxes and pitfalls; however, they were the most vibrant and fulfilling years of his life. He was married to the most exciting and beautiful woman he had ever encountered—and there had been many. There was nothing at which she couldn't succeed—world-famous model, actress, musician, best-selling author, mother, and wife. She was everything any man could have wanted, yet he had driven her away.

She always posed a challenge to him. For the most part, she drove him to madness, yet at times, he found he could make love to her endlessly. Shanna was that kind of woman. She was headstrong, confident, intelligent, ambitious, gentle, beautiful, vulnerable, passionate, and, most of all, sensual. The list of adjectives could go on and on—all so contradicting but true. So how could this day have come, the day when the woman of his dreams would marry another man?

Erich turned to let the hot water droplets beat into the back of his head, washing away the remaining shampoo, wishing it would also rinse away all images of her. Unfortunately, he knew that was impossible, for she was too much a part of his soul, his heart, his body, and his mind to ever obliterate her from his memory.

Reaching down, he turned off the marbled faucets while feeling blindly for a thick warmed towel left by his maid. Stepping out of the shower, his foot met one of the miniature oval Oriental rugs adorning the cool tile of his bath as he wrapped the towel around his waist. *Only a Shandon,* she had always said, *would have rugs of this expense in their bathroom to be dripped upon several times a day.* Erich shook his head in frustration. He had to get her out of his mind. *Of course,* she would always continue, *only a Shandon can do a lot of things that the average person could ever dream of doing in ten lifetimes.* He gave up. She would forever haunt his thoughts, and trying to forget her was useless. The image of her would never leave him.

Shedding his towel, Erich wrapped himself warmly in his Lauren robe and padded lightly into his magnificent bedroom suite overlooking the twinkling lights of New York City. Pouring a stiff drink from the crystal bar set, also left by his attentive maid, he placed a classical CD into the stereo and settled back into the enveloping

pillows on his bed. Again, the remembrance of many years of pleasure he had shared with her in this room drifted through his mind.

Tonight, he was alone for the first time in many nights, purposely ignoring phone calls from his current mistress. In retrospect, Erich began to reflect over his life with the only woman he had ever loved—his former wife, Shanna Somers.

# CHAPTER 1

Shannan Masterson loved life as a teenager. Her days were filled with school, the drama team, cheerleading practice, and her dogs. She had a passion for living and experienced each day to the fullest. Rising at 5:00 a.m., Shannan would go for a morning run with her two wolfhounds and then have a full day at school. She arrived home late in the afternoons and took a quick swim or a workout in the family's gym. Her evenings were normally spent with her two half brothers, Tony and Todd, while their parents attended the society functions that had become their ultimate addiction.

The siblings existed in a difficult and dysfunctional upbringing in that they rarely saw their mother and father and, when they did, were subject to public scrutiny. Tony, Todd, and Shannan had become used to living with overly ambitious parents, who were so completely self-absorbed with success in their own lives, that their children were often brushed aside and usually forgotten.

Only in instances where the image of a "well-rounded family" fit into the overall picture of advancement that the parents envisioned for themselves were their children brought into the circle of events. Tony, Todd, and Shannan were always called upon to appear on the annual Masterson family Christmas card or to pose for any corporate or political brochures that would enhance their father's campaign for success. The siblings' only salvation was themselves. Their love for one another made up for the lack of encouragement and acknowledgment they received from their parents. Tony, the older of the two sons from his father's first marriage, was very sheltering over his brother and half sister. He felt especially protective of Shannan, for she was so fragile in his eyes and completely unaware of the dilemmas that awaited her.

Tony cared deeply for his brother as well. Todd, however, kept mostly to himself, engrossed in his artwork and music. He often secluded himself inside his room with his paintings while heavy metal music blared from inside. Todd skipped school regularly, drank excessively, and, as Tony suspected, had already began using drugs. Marijuana had been a mainstay in Todd's life for several years, and now his brother feared that harder substances had begun to take over. Tony and Shannan eagerly encouraged Todd to enter his paintings in local art shows. They even went so far as to submit his work without his consent, but Todd was always too drunk, high, or hungover to attend any functions. Eventually, they gave up and let their brother create his masterpieces in the inner sanctum of his own personal hell.

As expected, Todd's behavior and actions did not please his parents or his father's law partners and political advisors. He was frequently in trouble with the police, and his continuing lack of interest in school left them doubting he would ever attend college. They were correct in their guess, for Todd had no intention of continuing his education and held little interest in even finishing high school. He was nothing like his brother. Tony had already been accepted to Vanderbilt University Law School and would start in the fall, following in his father's footsteps of pursuing a legal career.

*Shannan would most likely enter into the world of fashion design or a similar field,* Tony often thought. She was passionate about style and had been designing patterns and creating outfits at the early age of thirteen. Tony frequently teased his sister about the numerous scarves, shoes, belts, and designer fabrics scattered about her huge bedroom. She longed to be a model and undeniably fit the role. Everywhere Shannan Masterson went, she captivated the immediate attention of all that saw her. Jackie Masterson was well aware of the attention her daughter received, and she inwardly seethed with jealousy over Shannan's beauty. Whether they were together shopping or at a fashion event, Jackie was always conscious of the numerous stares and compliments that Shannan received. It was not fair, Jackie thought, fate had dealt her too many cruel blows.

Life had been tough for Jackie Somers until she met and married Jackson Masterson, a successful attorney with a prominent law firm in Nashville, Tennessee. Since their marriage, she had pushed him to seek the higher recognition she felt he could gain by running for public office. *Jackson was the perfect candidate for political limelight,* Jackie thought. He was a handsome tall man with a muscular build, striking features, and a charismatic personality. Jack had competed in local elections and had only been narrowly defeated, so his ambitions of seeking public office were highly probable. Jackie made a solemn vow to herself that she would not rest until her husband achieved the political success he so deserved.

Jackie Masterson had always been ambitious, and she loved reaping the rewards that came with being the wife of a prominent and successful attorney. Being a socialite suited her perfectly. She became a member of the Nashville Women's Club and the Cheekwood Garden Club and a volunteer for the symphony, the ballet, and the opera. She lunched frequently with her friends—Tootie Billingsly, Lura Tallingsworth, and Bebe Cheek. Jackie was elated that she had finally been accepted by the upper crust of society. She had finally made it. These were the happiest times of her life.

# CHAPTER 2

Born into a middle-class family in San Francisco, Jackie had always dreamed of living the life of a well-to-do woman. Her father, William Somers, had worked as a loan officer for California National for over thirty years until he died of a heart attack during her junior year of high school. Jackie's mother, Elizabeth, took a secretarial position with the electric company after his death to support their daughters, Jackie and Sabrina. Their father's pension and insurance benefits didn't adequately cover the numerous debts the family had incurred; his wife had been forced to get a job. Elizabeth died of cancer four years after the death of William, leaving the two sisters to fend for themselves with no inheritance to ease their plight. Hungry, eager creditors quickly consumed everything their parents had worked for over the years to bring their financial affairs current.

Sabrina set out immediately in search of a new life. She changed her name to Sable, a name she had once heard belonged to a very famous exotic dancer. Sable immediately acquired a job at the Bay Racquet Club as a cocktail waitress. The tips were meager, but her acquaintances were many. Within a year, she met and married the successful Canadian businessman, Markus Chandler, who was in San Francisco conducting business. He was a multimillionaire and extremely handsome. In his midfifties with silver hair, a dark complexion, and lean frame, Markus Chandler was the most striking and distinguished man Sable had ever seen. He was instantly charmed by Sable's soft, sexy ways and fell blindly in love with her the moment she sidled over to his table and crooned in a much-practiced British accent, "May I offer you something?" In time, she mastered the accent and claimed it as her own to forget the past.

After Markus divorced his wife of twenty-seven years, he eloped with Sable to the Caribbean. They honeymooned there for three weeks before returning to the sprawling Chandler estate in Montreal. They vacationed at their summer cottage in Nova Scotia and spent cozy winter days on Copper Island, off the coast of Victoria. Markus loved his island and the seclusion it offered. The newlyweds spent many chilly days curled up in front of one of the many welcoming fireplaces throughout the ancient castle. Jerome, the butler and overseer of the remarkable estate, had been with the Chandler family since Markus was a small boy and regarded him as a son. He liked the new Mrs. Chandler; she was young, pretty, and treated him as a family member rather than as a servant. Markus absolutely adored his new bride. He loved her well-rounded figure and never grew tired of her eagerness in bed. She

aroused passionate fires in him that he thought had forever been extinguished. During his boring long marriage to Lillian, he had yearned for the sexual excitement he found in Sable. Markus was so grateful to God for bringing her into his life. The endless high-priced call girls he had sought out during the past years of unhappiness had only provided loneliness and emptiness. He had prayed for an escape, and now it was his turn to reap the happiness he so deserved.

Markus loved the way Sable draped her full ample breasts over his face, inviting him to suckle and kiss each one, showing no favoritism with his warm tongue. He could barely keep from exploding when she caressed his entire body with her long fingers. She loved stroking him gently as she sang, "I've got a crush on you, sweetie pie." Sitting atop of him, she would kiss her husband hungrily while plunging him inside of her. Rapid spurts of ecstasy would flood through her body, leaving both of them breathless until Sable would eventually collapse on his moist chest. Nothing she did failed to amaze him. For many reasons, Markus loved her dearly, but nothing made him happier than the day she delighted him by announcing that he would again be a father at fifty-seven years of age.

Copper Island was Sable's favorite of all the places she and her husband owned or visited. It was her island paradise. She made a vow that she would someday retire there and live out her final days.

She loved staring out into the restless sea and hanging fog, feeling the cold mist on her face and listening to the distant sound of foghorns and answering ships.

She also insisted that this was where she wanted to have their baby despite Markus's vehement objections. He feared that complications would arise, and the nearest doctor was miles away on mainland Victoria. Sable was insistent, however, and assured him that there was little to worry about. Women had babies every day, and at twenty-two years old, she was in excellent health. She finally relented and allowed Markus to hire a nurse to move in with them, but she was determined to have her baby at the castle.

Sable had an easy pregnancy, just as she had predicted. Markus was the typical nervous father-to-be and pampered her constantly. He rubbed her feet in the evenings in front of the fire, spread warm oil over her body, ran hot bubble baths for her, and ordered the chef to prepare his young wife anything she desired. He enjoyed walking along the shore with her in the evenings, watching the sun sink into the distant horizon.

After their strolls, they would sneak away to their enormous bed where they giggled and fondled like two teenagers. Markus made love to her gently and delighted in the fact that she was still so interested in sex. In the latter months of her pregnancy, he entered her from behind so as not to hurt the baby. This seemed to satisfy Sable all the more. After their lovemaking, he would rub her enlarged belly softly and caress her swollen breasts until she drifted off to sleep.

Finally, in the spring, Sable gave birth to a seven-pound daughter during a simple delivery. They named her Catherine Geneva Chandler after Markus's two

grandmothers. She was a beautiful baby with fat cheeks and copper-colored hair, which Sable thought fitting, considering the name of the island.

Markus's other daughter, Channel, lived in Toronto with her boyfriend and near her mother. She had never been close with her father, especially since Markus had divorced Lillian to marry Sable. Thus, Markus vowed to start right from the beginning to create a loving and lasting relationship with his new baby daughter.

Catherine grew quickly and delighted Sable with everything she did. Markus eventually resumed his business travel but thought of his young wife and new daughter constantly. He phoned them every day on the island, except when violent storms wrecked the telephone lines making calls impossible.

Sable was content on stormy days to play with her young daughter and converse with Jerome on the history of the Castle of Copper Island. These were the happiest times of her life.

# CHAPTER 3

Jackie was insanely envious of her sister's good fortune. *How could Sabrina be so damn lucky?* she muttered one night as she shoved a frozen dinner into her filthy microwave. She looked around miserably at her dingy one-room apartment located in the low-rent district of San Francisco, trying to forget the horrible ten-hour day that she had spent at the drugstore. Jackie worked as a salesclerk and hated every waking minute of it. She had always played second fiddle to her sister and sulked about the bad luck that had been dealt her way again.

Jackie simply could not believe all the good fortune that life had heaped into Sabrina's lap. *A rich husband, many new houses, and now a new baby,* she sneered as she lit a cigarette. *It makes me want to fucking puke,* she moaned as she exhaled. *I'll have it someday,* she said aloud as the high-pitched beep of the microwave sounded, reminding her of the contents inside. She sat cross-legged on her shabby bed, poking halfheartedly at her food and viewing the squalor of her tiny place sighing, *Someday, someday.*

The next morning, Jackie telephoned in sick to the drugstore, saying she had some sort of flu or virus. She wasn't lying entirely, for she truly felt utterly miserable when she thought of the recent events that had occurred in her life. Thinking of her sister's lifestyle and then comparing it to her own rotten existence made her physically ill. She finally managed to pull herself out of bed and stumble to her drab kitchen to make a pot of coffee. Knocking empty beer cans off the counter into the garbage pail below, she lit a cigarette and waited for the coffee to brew.

Suddenly, there was a knock at her door. "Yeah, who is it?" Jackie yelled between puffs.

"It's me, Miss Somers, your neighbor Ernie" came the wimpy reply from behind the door.

*Good God,* Jackie hissed, *that quirky little bastard hasn't stopped bothering me since the day I moved in. Why the devil doesn't he get a job or go jack off or something and leave me the hell alone?* "Yeah, what is it, Ernie?" she yelled from her kitchen.

"I . . . uh . . . well, I sort of got an extra newspaper this morning at my door, ma'am, and I thought you would like to have it," Ernie squeaked.

Jackie meandered toward her door and opened it slightly. Ernie eagerly tried to peek around to see if she was wearing the cheap pink negligee with feathers that he had seen her wear one day in the hall as she clicked her way to the garbage shoot in her stiletto heels. She stopped him before he got too far and said, "Just give me the goddamned paper and get lost, Ernie. I'm in no mood to deal with your shit today."

"Okay, okay, Ms. Somers," he giggled. "But someday, maybe . . . uh . . . me and you can . . . uh . . . get together sometime . . . uh . . . maybe?"

"When hell freezes over, you little prick!" she screamed while slamming the door in his face with the kick of a fluffy pink house shoe.

Jackie poured a steaming cup of coffee and lit another cigarette as she settled down on her bed and sifted through the *San Francisco Chronicle.* With her long days at the drugstore, it had been quite awhile since she had found time to look at a morning paper. She fumbled through the pages until she located the Classified Section and then began to scan fervently for a better means of support. She scoured through every ad until her eyes rested on an ad for a position that sounded extremely intriguing.

A firm in Dallas, Texas, was seeking a qualified secretary/receptionist and offered a salary way above what she was used to making at the drugstore. Jackie had always dreamed of meeting a handsome rich Texan, and she also wanted desperately to leave the dreary, foggy, and damp climate of San Francisco. The dry air of the nation's largest state seemed most inviting. No more drizzle for Jackie Somers, she decided to set her sights for the vastness and warmth of the Lone Star State.

Jackie telephoned the Dallas firm of Doyle Engineering and informed them of her secretarial abilities. She and Sabrina had both excelled at typing in high school, and she felt confident in her skills.

Jackie had also often helped her father with his accounting transactions when he brought home ledgers from his office. She informed the phone interviewer that she was coming to work for them without a shadow of a doubt and that she was certain she could handle the position. They were impressed with Jackie's determination and confidence. She was a young woman from California who was willing to relocate; at least they owed her a chance.

Jackie arrived in Dallas two days later after scraping together every last cent she could.

Gathering her belongings into some semblance of order and throwing them into a battered old suitcase, she boarded Continental Airlines, stopped over in Denver, then flew directly into Dallas Fort Worth International Airport. She left the terminal, hailed a cab, and headed directly for the high-rise office building in downtown Dallas, where her interview was to take place.

She was two hours early, but the company was impressed yet again at her persistence and hired her on the spot. The director of Human Resources, Helen Hayes, was somewhat concerned about Jackie's taste in attire; however, with a little discipline, coaching, and an increase in salary, hopefully her appearance would change. Doyle was a conservative firm, and Jackie was far from conservative. However, the interviewers saw potential and liked her spunk; thus, her new career had begun.

Realizing her financial situation, Doyle advanced Jackie her first month's salary, so she rented an efficiency apartment in the heart of downtown Dallas, ten blocks from her office. Although not in the greatest of neighborhoods, her new abode was

better by far than where she had lived in California. The tiny apartment seemed safe enough. It was clean, and she did not plan to stay there forever. *All I need to do is snag a rich oilman, and things will change for me,* she muttered one day while on her way to work. *I am not that choosy,* she thought, *as long as he is well hung and worth a few million bucks.*

Jackie worked diligently for Doyle; she was determined to succeed at something in her life. Even though she was still sickened with envy over Sabrina's good fortune, Jackie dropped a note of congratulations in the mail about the baby, but that was the last contact she made with her sister. She had never acknowledged Sable's new name or her new fortune, for that was the lifestyle Jackie wanted for herself. It was a dream she would never give up on, no matter how long it took to achieve.

Jackie made a few futile attempts at impressing the elderly Mr. Doyle Sr. by showing an occasional leg or extra cleavage as he stumbled past her daily on his way out of the building. But much to her chagrin, he never seemed to notice. *Now that's what I need,* she had mumbled miserably one day. *Some old fart who's too old to fuck. I could keep some sweet young thing on the side and still enjoy all the old bastard's millions.* She smirked to herself.

Jackie progressed well in her job and soon was promoted to an administrative assistant position working for one of the senior partners. She liked her job and the people she worked with. They stayed out of her way and she out of theirs. She worked hard, arrived on time, took only the permitted hour for lunch, and left promptly at the end of the day.

One Friday afternoon, Jackie left her office feeling content and optimistic about the weekend.

She had longed for some time when she could muster the energy to become more settled in her apartment.

Not planning to leave her place for the entire weekend, she stopped by the local market to get a few groceries and some wine. As she entered the store, a man in a blue pin-striped suit mowed her down as he tried to conceal his newly purchased cigarettes in his coat pocket.

"Good god!" Jackie yelled as she stumbled backward. The man grabbed for her, but it was too late. She had already fallen back against the building, running her black seamed hose and ripping her tight black skirt. "You fucking clumsy oaf!" Jackie screamed.

"I'm so sorry, miss. Are you all right?" the gentleman asked nervously.

Jackie eyed him meanly as he helped her get steady on her feet. "I wasn't watching where I was going," he said apologetically.

She glared at him and finally said, "Yea, I'm all right, I guess, just shaken up a little."

He continued holding her arm to make sure she wasn't hurt and noticed that her clothes and stockings were torn. "You tore my outfit, you jerk!" she accused.

The gentleman looked at her helplessly and replied, "I am deeply sorry, miss, and I will be glad to pay for any damage I may have caused in my haste."

Jackie continued to brush herself off as he watched her.

She was rather tacky, but she had an undeniable sex appeal, and she might prove to be fun.

"Listen, miss, let me make this up to you." The stranger handed Jackie his card and gave her the name of the hotel where he was staying. "I'll be finished with my business meeting around eight o'clock, and I'd love to take you out for dinner to make up for my bad first impression and possibly get to know you better."

Jackie looked him over carefully. He was very striking, and she thought he looked prosperous and nice enough, so she replied, "Fine, here's my number. Call me when you're finished with your meeting; I'd love to meet later." After all, he looked like a classy guy, and what the hell, she did not have anything else to do. They said good-bye, and Jackie decided to finish her grocery shopping after her chance meeting with the handsome businessman. She purchased fresh Italian bread, pasta, seasonings, and sauces, just in case her mystery man never called.

Her small apartment, although not as dreary as her place in San Francisco, awaited her in near darkness as she entered through the shadowed hallway into its interior. She had barely set her groceries on the kitchen counter when the telephone began to ring. She leapt to answer it as the last bag broke and its contents spilled onto her dingy yellow floor. *Fuck,* she muttered then, "Hello?"

"Hi there, it's your man from the grocery," he said. "I left my meeting early because I couldn't stop thinking about you. Would you like to meet me for dinner at Cafe Royal in an hour?" he pleaded. "I'll send the firm's limousine for you."

Jackie couldn't resist the idea of riding in a limo, so she eagerly blurted out her address and told him she would wait for the car at the entrance to her apartment building. She hurriedly yanked off her torn skirt and stockings, then ran through her small dwelling, pulling her blouse over her head without stopping to unbutton it. While her tub filled with rust-colored water, she gathered her hair into a haphazard heap on top of her head and emptied cheap bath oil into the running water. At last, Jackie plopped down into the sudsy brown water and washed with one hand while polishing her toenails scarlet with the other.

After her bath, she rushed to her closet, selected a hot pink knit dress, and wiggled into it. Her hands were shaking so that she was barely able to fasten the garters onto her black fishnet stockings. She finished applying another coat of makeup, crammed her feet into a pair of hot pink pumps, grabbed her coat, and rushed out her door, clicking down the narrow steps to the lobby.

The company car arrived precisely at 7:00 p.m. with Jackson waiting eagerly in the backseat.

They spent the evening drinking, dining, and dancing—three activities that Jackie was most proficient in.

Jack couldn't take his eyes off her. She was the cheapest woman he had ever been out with, yet she was as smooth as Southern Comfort over ice. *Yes, she definitely has potential,* he whispered as he watched her breeze through the dining room of the

restaurant returning from the ladies' room. Before the evening was over, Jack had fallen for Jackie and decided to invite her to return to Nashville with him.

She cared for him too, but mostly, she loved his wealth and the advance in social status he offered. They went to his hotel room after dinner and enjoyed an evening of pure passion. Jackie was insatiable, and Jackson was more than willing to satisfy her desires. They made love with wild abandon, both meeting each other's needs, until at last they collapsed in utter exhaustion as the first light of day peeked through the blinds.

Jackie awoke later that morning with a splitting headache, finding herself alone in bed. She heard the sound of running water and realized that Jackson was in the shower. He emerged soon with tiny beads of water still lingering on the hairs of his chest. He bent over and kissed her hungrily and informed her that their breakfast would be arriving via room service shortly. Jack cancelled his meetings, so they spent a leisurely morning in bed, eating and making love until they were both too weak to go on.

They were engaged within three months and planned to marry soon. Jackie was delighted to learn that Jackson was a successful attorney in Nashville, and she looked forward to being his wife. She resigned from Doyle Engineering, cleared out her belongings from her apartment, and flew to Tennessee with her fiancé. They were married at the Cheekwood Mansion with only a few of Jackson's legal partners and their wives in attendance. Jackie wore an ice pink-tailored suit that Jackson had picked out for her. It was simple yet more elegant than anything she had ever owned in her life, and certainly the most expensive.

The reception was held at Richland Country Club, and it was the most exciting day in Jackie's life. She was center stage at last and felt as if she would burst with happiness. After their wedding, the couple flew to Hawaii where they honeymooned for two weeks. Later, they returned to their new home in Music City and resided in the prominent Franklin Road District, the same neighborhood as the governor.

For the first time in her life, Jackie Somers Masterson believed that she had finally reached the top.

# CHAPTER 4

Shannan was comfortable and happy living her young years in prestigious surroundings. She thrived on the opportunities that were provided to her, naive to the undertones of her family environment.

Shannan Masterson had more opportunities provided to her on a daily basis than any other teenager in the city or country perhaps. Her life orbited around constant school activities, dog shows, and spending time with her two brothers. The siblings spent most evenings together, except when Todd chose to go out with friends to party or when Tony had to practice with his local rock band. But most nights, Shannan spent time with her older brother Tony, whom she adored. They would stay up late doing her homework and watching late-night television.

One evening, Tony and Shannan lay together on the sofa as they so often did after completing her term paper. They snuggled side by side watching Letterman covered by a quilt as the snow fell outside in the January night. Their parents were attending a society function as usual while Todd was out drinking and would probably not return home until the early hours of the morning.

Tony realized that Shannan should have been in bed by now, but he loved spending these special moments with her when he could have her totally to himself. He loved watching and feeling her lying beside him. She was dozing, exhausted as usual from her daily hectic schedule of school, cheerleading practice, horses, and dogs. It amazed him that she maintained an excellent grade point average with so many other activities in her young life. Tony marveled at her eagerness every morning when he drove her to school if Todd was too lazy or more likely too hungover to attend classes.

At fifteen, Shannan was the most beautiful girl Tony had ever seen. At age nineteen, he was at his sexual peak and was well aware that other guys were as well. Therefore, he kept a close watch on his beautiful half sister, trying to offer her the protection that he always had. For many years, it was Tony who rushed to her bedside in the middle of the night to shush her childhood screams when nightmares invaded her sleep. He was always there for her, the only person who had ever truly loved and cared for her.

As she moved slightly beside him now on the sofa, he watched her intently as she barely glanced at the show they were watching infrequently to smile at a funny comment or joke; then she would close here eyes again to snooze peacefully. Tony could feel the soft silk of her nightshirt next to his bare chest and began to stroke

Shannan muttered his name breathlessly, somewhat fearful, as he stopped momentarily and asked her, "Sweetheart, do you understand about sex?"

She replied slowly, "I think so."

He smiled gently, for he wouldn't hurt her for anything in the world, and said, "Baby, I want to take you to your room now and show you what love is all about. Do you understand that, honey?"

She whispered, "I love you, Tony, and I know you would never hurt me. I want you to teach me many things, especially this," as she kissed him on the cheek.

Tony clicked off the TV by remote, carefully picked her up, and maneuvered through the darkness upstairs to Shannan's room. He laid her on the bed and pulled back the covers. She quickly scurried under them waiting for him to join her. They had slept together many times in the past, especially when she was a child and would awake from a bad dream crying. It was always her brother who would come running instead of her parents.

Tony turned off the lights in the bedroom and bath then came to join her in bed. He quickly stripped out of his jeans and climbed in slowly beside her. Tonight would be different from any other night. Tony remembered the many times when he had held her while she lay screaming at the demons that haunted her during sleep. She had been so childlike then, so vulnerable, yet now she was a beautiful seductress with a woman's body but still so innocent. He shook his head to clear it.

Tony looked down at her. She penetrated his stare as he looked into her dark eyes; then bending down, he kissed her. Gently at first, as he wanted anything but to frighten her. She accepted his kiss and his tongue willingly and hungrily. Tony feverishly pulled the silk nightshirt from her and slipped her panties down her long shapely legs. She hesitated somewhat, but he calmed her by nuzzling in her ear, "It's all right, sweetheart." She relaxed and let him proceed.

Tony moved his right hand down again between her legs as his left hand held her head steady so his mouth could have easy access to hers. She caught her breath again as his fingers started to move in mysterious places. This time, she grew wet that prompted him to instinctively begin probing inside her as his palm moistened. Tony was ever so gentle as he penetrated her tightness with his fingers. Shannan hesitated at first but eventually became used to the foreign feeling. As she became wetter, he moved his hardness against her as she moaned deeply. It was now or never, he thought, although he hated like hell to hurt her. She lay poised and ready, wetter than she ever would be. Now was the time. But could he do it? Tony shuddered now. Fucking one's sister was serious business; however, not everyone had a sister like this.

With his mind made up and with no last delay of the main event, Tony moved downward, lowered his head between her legs, and allowed his tongue to perform as his fingers had done seconds before. Shannan lost control. She started moaning and begging him "please" over and over when at last he could stand it no longer. Rising, he positioned himself over her. She lay below him not really knowing what to

expect as he began to enter her. He moved slowly at first, feeling the resistance of her virginity. He dreaded causing her pain, but she would experience it sooner or later, and he would be far gentler than any of the guys she would eventually encounter.

Tony tried to prepare his sister for the discomfort she would soon feel; however, she was much too worked up to listen to him. He finally kissed her ear, then her cheek, and decided to proceed with the inevitable. He held her wrists above her head and positioned his mouth above hers to squelch a scream. Finally, he plunged deep in one thrust while covering her mouth with his as she tried to cry out in pain. He watched as tears poured from her eyes while continuing to keep his mouth upon hers. He kept moving his lower body to somewhat ease the pain she felt, and eventually, her body joined with his in a rhythmic movement. Tony continued to speak to her in soft tones as he made love to her very gently, eagerly, and deeply. He was determined not to scare her the first time by being too rough, yet he was persistent in making her feel pleasure.

Shannan met Tony's thrusts with enthusiasm after the initial pain, for she had never felt so loved or complete in her life. She did not know what was taking place within her body, yet she knew it felt sublime, and she trusted her brother completely. As they kept moving together, Shannan began to feel a tingling between her legs like nothing she had ever experienced before. Tony sensed the beginnings of an orgasm too and pounded ever harder. Suddenly, an explosion of sensations with indescribable measures blew up and moved rapidly through Shannan's body touching her very soul with ecstasy. She couldn't believe this exquisite sensation and felt as though she had elapsed into another world, a sort of transcendental state. Tony, so moved by her reverberating climax, soon followed and, with a loud groan of pleasure, collapsed and lay in a sweaty heap on top of her.

They made love again, several hours later, while Shannan was still half asleep. Tony had never really slept, just drifted in and out of a dreamy consciousness. Neither of them were aware that their brother Todd had stumbled in just before dawn and looked in on them while they embraced each other in their nakedness and innocence. Saying nothing, Todd closed Shannan's door and retreated to his own room. Before sunrise, Tony rose in silence, tugged on his jeans from beside the bed, then stood looking at the sleeping beauty in front of him. God, how he loved her. He bent down, kissed her on the cheek, then turned to leave. Turning back to look at her once more made him wonder if he had done the right thing before sneaking silently back to his room.

# CHAPTER 5

For the next few weeks, Tony and Shannan enjoyed their afternoons together. When she arrived home after school, Tony would join her in her room and make love to her. Feelings of misgivings began to invade his conscious about the illicit affair he was engaging in with his half sister. Yet his infatuation with her overcame his mental taunting to the extent he couldn't resist her. She trusted him so completely and was so much a part of him that he buried the guilt that was killing him inwardly.

When Shannan's birthday arrived in March, her father was out of town as usual, which meant her brothers and mother would be the ones to wish her happiness on such a special day. They took her to Mario's Italian Ristorante where they all enjoyed a dinner of steaks, lobster, and desserts accompanied by plenty of wine and afterdinner drinks.

Later, the group assembled together in the library of their home for more liqueurs, gathered around a warm, inviting fire to honor their princess with her birthday gifts. Tony gave her a diamond bracelet, which Jackie thought a bit extravagant. Todd presented her a portrait of herself that touched her deeply; her mother handed her a little box that contained the keys to a BMW convertible that she would receive after passing her driver's test. Jack called from Chicago with birthday greetings wishing his daughter well and a pleasant good night. He did not know when he would be returning to Nashville; however, he promised to take her out on the town, just the two of them when he came home.

As the evening began to expire, Todd announced that he had plans and needed to be on his way.

Kissing his sister good night, he drew back briefly with his hand still on her cheek, looked deeply into her eyes, but said nothing. Turning, he grabbed his leather jacket from a chair and disappeared down the marbled hall and out the front door. Jackie stated that she was retiring to her room with a massive headache.

Her children knew that she was actually retreating to the private bar in her room to down her pharmaceutical collection of pills with a shot of vodka, which was a staple at her bedside. They bid her an unenthusiastic good night and watched her stumble up the stairs to her room. Tony and Shannan found themselves alone by the fire in the library. Tony rose to go refill their drinks, but this time he replaced Shannan's wine with brandy and brought it back to her as she stretched lazily in front of the comforting fire.

While Tony stood watching her, he realized that this had been a happy night for his sister. One's sixteenth birthday was special, and Shannan had enjoyed a wonderful night with her family. She had even tolerated her mother for an evening, despite Jackie's endless comments about not looking much older than sixteen herself, while downing several martinis. Tony felt very drawn to Shannan now as she lay in the fire's glow, her skin almost luminescent, and her body more inviting than ever. She was a woman now, and he was addicted to her more than ever, as she was to him.

He knelt down and began to caress her, stroking her hair, face, and then moving his hands up and down her body. He pulled her cashmere sweater over her head and examined her excited nipples under a silk bra. His mouth moved downward, stopping to place light kisses along her ribs and stomach as she arched her back in pleasure.

He looked up at her then and thought how utterly beautiful she was and how genuine his love was for her. He unbuttoned her skirt and slid it down along with her panties as his mouth found a resting place between her legs and his tongue began its usual journey within the folds of her moistness. She began to moan as Tony removed his clothing without missing a movement. Shannan responded eagerly for they were both feeling the effects of the alcohol, and it fueled them beyond the limits of their passion.

Tony continued fondling her as she wriggled under him in anticipation, holding on to his muscular arms and whispering softly in his ear. He held her down on the floor in front of him as he looked into her eyes and caressed her face. His hands moved over every inch of her as she writhed in anxious desire awaiting his entrance. He licked her breasts then ran his fingers through the dark curls between her legs while his fingers performed an inspection inside of her again. She was crazy for him now, and he knew she could not wait another second.

He entered her quickly, sharply, causing her to gasp, then plunged heavily into her. This scared her a little, but she guessed it must have been the alcohol that provoked a more aggressive entrance. She was right, of course, for as he plunged heavily into her, she clawed desperately at his defined back leaving a trail of red marks. They made love for another hour, giving to each other wholly and desperately, until they both finally collapsed in complete exhaustion.

Tony nuzzled Shannan's ear in the dwindling firelight, and she smiled sleepily. She's so sweet, he thought, and he dreaded like hell breaking the news to her that he would be leaving soon for a nine-month tour of Europe. His band had been invited to play in London, Paris, Berlin, and Amsterdam. He would have to postpone continuing college until next year, and he hated delivering that news to his parents. Shannan would be lost without him, but it was imperative that she start her junior year in the fall. He still had a couple of months, however, to drop the news on them all.

Tony was going to have a serious discussion with his brother and force him to clean up his act to be there for their sister during the upcoming months. As a steady

pouring of sleet pelted against the library window, they lay together into the night cuddling by the fading glow of the fire, looking at each other lovingly, and realizing they should each be retreating to their respective bedrooms very soon.

Jackie had never achieved the peace of sleep that night since retiring to her bedroom. In her restlessness, she pulled back her bedcovers, slipped into a silk robe, and drifted down the stairs in search of more vodka and ice. She stopped as she approached the top of the stairs, quite certain that she had heard voices down below. When she reached the landing, she collapsed suddenly in shock to her knees. She peered down through the mahogany banister watching in startled belief her daughter and stepson entwined naked on the floor in front of the fire. Jackie couldn't believe her eyes.

She perched on the top step transfixed, looking down. She remained there in silence watching them caress each other, Tony still holding Shannan tenderly. Jackie kept where she was, hunched down and silent, clinging tightly to the railing as her knuckles turned white in an effort to restrain herself from running down the steps and screaming at them. She was insanely envious of her daughter; however, she could never have imagined even in her wildest dreams anything like the scene before her, yet what she was witnessing was very real indeed.

Jackie lingered on the stairs for a while watching them until she could stand it no longer. She eventually crept silently back to her room, carefully closing the door and locking it. She moved slowly across the thick carpet, removed her robe, and sat down in stunned silence trying to piece it all together.

She had just witnessed incest. Well, they were only half brother and sister, but that counted, didn't it? Why would they do such a thing? Were they just two curious teenagers experimenting with sex? Or was there more to their relationship than met the eye? Should she confront them or tell Jack and let him do it? Jackie dropped her face into her hands, her head swimming from what she had just witnessed, too much alcohol, and numerous sleeping pills. Her temples throbbed, so she decided that a couple of Xanex wouldn't hurt, so she downed them with her watered-down vodka. She fell over with a sigh, passing out almost immediately. In the morning when Jackie awoke, she wondered if it had all been a bad dream.

# CHAPTER 6

Everyone resumed their usual schedules the next morning. Tony, Shannan, and Todd all left for school, albeit a little late, groggy, and hungover from the night before. Tony dropped his brother and sister off at their high school, then drove on to his college classes a few miles away. He was driving his father's Mercedes while Jack was out of town, so Tony parked a distance from the campus. The walk in the morning air would help to clear his head.

He thought of his sister and their night together as he walked and most of the morning as he nodded, trying to stay awake during his classes. Shannan did the same during her classes as her head pounded from the numerous drinks the night before. She had thoroughly enjoyed her sixteenth birthday.

This had been a special birthday in that she had spent it with her entire family with the exception of her father. Her moments with Tony had meant the most to her, for she had never felt so loved or so complete in her life. Her brothers meant the world to her, and she longed for the summer months when they could spend more time together.

Jackie finally crawled out of bed around noon, barely touching her breakfast, which had been left on her bedside table by the housekeeper. She dressed slowly, pulling on a Donna Karan skirt and blouse, then headed down the stairs carefully, still slightly inebriated and dizzy from the night before. When she reached the landing of the staircase, vivid images from earlier in the morning appeared wildly in her mind. She still couldn't believe what she had seen, and she was having a difficult time trying to separate reality from what she hoped had been a dream. Jackie wandered cautiously into the library trying to remember the events from the previous night while trying to keep her head from swimming and her stomach from reeling.

Suddenly, everything came back to her. She had watched her stepson and daughter having sex here in front of the fire last night. Still not trusting or believing in her memories, she knelt in front of the fireplace and sniffed the carpet trying to identify any scent that would substantiate her doubts. Then finally, she smelled it— the unmistakable fragrance of Tony's cologne still on the carpet beside the hearth mixed with the familiar scent that Shannan wore. *I knew it,* she whispered. *They actually did it!*

Jackie meandered over and sank down onto the soft leather sofa in front of her husband's massive cherry desk to contemplate the situation. She would have to wait

until Jackson came home, for she knew she could not deal with this disgusting matter on her own. Her mind slowly began to formulate a plan.

*Yes,* she hissed out loud, *I will wait until Jack gets back.* Jackie rose from the sofa a few moments later, mixed a drink from the liquor cabinet, then drifted toward the kitchen to plan the weekend menu with their cook.

Shannan and her brothers arrived home from school at the usual time that afternoon. Todd retreated to his room to smoke a joint, and Tony ushered Shannan quickly up to her room. She assumed they were going to follow their usual routine and make love, so she began to strip out of her clothes.

Tony stopped her abruptly and held her close.

"Sweetheart, I need to talk to you," he said solemnly. He pulled her down to the bed so that she sat close beside him; then he looked deeply into her eyes.

"What is it?" she questioned.

"I have to leave for a while," he answered.

Shannan looked at him wide-eyed. "Where are you going?" she demanded.

"I'm leaving on tour, honey; the band has been booked for a nine-month gig in Europe, and I can't pass this up."

"Oh, Tony," she cried as she clung to him, "you can't leave me. I'll go with you!"

Tony had known this would be tough, only he hadn't realized how hard it would actually be. He explained to her that she had to stay in school and that he would only be gone for nine months and would return as soon as possible. Shannan cried desperately and fell into his arms, shaking as she sobbed. He held her close until she fell asleep a few hours later.

Shannan awoke in darkness not knowing where she was. Her swollen eyes recognized the familiar shapes of her bedroom as she began to recall what Tony had told her. She smiled then, whispering, "Thank God, it was only a dream." As she sat up in bed, a stream of light broke across the room as Tony entered carrying two glasses of wine accompanied by a chilled bottle. "What time is it?" she said softly.

"Nine," Tony responded. "You fell asleep," he said, "and I helped you change into something more comfortable."

Shannan looked down then and realized she was wearing the same white silk nightshirt she had worn the first night they were together. The look on his face told her that what she hoped was only a dream had been very real indeed. "We didn't—?"

"No," he said hurriedly, "we were both too upset."

"Good," she sniffed, pulling the covers over her head, sliding down into the fluffy goose feather comforter.

Tony approached her bed and sat the tray of wine on a table by the window overlooking the garden below. "Now, Shannan," he said softly, "you're acting like a baby."

"You're leaving me, you bastard!" she hissed.

"Here," he said, handing her a glass of wine. She rose up and took it without hesitation and sipped delicately, watching him over the rim of the crystal glass. "I

know you think I'm abandoning you," he said, "and I am, but this is the opportunity of a lifetime, and I just can't pass it up."

"You could take me with you," she repeated, but he only shook his head.

They finished the wine as Tony tried to explain that he would be on the road for too long and that she could not afford to delay her education. He finally convinced Shannan that his trip was a wonderful opportunity, and she agreed that it would be exciting for him and only enhance his career as a musician. Tearfully, she finally fell asleep in her brother's arms, clinging to him until the pink streaks of dawn intruded the darkness of her bedroom. Tony left her at daylight and went to his room to pack. He had not told her about the call from his agent, changing the date of his departure. That date was today.

# CHAPTER 7

W hen Shannan finally awoke later in the morning, she realized that she had slept through two of her classes, but she didn't care. She was still upset over Tony's trip to Europe. She swung her long legs out of bed and stood up. Her white silk nightgown fell loosely around the tops of her thighs as she padded slowly into her mauve marbled bathroom. Her head was heavy from the wine she had consumed the night before, so she splashed cold water from the faucet onto her face while a steaming shower ran behind her. Shannan still could not believe that the only person she counted on in the entire world was leaving her for such a long time.

The whole upcoming summer had been planned around spending time with her two brothers.

Her dreams of them relaxing on the family houseboat, skiing, swimming, and racing their jet skis were gone. Shannan had already begun planning a huge gathering, inviting their best friends to join them on the law firm's chopper, which would whisk everyone to their lake house for an unforgettable party. Now it was all ruined. She stepped carefully into her shower, which usually ran too hot; however, this morning, the temperature was perfect as she stood in the warm spray and thought of Tony, wondering when he was leaving.

Tony had informed Todd about his leaving the country that morning before Shannan came down to breakfast. He encouraged his younger brother to look after their sister in his absence. Todd had never revealed what he had seen take place between his brother and sister the morning he had stumbled into the wrong bedroom. After all, everything was cool with him; he didn't care who fucked whom.

Todd assured Tony between draws on his joint that he would do his best to protect Shannan and shield her from imposing threats from high school punks, who would undoubtedly attempt to take advantage.

Hearing Todd's comment as somewhat sarcastic, Tony only hoped and prayed that his brother would clean up very soon.

Tony was scheduled to leave with his band later that afternoon, so Shannan and Todd left school early, catching a ride home with friends. They arrived at their home on Franklin Road just in time to see their yardman heaving large suitcases into their father's Mercedes. The whole family would see Tony off at the airport; however, their father hadn't yet arrived from his office downtown where he was in the midst of taking a deposition.

Shannan and Todd bolted out of the car and hurried into their palatial home, entering the main foyer. Jackie came clicking down the stairs hurriedly in charcoal suede pumps and a tight gray sweaterdress. She barely paused to greet Shannan and Todd in her haste to the coat closet to retrieve one of her many furs. She chose a full-length silver fox and retreated onto the front verandah to smoke.

Between puffs, she watched Ben, the landscaper, finish loading the bags.

Todd and Shannan looked at each other and rolled their eyes. Tony eventually came lumbering down the stairs, awkwardly dragging another suitcase behind. He also struggled with a handheld satchel accompanied by two smaller totes on his shoulders. "You need some help, man?" Todd exclaimed as he bolted up the stairs to help his brother with the cumbersome bags. Todd assisted Tony down the stairs where the remaining suitcases were heaped into the trunk by the elderly yardman while the rest of the family piled into the car.

When the group was finally ready to depart, a Yellow Cab came speeding and honking through the circular driveway bearing Jackson Masterson. Jackie mumbled a "thank Jesus" as she exhaled on a cigarette. Jack leapt from the cab into the Mercedes and was able to join them after all on the short trip to Nashville International Airport. They all watched in the waiting area as Tony boarded a Delta jet en route for Paris heading on to Frankfurt, where he would begin his tour, traveling by train thereafter. He tried to remember if he had forgotten anything and worried about the musical equipment that was already on its way by ship.

The rest of the band was leaving the following day and would meet Tony at the hotel. He was more than a little apprehensive about being away for nine months; however, he knew it was something he must do before becoming strapped by the constraints of law school. His relationship with Shannan had been unbelievable, and he would never get over the experience itself or over her. She was incredible. She was sexual. She was vulnerable, and she needed someone to take care of her. He would worry about his sister. His thoughts of her carried him upward through the clouds as the big jet pierced the silver blue of the afternoon sky.

# CHAPTER 8

In Tony's absence, Shannan sought comfort and companionship in Todd. He was usually stoned or drunk, so there wasn't much solace there. She went to his room daily after school hoping to find him painting or drawing, but he usually went out with his friends or came home and drank until he passed out. Jackie wouldn't let her daughter drive the BMW to school, so Shannan resorted to bumming rides home after classes because she couldn't depend on her brother to stay for the entire day of school or even show up at all.

She didn't have any real close friends to confide in despite her popularity. She really preferred keeping to herself. So without Todd's companionship, Shannan felt completely alone. With no interest in the countless boys who asked her out, she found solitude in retreating to her room daily after classes to read or watch television. Occasionally, she chose to venture outside for long walks with her dogs where she thought of Tony.

Shannan fell asleep early in the evenings after writing long letters to her brother, realizing that she was more tired and less energetic than usual. She was sure it was the strain of school and Tony's absence that attributed to her lethargic demeanor and nauseous existence most of the time. In the mornings, Shannan usually rose early. She would go for a run, then come back to the house for a shower, then appearing in the kitchen all bouncy and glowing to consume a wonderful breakfast prepared by Fanny, their housekeeper and cook. Lately, Shannan found it impossible to rise at her usual time, due to the fact she was so squeamish in the mornings, that she did not dare go near the kitchen for fear that she might be sick.

Fanny was very fond of Shannan. She also cared deeply for the two brothers; however, Shannan was special, and Fanny was sorry that the child led such an unstable life. In Fanny's eyes, Shannan's existence consisted only of her studies, after-school practices, her brothers, and her animals. She had no real friends except for her swim coach, Tim Richards, who had a mad crush on the girl despite Shannan's obvious disinterest in him. He frequently dropped Shannan off after school and hung around the pool with her until she left him to retreat to the inside of the house.

At twenty-seven, Tim had the body of an Olympian, a great tan, and was a very attractive young man. He was wild about Shannan and desperately wanted to date her. So far, all she allowed from him was a frequent ride home and very limited visits. He vowed to be patient though, for she was a beauty worth the wait. Fanny protectively

watched Tim and Shannan around the pool from the kitchen window and secretly harbored an unsettling feeling about the handsome coach. Although her fears were unfounded, they still existed, and she was determined to keep an eye on the young couple.

Fanny constantly griped and complained about Shannan's dogs, loud music, and clothes strewn all over creation. Of course, the heavyset elderly black woman's arguments were in good humor, for she loved the girl as if she were her own and tolerated the untidiness. Fanny had been employed by the Mastersons for over thirteen years, and Shannan had only been a toddler when Fanny started for the noted family.

Shannan was usually the first one down to breakfast in the mornings, and she was usually in a chipper mood. She never complained unlike her mother, who had been round and round with Fanny since her arrival. Nothing ever suited Jackie. Fanny had finally reached the conclusion that the lady of the manor was a miserable person who would never find comfort in anything life had to offer.

Fanny had begun to worry about Shannan of late. The young woman did not act her usual carefree self and was noticeably not as energetic as usual. The wise old black woman suspected with horror what was possibly wrong with the girl, for she had changed the bloodstained sheets the morning after Shannan and Tony's first night together. Initially, Fanny had surmised that Shannan had started her period in the night; however, there had been a masculine odor in the bedroom that she would never forget. Now, the old woman dwelled on the possibility of this child carrying a child, and the thought terrified her.

Fanny wondered if she had mistaken the relationship between Shannan and her older suitor, Mr. Richards, and if he could have taken advantage of her. Fanny decided not to mention her suspicions to anyone, just as she had never mentioned the morning she discovered the bloody sheets.

One evening, Shannan wandered toward Todd's room hoping to chat with him. She was lonely and depressed, and she needed his companionship. She went to his bedroom after their parents had gone out for dinner and tapped lightly on his door. He didn't respond, so she knocked a little harder.

Finally, she called out his name and pushed the door open gently, then called to him again. There was still no response, causing Shannan to feel a slight sense of terror, instinctively sensing that something was wrong. She pushed the door open slowly and entered Todd's room with dread.

He was lying in his bed peacefully, almost like a child. Shannan approached him slowly, looking only at Todd's face, thinking how handsome he was. She whispered his name, knowing that something desperately was wrong. She moved to his bedside and reached out, gently touching his face. His skin was soft with slight stubble, which tickled her fingers as she stroked his cheek. His skin was cold, and he was completely lifeless. Shannan drew back as if bitten but then realized that it would make no difference.

She rose up and began to brutally beat against his chest, hoping to forcefully will him back to life. It was useless. Todd was dead. He had apparently died of a drug overdose, for Shannan noticed dirty syringes and empty whiskey bottles around his bed. She collapsed on top of her brother, hugging him and sobbing hysterically. She held him lovingly as her tears spilled onto his neck and trickled down his motionless torso.

Shannan stopped crying and lifted herself from Todd's body, realizing that it would do no good.

She sat beside him for a long time, just looking at his face, rubbing her fingers along his jawline, and remembering all the good times that the three of them had shared. Finally, around midnight, she willed herself away from her dead brother and paced around the room to think about what she should do.

Shannan was close to no one except her brothers, and now one of them was gone forever.

Tony could not be reached, so she would have to tell her parents and contact the proper authorities. Shannan was devastated and grief stricken, yet she remained strong. She made her way to her parents' room and knocked gently at their door. Hearing no answer, she opened the door and peeked in. The bed was empty. *Typical,* she moaned. Shannan went back to her room, locked the door, and called the police.

The paramedics arrived in less than fifteen minutes in a wail of sirens and took Todd's body away. Jackson and Jackie arrived home shortly afterward and reacted in stunned disbelief to the news of their son's death. Shannan remained intact until after the medical team had left the premises; then she lost control. She became hysterical and seemingly half crazed while her parents tried to comfort her.

She finally collapsed on the floor of the entry hall where she had given her report to the authorities. Jack leapt quickly to her side, scooped her up into his arms, and carried his distraught daughter to her bedroom.

He placed her gently on her bed and covered her with a quilt. She was dazed and unbelievably anguished, so Jack left to retrieve two sleeping pills from Jackie's bedside table. He hurried back to Shannan and saw to it that she took the pills, accompanied by a sip of brandy to ensure her sleep. He shook his head in despair as he turned off his daughter's bedroom light and headed back to his own room.

The next few days would be tough on them all, he thought sadly.

The memorial service was held at Woodlawn Cemetery with a mass of mourners in attendance. Jackson, Jackie, and Shannan stood motionless and silent as the casket was lowered into the ground. Jackie, dressed in a black Dior suit, stood stoically beside her husband honoring her second son. Shannan, sedated heavily by her doctor, had managed to stand beside her parents at the chapel ceremony and at the graveside in a seemingly catatonic state. She just stared transfixed at her brother's casket, not believing that this horrible tragedy had really happened.

The family, as well as the grief-stricken onlookers, watched sadly as the young man's coffin disappeared from view. Everyone considered Todd's death an

unfortunate loss of a young life. Shannan plucked a single white rose from one of the arrangements and flung it down into Todd's grave as she staggered forward away from the group. *Good-bye, dear brother,* she whispered. *I'll miss you.* She then crumpled to the ground beside the foreboding hole. Spectators gasped and gathered around her in confusion. Her parents just looked at each other in embarrassment and walked slowly over to help their daughter to her feet.

# CHAPTER 9

Tony was unable to attend the funeral, and he was miserable sitting alone at his hotel in Paris, thinking about Todd and how much Shannan must be suffering. He had no way of getting home to his family, so he desperately prayed to be there in spirit, if only for his sister's sake. He knew how tough Todd's death would be on her, and he hated the fact that his schedule hadn't permitted him to be there for his only brother's funeral and for not being able to comfort Shannan. Tony sat on his bed in the posh suite with his head bowed into his hands, and he wept bitterly.

What a mess all their lives had become, he thought unhappily. He rose and reached for a bottle of scotch from the bar beside his bed. He downed a couple of shots, then collapsed on a Chippendale chair beside the window overlooking the Champs-Élysées. As he drifted into an intoxicated sleep, Tony dreaded the months ahead and wondered if he would be able to survive the tour and if his poor sister would be able to survive his absence.

In the days following Todd's death, Shannan became an utter recluse. She remained in her bedroom and didn't emerge for any reason, except for early morning walks with her hounds. She found solace in her canine friends, for they were her only companions. Only when she was sure her parents were gone would she sneak downstairs to the kitchen searching for something to eat. Although she really didn't *feel* like eating, her body was begging for nourishment to the point Shannan felt she would collapse unless she ate. She would then escape back to her room by midmorning where she either returned to bed or sat and stared out the window at the green manicured grounds of her family's estate.

It was June, and Shannan was out of school, so she found no reason to participate in her usual daily functions. Fanny became increasingly worried about the girl, especially when she didn't get out of bed for any length of time during a two-week period. Shannan was sick most of the time, so she just stayed in bed, curled around her pillows as the days passed. The Fourth of July came and went while Shannan chose to stay in her room and withdraw from the family barbecue. Tim Richards dropped by often to visit, but Shannan ordered Fanny to send him away, also ignoring his persistent phone calls.

On a muggy day in early August, Shannan decided to go for a swim. Fanny was at the market. Jack was away on business, and Jackie was out lunching with friends. Shannan ventured down to the pool and slipped into the cool water. She laid her head against the side, closed her eyes, and listened only to the faint hum of a weed

eater in the distance. Suddenly, she felt strong hands grip her shoulders, massaging gently as she struggled to raise herself. Looking up, she was blinded by the sun, visualizing only the silhouette of a man above her. Squealing and pulling away, she recognized the muscular build of her swim coach, Tim Richards. "Good god!" she exclaimed. "What are you trying to do, scare me to death?"

Grinning his broad toothy grin at her, he replied, "Just trying to make you feel better, babe."

"I feel fine. Thanks," she said as she swam to the opposite end of the pool.

Stripping out of his shorts, Tim eased into the water and dove under, swimming along the bottom of the pool until he reached her. Surfacing and splashing up right in front of her, he placed his arms on either side of her body. He was inches away from Shannan's face as he reached over to kiss her. "Tim, please," she begged, turning her head.

"Oh, come on, baby," he responded, taking her face in his hands and forcing his mouth upon hers.

"Don't!" she ordered, trying to push him away.

Tim jerked back and splashed water angrily into her face. "What's wrong with you, bitch? I've tried to be nice to you, be a friend to you, and even defend you when other students make fun of you because you're so fucking strange!" he yelled.

Saying nothing, Shannan lifted herself from the pool, collected her towel, and began to make her way up the path to the house.

"Hey, wait a minute!" Tim called.

She ignored him and proceeded along, hurrying her pace.

Reaching her bedroom at last, Shannan exhaled heavily, nervous and shaking over what had just transpired. In the air-conditioning, she was chilled, so she went to draw a hot bath. Slipping out of her swimsuit, she pulled on her robe and, while brushing her hair, padded into the bedroom to turn on some music.

There, in the middle of the room, stood Tim. Shannan gasped, dropped the brush, and pulled her robe together. "You didn't think I was going to give up that easily, did you?" He smirked.

"Get out of here," she said calmly but forcefully.

"Oh, come on, baby. Don't you think it's about time you give it up?" Tim teased.

"I mean it," she said, nervous by his presence and comments.

He took a step toward her as she leapt for the bathroom. Slamming the door behind herself, she didn't realize that her sash was caught, prohibiting the door from closing. Tim advanced quickly and pushed the door open with his powerful arms. "Go away, please!" Shannan screamed, crying now. With a mighty shove, he burst through the bathroom door, grabbed hold of the dangling sash, and pulled her roughly to him.

"Now I've got you, my pretty," he sneered as he forced his mouth on hers again, pulling the robe from her naked body. This time, she could not get away from him, but she struggled desperately as steam filled the room. Tim finally stopped kissing

her and looked down at her body. She tried to shrink away from him in shame, but he held her tight and took in every inch of her with his dark eyes. "Good god, what has happened to you?" he berated.

"Tim, *please* leave me alone," she cried. He ran his hands over her, taking in her anorexic features everywhere except the little round tummy she now had. He placed one hand behind her buttocks while his other found her crotch and fingered it eagerly. Shannan just whimpered, knowing it was useless fighting him.

Down below in the courtyard, the sounds of her mother and Fanny arriving home drifted up through the trees. Disappointed, Tim pushed her roughly away, muttering, "You're not even worth my time, bitch!" He left her room angrily and hurried down the main staircase, nearly knocking over the elderly housekeeper with her groceries. Jackie, still on the front landing, watched Tim speed away in his red Porsche.

Fanny, concerned about Shannan, urged her mother to go and check on the girl. Jackie was bored with Fanny's incessant complaints about her daughter's behavior. "She is just feeling sorry for herself," Jackie muttered irritably. "The rest of us have gotten on with our lives since Todd's death, and it's time she does the same," Jackie stated as she checked her lipstick in a gilded mirror hanging in the foyer.

"I'm going upstairs, Fanny," she called out as she turned and headed up the winding staircase to Shannan's room. Jackie finally decided to go up and confront her daughter about her reclusive behavior and order her to come out of that room. Fanny wondered if she should have ever mentioned her concern over Shannan, for she was well aware of the animosity between the two women. She simply kept putting away the groceries as her old black hands shook with worried anticipation.

Shannan was sitting on the side of the tub still shaking from her encounter with Tim. She swirled her fingers through the scented bubbles as the water level rose. She allowed herself to slip into a peaceful daydream, listening to the sound of the running water and thinking of happier times spent with her two beloved brothers. Reaching over, she turned off the marbled faucets then stood letting her silk robe fall to the floor. Shannan was about to step into the hot foamy suds when her mother burst into the steamy bathroom. Both women stared at each other in shocked silence as Jackie's eyes took in the form of her pregnant daughter. Shannan was nearing the fourth month of the pregnancy, and despite her thinness, there was still no mistaking the growing shape of her stomach.

For months, Shannan had been nervous and frightened about the changes that were taking place within her body. She knew that she had felt very different for quite a while, only she did not know why.

With the steady onslaught of tragedy that had occurred over the past few months, Shannan consciously overlooked physical changes, dwelling solely on the ache in her heart. Unfortunately, her emotional torture was only just beginning.

Jackie finally broke the silence of the awkward moment by hissing, "Good god, you little slut!"

Shannan stared back at her mother in shock and disbelief as a buried rage began to build within her.

"Well?" Jackie forced. "What have you got to say for yourself, you little whore?"

Shannan stared into the black coldness of the older woman's eyes and responded in a calm threat, "Get out of my room, Mother. Now!"

Jackie remained where she was, lowered her gaze, and stared at her daughter's swollen stomach, knowing full well that her own stepson had planted the baby growing inside. She became nauseous just thinking of the nastiness of it all and felt the oncoming of a migraine. "Just who in the hell are you trying to fool?" Jackie sneered accusingly. "I saw it all that night by the fire. You and your loving brother entwined in a passionate naked embrace!" she hissed evilly.

Shannan rose, reached for a towel, wrapped it carefully around her body, and then looked straight into the devilish eyes of her mother. She advanced toward Jackie as an eerie feeling came over the room. "So you know then," Shannan stated bluntly.

"Yes," she responded, not liking the vicious look in her daughter's eyes.

Shannan slipped past her, then proceeded into the bedroom, and stared out the window.

Jackie approached her daughter and said in a more compassionate tone, "Shannan, you know that you cannot keep it. That would be the most disgraceful and damaging thing that could ever happen to our family. Why, just think what it would do to your father's political career? I never mentioned to him that I watched you and your brother screwing around, and I don't want you to breathe a word of this to anyone! Do you understand me, young lady?"

Shannan turned from the window and faced her mother. "Yes, I do," she replied.

"Good," Jackie said. "Now, I want you to start gathering some of your things together, and I'll send Fanny up later to help you pack," she continued as she opened the door to go.

"Where are we going? What are we going to do?" Shannan uttered through the tears that were beginning to trickle down her face.

Jackie shook her head in annoyance and simply responded quietly, "Leave."

When Jackie left the room, Shannan knelt down beside her bed and wept loudly as her poodle came over and licked her tears, trying hard to comfort his mistress. She put her arms around him and cried even harder into his curly fur. Shannan was extremely confused and terrified of the events to come and wondered how she would bear them without her brothers to cling to. The cruel words of her mother still rang in her head, remembering Jackie's accusing tone in recanting the night by the fire. An imagined witchlike laugh tore through her thoughts as she again heard the words, *You deserve exactly what is going to happen to you!* Shannan shuttered and tried to envision a moment in her life when she would be happy again.

# CHAPTER 10

Jackie took Shannan to their family doctor the next morning, and his report was more shocking than she could have possibly imagined. She had figured her daughter to be about three or four months along and was stunned when he announced that the pregnancy was just entering the sixth month. Jackie could have fainted. She had never dreamed that such a thin girl would be delivering a baby within three months, yet she trusted the old doctor who had helped deliver the mother-to-be he was examining now.

Shannan was scheduled to start back to school in a couple of weeks, and now Jackie's mind raced wondering what she should do about the situation at hand.

When they returned home, Shannan retreated to her room in exhaustion and humiliation while her mother began to devise a plan. Jackie arranged for her and her daughter to leave for Phoenix the following day. She lied and explained to Jackson that she had an elderly aunt who was dying with respiratory ailments, and she needed to go and be by the old woman's side. "After all," Jackie explained to her husband between drags on her cigarette, "the trip will appear empathetic and caring to your partners, which will undoubtedly leak to your voters."

She further explained that by taking Shannan, she could spare the girl the embarrassment of probing questions regarding Todd's death by her classmates if she returned to school. "Besides," Jackie continued, "a change of scenery will help her emotional state immensely." Jackson agreed that it would probably be best if his daughter did start back to school after the holidays, and Jackie was relieved that he bought her story so easily.

Jackie decided that her scheme would work out perfectly. Shannan could have the baby in Arizona and be back in Nashville by January to continue her junior year. She could study under a private tutor out west and, with any luck, would be back on schedule with her classmates. The baby was due in November, so they could return home easily by Christmas.

Jackie and Shannan boarded an American Airlines flight the next morning and left for Phoenix as Jack stood at the gate waving, although neither of them noticed. Shannan maintained a trancelike stare, and her mother chain-smoked until they reached their seats in first class. Jackie snubbed out her last cigarette while motioning to the stewardess, requesting a cocktail. The two women ignored each other completely as the big jet left the ground and headed west.

They arrived in Phoenix in less than three hours, landing at Sky Harbor Airport, emerging into a temperature of one hundred degrees. Jackie leased a Lincoln Town Car and headed toward the Scottsdale Marriott Resort. She had already contacted a local obstetrician recommended by their physician in Nashville, and Jackie planned to phone him upon their arrival at the hotel. Shannan was terrified of what was to come, and she sat quiet, looking out at the desert landscape as they drove along.

They checked into a two-bedroom suite, and Shannan immediately collapsed on her bed, exhausted from the trip as well as the recent tragedies that had occurred in her life. After Jackie tipped the bellman for delivering their luggage, she grabbed the Yellow Pages and went out onto the balcony to smoke a cigarette. Flipping through the voluminous book, she tabbed the pages that held the numbers of local adoption agencies. She planned to call them all the next day as well as consult with the doctor on referrals.

The next morning, Jackie faced another hot Arizona day as she left to go out and make arrangements for the adoption of her grandchild. She shuddered, thinking of herself as a grandmother, but was comforted in the fact that this nasty interruption in her otherwise perfect life would be a deep secret kept from all who knew her. Shannan stayed in the hotel suite feeling utterly miserable and depressed beyond belief. She hated her life and despised herself for being in this horrible predicament. She had tried to phone Tony but found it impossible to reach him. A part of her wanted to inform him of her dilemma, although in a way she was glad that he did not know and probably never would.

On the other side of the world, Tony Masterson was nearing the end of his tour and couldn't wait to return home to see his sister. He had missed her desperately and had worried about her constantly. He had tried to reach her several times from several stops during the band's stint in Europe but had been unsuccessful. On one occasion, he had been able to get a call through to their home but was informed by Fanny that Shannan and her mother were out of town and Jackson was in unending political meetings.

Tony had finally resigned himself to writing letters to his beloved sister, hoping desperately that they would reach no one else.

Shannan and Jackie barely spoke to one another for the next three weeks despite being cooped up together in their suite most of the time. Shannan was ill and extremely weak most days. Jackie spent most of her time reclining on the patio, reading magazines, drinking martinis, and smoking imported cigarettes.

One afternoon in late October, Shannan's water broke while she padded from the living room to her bedroom. "Oh my god!" she screamed and slumped to her knees crying. Jackie came running from the patio and stared at the puddle on the floor between her daughter's legs. Shannan remained crumpled on the floor in pain as a contraction spread through her abdomen. The baby wasn't due for another few weeks, and both Shannan and Jackie were worried. After phoning for an

ambulance, Jackie helped her daughter to her feet, led her to the couch, covered her with a blanket, and waited for the paramedics to arrive.

Shannan writhed on the sofa screaming in agony while continuous contractions tore through her young body. Jackie did little to comfort her daughter as her only concern was getting this mess over and done with as soon as possible. As she paced the room and downed vodka, Jackie became even more agitated when she realized that she was out of cigarettes.

The medical team arrived within minutes and carried Shannan away to Saint Joseph's Hospital where she gave birth to a four-pound baby girl. She passed out immediately after the baby entered the world, and she never even saw the tiny face of the child before the nurses whisked her away to the neonatal unit. The infant would remain there until the adoptive parents arrived who would raise her, nurture her, and love her for the rest of her life. The child would probably never know the woman who gave birth to her and would wonder about her forever.

# CHAPTER 11

Jackie and her daughter returned to Nashville when Shannan was strong
enough to travel. The young woman had endured more than the physical and
emotional trauma of pregnancy and childbirth.

Shannan showed the beginning signs of suffering from a mental breakdown
although her mother didn't seem to notice. Because of the combined stress of Tony
leaving, Todd's death, the pregnancy, and the agonizing delivery, Shannan reeled
into a dark world within herself. Her loneliness and despair caused her mind to
falter, allowing the tragic recent events to vacate her memory. After their arrival back
at home, Shannan secluded herself in her room, hiding from everyone and
everything that had caused her such incredible pain.

Jackie felt reborn and triumphed in her victory over her lie to Jackson regarding
their trip. She reported that all had gone well with her ailing aunt in Arizona and
that Shannan seemed to have healed emotionally and was able to return to school
after the first of the year. Nothing could have been further from the truth. Shannan
continued to drift further and further out of consciousness trying to shield herself
from the emotional trauma she had suffered. Her frustrations turned to anger, and
a slow boiling pot of hatred began to rise within her soul for her mother—the
woman who had contributed to the pain in her life.

The family celebrated a dismal Christmas that year, and with the absence of Tony
and Todd, Shannan grew more distraught and distant than ever. She retreated to
her room as often as possible; however, when confronted about her reclusive behavior,
she became defensive and angry. The fights with her mother became more frequent,
bringing out a violent side of the girl that the family had never witnessed.

Shannan slipped down to the kitchen one morning thinking the house was
empty and was confronted by Jackie who offered a snide remark about laziness.
Shannan ignored her mother and proceeded to the sink for a glass of water.

"So who do you think you are, missy? A lady of leisure or something?" Jackie
snarled as she sipped on her early morning cocktail.

Shannan continued to avoid her mother and scrambled to get a glass and plate
of food together in order to retreat once again to the sanctity of her room.

As she moved toward the door, Jackie grabbed her daughter's arm and wheeled
the girl around, causing Shannan to spill the contents of her plate. "What is it, you
slut? Are you still missing your dearly departed brother or the brother you were
sleeping with?" she spat.

The silent rage that had been building in the young woman over the past months finally reached an eruption point. She jerked away from her vicious mother and reached for a knife that was lying on the kitchen counter. Facing her mother with all the rage of a lion, Shannan pointed the butcher knife at Jackie, holding it mere inches from her face.

Dropping her vodka tonic, Jackie backed into the wall facing her daughter and hissed, "You vicious bitch!"

Shannan continued to hold the knife on her mother and whispered, "How dare you say such things to me! You have never been any kind of mother. Why, an alley cat is a better mother than you!"

Jackie remained silent but held a vigilant stare into her daughter's eyes. Shannan moved stealthily around her, still holding the knife close to Jackie's throat.

At that moment, Fanny entered the kitchen with the laundry she had collected throughout the household. Startled, she gasped at the two women enthralled in an altercation. "Why, what's going on here?" the old black woman said quietly.

"Nothing," Shannan responded. With that, she laid the knife on the table and left the room. Jackie looked at her housekeeper, threatened her to keep quiet, and quickly exited the kitchen and headed for her room. Collapsing in a chair, Fanny placed her face into her hands and muttered, *Lordie, lordie.*

The month following the holidays didn't offer a very bright beginning to a merry New Year for the Masterson family. Shannan's outbursts toward her mother continued, and after deliberation by her parents, they agreed to commit her to a facility for psychiatric evaluation. It had been mostly Jackie's suggestion, for she was sick of the everlasting weaknesses of her daughter and the constant competition between them. This way, Shanna would be out of her hair for good.

Jack leased a private jet, and he and Jackie flew with Shannan to Bristol Heights in East Tennessee. They committed their daughter into the psychiatric ward to undergo months of treatment and evaluation by qualified therapists. Shannan regressed more than anyone could have imagined and continued to do so until Tony returned from Europe.

He had phoned many times during his tour but had only spoken to Fanny, whose comments were vague. Tony had reached Jack briefly while Shannan and Jackie had been in Arizona, only his father had little or no news to report. His heart ached for his sister and thoughts of her plagued his mind.

Something was definitely not right; he felt her pain and longed for the end of the week when he could hold her in his arms again and protect her from whatever hell she was experiencing.

# Chapter 12

Tony bit his nails as his cab raced through the streets of Paris, rushing to get him to the plane on time. He thought this day would never arrive—the day when the tour was over and he could return to the States and to Shannan. He had played his heart out, and his band had become an overnight success. His agent had already arranged contracts with several record producers in the United States as well as Europe. It would be up to Tony and the guys to decide whether they wanted to pursue their music careers or corporate ones.

The taxi dropped Tony off at Orly Airport, and he raced to his gate, barely catching the jumbo jet that would take him home. After a brief stop at LaGuardia, Tony's plane finally touched down in Nashville, where he was met by the drizzly cold bitterness of a mid-January evening. Tony had left word with their housekeeper that he would be returning; however, looking quickly around, he saw no familiar faces, so he raced to grab yet another cab.

Entering the big gates to his home on Franklin Road, Tony stared at the massive house and looked in wonder at the shimmering ice that clung to the shrubs as the lights from inside reflected off the bushes. Paying the driver before he had even stopped, Tony jumped from the car, grabbed his bags, and raced up the front steps, slipping a little as he struggled with the door.

Inside, Jack was sitting by the fire reading a book and smoking a cigar in his library. Hearing the front door, he rose to go greet his son. Tony was upon him before he had barely risen from the leather chair. The two men embraced as Jack remarked how well his son looked.

"Where's Shannan?" Tony asked, ignoring his father's comment. "Where is she?" he asked again.

Jackie suddenly appeared from the kitchen, holding a fresh vodka tonic with an evil smirk on her face. "Well, welcome home, sailor," she cooed.

"Hello, Jackie," Tony responded halfheartedly. "Where is Shannan?" he asked for the third time.

Jack and Jackie looked worriedly at each other. "Son—" Jack began.

"Where the hell is she!" Tony demanded.

"Son, she's in the hospital," the older man answered.

"What! What's wrong with her?" Tony said becoming terrified.

Jackie, barely able to contain herself any longer, replied, "She went crazy, dear. She tried to kill me."

Tony advanced on his father. "If you don't tell me where she is, you son of a bitch, I'll kill you both!"

"Calm down, Tony," Jack ordered. "Shannan couldn't cope with things after you left. I guess with the death of Todd and your abandoning her, she just couldn't take it any longer. She's in Bristol Heights psychiatric hospital."

Not believing what he was hearing, Tony collapsed on his father's chair running his hands through his hair trying to comprehend what they were saying. "I'm going to get her," he moaned.

"You can't do that, son," Jack responded. "She's not well. The doctors say she will have to stay there about six months."

"Over my dead body!" Tony yelled. Stepping over his bags in the foyer, he made his way through the kitchen to the garage as his father and Jackie followed in hot pursuit.

"You can't do this, Tony," Jack ordered, grabbing his son by the arm. Pushing him backward into the garbage cans, Tony got into their Mercedes, raised the garage door, and squealed backward down the driveway. Reaching the main road, he pointed the automobile east and headed toward Knoxville. Jackie helped her husband to his feet, and the two of them watched in silence as Tony sped away into the winter night.

The next morning, Tony arrived at Bristol Heights, hours before the facility opened to visitors.

He dozed in his car as sleet pounded against the windshield, thinking of what to say to his sister. The alarm on his watch went off, waking him with a start. The rain was still coming down as he moved the Mercedes closer to the entrance of the big gray building. He entered the security area, gave his name to the guard, and explained that he was there to see his sister.

The security officer noticed his unkempt appearance and offered him the use of a restroom to freshen up. Tony, embarrassed by the man's comment, made his way to the men's room hoping to make himself more presentable. When he looked into the mirror under the dim lights, he was shocked when he saw his reflection. His eyes were bloodshot beyond belief, now remembering that he hadn't slept in over forty-eight hours. The stubble on his face made him look more like a beggar than a rock star, and his whole body ached from the jet lag. *Oh, well,* he muttered to himself, *I'll just have to do the best that I can.* Splashing cold water on his face and brushing his hair, he felt a little better, so he left to go find the visitor's area.

Tony was escorted down a dingy, poorly lit corridor and led into a locked room full of patients of various ages in faded blue jumpsuits. The guard pointed to a far corner where a young woman sat alone and motioned to him that that was her. Tony made his way across the room. Sensing that she was being watched, Shannan turned and stared at him. She looked pale, cowed, and withdrawn. Tony stopped where he was, then advanced slowly toward her again.

She showed a faint sense of recognition as she moved toward him in a trancelike motion. He held out his arms to her, and she practically fell into them, sobbing uncontrollably and shaking violently.

"Oh, Tony," she cried, "where have you been?"

Tony held her tightly, reassuring her that he would never abandon her again. "Baby, baby, what are you doing here?" he whispered in her ear.

"They sent me here, Tony, after—" She hesitated, not remembering what events had transpired to result in this. "Just get me out of here," she pleaded.

"I will, honey, I will," Tony promised as he continued to comfort his little sister.

# CHAPTER 13

The next few months were a living hell for the Masterson family. After Tony returned home with Shannan, the confrontations continued between mother and daughter. Shannan's relationship with Jackie became increasingly violent, and the entire household wondered at times if they would eventually kill one another. The young woman acted as if she existed inside another world, her sporadic behavior prompting her to react aggressively with anyone offering confrontation.

Tony was very perplexed by his sister's behavior. Often when he tried to console and comfort her, she pushed him away in anger and frustration. They never resumed their sexual relationship that was a tremendous disappointment to Tony. He loved Shannan so much, and her total rebuff of him was heartbreaking, especially when he attempted to hold her, she shrank away from him in fear. He sat alone in his room at night believing that everything they had experienced together had been totally forgotten by her. Blocking his pain with whiskey, he convinced himself that Shannan had buried the memories of them loving each other, ignorant of the reasons why.

Jackson and Jackie pushed to recommit their daughter to the psychiatric hospital, but Tony adamantly objected. Shannan's rebellious attitude had finally gotten the best of them, and Tony felt he was losing ground rapidly. Out of desperation, he finally called his aunt Sable in New York to see if she could influence Jackie in the least. Sable, recently widowed, had relocated to Manhattan and become a very powerful woman in her own right. She offered the perfect solution; Shannan should come live with her.

As predicted, Jackie vehemently voiced her opinion about her daughter's relocation to New York.

Her intense hatred of her only sister fueled her outrage against the move. Tony argued with his father that Sable could offer Shannan a secure environment, not to mention a very influential lifestyle. Jackson eventually overruled his wife and granted his approval for his daughter's move. It became apparent that Shannan desperately needed to start her life over and exist without anyone knowing what she'd been through. With this arrangement, she could complete her high school education, heal emotionally, and be healthy enough to enter college the following year.

Shannan had always dreamed of living in the fast-paced lifestyle of Manhattan and was delighted that her parents would actually allow her to move north. She had only met her aunt a couple of times; however, through the years, Sable had sent her niece lavish gifts on special occasions, and Shannan sensed they would be very

close. Jackie was incensed that Jack had actually succumbed to Tony's pleas, declaring that everyone was against her. She drank continually that only added to her paranoia.

Shannan left for New York as soon as possible, extremely anxious to see her aunt. She wasn't aware that Sable was equally as anxious to see her. Sable had been planning for her niece's arrival for weeks. She planned to show the girl everything that the Big Apple had to offer.

Sable arrived at LaGuardia in her limousine, eager to greet Shannan and escort her back to the penthouse on Park Avenue that she had shared with her dear Markus. Her driver returned with news that Shannan's plane was delayed, so Sable relaxed in the voluptuous leather of her car and thought of the past.

Life had been good to her, she thought; her only disappointments had been the early loss of her beloved Markus and the distant relationship with her daughter Catherine. Sable had found nothing but utter disappointment in her only child. Catherine was selfish, controlling, and bitter, often reminding Sable of Jackie. From her letters, Shannan had seemingly been a very loving young woman, and Sable sincerely hoped that their relationship would fill the void in her life for a daughter. The chauffeur's gloved hand jolted Sable back into reality as he tapped on the window, motioning to her that the plane had arrived.

Shannan was overjoyed to finally be in the city she had always dreamed of, albeit Sable was somewhat of a stranger to her, and she was apprehensive about this new adventure in life with her mother's younger sister. The two women recognized each other instantly as Shannan exited her gate and moved to greet her aunt. Sable looked beautiful in a light blue Channel suit and floor-length silver mink coat. Shannan caught her breath as she took in the beauty of the older woman. Sable reached out to embrace her niece in a gesture of welcome as well as comfort. She realized what the young woman had been through in the previous months and understood the turbulent relationship between Shannan and Jackie. Sable knew her sister well and grieved over what Jackie's vindictive nature had done to the girl. She shuddered thinking of what Shannan had endured in her lifelong relationship with a mother whose ambitions outweighed any feelings of motherhood.

Timothy, Sable's chauffeur, arrived promptly to assist the two women with their baggage and usher them to the awaiting limousine. The drive to the Chandler penthouse provided a buffet of new sights and sounds to Shannan Masterson. She loved New York the moment the car exited the airport, and she spotted the magnificent skyline that only Manhattan claims as its own. They arrived at Sable's apartment on Park Avenue, and Shannan marveled at the beautiful structure of the building. Markus had purchased the property many years before as an investment and as an alternative to hotel suites when in town on business or social functions.

Sable had used the penthouse while on fashion shopping sprees or charity functions. She had also traveled to New York frequently in hopes of seeing her daughter. She longed for the day when Catherine would take leave from her legislative duties in Washington and shuttle north for dinner, a play, or just a quiet

drink at a piano bar. Unfortunately, Sable was always met with disappointment, for her daughter never showed. Catherine was so much like Jackie that it unnerved Sable. Both women were so self-absorbed and ambitious that it caused Sable to wonder if the heavens had mistakenly awarded the wrong daughters to the wrong mothers. Sable and Shannan were much more the likely pair; so undoubtedly, an inevitable bond soon formed, and the two women became inseparable.

# CHAPTER 14

Sable and Shannan went everywhere together. They attended parties, formal dinners, and endless society functions linked with Sable's various charities. At every event the two women attended, they were blinded by the flashing cameras of the paparazzi who delivered pictures of the famous widow and her niece to the society pages of New York. Sable used her prominence to introduce Shannan to everyone of importance in the city. The elite class to which Sable was so much a part of now became her focus for an entirely different reason—making her niece famous.

One afternoon while attending a fashion show, Sable bumped into Eileen Ford, the founder of the infamous Ford Modeling Agency. Sable persuaded Eileen to meet with Shannan the following day and, for the favor, promised to make a generous donation to the Ford Agency's favorite charities. The two women shook hands, and after purchasing several designer dresses, Sable summoned her limousine driver and headed back to her penthouse, eager to tell her niece the wonderful news.

Shannan was thrilled to hear Sable's ecstatic news about the Ford Agency, so the two women decided to dine out and celebrate. Sable had no trouble reserving a table at Tavern on the Green, and they enjoyed a fabulous evening out together on the town. They returned home early so that Shannan could get plenty of rest before her big meeting the next morning. Both women were so excited that neither of them slept very much.

Eileen Ford was enchanted with Shannan and signed her on the spot. The agency had her change her name to Shanna Somers, and they put her to work immediately. She graced the covers of numerous magazines and quickly became a spokeswoman for Blackglama furs, Rolex watches, Jaguar, and eventually landed the cover of *Sports Illustrated*.

Shanna had never been happier in her life, and Tony also reached the pinnacle of success with his band. He relocated to New York City to be near his sister and purchased an apartment on Seventh Avenue.

Shanna eventually joined his band as the lead singer, and together, they became as famous as the Osmond siblings and the Carpenters, touring across the country as their popularity soared. Tony and Shanna maintained a hectic pace on the road, and in order to keep up with their busy schedules, they both began to use cocaine to stay awake and alcohol to achieve sleep. Tony also experimented with heroin but kept it hidden from his sister.

When at home in New York, Shanna and Tony attended every party and club in town and were honored with drinks on the house and their drugs of choice served in private rooms. Shanna predictably contemplated moving into Tony's apartment, much to Sable's disapproval. Sable received several phone calls from Eileen Ford complaining about Shanna's absence from numerous photo shoots that had cost the agency thousands of dollars from huge clients. One day, while lunching at the penthouse, Sable confronted her niece about the missed modeling assignments. Shanna grew defensive and nervous.

Sable continued to scold Shanna for the daily reports in the newspapers and tabloids publicizing her and Tony's endless partying and suspected drug use in nightclubs around the city.

The argument caused Shanna to revert back into memories of her mother constantly harassing her about everything until she finally lost control and screamed at her aunt, "Leave me the hell alone!"

Immediately sorry for her outburst, Shanna started to cry. Sable placed her napkin in her lap and went to her niece's side. "It's okay, sweetheart," she said gently. "I didn't mean to hurt you. I'm just so very worried about you. I love you very much, Shanna. You're like my own daughter."

Shanna looked tenderly at her aunt and said, "Oh, Sable, I'm the one who's sorry. I've behaved so badly after all you've done for me."

Sable took Shanna in her arms and held her tight. "I don't want you to move, Shanna. In fact, I forbid it! Moving in with your brother would be a terrible mistake."

Shanna looked at her aunt with tearful eyes. "Why?" she asked.

"It wouldn't be a good arrangement, sweetheart. I've heard about the drugs, Shanna, and I don't want to see you ruin your life by getting involved in that scene. You have too much going for you and too much to offer the world and the people who love you. And don't forget how drugs destroyed your brother Todd." Shanna once again began to cry while Sable held her close and whispered, "It's all right, love. Everything will be all right."

# CHAPTER 15

It was 1980, and the winter Olympics were in full swing. Shanna flew to Lake Placid, New York, to pose for a fur layout and make public appearances. The whole town was crowded with tourists, spectators, and security. After shooting her layout, Shanna was ushered hurriedly from one event to another by bodyguards and a chaperone. By the end of her third day, she was utterly exhausted and asked to be excused so that she could retire early.

Her suite at the Breckenridge was warm and cozy, and a roaring fire awaited her as she entered and shed her parka. A bar stocked with the world's finest wines and liquors beckoned to her, and she eagerly poured a brandy. Pulling off her boots, Shanna collapsed in the chaise lounge beside the fire. She pulled the fur that was thrown from the back of the chair and wrapped it around herself. As she sipped her brandy, she picked up the phone and called her brother. At his apartment in New York, there was no answer, so she left him a message. After hanging up, she considered calling Sable, but she was just too exhausted. Snuggling down farther into the chaise, she quickly fell asleep.

The fire popped loudly, waking Shanna from a sound sleep. She had been dreaming that she was a participant in the Olympic Games, ice skating to the classical masterpiece, "Rhapsody on a Theme of Paganini." She yawned loudly, still hearing Rachmaninoff's music play in her head. It was after midnight, and she was starving. There were only snacks left on the side of the bar, none of them that would prove to be very filling. Desiring some fresh air anyway, Shanna decided to go for a moonlit stroll through the snow and search for an open bar or deli.

The night was cold but clear, and there were a million stars overhead. Shanna took in a deep breath and ventured down Vancouver Avenue looking at the many beautiful resorts, all filled with excited visitors. People were scurrying everywhere despite the late hour, and Shanna felt content just being able to observe them all. Suddenly, two young boys ran past in a race to get to their hotel. One of them bumped against her roughly causing her to loose her footing in the snow.

As she struggled to regain her balance, she felt wildly for the rope strung along the sidewalk, protecting pedestrians from slipping down the embankment on either side of the street. Shanna did finally manage to grab onto the rope, but only after her feet had slipped over the side. Her gloved hand couldn't hold on to keep her from sliding down the hill and into the drift below.

Shanna lay at the bottom of the gully for several minutes, shaken by her fall. When she finally tried to stand, it was difficult to maintain her footing, and she slipped several times trying to raise herself.

When her feet finally managed to hold her steady, she looked upward from where she fell. It was only about ten or twelve feet back up to the sidewalk; however, the embankment was completely covered with snow, and there was nothing on which to hold. It was nearly 1:00 a.m., and most of the tourists had gone in for the night. Shanna yelled for help over and over, but with the wind blowing and the decreasing number of people milling about, no one heard her calls. Shivering, she finally sat back down and began to cry.

# Chapter 16

Erich Shandon had grown up with every privilege life had to offer. Born into affluence to Alexander and Elise Shandon, he was their only son and, in their presence, was treated like royalty—not too much different than the way he was revered by society. Erich had been a spoiled child, not only by his parents but also by his older sister Victoria. By the time he reached manhood, he in turn demanded to be the center of attention by all who graced his presence.

The Shandon wealth began with Erich's grandfather Lucas who had come to America from England and began working in a bank in Boston in the 1800s. Lucas's financial savvy and sharp mind for business soon advanced him to the position of bank president and quickly became a partner in most major land acquisitions in the east. His love for expansion and growth sparked an interest in architecture and engineering. He worked with the greatest professionals in the country, so with the birth of his first and only son Alexander, Lucas vowed that this boy would become one of the greatest architects the world had ever known.

Lucas Shandon's empire continued to grow until his death in 1900. By then, his son Alexander had completed his education with degrees from Harvard and Vanderbilt and was running Shandon Incorporated from his father's New York office. Although based in Manhattan, Shandon Incorporated also held offices in Los Angeles, London, and Tokyo. Alexander ran his father's company like a finely honed machine and maintained excellent relationships with the many clients in the United States and abroad for whom they designed buildings.

Eventually, to the delight of New York society, Alexander met and married Elise Wentworth, the daughter of a banker his father had done business with and admired as a friend. Elise was the perfect wife for Alexander. She, also the product of an elite upbringing, fit well into his lifestyle and was the toast of the social circles in which they traveled. They had homes in Manhattan, the Hamptons, Newport, Palm Beach, and Beverly Hills. Their lives together were made even more perfect by the births of their two children, Victoria and Erich.

Both children were raised in the lap of luxury. Victoria, the eldest of the two, attended the best schools, excelled in ballet and art, and became an accomplished horsewoman. Erich, although not quite as fluent in his studies as his sister, also attended the finest academies and boarding schools. In his senior year, while

finishing college in Switzerland, he won first place in an international competition for his downhill skiing team. Erich had always loved the winter sports, such as skiing, hockey, and speed skating, which was why he decided, before starting his career in his father's company, to attend the 1980 Winter Olympics in Lake Placid, New York.

# Chapter 17

Erich and his friends arrived in Lake Placid with skis, snowsuits, parkas, and tons of baggage.

They rented a large chalet atop a high slope not far from the festivities. The young men considered this trip to be their last before assuming their expected roles within their fathers' businesses. They had all graduated early from their last semester of graduate school, and they planned to celebrate. Upon arrival, Erich called the local restaurants and liquor stores and had all their favorite gourmet foods and liquors delivered to the chalet. The only adult figure in their presence to witness all the debauchery was Bentson, Erich's valet.

Bentson was a kindly old black gentleman who had been a servant with the Shandon family for many years and had been by young Erich's side since the lad had taken his first step. Bentson was very fond of Erich and wanted his charge to enjoy himself, yet he feared this would be a trip they would never forget. The young men partied nonstop, attending most of the events drunk and disorderly; however, their behavior was tolerated because of who they were.

One evening before retiring, Bentson decided to take a walk in the night air. Erich and his friends were still out visiting the bars, and although it was well after midnight, the old man felt restless.

He couldn't tell if it was out of concern for Erich or if he was just feeling old. The wind calmed as Bentson strolled along the snow-covered sidewalk. He wasn't too far from their chalet when he heard a soft moan down below. He looked down as he held on to the rope beside the walkway and saw a crumpled figure below.

"Hello! Are you okay?" yelled Bentson. There was no response, so the old man yelled again.

Finally, the woman at the bottom of the slope turned and looked up at him. "Help me!" she cried.

"Hang on, miss. I'll get you out of there!" Bentson turned to see if there was anyone close by to assist him in rescuing the young woman, but there was no one around. He realized that he would have to help her on his own, so he turned back to the ropes that were lined along the sidewalk. Quickly unhooking a cord from the iron posts holding them in place, he then hooked it to the end of another rope. With both ropes being held by the post, he lowered himself downward to the helpless woman.

"Are you okay, miss?" he asked as he neared her.

She appeared to be all right except for being bitterly cold and having a sprained ankle. "I think so," she whimpered. "Just please get me out of here!"

Bentson assured her that she would be all right now, and he proceeded back up the hill with her in one arm and the rope in the other. Slowly, they made it back up the snowy hill with her clinging to him and limping badly.

When they arrived at the top, they both collapsed on the sidewalk in exhaustion. Shanna introduced herself to Bentson and thanked him profusely for rescuing her. He helped her to her feet, but she couldn't stand on her own. Bentson insisted that she come back to the chalet with him so that he could watch over her until the morning, at which time they could call a doctor.

Once back in the chalet, Bentson placed Shanna gently on the foldout sofa by the fire. He prepared a roast beef sandwich for her and served it with a glass of burgundy wine. Shanna sipped the wine, allowing it's richness to envelope her sore body. She also enjoyed the food, and it soon relaxed her enough to where she fell asleep.

Erich and his friends stumbled back to the chalet around 4:00 a.m. after consuming large amounts of alcohol accompanied by several young ladies. Erich escorted most of his friends to their respective rooms; however, he decided to stay up and pour himself another drink. He looked down and saw Shanna on the sofa and was instantly taken with her beauty. He thought she was probably an admirer who had followed them home, so he quickly shed his clothes and climbed into bed with her.

Moaning, Shanna stirred softly beside him, and he smelled her sweet perfume. She was somehow different than the usual girls who lusted after him; she was beautiful and sexy, no doubt, but there was a softness and a sweetness about her. She moved again and was now facing him on her side. Her long brown hair trailed behind her on the pillow. He stroked it with his fingers; it was silky and smelled of flowers.

He then ran his hand across her face thinking she was the most enchanting creature he had ever seen. Erich glanced down and noticed that the young woman was wearing one of his white cotton dress shirts with his monogram on the cuff. Who was this delicate creature that obviously knew him enough to help herself to his wardrobe?

He continued touching her face while she slept and eventually moved his hand downward. He unbuttoned the top button of the shirt and, reaching inside, cupped a soft full breast. The young woman moaned again as Erich felt himself grow hard. He gently rolled her onto her back, unbuttoned the rest of the shirt, and ever so gently climbed on top of her.

Shanna had been sleeping deeply due to the wine Bentson had given her, but she slowly began to drift back to consciousness, sensing something was terribly wrong. She woke up in terror with a strange man straddling her, kissing her, and caressing her entire body. Shanna let out a scream and started clawing at the maniac who was trying to rape her. Erich was just as startled as she, so to avoid being scratched

to pieces, he pinned her arms above her head. This frightened Shanna even further, and she screamed even louder.

The other occupants of the chalet rushed into the room, and after flipping on the light, Bentson roughly pulled Erich off the young woman.

"What the fuck's going on?" Erich screamed.

"You've got it all wrong, sir," Bentson replied. "She's not what you think, Mr. Erich."

"Then who the hell is she?" Erich bellowed again.

"She's a young woman who had an accident tonight, and I assisted her," Bentson replied helplessly. "I brought her here for the night. I didn't think you would mind, sir," the old man continued.

Erich ran his fingers roughly through his hair shaking his head. "It's all right, Bentson. You did what you thought was right; I'm the fool here," he said. He looked sorrowfully at the frightened woman on his sofa bed and said, "I'm sorry, Mam. I thought you were someone else, and I screwed up."

Shanna shyly responded to him, saying, "It's all right. Should I go?"

Bentson hurriedly answered her, "No, miss. You have to stay here and not put any weight on that ankle until we can get you to a doctor in the morning."

Bentson covered Shanna again with a comforter and turned to his boss, saying, "Mr. Erich, I suggest that you retire to your own room now. It's late, and we all need to get some rest."

Erich nodded saying, "You're right, Benson, and I'm really sorry, Mam," he said nodding to Shanna. She nodded back and slid down in her bed, pulling the blanket up to her chin. Bentson helped Erich to his room, then turned toward his own bedroom, turning off the lights.

# CHAPTER 18

The next morning, the entire group awoke with hangovers from the night before. Erich rose to face the day with a splitting headache trying to remember what had happened the night before.

Fortunately, Bentson had placed aspirin and water by his bedside in anticipation of his condition. Erich downed the aspirin and began to ponder upon what had occurred earlier. He remembered attending the last of the skiing events, then visiting every pub en route back to his chalet. His memories honed in on one particular sight, the beautiful young woman he had encountered in his own place last evening. Erich could not take his mind off her. She was the most beautiful woman he had ever seen.

Finally, he harnessed enough strength to raise himself from his bed and venture forward into the living room where he had at first encountered this exquisite beauty of his dreams. Stumbling into the large vaulted living room, he looked toward the foldout sofa where he had last seen her. She wasn't there. The entire room was reassembled, and everything was in place. Did he imagine the entire ordeal?

Erich didn't think so, for he still smelled her on his hands and body. She had to have been real.

"Bentson!" he yelled. There was no answer. "Where the hell are you?" he bellowed while moving toward the bar. Erich poured himself a vodka and orange juice to help ease his mind while he sorted things out. It was all starting to come back to him. Bentson had rescued a woman from a fall and had brought her here. Yes, it was all so simple, but where was she now?

Finally, Erich collapsed on the sofa and turned on the TV. At the same moment, it seemed, the phone rang. It was Bentson. "I'm sorry, Mr. Erich, but I just got the young lady to the doctor, and he says she's ready to go."

Erich sighed and took another drink. "Very well, Bentson, what next?"

The old man responded, "Well, sir, I think I'll just take Madam back to her hotel and let that be the end of it."

"Very well, Bentson, but I don't think that will be the end of it," Erich answered.

"What do you mean, sir?" he asked.

"I mean that I would like to get to know this young woman in more detail. Pull strings, man, and get her for me!"

"Very well, sir," Bentson responded.

Bentson did pull strings, and over the next few days, Erich and Shanna were inseparable. She forgave him for his indiscretions and they attended all the remaining events together and were the toast of every festivity. Erich was enamored with Shanna and she with him. They enjoyed front row seats to all the remaining Olympic events, and Shanna had never experienced a more exhilarating time in her life.

Erich could hardly bear to let Shanna go when their time at the games were over. She had to return to Nashville and resume her schooling at Vanderbilt, and he had to get back to his father's company in New York. Erich desperately wanted to see her again, and before she boarded the plane to return home, he begged her to come and stay with him in Manhattan when she had modeling jobs. He promised to visit her in Nashville as soon she has a break between semesters.

Erich stood in the airport and watched as Shanna's plane disappeared into the distance. Never in his life had he felt this way about anyone. It must be love, he thought, because he had never hurt this much or been this lonely in his entire life. On his way out of the airport, he stopped at the ticket counter and purchased a ticket to Nashville for the following weekend. He had to see her again, and it had to be soon.

# CHAPTER 19

Shanna was both delighted and surprised to see Erich so soon after their meeting in Lake Placid.

He arrived after her final classes on Friday, and they spent the winter weekend together watching movies, ordering takeout, and going for long walks in the snow. Shanna was nervous at first when Erich suggested they share the bed; however, remembering her fear when he tried to force her before and sensing that she was inexperienced just made him all the more intrigued by her.

She was so beautiful and famous yet so shy with everyone she met. Erich was convinced that she was a virgin, and he vowed to be the one to make love to her for the first time. Shanna was grateful to him for not pressuring her, and his patience and kindness toward her made her love and trust him all the more.

They spent their first winter together every weekend with either Erich traveling south or Shanna going to New York. The press was having such a field day with their relationship with the romance between the handsome millionaire playboy and the beautiful model that the couple spent most of their time in the privacy of their apartment. They didn't seem to mind; however, they were so enamored with one another that the rest of the world didn't seem to matter. In bed, Erich was passionate and made Shanna feel loved and more fulfilled than she had ever felt in her life. She still had not allowed him to completely make love to her, yet something inside of her stopped him every time that he was close to entering her. She would beg him to stop, often crying when she had to deny him.

Eventually, Erich grew frustrated with her and accused her of teasing him to the point of insanity.

On Shanna's birthday in March, they hired a limo and celebrated the occasion with Tony and a few of Shanna's friends at a trendy restaurant in Nashville. They also visited several bars and didn't return to Shanna's apartment until way after midnight. Tony said good night and headed upstairs to his own apartment in the same building. He was worried about his sister; although he liked Erich well enough, there was something about him that he didn't trust.

Shanna had consumed a lot of champagne that evening, and Erich had certainly downed a large amount of whiskey. He poured another drink as he watched Shanna teeter toward the fireplace. The flickering light from the flames silhouetted her body underneath the silk dress that she wore, showing every curve that God had given her. Erich began to get sexually excited. She felt his gaze and turned toward

him. Feeling playful, Shanna slipped out of her dress and let it drop to the floor. Still sipping on her glass of champagne, she stood in front of him in the firelight with nothing on but her underwear and her sheer stockings.

Erich could stand it no longer and moved to her. He took her into his arms and crushed her lips with his own. His tongue hungrily met hers as he took her breath away. He pulled her to him and violently ripped off her bra and panties. Shocked by his aggressiveness, Shanna moved back from him slightly as she watched him roughly pulling off his trousers and ripping open his shirt.

For the first time in their relationship, he frightened her. "Erich, what are you doing?" she whispered.

"I'm going to fuck you, sweetheart," he replied.

"No! Erich, no, you can't do this!" she begged, starting to cry.

"Shut up, you little prick tease, I've waited long enough!"

"Erich, please!" she screamed. "I'm not ready!" He pulled her roughly to the floor and held her wrists in his hands while his lower body tried to get between her legs.

She fought him viciously and managed to free her hand long enough to put deep painful scratches across his chest. Furious, Erich slapped her hard across the face causing her lip to bleed. As she looked at him in horror, he realized what he had done and immediately let her go. Hysterically, Shanna staggered to her feet with blood dripping steadily from her mouth. She grabbed Erich's torn shirt and headed for the door. As she ran down the hall frantically making her way to the elevator, she pulled what was left of the cotton shirt around her naked body.

Erich scrambled to his feet, tugged on his pants, and ran after her. He saw her at the end of the hall and headed toward her. Shanna panicked when she saw him, and since the elevator had not come, she ran down the stairs into the cold night. When Shanna reached the parking lot, Erich was hot on her trail, and being barefoot, she could not go very far on the icy pavement. He finally reached her when she collapsed beside a parked car. By then, she was sobbing uncontrollably and screamed when he grabbed her. "Shanna, it's okay," he said trying to comfort her. "I'm so sorry, baby. I don't know what came over me! I'll never hurt you again, sweetheart," he cried. Shanna just looked at him with tears pouring out of her eyes.

Suddenly, the night was filled with sirens and anxious neighbors gathering around to see what all the commotion was about. Someone had recognized the couple and had already alerted the media. Both Shanna and Erich were humiliated by what had happened, especially when they realized that they were standing in the middle of a parking lot drunk, bleeding, and half dressed.

The police arrived, and bright lights were everywhere. Erich held Shanna close and begged her to forgive him. She looked into his eyes and realized that they both had probably been at fault and that things had just gotten out of hand. An officer asked her if she was all right, and she assured them that she was.

Tony finally arrived after being alerted by a neighbor that his sister was standing nearly naked in the parking lot with her rich boyfriend. He was terrified when he

saw blood on her and was outraged when he learned that Erich had struck Shanna. She assured him that it had all been a misunderstanding and asked him to help her get back inside. Tony ushered them both back into the building through the long stream of policemen and reporters that had gathered outside the condominium. He helped Shanna into bed and gently washed her face with a warm cloth. After giving her two aspirin and some cold water, he sat with her and stroked her hair until she fell asleep.

Back in the living room, Erich had poured himself another drink and sat watching the fire die down. "You, son of a bitch," Tony sneered as he entered the room. Erich ignored him and continued to sip on his drink. "You listen to me, motherfucker," Tony spat, "you ever hit her again, and I'll kill you! You got that?"

Erich turned slowly and softly said, "I'll never hit her again, Tony. I lost control because I love her so much and I wanted her; I just wasn't willing to admit that she wasn't ready for me."

Touched by his remark, Tony turned to leave. "In a way, I understand," Tony responded. "But just remember, you've been warned."

With that, he was gone.

Erich finished his cocktail as the last ember in the fireplace grew cold. He went into the bedroom and looked down at the woman he had grown to love sleeping so peacefully. He climbed quietly into bed putting his arm around her. He gently pulled her close to him as she moaned softly. "I love you," he whispered softly. Her eyes fluttered open for a moment as she realized that he was beside her. His strong arms were comforting, and she felt certain that he truly loved her. But as she drifted back into sleep again, an inner voice began to haunt her thoughts making her wonder about the man who shared her bed and now her life.

# CHAPTER 20

The winter snows melted, and spring brought forth new growth. There was never a more joyous and social event in all of New York society than the anxiously awaited Shandon Ball at the home of Alexander Shandon on Park Avenue. Erich had known for a long time that he wanted to invite the love of his life to attend the party but also realized the extent of his mother's vehemence in the matter. He knew that she would be adamant that he escort Blaine Edwards, the woman that they had always hoped he would marry. She was the daughter of a wealthy steel magnate, and her father was a good friend of Erich's father.

Erich detested Blaine. She was boring, snobbish, and well-bred. He wanted someone exciting, exhilarating, and alluring. Shanna was that woman. She ignited flames in him that had never been lit before. As the date of the ball drew near, Elise continued to press Erich to invite Blaine; after all, she was awaiting his invitation. But, Erich could not conceive of going with anyone other than Shanna.

As the date grew ever closer, Erich decided to override his mother and invite Shanna. He decided to take her to New York weeks before the ball so that his parents could meet her and see for themselves how utterly charming and beautiful she was. Erich knew instinctively that his mother and sister would hate Shanna; however, something inside of him felt that his father would see the love that he felt for her and, with any luck, would be on his side.

Nature produced a beautiful spring that year, and in mid-April, Erich decided to fly Shanna up for the inevitable meeting with his parents. His sister Victoria was due back from a shopping spree in Paris, and his family planned to spend the upcoming weekend at their manor on Southampton. Erich and Shanna arrived at his parents' estate just in time for afternoon tea. Elise and Victoria were seated on the verandah overlooking the ocean when the couple approached.

As expected, the women were cold to her; however, both of them had to admit that she was intoxicatingly beautiful and intelligent. Erich's father, Alexander, was warmer to her although he did point out to his son that her lack of breeding and lineage would make it impossible for her to become a permanent member of their family. Nonetheless, for once in his life, Erich stood up to his parents and insisted that Shanna was to be his date to the infamous ball.

The evening went off without a single hitch, and Shanna arrived looking lovelier than Erich could have imagined her to be. Her dress was a floor-length strapless

blue velvet Dior trimmed in gold, and it molded her body perfectly. She was a vision as she entered the hallway of his parents' estate.

Shanna and Erich enjoyed the event immensely as they danced every dance together. His mother was dismayed that he hadn't spent more time in getting to know Blaine Edwards; however, she tolerated her son's actions for the night so as to not create a scene.

After the ball, before Erich accompanied Shanna back to her room at the Plaza, he cornered her and demanded to know what her intentions were for their relationship. She confessed to him that it would be difficult for a while with her having to pursue her education at Vanderbilt, model, and still perform in Tony's band.

Erich couldn't bear the thought of them being apart so much so he eventually persuaded Shanna to hire a private tutor to get her through her final studies at Vanderbilt and to get her own apartment in New York so that he could be near her all the time. This made perfect sense to her in that most of her modeling jobs were in the city and many of the band's gigs were there too. She leased a charming place on Madison Avenue, not far from where Erich lived on Fifth. Everyone was happy with the new arrangement, except for Tony and Erich's parents.

Tony had been worried about Shanna's relationship with Erich since the night he found her bleeding and half naked in the parking lot. He no longer liked Erich; in fact, he despised the man for the way he was controlling his sister. In Tony's eyes, Erich Shandon was a dominating rich snob who was pulling Shanna further and further away from him. He had always loved her and couldn't bear the thought of her being with another man; however, there was nothing he could do. It was out of his control.

Jackson and Jackie were elated with their daughter's relationship with the rich playboy from one of the finest and most respected old money families in the country. Jack still harbored political aspirations and looked forward to hopefully being linked to the Shandon family while Jackie bragged endlessly to her friends about her daughter becoming the next Mrs. Erich Shandon. Little did she realize that her boastful comments were not too far off the mark.

Elise Shandon was livid about her son's relationship with the supermodel, and she complained endlessly about it to her husband and Victoria. Erich's father was convinced that his son was just sowing his wild oats with the starlet and would settle down with a respectable woman eventually. Elise, however, had seen the look in her son's eyes the night he danced with Shanna at the ball and never taking his eyes off her.

Shanna had never been happier with her life after the ball. She loved living in New York, and Erich had never been kinder to her. He took her to the finest restaurants. They attended the opera, Broadway musicals, and the many social functions that Erich was invited to. Shanna was the toast of every party, and Erich was proud to have her at his side. He loved showing her off to his Harvard friends, and

they were all envious and impressed that he had landed such a beauty. On one occasion, one of Erich's college buddies made an ardent pass at Shanna that Erich overheard. After a heated argument, he knew that his mind was made up. She was going to be his and his alone; he would see to that.

# CHAPTER 21

Shanna was busier than she had ever been in her life. Modeling jobs continued to roll in at a steady pace that frequently sent her to London or Paris. Her tutor forced her to keep up with her studies to ensure graduation in the spring, and Tony booked her as often as possible to sing with his band. The rigorous pace was beginning to take its toll on her, and Erich was furious that she had so little time to spend with him. Shanna was weary, but she felt she had no choice but to continue to try and do it all in order to meet all the expectations that were required of her.

Finally, the strain of Shanna's schedule wore her down, and she collapsed onstage after a Friday night set at Tony's club in Greenwich Village. Terrified, Tony rushed to her side and carried her backstage. His immediate fear was that she had tried the ever-present drugs that were always available in the club and among his fellow band members. Tony had even become a heavy drug user himself, but he did not want Shanna near that scene, not after what had happened to their brother Todd so many years before.

"Shanna, sweetheart, can you hear me?" Tony pleaded with her.

Shanna opened her eyes and looked around slowly. "Oh my god, Tony, what happened?"

"You fainted, baby. Are you okay?" he asked.

"I think so. I'm just so tired, Tony," she moaned.

"I'm going to call a limo and take you home now."

"Take me to Erich's," she said. Disappointed, he assured her he would although he still was wary of Erich Shandon since their horrible fight in Nashville.

Tony phoned Erich from the car and told him he was bringing Shanna to him after her fainting spell. Bentson was at the door to greet them when they arrived, and Erich hurried from his bedroom pulling on his robe. He ran to her and hugged her close to him as they entered the foyer. "Baby, baby, are you all right?" he uttered.

"I think so," she replied weakly.

"Benson, take her to my room and make her comfortable. I shall be there momentarily," he instructed the old man. Bentson led Shanna through Erich's formal living room and down the hallway to his suite. Tony watched her go and hoped she would be all right.

Erich motioned Tony in, went to the bar, and poured them both a scotch. "What happened?" Erich asked coldly.

"She fainted onstage, just tired, I guess," Tony replied.

"Tired? Tired, you say!" Erich shouted. "What are you trying to do, kill her? She's already working her ass off with school and modeling, and then you want her to perform in your fucking two-bit band on weekends? She can't take much more!"

"I know," Tony mumbled. "She just loves it so."

"She doesn't love it, goddamn you!" Erich yelled, "She's just doing it to fucking please you, and I'm saying it's over! Do you understand me? It's over!"

Tony set his glass down and turned to leave. "I'll talk to Shanna about it tomorrow. Please have her call me when she's feeling up to it," he said quietly. Tony made his way to the door with Erich in hot pursuit of him.

"Maybe I didn't make myself clear to you, Tony. Shanna is through with the band, and after graduation, I'm going to see to it that she's through with modeling too. In fact, I'm planning on taking her away for the entire summer where she can rest and we can escape from the world for a while, and that means you, your fucking band, and the fucking paparazzi!"

Tony walked out the door and just said, "Please tell my sister to call me."

Erich pampered Shanna the entire weekend. She had breakfasts in bed, long hot steamy baths, massages, facials, manicures, pedicures. Erich spared no expense in making her comfortable and feeling completely like a princess. He had five-star meals catered in where they dined by candlelight under the stars on his balcony with only the world's finest wines and liquors served. He delighted in spoiling her and having her all to himself.

By Sunday morning, she was so relaxed and happy she would have promised him the world, and she did. They lay wrapped in each other's arms as the first rays of light from the spring morning peeked through the window blinds. Shanna snuggled naked next to Erich's hard body and loved the feel of his strong arms around her waist. He had taught her many ways to pleasure him sexually without actually having intercourse. Erich had grown used to her reluctance in going all the way with him before marriage, and he secretly delighted in being the first for her although he didn't plan to wait much longer.

He sensed Shanna was awake and kissed the tip of her ear, making her smile. "Good morning, sweetheart," he whispered.

Shanna just moaned and rolled over to kiss him. As she turned, the light from the window made a dazzling sparkle across the room, and she looked down to see what had caused the prism. There on her finger was the largest diamond ring she had ever seen in her life. "Oh my god, Erich!" She breathed, "What is this?"

"What do you think it is?" he teased.

Shanna was speechless as she looked at him with tears in her eyes. "Oh, Erich" was all she could say.

"Well?" He probed, "Will you or won't you?"

"Marry you?" she cried.

"Yes, my love," he smiled.

"Oh yes!" she squealed. "Yes, yes, yes, yes!"

He held her close as she cried and laughed simultaneously. "And that's not all, my sweet. I'm taking you away for the whole summer to my father's private island in the Caribbean where we can be alone and the rest of the world can't bother us. Do you accept that too?" He laughed. Shanna just held him tighter, continued to cry, and whispered yes, over and over into his neck.

# CHAPTER 22

After Shanna's graduation from Vanderbilt, Erich stayed true to his word and whisked Shanna away to the Caribbean where they planned to stay the entire summer. Vanilla Island was owned by a group of American millionaires who used the island for corporate entertaining, and Erich's father, Alexander, had been one of the founders of the original concept. Although the Shandons still didn't entirely approve of Erich's relationship with Shanna, they realized that forcing them apart would only drive them together all the more. Alexander had finally persuaded Erich's mother Elise to let them go, and she eventually had given in to her husband.

When Erich and Shanna arrived on the island, Shanna was overcome by the indescribable beauty of the place. Everywhere one looked, there were breathtaking views of the ocean, rolling green hills, cobblestone streets, charming shops, and restaurants and flowers everywhere. Shanna was thrilled by the quaintness of it all, and much to her delight, there were no cars, only horse-drawn carriages. The Shandon villa was on the far side of the island from where they landed, and as they made their way through the village in a carriage pulled by a beautiful white horse, Shanna felt as if she'd become a part of a fairy tale with her handsome prince by her side.

When the couple arrived at the villa, Hattie, an elderly Jamaican woman who had been their housekeeper for many years, greeted them warmly. Erich ran to Hattie and hugged her warmly. They had always been close, and she had spoiled him rotten in his younger years. "Ah, it's good to see you, my boy," she said in her thick island accent. "And just who is this lovely lady you've brought down with you?"

Erich took Shanna by the hand and pulled her close to them. "Hattie," he beamed, "this is my fiancée, Shanna Somers." The older woman reached out and took Shanna's hand, kissed her on both cheeks, and told her how glad she was to meet her and to have her on the island. Tears filled Shanna's eyes, for she was touched by the tenderness the housekeeper had extended to her.

After welcoming them, Hattie left to go and tend to their rooms. Erich led Shanna out onto the sprawling verandah overlooking the ocean where a bottle of champagne sat chilling in a silver bucket. He poured them both a glass, and they sipped on the golden beverage as they stared out at the awesome view that lay before them. Shanna turned to Erich and whispered, "I feel like I'm in a dream."

Erich set down his glass and took her in his arms. "It's real, sweetheart, and I'm going to make this a night you will never forget!"

"Oh, Erich, my love, I don't know how you can make it any more spectacular than it already has been," she murmured.

"Just wait and see, but promise me, Shanna, that you will go along with everything that I have planned for this evening, will you?" She giggled and promised she would; however, she had no idea what lay in store for her, for this was a man of many surprises and one who wouldn't take no for an answer.

Their dinner was served on the verandah, and the couple enjoyed a feast of lobster and shrimp in rich sauces, steamed rice, and fresh vegetables accompanied by fine wine. For dessert, Hattie prepared a fondue pot with bubbling chocolate surrounded by a grouping of exotic fruits for the dipping that she served with warm brandy. After their meal, Erich and Shanna decided to take a stroll on the beach to try and walk off some of the calories they had consumed as well as to clear their heads from the alcohol.

The night was warm and breezy, and they held hands as they walked along the beach. After they had gone approximately half a mile, Erich turned toward Shanna and pulled her to him and said, "Sweetheart, I think you know why I brought you down here, don't you?"

She looked at him, somewhat puzzled, and responded, "To be alone and get to know one another better?"

Erich looked up at the stars for a moment then looked back into her beautiful blue eyes. "I *want* you, Shanna, and I can't wait any longer to have you. I'm a man, and I *need* to have you sexually, completely."

Shanna looked away briefly, but he turned her back around to face him. "Do you hear me, sweetheart? I *have to have you*, and it has to be tonight."

Tearfully, she looked at him and said, "But Erich, we're not married yet, and I'm not sure I'm ready."

Erich stared out into the sea in silence, then turned to her, and said, "Then let's marry ourselves."

"What?" she answered in surprise.

"Let's commit ourselves to each other right now under this blanket of stars, beside the presence of this magnificent ocean, and under the watchfulness of God's almighty presence right here and now!" Erich proclaimed. "Please, Shanna," he begged, "let's do our own private ceremony right here and now, and then we'll do it for everyone else when we return."

Shanna looked at him with tears in her eyes, touched by the spiritual side of him she had just encountered. "All right," she whispered.

Thrilled by her willingness to go through with his plan, Erich sat her down on a boulder while he scurried around to make hurried and rugged preparations. He returned with an armload of brush that he placed at her feet and surrounded it by a long train of ivy he had found encircling a nearby tree. In her hair, he placed a

beautiful white flower, which to him symbolized her virginity. After lighting the brush, Erich pulled Shanna to her feet, took her hands in his, and stared at her beauty in the firelight.

For a few moments, they just stood gazing into each other's eyes listening to the waves crash against the shore and to the popping of the fire at their feet. Finally, Erich spoke, "Shanna, I just want you to know that I love you more than anything, and I want you to be my wife, now and always. Will you let me be your husband, your protector, your lover, and your friend, forever and ever?"

Shanna stared back at him, her eyes never leaving his, and answered, "Yes, my love, now and always."

Erich kissed her hands and, in addition, asked, "Do you have anything to say to me, sweetheart?"

"Yes," she whispered quietly. "I just want you to promise that you will never hurt me and that you will always be there for me until the end of time."

Erich took her into his arms, held her tight, and whispered to her, "You know I will, baby. You know I will."

# CHAPTER 23

The couple walked hand and hand back to the villa where Erich led her to their bedroom. He motioned for her to go on inside and that he would return momentarily. She entered and was amazed at how beautiful everything looked. The room was bathed in candlelight. Garlands of tropical flowers were strung around their bed, and a warm bubble bath with floating rose petals waited for them. Although Shanna was nervous, the beauty of the room brought a sense of tranquility to her. She looked around and saw that Hattie had laid out a beautiful pink silk nightgown and robe on their bed, which she had made with the most beautiful linens Shanna had ever seen.

Erich tapped slightly on the door and entered with a silver tray bearing champagne and strawberries. Shanna smiled at him as he set the tray down and moved toward her. "Are you happy, sweetheart?" he asked.

"Yes," she replied quietly. Realizing she was tense, Erich held her for a moment then motioned toward the bathtub. He led her to the tub, removed her clothing, and eased her into the hot steamy water. He watched as she settled into the suds and caught his breath as the bubbles glistened around her naked breasts.

Erich turned and brought the tray and set it on a marble table beside the bathtub. He then slipped out of his clothes and slid into the water with Shanna. As the water swirled around his hard body, he pulled her to him and kissed her tenderly. Erich felt her slowly began to relax into him, so he began to softly stroke her hair and touch her breasts. He noticed himself starting to get aroused, and he knew he did not want to rush the event, so he pulled away and suggested they have some champagne. They bathed slowly, washing each other, touching, and kissing.

Eventually, Erich suggested that they get out of the water before they shriveled away to nothing, and Shanna giggled as he helped her step out of the tub and toweled her dry. She went to the bed and slipped into the pink nightgown as Erich wrapped a towel around his waist and followed her.

They sat on the bed together looking into each other's eyes and sipping the last of the champagne.

"Shanna," Erich began, "I love you very much, and I want more than anything to make you happy, and I don't want tonight to be anything less than perfect."

Shanna didn't respond but leaned over and kissed him softly on the lips. "Everything is perfect, Erich," she whispered.

Shanna moved her kisses from his mouth and down along his neck. Her tongue made little traces along his shoulders as her hands caressed his chest. Erich's entire body tingled as he watched his wife's head move down his stomach as she continued to cover him with wet kisses. When her tongue reached the top of the towel, he trembled and felt himself grow hard. Finally, when he could stand it no longer, he reached down and pulled her up to face him, then kissed her hungrily on the mouth. She kissed him in return as they fell back into the luxurious bedding.

Erich removed her nightgown as his towel easily fell away. He stared down at her magnificent body in the candlelight and looked into her eyes. She returned his gaze with a look he had never seen before, a look of hunger and lust for him that he had awaited for so long. The joy in him spurred his ardor; knowing that she was ready for him, he kissed her again while moving his hands over her lean body. He reached down between her legs and let his fingers begin to move gently along the pink folds of her womanhood as she moaned. Erich then spread her thighs apart and moved on top of her. She didn't show any of the hesitancy that he had expected, convincing him that she had truly accepted him as her husband and was ready to give herself to him totally.

He entered her slowly at first, and she gasped only a little as he penetrated her. Erich looked into her eyes once again, then lowered his mouth to hers, and pushed his way gently inside of her. Shanna moaned softly as Erich quickly began to move his hips with rhythmic motions. Her body soon joined in with his, and they became as one—connected in spirit, mind, and eternal love.

Erich's passion for her was unbridled, and he found it hard to contain his climax, wanting to pleasure her first; however, she was far more into him than he ever could have imagined. As he continued to move against her, he began to softly pinch her nipples with his fingertips, and she whimpered as they hardened beneath his touch. The tingling seemed to move rapidly down through her body until it reached where they were joined together, and she screamed in surprise as the sensation erupted there and then tore through her entire being. Erich, unable to hold on any longer, came in her with such a force that he too yelled out in surprise and joy then arched his back, praying that this feeling would never leave him.

After a few moments, Erich lowered himself and lay on top of Shanna, and the silvery glow of the moonlight beamed down upon them, their bodies glistening.

# CHAPTER 24

The next few weeks were the most blissful times of Shanna's life. She and Erich were inseparable, and their moments together were the most passionate that either of them had ever known.

They made love almost continuously and were amazed at the insatiable appetites that each of them harbored for one another. Hattie was amused that the young lovers rarely left their bedroom, and she delighted in preparing them special meals that she left by their door daily, accompanied by fine wines and tropical drinks.

When they did emerge from their room and left the villa, they took long strolls on the beach where they would watch the sunsets and talk about their wedding and what the future held. Erich took Shanna to the stables on the island where his father kept several of his once prize-winning stallions that had been retired to the island but were still magnificent animals. Often, Hattie would pack a lunch of imported cheeses, wine, fresh bread, and local fruits for them to carry on picnics when they would take the horses on long rides throughout the enchanted green hills.

Some days, Erich would have a horse-drawn carriage waiting to carry them into the town, which was a quaint village with cobblestone streets and exquisite shops. They would walk hand in hand peering into windows and sampling the delectable edibles offered by the street vendors along the way.

One afternoon, while Shanna sat sipping a spiced rum drink and a scone at a café, Erich disappeared into a vintage jewelry shop only to appear later with the most beautiful antique cameo Shanna had ever laid her eyes on. "Oh, sweetheart, it's beautiful!" she exclaimed. Erich beamed, for he delighted in spoiling her and making her happy.

And Shanna was happy, happier than she had ever been. She felt like she had finally reached nirvana, and she never wanted to return. Vanilla Island was her Eden, a paradise that only a privileged few ever get to experience. But even in the original Eden, there were upheavals, and Shanna wasn't prepared in the least for what she was soon dealt.

After being on the island for almost two months, Shanna awoke at dawn with an upset stomach. This was a sickness she had never felt before; however, somewhere in the dark shadows of her mind, it felt vaguely familiar. For several days, she couldn't eat any of Hattie's wonderfully prepared meals, and she felt absolutely drained of energy—to the point that she would not even accompany Erich to the beach for their daily walks. Erich became increasingly worried about her and expressed his

concerns to Hattie one morning while he sat on the verandah sipping coffee. The old woman had her suspicions about Shanna's illness and had decided to speak to the girl herself as soon as she could find time to be alone with her.

Hattie finally sent Erich into the market for some herbs that might cure Shanna's queasiness and help her regain her strength. He agreed and left shortly after breakfast to retrieve the things from a list the housekeeper made for him. While Erich was gone, Hattie ventured into the couple's bedroom to find Shanna still in bed lying there, looking positively green. "You all right, sweet child?" the older woman spoke in her West Indian accent. Shanna just moaned and rolled over on her side.

Hattie moved to the bed and sat down on the edge. She reached over and patted the younger woman's backside and said softly, "I want you to drink this, sweetheart. I think it will make you feel better."

Shanna rolled over to see Hattie holding out a tiny crystal goblet containing an olive-colored liquid. "What is it?" she inquired softly.

"It's an old island herbal recipe, my dear. Drink!"

Shanna reached forward and took the glass, raised it to her lips, and drank. It was sweet yet bitter at the same time. She made a face but smiled as she handed the goblet back to the old woman. "Thanks, Hattie," she whispered, grinning a little.

The housekeeper still sat on the edge of the bed looking at the beautiful young woman in front of her, not knowing where to begin. Shanna just stared back at her and finally asked, "Hattie, what is it?"

Looking down, Hattie softly asked, "My dear, when is the last time you had your monthly?"

"What?" Shanna responded, shocked at the question.

"I'm asking you about your menstrual cycle." She continued, "When was the last time?"

Shanna sat up, fidgeted, and responded, "I honestly don't know. I think it was way before I came down here."

"Well, with that being about two months ago and with the way you're feeling now, I'd say you were with child," the old woman said assuredly.

Shanna just stared at her in amazement but then realized that Hattie was right! Shanna put her head in her hands and started to cry. "Oh, Hattie," she whimpered miserably, "what am I going to do?"

The old woman just stood up, laughed, and responded, "Oh, child, this happens every day; women have babies all the time! Master Erich will be thrilled!"

Shanna sprang up after her. "Oh, God, Hattie, you cannot tell him, not yet!" The older woman was somewhat confused, but she agreed not to say anything at all. She left Shanna alone then, still chuckling softly at the young woman's naiveté.

After Hattie left, Shanna got up and went to the bathroom. There she splashed cold water on her face and looked at herself in the mirror. The person staring back didn't even look like the same girl that had come here just a few weeks ago; now she

appeared tired, gaunt, and pale. She padded softly back into the bedroom and sat down on the window seat to stare out at the ocean. The day was gray and misty, not too different from the way she felt.

Erich returned from town and immediately went to look for his bride. He found her seated by the window and immediately went to her. He knelt by her side and took her hand in his, kissing it. "How are you feeling, sweetheart?"

She smiled at him and answered, "A little better."

"I brought back some special treats for you from town, which should make you feel better; Hattie is preparing a tray now."

Shanna didn't comment; however, she just stared into his eyes, touched at the love pouring out from them. With tears in her eyes, she said softly, "Erich, we have to talk."

He just looked at her in amazement and answered, "What is it, babe?" Not answering him yet, she stood and walked away, then turned to face him. He followed, anxious to know what she wasn't telling him. "Shanna, what is it? Are you sick? Do you want to leave me? What? Damn it!" he said raising his voice.

"I'm pregnant," she replied meekly.

Erich just stared at her in disbelief. "You're what?" he implored.

"I said I'm pregnant, at least I think I am," she answered.

Erich was stunned and silent for a moment then Shanna started to cry. He pulled her to him and held her tight, gently rubbing her hair as she cried into his shoulder. He comforted her as best he could for a few moments, then asked hesitantly, "Are you sure, baby?"

Shanna stepped back from him slowly and wiped her eyes. Erich noticed that her tears had stained the beautiful silk pajamas that she wore. "No, I'm not sure, but by all calculations, I guess I am," she replied finally.

Erich paced around the room running his fingers roughly through his hair. "So what does that mean, Shanna? Are you or aren't you?" he demanded.

"Well, I'm not sure just yet, but we've been on the island for over two months now. We've never used any protection, and I haven't had my period since before we left," she said, starting to cry again. "What are we going to do, Erich?" she asked tearfully.

Erich didn't respond to her at first as he continued to pace around the room. He finally stopped in front of the window and turned to her and snapped, "How in the hell could you let this happen?"

Shanna was taken aback with surprise by his question and stood in silent shock for a few moments. Finally, she approached him and said angrily, "How could *I* let this happen? Was it all up to *me*, Erich? Did you think that we could just fuck over and over and nothing would happen?"

Erich was furious that she would take that tone of voice with him and be so crude with her remark. "We didn't fuck, goddamn it! We made love, or at least I thought that's what we were doing, and I assumed you were on the pill or doing something to prevent getting pregnant!" he yelled.

Shanna just stared at Erich in disbelief as he poured himself a shot of vodka from a decanter and swallowed it angrily. A long silence fell between them as neither of them said anything. Erich finally sat down at the window and poured himself another shot. Shanna approached him and put her hand on his shoulder and said softly, "I wasn't sure what I was supposed to do, Erich. Our being together as man and wife . . . making love took me by surprise. It has been so intense and powerful that I really didn't think of anything else."

Erich stood abruptly, startling her, and replied, "Well, you had better think of what to do now!" With that, he grabbed his windbreaker and stormed from the room, slamming the door.

Shanna was absolutely stunned by her husband's behavior. She had seen that side of Erich before, but she had never expected him to react so cruelly toward her, especially when this was half his fault! She approached the window again and looked out into the nasty weather. She didn't see Erich; however, she soon heard his motorbike fire up and spin out of the gravel driveway. Depressed and lonely, she also poured herself a vodka, mixed in a little juice, and, sipping it slowly, returned to her bed.

She moped around their bedroom all day lying in bed, sitting by the window and sipping her drink. Just before dusk, Hattie came in to check on her and was amazed at how miserable the young woman looked. She forced Shanna out of bed and into a hot bath, where she helped her bathe and wash her hair. Shanna started to argue with her; however, she was too tired and somewhat tipsy to protest much. The older woman helped her out of the tub and ushered her into the bedroom where she wrapped her into a plush robe and settled her onto a chair. Hattie had set out a tray of sweet crackers, cheeses, and teas for her, so Shanna nibbled and sipped in silence as she watched the older woman change her bedding and lay out clean clothes.

Hattie finally broke the silence by saying, "It's almost dinnertime, and I'll be serving you and Master Erich out on the porch tonight."

"Did he come back?" Shanna asked halfheartedly.

"No, but he'll be back," Hattie assured her. "He loves you Mrs. Shanna, and he ain't going to go far as long as you're around and carrying his baby. He's just in shock, that's all," she said while tucking in a crisp white sheet. At the mention of the baby, Shanna began to cry again. Both she and Hattie looked up suddenly as they heard Erich's bike pull up outside. "There he is now, honey," Hattie said. "Now you just put on this pretty dress that I laid out for you and come on down to dinner in half an hour." With that, the old woman picked up the dirty laundry and turned to go.

Reluctantly, Shanna sat down her teacup and began to get ready. The outfit Hattie selected for her was beautiful, and she smiled at the old woman's thoughtfulness. It was a dainty white eyelet dress with a low-clinging neckline and tight-fitting waistline that came down to her ankles. Shanna looked at herself in the mirror and smiled at how innocent and pure the dress made her look but was

reminded that if she *was* pregnant, then her innocence was long gone. She sighed sadly and reached for a strand of pink pearls from the dresser, a gift Erich had given her in New York. She fastened them around her neck, ran a brush through her hair, then turned to go downstairs. Although she dreaded the confrontation, she would have to face her husband eventually and discuss their problem.

Shanna opened the door and caught her breath, for there stood Erich. He was drenched from head to toe but smiled sheepishly at her as she looked at him in surprise. She said nothing but stepped back to let him in. "Where have you been?" she finally asked to break the silence.

Erich stripped off his jacket and then peeled out of his shirt as he stared at her. "I've been out riding in the rain all day thinking about you, about us, about the baby," he said softly. Shanna said nothing as he continued. "And I've been thinking, sweetheart, that's it's okay. It's going to be okay."

"What do you mean?" she asked.

"I mean that we'll have our huge wedding when we get back; then it will be official. I'll sweep you away on a fabulous honeymoon, and everyone will think you got pregnant then," he answered confidently.

Shanna just stared at him in amazement. "Are you serious?" she replied. "Are you insane? And what are people going to think when I have this baby in six months? It won't work, Erich. Everyone will know anyway."

Frustrated, Erich ignored her and continued to come out of his clothes. Shanna paced around him and continued to pummel him verbally with questions. Finally, in anger and irritation, Erich grabbed Shanna and threw her down upon the bed and covered her mouth with his own. She struggled against his hard and now-naked body that only managed to arouse him. He tried to remove her dress; however, the fabric and tiny buttons made it impossible.

Shanna continued to try and wiggle away from him, but he held her firmly underneath his body. "Erich, please," she begged, "let me go!"

He sneered at her and responded, "Why, what harm can it do now?" She smelled beer on his breath and wondered how many six-packs he had consumed that day.

Suddenly, Hattie rapped softly on the door announcing that dinner was ready. Shanna lay quietly with Erich still sprawled on top of her. "We'll be right down, Hattie," he said. With that, he moved off Shanna, and she quickly rose to her feet, wobbling a little. She was shaking as he got up and stood beside her. He kissed the side of her head and said softly, "I'm going to shower, baby. Go on down, and I'll join you in a minute." Erich went to the bathroom and closed the door as Shanna just stared after him in silent confusion. She moved to the mirror, wiped the tears from her face, straightened her dress, then went downstairs for dinner.

Shanna was seated at the table when Erich arrived out on the verandah for dinner. Hattie had arranged a beautiful table with crisp linens, tropical flowers, polished silver, fine china, and crystal goblets. She even had a bottle of their finest champagne chilled and waiting in a copper stand. Hattie knew that the day had

been difficult for both of them, so she wanted to make the night as special as possible for the young couple.

Shanna didn't look up when Erich approached nor when he kissed her cheek before seating himself. He reached immediately and poured them both a glass of champagne, and only when he raised his glass to hers did her eyes meet his. "I'm sorry, baby," he said. "Let's forget everything from today and just enjoy this evening." Shanna still didn't utter a word; however, she did pick up her goblet and touched it to Erich's glass before downing the entire thing. "Thirsty, are we?" He smirked as she reached for the bottle and poured herself another drink. This one she just sipped as she just sat and stared at him.

Erich also poured himself another glass full of the golden liquid then reached for her hand. They held hands for a few moments and just stared out at the beach, listening to the waves as they crashed into the shore. Hattie brought their appetizers of caviar, oysters, and imported crackers and noticed the somber atmosphere surrounding the two young lovers. She hurt for them for the old woman had grown to love Shanna and Erich had always been like a son to her, for she had served their family for many years.

Each of them only picked at their food even though they were both starving.

Hattie came and removed the plates, and when she returned to the kitchen, Shanna finally spoke. "Erich," she said quietly, "we can't just forget it."

"Forget what?" he said halfheartedly as he poured them each another glass of champagne.

"About this child!" Shanna reiterated.

"I don't want to talk about it tonight," he replied irritably.

Stubbornly, Shanna continued, "I've made a decision, Erich. I want an abortion," she said simply.

It was as if the world stopped turning and the air hung as heavy as a London fog as Erich turned to face her with a look she prayed she would never see again. His eyes were black as he stared hard at her and asked her heatedly, "What did you say?"

Fearfully, she answered, "I said I think I should have an abortion, at least this time. We can always have other children, Erich." He continued to stare at her with a devilish look that made her shiver. She started to open her mouth to speak again when the blow came before the words came out. Erich smacked her so hard across the face that she jerked, knocking her champagne glass over, sending it shattering against the floor.

Shanna was so stunned that it took her a few moments to realize what had happened, her head swimming both from the blow and the champagne. She stared up at her husband in disbelief with blood trickling from her lip. "How could you even think of such a thing?" he asked in an evil tone. "You would kill a Shandon? You bitch!" he bellowed. Shanna was mortified and didn't know what to do. She saw Hattie from the corner of her eye coming from the kitchen, so she decided to make her move and escape from this madman who claimed to love her.

As the housekeeper approached the table, Shanna sprang from her chair and bolted down the steps of the verandah, heading down the beach. Erich was furious and took off after her in hot pursuit.

Hattie screamed at him to stop, but he ignored the old woman. When Shanna realized Erich was after her, she started to run; however, the tightness of her dress wouldn't allow her to put much distance between them.

She spotted a clump of boulders and decided that her only way of escaping would be to climb up and away from him. Shanna barely made it to the first ledge when she looked down and saw Erich below her. Frantically, she tried to pull herself up higher onto the rocks to no avail. Her dress ripped, causing her to slip; and it was then that Erich grabbed her ankle. "Shanna, come down from there before you hurt yourself," he begged.

She struggled against him crying, "Get away from me, you bastard!" Erich continued to keep a tight grip on her leg when all of a sudden, she tried to kick free of him, losing her footing and falling down hard against the sand.

Shanna hit the ground with such force that it knocked her unconscious. Erich was terrified at the sight of his wife's lifeless body lying on the beach, and he was deathly afraid of the damage he had caused to her and possibly his unborn child. In a panic, Erich scooped her up into his arms and raced back to the villa with her as fast as he could. As he approached the verandah, he screamed for Hattie and instructed her to call a doctor. Since there were no hospitals on the island and only two practicing doctors, Erich feared for the worst in their situation.

He placed Shanna tenderly in their bed, and he and Hattie waited anxiously for a doctor to arrive.

The old woman sat nervously by the window wringing her hands as Erich paced nonstop, drinking whiskey. Finally, there was a knock at the door, and Hattie raced to open it. Dr. Meadows had come. He was an old friend of Erich's father and had been semiretired and living on Vanilla Island for years.

Hattie quickly ushered him in and told him what had happened with Erich's fiancée.

Erich, not long on patience, grabbed Dr. Meadows by the arm and pulled him in the direction of Shanna's room. He explained to the doctor that he and Shanna had just been out for the nightly stroll, and they had had too much champagne and had gotten silly on the rocks, causing her to fall. Dr. Meadows nodded, and as he started into the bedroom, Erich stopped him and said, "Oh, and Doc, I think there is a chance she might be pregnant." The doctor gave Erich another silent nod, went into the bedroom, and closed the door.

Erich resumed his pacing and drinking while the doctor examined his wife. Hattie sat on the window seat and gave the young man an ugly stare. "What?" he questioned her. The old woman said nothing and looked away. "I asked you a question, Hattie," Erich continued. "What was that look for?"

Finally, the elderly woman could hold her tongue no longer, even if he was her employer, and replied, "I know what you did to her, Mr. Erich; I heard the glass break and saw the blood on her lip. You ought never to hit a lady like that. I know what you did to her on that porch, but I don't know what you did to her out there," as she motioned toward the beach.

Erich could take it no more. He collapsed on a chair, put his head in his hands, and started to cry.

Hattie rose and went to him, putting her arm around his shoulders, for despite his cruelty, she felt sorry for him. Eventually, Dr. Meadows reappeared from the bedroom, and he was wiping his hands dry on a towel. Erich sprang from his chair and immediately approached him saying, "Well, how is she? Is she all right, Doctor?"

Dr. Meadows looked at the young man solemnly and answered, "Yes, son, she'll be fine. She just needs lots of rest."

Immediate relief washed over Erich, but he had to know. "And the baby? Was there one?" he asked.

"I'm sorry, Erich," Dr. Meadows replied. "There was, but she lost it."

Disappointment showed on Erich's face; however, he was relieved that Shanna was going to be all right. "Can I see her?" he asked.

"Yes," the doctor answered, "just don't get her excited."

Erich shook the man's hand then headed down the hall toward the bedroom. Upon entering, he noticed that Shanna was lying on her side, her back to the door. Her shoulders were heaving, and he realized that she was crying. Not knowing quite what to say to her, he approached slowly and sat on the edge of the bed.

Shanna knew it was him, but she didn't turn over nor did she say a word. He spoke first and said, "I'm so sorry, sweetheart." She continued to ignore him, so he moved to her and turned her to face him. He immediately felt sick at seeing the ugly bruise on her mouth from where he had hit her. Her eyes were dark and sad as he reached down and pulled her close to him and held her gently in his arms.

They sat that way for a long while before Erich finally spoke to her and said, "Baby, I will never hit you again. I promise. I want us to get past this whole ugly episode and put it behind us."

Shanna finally looked up at him and spoke softly, "I do too." Then she fell asleep in his arms. Erich stayed awake for a long while thinking about what had happened, and he decided that as soon as Shanna was strong enough to travel, they would leave the island and return home to plan their wedding.

# CHAPTER 25

When Erich and Shanna returned to the States after their summer in paradise, their lives were anything but normal. Erich went back to work at his father's architectural firm in New York, and Shanna returned to her hometown in Nashville. She resumed her modeling career on a part-time basis and began singing again with her brother's band.

Tony was thrilled to have his sister back in town and loved the time they spent together recording and writing music. He noticed a change in her; however, although she was still the same vibrant and beautiful girl he had always loved, there was now something different about her, something more deep, sensuous, and mysterious. Shanna was delighted to be back in her brother's company for she had missed him; they had always been close, and she didn't feel complete without Tony in her life.

They still had their apartment together at the Rokeby in Nashville; but now that Shanna was back in town, still modeling, planning her wedding, and making a splash with the band, the press hounded her constantly. Every time she left her building to attend classes or go to the airport, cameras flashed incessantly, and reporters screamed her name. Tony tried to shield her as much as possible; however, his popularity was soaring as well, so their problem seemed to be compounded when he was with her.

Finally, Tony's manager suggested to them that they purchase a beautiful historic property that had just come on the market that was previously owned by a country music artist who had built a state-of-the-art recording studio located on the grounds as well as a newly installed security system. It almost sounded too good to be true, and when Shanna heard the name of the property, Hounds Run, she knew it had to be theirs.

Naturally, Erich was not thrilled about Shanna and her brother becoming partners in real estate nor was he happy about her spending so much time in the music industry. In his opinion, modeling was bad enough; now his fiancée was a rock star. However, when he learned that she had recorded with artists; such as Dan Fogelberg, Don Henley, Nancy Wilson, and others, he was somewhat impressed. Erich was very amazed when he heard her remakes of some Barbra Streisand hits, for he had never realized what a vocally talented woman his future wife was. Nonetheless, he wanted her to concentrate more on becoming his wife and a socialite and less on being a glamour queen and recording phenomenon.

On weekends, Shanna flew to New York to be with Erich and make arrangements for their wedding. Thankfully, Elise, her future mother-in-law had stepped in and was doing most of the planning herself. The date was set for the following May at Saint Patrick's Cathedral on Fifth Avenue, and Elise was inviting over 1,500 guests for the nuptial. The reception was to be held at the Shandon's Long Island estate where only an elite few hundred would be invited. Shanna didn't have much of an input toward the happenings whatsoever, and she really didn't care; for in her mind, they were already married, and this event was just a formality.

On her weekends in New York, Shanna and Erich spent much of their time selecting china, crystal, and silver and were on the bridal lists of every major store in the city. Most of their decisions were made either in the privacy of their own apartment or at the Shandon's place because the press followed them everywhere. Erich hated the media. He and his parents were humiliated that a family of their status was on the news at every waking hour and in the tabloids on every corner. The intrusiveness of the cameras left them feeling as if they were experiencing photogenic rape at every turn. Erich's sister and mother nagged at him constantly about the embarrassing position they were now in and reminded him continually that he had let the family down by marrying out of his social class.

As the holidays approached, Erich and Shanna found themselves in even more of a social whirlwind with parties, dinners, and appearances. It was a draining time for both of them, yet oddly enough, they dealt with the pressure and got along well together except for a few minor spats about wedding decisions. Erich loved showing off his beautiful fiancée to his corporate friends and old college buddies. She looked smashing at every event they attended, and the cameras loved her.

Shanna's classes were over, and she had completed her midterm exams, so she accepted a couple of modeling assignments and offered to do a benefit concert with her brother. Unfortunately, her plans coincided with what Erich had in mind, and he was livid when he learned of the commitments she had made. "You're not doing it," he bellowed one afternoon over lunch in Manhattan. "You have disgraced me and my family enough by bringing your celebrity into our lives, and I'm telling you, it's enough!"

Shanna, although not entirely shocked by his outburst, was hurt by his comment; she had never meant to disgrace anybody. She was simply doing her job. They had been getting along so well, and Shanna didn't want to rock the boat, so to speak, so she agreed to cut back her modeling and recording work until after the first of the year. This did not appease Erich, for he looked at her in amazement and said, "You're not getting it, are you? I'm telling you, Shanna, that it is over. This modeling career of yours and these insane plans of becoming an international rock star with your brother are history!"

Shanna knew that arguing with Erich was useless, especially when he was indignant on a subject, so she let the matter drop for the moment. She agreed to put

her careers on hold until after their wedding, but she began to feel something inside of her starting to crumble, her dreams on the verge of shattering.

That night, she called Tony and told him she wouldn't be able to record or sing with him or the band until after she returned from her honeymoon. He was devastated over the news and could tell that a spark inside of her had slowly started to dim. They agreed to talk more about the subject when she returned home for the holidays.

On Christmas Day, Shanna introduced Erich to her parents. She had never reconciled with them after her brother Todd's death and the insanity that they forced upon her by placing her in a mental institution. Thankfully, she had never regained her memory over her pregnancy at age sixteen and the traumatic episode of giving birth to Tony's child.

Erich had never known the reasoning behind Shanna's alienating her parents from her life nor her reluctance in introducing him to them. He knew by what she had said that they were a dysfunctional family, yet Jackson Masterson was a prominent Nashville attorney, and his wife Jackie was a well-known socialite around town. They were no means in the same class as his family; however, it appeared to him that they had made the most of their lives without being born into social privilege.

Shanna and Erich had spent Christmas Eve morning with Sable, enjoying a delectable holiday brunch at the Plaza. The threesome then all delighted in a handsome cab ride through Central Park in the snow making it all the more special. Erich and Shanna later attended his mother's annual black-tie dinner in the Hamptons, to which Sable was also invited, but she had already planned to fly to Palm Beach to celebrate with friends. The next morning, the young couple flew south, much to Shanna's dread.

The Mastersons could not wait to meet their future son-in-law. They had never dreamed that their daughter would marry into such prominence, yet she was engaged to one of the most sought-after bachelors in the world. Jackie was envious, naturally, but she was also thrilled that her placement on the social ladder would be raised a notch or two. Jackson was equally enthused over his daughter entering into an entirely new economic realm; however, he was more excited about all the new clubs he would be allowed into and the new connections he would undoubtedly acquire.

The entire Masterson household had been in a hubbub with the news of Erich and Shanna's arrival. At his sister's request, Tony had phoned his father at the law office and told him that they would all be coming on Christmas morning. Jackie had spent weeks preparing for their visit by ordering the finest champagne, beluga caviar, pates, smoked salmon, and a huge roast duck. For the first time in years, she had brought in prominent designers to decorate their massive entry hall, the yard, a huge tree, and nearly every room in the entire house. Jack had never seen his wife so excited about anything in her life, and he did not even mind the exorbitant bills that accrued as a result of her efforts.

On Christmas morning, Jackie was up at dawn making sure that everything would be perfect for the arrival of her future son-in-law. She had their housekeeper Fanny

busy making homemade stuffing, rolls, and desserts way before the sun was even up. By 10:00 a.m., only after Jackie was certain that everything was perfect, from the frosting on the cake to the place cards on the table, did she race upstairs to get ready herself.

Jack was up and buttoning his shirt when she entered the bedroom looking disheveled but excited. She barely acknowledged him as she shed her flour-covered clothes, pulled on a bathrobe, and went to run a bath. She reappeared a moment later and headed to the bookshelf where she kept a decanter of vodka stashed, still ignoring her husband as if he wasn't there. She poured a shot into a glass of juice she had brought from the kitchen and headed back toward the bathroom. This time, when she passed him, Jackson reached out, touched her arm, and said, "Don't overdo it today, Jackie, please."

"Fuck you, Jack," she replied, continuing on to the bathroom and slamming the door.

Tony collected Erich and Shanna at the airport in his new Mercedes and drove them to the Masterson home on Franklin Road. Shanna was a nervous wreck and didn't know how she would ever make it through this holiday without totally losing her mind. She had consumed as much champagne as Erich would allow her to drink on the plane, but it still had done little to calm her nerves. Tony was on edge too and had smoked a joint earlier in order to help him deal with his parents. They entered the big iron gates just as a light snow began to fall, and they all marveled at the beauty of the stately home with its festive decorations.

Jackson was waiting in his study nursing a scotch and smoking a cigar when he heard the Mercedes in the driveway. He rushed to the front door to let them in and couldn't believe the excitement he felt over seeing his daughter again and meeting her fiancé. It had been a long time since they had parted ways, and he had missed her more than he had realized. He watched them get out of the car and felt an unexpected rush of anticipation well up inside.

As they entered, Jack and Tony embraced as a father and son would; then he approached his daughter hesitantly not knowing what to do or say. Finally, she spoke, saying, "Merry Christmas, Daddy."

With that, Jack pulled her into his arms, hugged her tightly, and cried. She finally pulled away from him with tears in her eyes, but smiling, and said, "Daddy, this is Erich, my fiancé."

Jackson shook hands with his future son-in-law and was relieved that the younger man seemed genuinely glad to meet him.

After taking their coats, he finally ushered them all into the formal living room where Jackie's massive tree stood covered in ornaments. Tony, Shanna, and Erich placed the gifts they had brought underneath it and complimented the décor of the entire home. Jackson explained to them that Jackie had gone crazy that year with decorations and that he was near bankruptcy because of it. They all laughed as he excused himself to go and make drinks and locate Fanny.

He returned shortly with a tray of champagne flutes followed by the elderly housekeeper carrying an ice bucket with a chilled bottle of Dom Perignon. Shanna rose immediately and went to the old black woman and took the ice bucket from her. She then gathered her in her arms, and the two women held each other for several minutes, swaying back and forth and crying. For many years, Fanny had been Shanna's only friend and the main reason the young woman had not committed suicide after Tony left her and she had learned of her pregnancy.

Jack ceremoniously announced that he was ready to pour a toast and ordered Fanny to summon Jackie. The old woman turned and was about to head up the grand staircase when she saw the lady of the house exit her bedroom, and Fanny heaved a sigh of relief at not having to struggle up the stairs with her advanced arthritis.

Jackie arrived in the living room looking beautiful in a black wool pantsuit with her silver hair swept up in an elegant style. Ignoring her family, she strolled immediately over to Erich, stuck out her hand, and introduced herself. He politely took her hand and kissed it gently, stopping to notice the garish diamond ring she always wore. Jackie could not take her eyes off him, for he looked much more handsome than the pictures she had seen in the newspapers and magazines.

Jack eventually broke her gaze from the good-looking young man and indicated that she needed to greet her children. Jackie had purposefully focused her attention on Erich because she was uneasy around Tony and desperately wanted to avoid any uncomfortable contact with her daughter. The half siblings stood side by side until their mother had no choice but to acknowledge them.

Finally, Jackie moved to Tony, gave him a hasty brush on the cheek with her lips, and wished him a Merry Christmas. Then, with all the fake motherly love she could muster, she grabbed Shanna and hugged her tightly, telling her how thrilled they were to have her home. After their supposed tender embrace, Jackie pulled back and said, "Now, let's have some champagne, shall we?"

The rest of Christmas was tolerable for Shanna; her mother drank quite a bit and flirted shamelessly with Erich, and her father, although inebriated too, was cordial and charming. She and Tony stuck close by one another, watching their parents' behavior and drinking excessively themselves. Shanna covered for her brother while he occasionally went out to sneak a joint, never taking her eyes off the others.

The dinner was delicious, and everyone seemed happy with their gifts. Erich and Shanna gave Jackie a diamond bracelet, Jack a fine bottle of scotch; and Shanna brought Fanny an antique quilt and some dusting powder. At the end of the day, as Erich drove Tony's car, he seemed satisfied with his future in-laws, and Shanna and Tony couldn't have been more relieved that the ordeal was over as they headed home to Hounds Run.

# CHAPTER 26

The marriage of Erich Shandon and Shanna Somers was one of the most celebrated unions to ever take place in New York City. The young couple had become American royalty, and the public could not get enough of them. One week before the wedding, Shanna found that she had grown petrified of the press and she had become secluded within the walls of her apartment because if she ventured out, she was instantly surrounded by reporters and photographers at every turn. Just peering out of her window to check the weather resulted in cameras flashing and voices yelling up at her.

The incessant scrutiny of her life began to wear her down, and Shanna cried constantly to Sable that she was the most miserable woman on earth. Sable was patient and reassured her niece that everything would die down after the event and that she was probably only experiencing prewedding jitters. Shanna was still miserable, and to make matters worse, her future sister-in-law and mother-in-law saw the need to insert their insidious comments about her not fitting into their social circle every opportunity they could.

On the morning of her wedding, Shanna was surprisingly calm despite all the hustle and bustle all around her. The days leading up to the present had been so hectic that she felt a great sense of relief that the intense chaos of her life would somehow slow down after today. She had spent the night at her aunt's apartment that had fooled many of the media hounds that trailed her constantly; however, a relentless few had found her and lingered hungrily outside the doors of Sable's building.

Sable had done everything possible to assist her beloved niece with her wedding plans and to shield her from everything she could. Jackie had phoned several times demanding to speak with Shanna over not being included in the ceremony, but Sable had refused to speak with her on the subject. The Mastersons would be in attendance; however, Shanna's brother was giving her away.

Tony had agonized for weeks over Shanna's upcoming marriage. He despised Erich Shandon, for he had seen the way he treated his sister, and he innately felt that there was more to his abusive nature than met the eye. Tony loved Shanna more than anything in the world, and he would willingly die for her.

He planned to speak with her before the ceremony to make sure she felt confident about the marriage and to ease his own mind over the deep fear he felt for her future.

He called Shanna at Sable's the morning of the wedding but was told that Ms. Somers was indisposed at the moment by the housekeeper. Shanna was more than a little *indisposed*; she was in the middle of a frantic array of people who were trying to prepare her for the biggest day of her life. After the hairdresser, nail technician, designer, and makeup artist had put their final touches on every last detail of her appearance, she stood looking at her reflection in a large mirror.

Her aunt entered the room behind her and, with one wave of her hand, dismissed the others from the room. She went to stand behind her niece, and together, they looked at their reflections. "You look beautiful," Sable whispered.

Shanna just smiled and looked tenderly at her. "I would be nothing if it weren't for you," she responded.

"Now that's not true," Sable argued. "I just made introductions. You did the rest by impressing the hell out of everyone!" The two women hugged for a moment before Sable's butler came and announced that a car was waiting downstairs to take them to the church.

When Shanna, Sable, and her bridesmaids arrived at the cathedral, none of them could believe the mass of supporters that waited outside. Photographers and reporters swarmed everywhere, and helicopters hovered overhead awaiting her arrival. The limousine driver swung the long vehicle around to the back of the church where Shanna and the others made a mad dash into the building. The wedding coordinator ushered them immediately into a small room off the main auditorium where they were to wait for their cues to enter at the appropriate time.

Erich and his groomsmen were assembled in a room on the opposite side of the building where they also waited anxiously for the ceremony to begin. Tony paced nervously in a small meditation garden still wanting desperately to speak to his sister before walking her down the isle. He finally decided that he had to go and find her so that they could spend a few moments alone together before he must give her away. He ventured through the hallways until he found the little room where he overheard the excited chatter of the ladies inside. Before he could knock on the door, it flung open, and eight excited young women flew past him in long beige satin evening gowns.

Tony looked inside after almost being trampled by the bridesmaids and saw his sister standing alone, surveying her reflection in a large mirror that stood in the corner of the room. Her beauty took his breath away as he entered silently and closed the door behind himself. He walked over and stood behind her, and she smiled sweetly when she saw him. He put his arms tenderly around her waist and softly kissed the back of her neck. She sighed as chills ran through her body; then she turned to face him.

"Dear, sweet brother, well, today's the day, isn't it?" she said softly.

"Yes, it is, my dear," he responded. "Are you sure you want to go through with it?"

Shanna giggled somewhat at him and replied, "Well, of course, I'm going through with it. Do you think I'd back out now? With all this shit that's been arranged just for

me? Why, they really would commit me if I backed out now, and Erich, well, he'd probably hire a hitman to kill me!" still laughing.

But Tony wasn't amused. "That's what I'm afraid of, Shanna," he said in all seriousness. "I fear that Erich will really hurt you someday."

He took her hands in his and forced her to look at him. "Listen to me, sweetheart. I love you with everything that's in me and with every fiber of my being. You and I are a part of one another, and I would do anything humanly possible to protect you, and know this, Shanna," he said looking deep into her eyes, "I will kill Erich Shandon if he ever lays a hand on you again."

The words he spoke to her and his piercing gaze made Shanna shudder as she looked away from him. He turned her face back to his, and before she could catch her breath, his mouth was upon hers, kissing her lovingly but forcefully. Something about their kiss was briefly familiar and pleasurable to her, but then a wave of panic came over her as she pushed him back. "Oh my god, Tony, what was that?" she implored.

"I just love you so much, baby. I just wanted you to know how much!" he replied.

"I love you too, Tony, but you *are* my half brother, and I'm about to be a married woman, so we must behave!" she snapped at him teasingly. Just then the wedding coordinator appeared in the doorway and informed them that it was time for the ceremony. Tony and Shanna looked at each other lovingly once more, then walked arm in arm toward the sanctuary.

# CHAPTER 27

The wedding occurred without incident as the large crowd witnessed the marriage of the most celebrated young couple the city had ever seen. The audience was full of political dignitaries, business magnets, celebrities, and even a few members of the royal family. The guest list to the reception following the ceremony was as impressive as any White House dinner, and the party was rumored to rival anything the Vanderbilt's or the Astor's had ever thrown. As the couple exited the cathedral as man and wife, the crowd and the hordes of media outside went wild. For miles around, the city seemed to be in a frenzy; and everything to Shanna was a complete blur as Erich ushered her quickly into an awaiting limousine.

When they were safely inside and had managed to catch their breath, Erich turned to her and asked, "Are you all right?"

Shanna was shaking but replied, "I think so."

He reached for the bottle of chilled champagne that the driver had prepared and filled a crystal goblet. "Here, sweetheart, this will make you feel better," he said. She took it and smiled at him. They rode in silence just holding hands and catching their breath en route to his parents' home on Long Island.

As they entered the gates to the Shandons' estate, theirs was the first of many black limousines to enter the winding driveway leading up to the main house overlooking the ocean. Erich and Shanna were the first to arrive, and the servants had been instructed to take them immediately inside to freshen up.

Shanna was lead to a bedroom where Sable's makeup artist and hairdresser awaited her. She was touched up, restyled effortlessly, and then led back out to rejoin her groom and wedding party.

Erich met her immediately as she emerged from the house, and he stayed by her side as they greeted and mingled tirelessly with their guests. The lawn was sprinkled with white gazebos where imported hors d'oeuvres were displayed and beautiful fountains were everywhere, bubbling continuously with only the finest champagne. Elise Shandon had seen to it that only the best chefs in New York were acquired to cater her son's wedding reception. Although she did not approve of the bride, she loved her son and longed for him to be happy on his special day. She also wanted to make sure that a party of this magnitude that bore her name was carried off with elegance, grace, and style.

The entire event was going beautifully, and Elise was more than pleased with the outcome, except for the presence of her newly acquired in-laws. Shanna had finally

relented and allowed her parents to be present at the wedding; however, she had insisted that they not attend the reception, fearing how they would behave. The Mastersons crashed the event anyway, and Shanna's prediction proved accurate; their behavior could not have been more despicable.

Jackie made a drunken spectacle of herself by dancing with unattached men and bragging about now being related to the notorious Shandon family. Jack ignored his wife, got drunk himself, and flirted with every available socialite he met. Eventually, the guests grew tired of their antics and started to complain to their hostess. Elise Shandon was incensed and disgraced over Jackson and Jackie's behavior, so she discreetly asked her butler Collins to arrange for their exit. They were escorted quietly from the party and delivered promptly back to their hotel in the city.

For hours, Shanna and Erich circulated with their guests until Shanna finally informed Erich that she needed to rest. When she finally did sit down, she was amazed at how tired she actually was. Word finally got back to her about her parents' behavior and when she heard how impolitely they had acted, she was horrified. Shanna immediately started to cry, which brought Tony racing to her side. He had been watching her all afternoon and was aware of their parents' abrupt and invited departure, so when he saw her break down, he knew exactly what had upset her.

When he reached her, Tony urged his sister to go inside to get out of view from the other guests. She followed him into the garden room of the house and cried as he held her. "I knew something like this was going to happen," she wept. "I just knew it!"

Tony continued to hold her against him, trying to comfort her. Erich soon missed his bride, went to look for her, and was angry when he saw her crying in her brother's arms. He immediately pulled her away from Tony and asked her what was wrong. She explained to him what had transpired and apologized profusely. He told her that it wasn't him that she needed to apologize to but his parents. She agreed and tearfully followed him back out into the crowd to locate them.

They finally found Elise and Alexander chatting pleasantly with the governor and his wife; however, when Shanna pulled them aside to say she was sorry, they snubbed her and walked away.

She was crushed by their reaction and started to cry again. Erich approached her and whispered to her to forget the incident and to go on with their party. She painfully agreed and followed him to go and rejoin their friends.

The crowd eventually began to dwindle after a sit-down dinner and hours of dancing in the magnificent ballroom. The couple finally departed in a limousine back to the city amid showers of rice and rose petals. Despite their exhaustion from the eventful day, Erich was still eager to get his new bride into bed in their suite at the Plaza Hotel.

Erich and Shanna left the next morning on the Concorde en route to London. From there, they honeymooned throughout Europe for three weeks, then flew back

to Vanilla Island for another week of bliss together before they each had to return to their careers. Although their time together in London, Paris, and Rome had been wonderful, they always seemed to find each other on the island, where they grew as close as two lovers could become. Erich made love to her incessantly and longed for her to conceive again, for he desperately wanted her to have his child.

Shanna was somewhat less enthusiastic about a baby, not wanting anything to jeopardize her modeling career nor the sought-after transition she hoped to make for herself in the film world. After their honeymoon, Shanna began to grow restless in New York. She longed to pursue other directions in her profession, so she eventually persuaded Erich to relocate to Hollywood so that she could possibly make a name for herself in movies. Erich was reluctant at first but, after speaking with his father, learned that they really needed someone to manage the West Coast division of Shandon Incorporated so that they could expand their operation. If Erich managed the office there, he could then oversee their expansion into Japan and the Orient.

Erich liked the idea of finally getting away from his father's overbearing ways and was excited about the opportunity of managing his own team, so he agreed to take the position. Shanna was thrilled that the whole situation worked itself out so effortlessly and that Erich had been easier to convince about the relocation than she originally thought. After selling their apartments in New York and saying good-bye to their friends in the east, the young couple headed west to begin a new life together.

During their first months in Los Angeles, Erich and Shanna lived in a luxurious suite on the top floor of the Beverly Wiltshire Hotel. While Erich ran his father's office during the day, Shanna searched for a place to live. In two weeks after working with one of the top realtors in Beverly Hills, she finally found the place of her dreams. When she and the agent pulled through the massive gates of an estate called Sky Hill, Shanna knew it had to be theirs.

The old mansion had been abandoned years earlier by Collette Juleson, the widow of Miles Juleson, one of the wealthiest businessmen in California. After Miles's sudden heart attack, Collette had been so devastated that she just left the mansion and all its contents and relocated to Paris. Collette had placed Sky Hill on the market via real estate agents, but due to the disrepair of the estate, the celebrities and prosperous lookers did not make offers on the property.

Despite its unkempt state, Sky Hill was a remarkable piece of real estate, and Shanna saw the unlimited potential that it beheld. The main house was over thirteen thousand square feet with nine bedrooms, a fabulous ballroom, an impressive library, a theatre, and an art gallery that held one of the most impressive collections in the country. The outer grounds contained a pool with adjoining cabana that overlooked the pulse of the city below, and along the back of the yard was a prize-winning rose garden that was now only a thorny mess of tangled bushes.

Shanna couldn't wait to tell her husband about her remarkable find, so she called him immediately after she finished viewing the estate. She was so excited

during their conversation that Erich laughed as she spilled out every detail about Sky Hill. Erich was familiar with the property, for his parents' had been friends of the Julesons, and he remembered them mentioning the splendor of the palatial home on several occasions. His only concern was the bad state of repair that it was in; however, Shanna assured him that she would hire only the best contractors and decorators in the city to restore the home. Erich couldn't say no to her, and the price was certainly reasonable enough, so he agreed to go see it with her the next day. He promised her that if he liked it as much as she did, then they would consider purchasing it.

Erich loved Sky Hill as much as Shanna, so they made an offer that was accepted immediately by Collette upon the contention that she could retain a few of Miles's favorite pieces from the art collection; however, the rest of the contents would go with the estate. The deal went through, and within days, the young couple moved into their new home overlooking the lights of Los Angeles and the Hollywood Hills.

Erich had never seen Shanna so obsessed with anything as she was with the restoration of Sky Hill. She worked tirelessly with contractors, landscapers, and decorators to create the perfect home for her and her husband. The furnishings Collette had left were exquisite antiques, so Shanna kept most of them but livened them up with new finishes and fabrics that she had imported from Paris. Erich was impressed with her efforts and allowed her to spend whatever she deemed necessary to make their home a masterpiece.

When the finishing touches had finally been put on Sky Hill, they decided to throw a party to show off their new place. Shanna put together the most impressive guest list and invited the most notable individuals in the area. The Shandon housewarming party was written up in every society page as being one of the most memorable soirees ever thrown in Beverly Hills, and Shanna was elated when she read the review of her party in the columns the next day.

# CHAPTER 28

After she had finished restoring and decorating her new home, Shanna began to grow restless with nothing to do. Her modeling assignments had been put on hold by her agent since her wedding, and Tony had put his band on hiatus temporarily while he vacationed in Mexico. His sister's marriage had depressed him, so he decided to leave the country for a while and allow her to start a new life without his interference.

Erich's new position in his father's company required him to travel most of the time. During his absence, Shanna spent most of her time alone at Sky Hill wandering through the large home making sure all was in place. She went on a few auditions for movie roles and finally managed to land some small parts in a couple of films. She did manage to acquire a lead role in a low-budget film; however, its explicit subject matter did more to hamper her career than enhance it. Finally, out of frustration, she phoned her agent in New York and informed him that she needed to return to the modeling world or she would go mad.

Erich was outraged that his wife wanted to resume a career in the fashion world and adamantly refused to allow her to leave him. They argued constantly over the subject, and Shanna cried frequently to him that he was controlling her life and ruining her career. He finally grew tired of her nagging and agreed to let her work only when he traveled.

Shanna's reentry into the fashion scene wasn't hard, and before long, she was once again the most sought-after model in New York. Her assignments took her often to Paris and Milan, and on a trip to Rome, she encountered a rich Italian playboy named Ricardo Belicci, the heir to the Belicci Collection, a European chain of fine jewelry stores. Ricardo was young, good-looking, and debonair, and he was an expert in seducing any woman he went after.

He noticed Shanna instantly when she entered Bolci Restaurante on the square where she was dining with two other models one night after a fashion shoot. Ricardo watched her throughout the evening, and after she and her friends had finished their meal, he ordered a bottle of Rémy Martin and had it delivered to their table. Shanna and her model friends all looked up to view the most handsome and striking man any of them had ever seen, but it was only Shanna's eyes that he connected with. She smiled and mouthed the words, *gratci*, as she raised her snifter to him.

Ricardo quickly left his bar stool where he was seated and meandered over to their table. The other ladies giggled as he joined them; however, Shanna remained

pleasant but leery. He charmed them with tales of his great exploits throughout Europe and the history of his family's business. They were all fascinated by him and remained mesmerized by his stories until way past midnight. Shanna and the other girls had early modeling calls in the morning and were quickly becoming sleepy and slightly drunk.

Shanna finally indicated that they should go and bid him good night, but Ricardo insisted that they go to some clubs to dance.

The other two girls said they were up to going out, but Shanna refused and insisted that she was returning to her hotel. Ricardo was clearly disappointed, and when Shanna's friends went to the powder room to freshen up before their car arrived, Ricardo moved closer to Shanna. He leaned near to her and whispered to her in Italian, "I want to see you again." She laughed and spoke back to him in Italian that she was very flattered but that she couldn't because she was married.

Ricardo was impressed that she knew his language, and he wanted her more than ever. "I will see you again, my dear," he whispered; then he led her gently outside, kissed her delicately on the hand, and placed her in a cab. When Ricardo rejoined her friends, he found out immediately at which hotel Ms. Shanna Somers was staying.

The next morning, when Shanna's alarm went off, she wasn't real sure where she was. Her head pounded from all the wine and cognac the night before, and she felt sick at her stomach. She rose and went to heat a cup of tea then went to the door to retrieve the morning paper. *Rome's Daily Newspaper* was by the door, but when she picked it up, she noticed there was something inside. She unrolled it carefully, and out fell a beautiful red rose, and dangling from its stems was the most gorgeous diamond bracelet she had ever seen. All that was attached was a small white card that read, "See you tonight, Love, RB."

Shanna was stunned and sat down to look at the bracelet. It had to be Ricardo. Who else did she know in Rome that would deliver such a gift when she had only just left him a few short hours ago? Of course, she had no intention of going anywhere with him, and she knew of no way to get in touch with him.

All she could do was wait until he called her and then thank him profusely, insist on returning the bracelet, and lastly to convince him that she could not go out with him. But she couldn't worry about Ricardo Belicci now. It was past 7:00 a.m., and she had to be at the photographer's studio in an hour, and she still felt like hell and had to shower.

Shanna rushed out the door of her hotel with her hair still damp, no makeup on, and wearing black leather pants, a white turtleneck, and a gray suede jacket. She still looked beautiful and turned heads at every corner. Ricardo's men were in the lobby watching for her and followed her to the studio where she would be working all day. They reported everything back to their employer, including the moment when she left her shoot seven hours later.

When Shanna returned to the Hotel Victoria, she was exhausted. She went straight to her room, changed into a comfortable robe, and poured a glass of white wine. She had almost forgotten all about Ricardo when suddenly, there was a knock at the door. Thinking it must be the maid, she tiptoed over and looked through the peephole. There was no face to see, just a bunch of brightly colored flowers. Curious, Shanna opened the door to a gentleman bearing the largest bouquet of roses she had ever laid eyes on.

"Oh my god, what is this?" she spoke in Italian.

"For you, madam."

Shanna accepted the huge vase of flowers from the mysterious man and handed him a gratuity in return. After closing the door, she inspected the bouquet for some sort of clue as to why she had received them. Then she found it; there was a note from Ricardo informing her that his limousine would pick her up promptly at 8:00 p.m. for an evening of dining and dancing. "My god!" she exclaimed, setting the vase onto the nightstand and collapsing herself down onto the sofa. "That man never gives up!"

She realized once again that she had failed to get any sort of number by which to reach Ricardo; so wearily, she came to the exhausted conclusion that she must meet this playboy, have dinner with him, and end this nonsense once and for all. He was obviously someone who wouldn't take no for an answer.

Shanna poured another glass of wine and ran a hot bubble bath. While the water ran, she went to search for an outfit to wear for her evening out with the Italian playboy. She chose a close-fitting black dress with crocheted sleeves, hem, and back. It was a sexy little number she had purchased in Paris, and with black pumps, it would be perfect. She went to check the water, and after turning it off, she thought about calling Erich. It was still early in Los Angeles, but when she rang his office, his secretary informed her that he was out. She decided not to try reaching him at Sky Hill because he usually worked out at his club before he went to the office, and she knew it would be hard to track him down there.

She dozed and sipped her wine while soaking in the tub for nearly an hour, thinking of how she would handle Ricardo over the next few hours. He was definitely charming enough but not someone she wanted to neither get involved with nor ruin her reputation or her marriage over. She would just enjoy his company while in Rome, then forget about him once she returned home.

The bath revived her, and once she was dressed and ready, she still had some time to spare to enjoy another glass of wine and nibble on some cheese. At 8:00 p.m., she slipped a black shawl around her shoulders, grabbed a black leather handbag, and headed downstairs to the lobby. The same man who had delivered the flowers was waiting for her at the front desk and eagerly escorted Shanna to the elegant white limousine parked outside. As she approached, Ricardo immediately stepped out of the car and reached for her hand. He looked dashing in a black leather jacket, dark slacks, and white dress shirt. He

kissed her lips softly and told her how lovely she looked, then helped her into the car.

Ricardo took Shanna to the best restaurant in town, where they dined by candlelight and listened to Italian music. He never took his eyes off her, and although she was flattered, she was also very embarrassed by his undying attention. After dessert, the waiter brought another bottle of the restaurant's finest champagne. When he served Shanna, a flawless diamond necklace poured out with the golden liquid into her glass causing her to gasp. Ricardo laughed out loud as she gently fingered the beautiful piece of jewelry out of the crystal and watched it drip all over the linen tablecloth.

"Ricardo, I can't accept this," she said bluntly.

"Oh, but yes, you can, and you will, my darling!" Ricardo replied enthusiastically. With that, he summoned the waiter that they were ready to go and informed Shanna that she was in for the time of her life.

"But we haven't even finished our champagne," she protested.

"Not to worry, *mi bella*, there's more where that came from!"

Ricardo escorted Shanna to the most exclusive nightclubs in all of Rome, and they danced and drank until she thought she couldn't go another step. In fact, she was literally staggering when they left the disco at 4:00 a.m. "Ricardo, please," she begged, "I must go back to my hotel."

Finally, he agreed that they'd had enough of Rome's nightlife and ordered his chauffeur to drive them back to the Hotel Victoria.

Ricardo practically carried Shanna to her room, and once they were inside, he quickly began to undress her. She protested at first; however, she was so tired and drunk that there was little she could do to stop him. He pealed off the tight black dress and marveled at her exquisite figure, accented by an elegant lace bra and with matching panties. He carried her to the bed and laid her down gently as he proceeded to take off his own clothing. This was one beauty that he could not wait to conquer, and he was almost there.

Ricardo turned off the lights in her hotel suite, poured them each another glass of wine, and proceeded to join her on the bed with the room lit only by the twinkling lights of Rome. Shanna was dozing quietly when he lay down beside her, and he once again admired her exquisite beauty.

He gently removed her underwear as she sighed softly. Her breasts were full and round against such a slim figure, and the mere sight of them made him grow hard. He played with her nipples, and they were firm and dark pink between his fingertips. She breathed heavily as he caressed her. Ricardo had been with many women, but this one took his breath away.

He moved his hands down along her rib cage while simultaneously brushing his lips against her smooth skin. He then slid his fingers farther south between her legs; and with his palms, he separated her thighs, then turned his fingers inward, and began stroking her. She moaned loudly as he touched her, and when he felt her

wetness on his fingers, he could wait no longer. He moved upward, still between her legs, and lowered himself gently but steadily into her. She sighed at his entrance but, in her hazy and sleepy state, did not protest. Instead, to his delight, Shanna instinctively began to respond to his movements; and together, their lovemaking heightened into a work of art as they both climaxed simultaneously. Shanna sighed contentedly in his arms and finally fell dead asleep as he gently stroked her hair. Ricardo eventually joined her in slumber as he sipped the last of his wine and watched the pink streaks of dawn begin to pierce the Italian sky.

Shanna awoke the next morning still entangled in Ricardo's arms. She looked at the sleeping Roman lying next to her; and although she felt terrible about what she'd done, she had to admit that he was the most handsome man she had ever seen and, from what she could remember, the most artful lover.

Shanna slipped out of bed without waking him and went to run a hot bath. It was after 10:00 a.m., and thankfully, she didn't have an early call that morning, just an appointment later to look at proofs with the photographer. If all the shots were as good as everyone expected them to be, then Shanna's assignment would be over in Rome, and she could catch a red-eye that night to return to New York.

When she finished her bath, Shanna returned to her bedroom suite to find Ricardo awake and appearing very chipper for what was an early hour of the day for him. He smiled beautifully at her and held out his hand for her to join him again in bed. "Ricardo, I can't," she said softly. "I have to be at the studio in less than half an hour."

He rose from the bed and went to her, walking across the room in unashamed nakedness. He pulled her gently into his arms and said softly, "I want to see you again. When are you scheduled to fly out?"

Shanna pulled away from him and sighed softly. "Ricardo," she hesitated, "we have to talk."

He looked at her surprised. "What is it?" he asked.

"I have to return home, and I don't think that we should see each other anymore; after all, I am a married woman."

Ricardo laughed and replied, "Ah, mi bella, such things do not matter to an Italian man."

"Well, they matter to me," Shanna responded as she pulled away from him and headed for the door.

"Good-bye, Ricardo. I am going home after my meeting with the photographer, and I would prefer that we just say good-bye to each other now."

He looked at her seriously and responded, "I understand how you feel, but I think that we have created something special that we cannot let go now. I *will* see you again, mi bella."

Shanna removed her hand from his and left the room. She hailed a cab outside her hotel, and on her way to the studio, all she could think of was Ricardo and how dangerous the future would be with him in it.

# CHAPTER 29

The jumbo jet touched down at LAX International Airport at daybreak, and Shanna Somers had never been so anxious in her life to return home. Her stint in Rome had been exciting for sure, but her excursion with Ricardo had left her disillusioned and bewildered over what she had done and worried over what repercussions her affair would cause. Shanna was happy to be back in her beautiful mansion overlooking Los Angeles and was relieved when her butler informed her that Erich was still in Tokyo and would not be returning for another week.

She missed her husband but wasn't ready to face him for fear he would sense by her actions that something was amiss between them. But she would have several days to recover from her reeling emotions and try to forget the dashing Italian who had nearly swept her off her feet. Shanna was exhausted from jet lag, and after eating a light breakfast and taking a hot shower, she went to bed and slept until nightfall. She awoke to a light rapping on her bedroom door as her maid informed her that Mr. Shandon was on the phone from Japan.

Shanna yawned and reached for the phone. She answered sleepily as the phone cracked loudly due to the great distance of the call; then she heard Erich's voice. "Hello, sweetheart. How are you?" Erich asked.

She sighed and replied, "I'm fine, a little tired from the trip, but I'll survive."

"How was Rome?" he inquired.

"It was noisy, dirty, and busy; but the shoot was successful, and I'm glad to be home. Speaking of home," she continued, "when are you returning?"

Erich replied, "Unfortunately, not until next week."

Shanna was quiet for a few moments, and Erich thought he had lost the connection, but he finally heard her voice softly say, "When you get back, we need to talk."

"Oh," he responded, "what about?"

"About us," she answered. "We're spending too much time apart, and I just think we need to discuss things."

Erich moaned, tired of hearing her complaints about that subject. "All right, Shanna, we will talk when I get back, but we've been through this before. Until you give up on wanting to be a star, we will never be together as much as we need to be. Like I've told you before, if you would quit modeling, you could travel with me constantly and be the wife you should be."

Shanna hated her husband when he berated her for wanting a career in show business, and as usual, his comment made her furious. But in her exhausted state,

she was too tired to fight with him, so she told him bluntly that they would discuss it when he came home and hung up. She knew that he would most likely call back, so she rang down to Andrew, her butler, and instructed him not to patch Mr. Shandon through if he should happen to phone again. While she had Andrew on the phone, she told him to bring her a dinner tray and then to instruct the rest of the staff that she didn't want to be disturbed until morning.

Without delay, Andrew delivered a tray of fresh seafood, a baked potato, salad, and a chilled bottle of white wine. While she dined, her maid ran a steaming bubble bath; and when Shanna finished eating and bathing, she went back to bed and fell into a deep sleep, dreaming of a handsome dark Italian.

Shanna awoke the next morning to the cold, wet nose of her poodle nuzzling against her cheek.

She giggled as she stroked his curly head. Shanna stretched in her bed and finally felt rested. She took her time about getting up and dressing, but she eventually made her way downstairs to start the day.

When she entered the foyer, the smell of roses hit her full in the face. There were arrangements of flowers everywhere, and the delivery man continued to bring them in. "Andrew!" she screamed. "What is all of this?"

Andrew appeared instantly from the kitchen wiping his hands on an apron. "I don't know, madam. They started arriving a half hour ago." When the deliveryman had set down his last vase, he gave Shanna a receipt to sign and handed her a card. The card read, "I will see you soon, love, Ricardo."

Shanna was surprised yet flattered by the actions of her newfound lover. However, she still felt a tremendous amount of trepidation over the affair she was about to continue. When he finally did call to inform her that he was at the airport with two tickets to Mexico, she didn't hesitate and agreed to join him.

Shanna and Ricardo flew to Mazatlan together where he had reserved a magnificent villa overlooking the ocean. They spent the days together strolling on the beach and their nights together dining out and making love endlessly. Ricardo constantly showered Shanna with jewelry, and she delighted in his unending attentions, yet she remained worried over the harm she was causing her marriage. Shanna loved her husband despite his controlling and often abusive behavior.

Erich returned from Tokyo exhausted and frustrated over his business dealings there. Upon landing in Los Angeles, he was eager to locate his chauffeur and head home to see his wife. He was sure that the stressed conversations that they had shared while he was away were simply a result of his being away much of the time and her pressing modeling schedule. He was determined to make it up to her when he returned home and encourage her to make the next trip with him back to Japan with a stopover in Tahiti as a second honeymoon.

Erich's limo driver was waiting for him as always, and as the vehicle pulled away from the airport, they drove past a magazine stand. Erich happened to glance out the window and noticed to his horror several cover stories about his wife cavorting

with her Italian lover in Mexico. Pictures of Shanna and Ricardo were everywhere, and he screamed for his driver to stop. Erich leapt from the car and quickly purchased as many of the magazines as he could hold, then jumped back into his limousine, and yelled at his driver to take him home.

When Erich arrived home at Sky Hill, he entered the magnificent marbled foyer and angrily flung the magazines everywhere. His servants just looked at him in pity and went about their chores. He went into his study, poured himself a scotch, and collapsed on his sofa while he tried to decide what to do about Shanna.

The phone rang, but he ignored it. Within seconds, a maid tapped lightly on the door and informed him that his mother was waiting to speak with him. Erich groaned and reached for the phone.

"What is it, Mother?"

"I suppose you've seen the news," Elise replied without even a "hello."

"Unfortunately, I have, Mom, and I don't know what to do. I love her, and I am brokenhearted." For once, Elise Shandon's heart went out to her son where his wife was concerned, for he sounded like a high school boy to her who had lost his best sweetheart.

"I'm truly sorry for you, son, but she's not worth it. Your father and I warned you from the beginning that she was cheap and not worthy of you."

Erich sighed and answered, "I know, but I am poisoned by her, and she is irresistible to me."

Elise ached for her son on her end, but she felt she owed it to him to encourage him to forget Shanna and move on with his life, with a woman who was more in his social league. "You must let her go, Erich," she warned.

"I am going after her, Mother. I don't know what I'll find when I get to Mexico, but I'm coming home with my wife," he replied.

Not wanting to hear those words, Elise simply wished him a safe trip and hung up.

The next morning, Erich chartered a private jet to Mazatlan and arrived before 10:00 a.m. If the paparazzi reports were correct, they were staying at a private villa in the hills. He had not had time to hire a private detective; however, with his money, he knew there would be someone on the island who he could bribe to tell him where to find them. Erich was correct. In fact, the taxi driver who picked him up at the private hanger knew exactly where Shanna and Ricardo were staying. In fact, the whole town had been humming ever since their arrival.

Erich was a bundle of nerves as the tiny cab wound its way up through the hills on the narrow roads to the villa that Ricardo had rented that overlooked the ocean. He didn't know what he would say to his wife or what he would do to her lover, but he knew it would not be a pretty scene. The cab driver pulled into the circular cobblestone driveway of the Mediterranean-style home. As Erich exited the vehicle, he handed the driver a one-hundred-dollar bill and told him to wait for as long as it took.

Shanna and Ricardo were seated on the terrace of the villa having breakfast and didn't hear Erich as he knocked on the front door. They were enjoying a meal of huevos rancheros, and Shanna almost choked on hers when she saw her husband come around the corner of the villa. "Oh my god!" she muttered. Ricardo turned in the direction that she was staring just as Erich made his way steadily toward them.

Ricardo stood as Erich approached only to get roughly pushed back against the wall of the terrace where he fell. Erich grabbed Shanna by the shoulders, looked her square in the eyes, and viciously asked, "What the fuck do you think you're doing?" She just stared at him blankly as Ricardo pulled himself up from the terrazzo floor of the terrace. He had hit his head against the wall and was groggy. Erich turned to him and, surprisingly in a calm voice, said, "Please leave us. I need to speak to my wife alone. I will not hurt her." Ricardo nodded and went inside.

Once he had gone, Erich turned to Shanna again and asked her, "Baby, what is this all about? What have you done to us? Do you love him?"

Tears spilled from Shanna's eyes as she put her arms around her husband and said crying, "Oh, Erich, I'm so sorry. This is a mistake. Ricardo means nothing to me. I've just been so lonely without you lately. He seduced me in Rome, and now it's come to this. Can you ever forgive me?"

Erich pushed her back so that he could look at her. "I love you, Shanna, more than any man has ever loved a woman throughout history; but I cannot tolerate your making a fool out of me. This little fling of yours is on every magazine cover, making you look like a whore; and that's not the kind of wife I want or deserve."

Shanna looked at him. Her eyes were the color of the water behind him and were now pools of tears. "But can you forgive me?" she whispered.

Erich didn't respond, but as he looked at his wife, he melted with love for her and roughly pulled her into his arms and kissed her more hungrily than he ever had in the past. She responded to his kiss, and as their tongues danced together, they knew that their love for each other would never die.

Erich and Shanna left Mexico together, and Ricardo returned to Italy where he would search for a new female conquest. He still held a fondness for Shanna Somers, yet her celebrity and marital status were too inconvenient for him. He was ready to move on. On the flight back to Los Angeles, Erich talked frankly to Shanna. He told her that he wanted her to join him on his next trip to Tokyo and that, as a surprise, he wanted to take her to Tahiti and Fiji for a second honeymoon. He also confided to her that he hated Los Angeles and wanted to move back to New York.

Shanna was delighted about the trip to the South Pacific and sadly agreed to move back east since her acting career had miserably failed. As they held hands, sipped champagne, and flew into the sunset, Erich informed Shanna that maybe acting just wasn't in her blood but that maybe motherhood was. He admitted to her that he wanted to start a family; and the sooner, the better. She smiled at the tenderness of his remark, and although the thought of pregnancy terrified her, she felt that their having a baby together would be a wonderful experience.

# CHAPTER 30

Erich and Shanna had a magical time on their journey to Japan. They stopped in Hawaii, Fiji, Tahiti, and Micronesia where they experienced the tropical splendor of the islands and the total coming together of two people in love. Erich held true to his promise of trying to get Shanna pregnant, and their lovemaking sessions were endless. They had the world at their fingertips; vacationing in paradise and alone with each other to discover endless possibilities.

Erich was so determined to get his wife pregnant with an heir that he wanted sex with her constantly. He had contacted several specialists on the matter, and he knew just exactly how to position her and just how often. Fortunately, the islands they visited were virtually uninhabited, so they were able to do as they pleased at the places they stayed.

Shanna was extremely happy to be away with her husband. She found his enthusiasm about having a baby very charming and eagerly participated in his diligence in impregnating her. Erich was so intent on getting her pregnant that he made love to her incessantly, and she delighted in his passion and his attentions. Their sexual eagerness with one another proved successful, for by the time they returned to the States, Shanna was six-weeks pregnant.

The move from Los Angeles back to New York was a happy one for Erich. Shanna was excited as well to get back to the fast pace of the city; however, leaving her beautiful home in Los Angeles made her sad. She had given new life to a magnificent estate, and she would miss living among the priceless paintings lining the hall gallery, the thousands of vibrant prize-winning roses in the gardens, and the magical view overlooking Hollywood that the mansion provided.

Shanna would forever be in awe of Collette Juleson for creating such a spectacular home and allowing her and Erich to purchase it from her at an unbelievable bargain. As promised, they had restored everything to its original splendor, including refurbishing all the priceless paintings and breathtaking sculptures situated throughout the mansion.

Shanna dreaded calling Collette to tell her that they would be selling the estate since she had entrusted its revival to the couple. When Erich saw how unhappy his wife was over losing her beloved mansion, he said to her, "We'll just keep it, my dear. It is a showplace, and we can stay here when we have to be in LA." Shanna was thrilled and happier than ever that she had a rich and generous husband who would allow her to keep such a magnificent house and also create the most spectacular penthouse in New York City.

The Shandon Incorporated building had been a fixture on Madison Avenue for over fifty years. Erich's grandfather had built the headquarters there, and it still stood as a historic landmark in midtown Manhattan. When Erich informed his father that he and Shanna were moving back to the city, Alexander Shandon was overjoyed to hear that his only son would soon be working by his side again in the family business. Erich had one favor to ask of his father, however; he wanted to develop the top three floors of the office building that had never been utilized to create a fabulous home for him and Shanna. Alexander didn't object in the least and even offered to provide the company's own architects and decorators to do the job.

Erich and Shanna leased an apartment close to their future home so that they could conveniently oversee the work being done by the many workers hired to create their perfect living space. Shanna had an easy pregnancy and even accepted some modeling jobs in between meeting with her decorator. She was always eager for Erich to come home from the office every day to show him the latest selections she had made for their new residence. Erich was also eager to arrive home every day to see his beautiful wife and was thrilled that she still wanted him sexually, even while pregnant.

Being back in New York suited them both, and Erich was so happy with the circumstances in his life that he decided to splurge a little and give his beloved wife the most extravagant gift to celebrate the birth of their child. Shanna had had a busy day and was napping peacefully on the sofa of their apartment when he came in. He sat down his briefcase and walked over to where she lay.

Kneeling beside her, he gently stroked her hair and her cheek and said, "Wake up, sleepyhead. I'm home."

Shanna sighed softly and opened her eyes. She smiled upon seeing him then said sleepily, "Oh, dear, have I slept that long?"

Erich laughed and answered her, "No, sweetheart. I'm home early. I've got a surprise for you."

Shanna sat up, tenderly holding her swollen belly. "What is it?"

"You'll have to get up and come with me; we're going for a little drive, my dear," he replied.

Erich led his wife out the door of their apartment building and into a waiting limousine. It was early spring, and the temperature was still starting to drop before nightfall. Shanna snuggled next to Erich inside the limo since she had forgotten to grab a jacket in their rush to get to where they were going before dark. Erich held her close and promised to give her his coat when they arrived at their destination.

"But where are we going?" Shanna demanded.

"You'll see" was all Erich would provide. As they headed toward the harbor, Shanna became more and more bewildered.

Finally, as their car entered the gates of the New York City Yacht Club, Shanna was sure they were going to a cocktail party, and she was hardly dressed for the occasion. She started to fuss at her husband for taking her to a social function when

suddenly they stopped beside the most beautiful boat she had ever seen. Shanna just stared in awe of the beautiful vessel. "Whose is this?" she asked.

"Why don't you step out and see?" Erich answered. He helped Shanna out of the car, and being eight months pregnant, she was a little awkward in her movements. She climbed out and again looked up at the beautiful boat and then her eyes caught the inscription in the side, The Shanna-McKenna. Tears started to spill down Shanna's cheeks as she looked at her husband and cried, "Oh my god, Erich, you bought this for me and for our daughter?"

Erich pulled her into his arms, looked into her eyes, and said, "Yes, my love; there is nothing I wouldn't do for you and the child you are about to give me. I plan on giving you the world and everything in it that you desire."

Shanna looked up at him tenderly, her eyes still moist and whispered softly, "I love you, Erich Shandon, and will spend the rest of my life doing everything I can to make you happy."

Erich replied, "I love you too, my darling," then he leaned down and kissed her long and hard as the setting sun sunk into the water behind the *Shanna-McKenna*.

# Chapter 31

Shanna gave birth to a six-pound baby girl whom they named McKenna Elise. Erich was ecstatic over the arrival of his first child and planned to spoil the little girl shamelessly for the rest of her life. When Shanna was released from the hospital, she and Erich took their new baby back to their temporary apartment.

Within a matter of weeks, they realized that their current home just didn't live up to the standards that they were used to, and their new penthouse would not be ready to move into for at least a year.

Although Erich knew his wife would not agree, he suggested that they move into his parents' estate in Greenwich, Connecticut. To his surprise, she did not object too much despite her ongoing conflict with her mother-in-law throughout the years. But at this point in her life, Shanna was willing to do anything to appease her husband and do whatever she had to for the benefit of her daughter.

Life at the Shandon mansion was easy for Shanna. The servants took care of the baby, and Elise constantly doted on her only grandchild and stayed out of her daughter-in-law's way. Shanna took short trips with Erich when he went away on business, and she enjoyed escaping the boredom that was ever present at her in-laws' house.

When McKenna turned two, Erich was approached by his father about a huge project that their company had secured in Kenya. Shanna was thrilled about the opportunity to go to Africa and couldn't wait to leave. She had never traveled there before. Although she had modeled for a swimsuit layout in the Seychelles, this would be her first trip to the continent. Elise was horrified over the fact that they would even think of taking the baby to such a remote place; however, Shanna insisted that she didn't want to be away from her daughter for the six months that Erich was assigned to work there.

They departed for Kenya with a stopover in London where Shanna wanted to spend a couple of days to shop for the trip. She bought so many clothes, supplies, and gadgets for them that she had to purchase an additional set of luggage just to transport it all. Erich scolded her lightly and kidded her by saying that Kenya wasn't exactly a wilderness and that the city did have most of the modern conveniences of home.

Nonetheless, Shanna wanted to be prepared and make sure that her family was well clothed and stocked for any emergency or necessity that should arise. Erich's father had arranged for them to reside at the home of a wealthy coffee plantation

owner who had been a business acquaintance for many years. The plantation comprised of three hundred acres and was over one hundred miles from Kenya; however, the company that Erich would be working for would be providing a chopper to transport him to and from the site each day.

When they finally landed in Kenya, Erich and Shanna were exhausted. The flight had seemed endless, and although McKenna had been content for most of the trip, she had grown restless and tired toward the end and had cried for hours.

A driver was waiting for them as they exited the plane and escorted the family to an awaiting Hummer where they rested while he retrieved their bags. The drive to the plantation house was bumpy and took over three hours. By the time they got there, McKenna was hysterical, and her parents were nearly delirious with exhaustion and weariness. It was pitch dark and in the middle of the night when they arrived, and it was difficult to get a clear picture of the house; but from what Shanna could see, it was beautiful.

The butler, or houseman as he liked to be called, was named Sabu, and he greeted them graciously as the driver helped them inside with all their luggage. Sabu was a slight man and very dark, but his demeanor was gentle and kind. He showed Shanna and Erich to the master suite where he had set up a crib for McKenna. He had left a silver tray of muffins and a hot pot of tea for them and offered to get milk for the baby. McKenna was sound asleep, so Shanna told him that they would be fine until morning and thanked him profusely. The beautiful bed in the suite was shrouded with white fabric and was adorned with the finest English linens. Shanna and Erich were so tired that they didn't even bother to unpack; they simply shed their clothes, climbed into the massive bed, and fell asleep immediately in each other's arms.

They awoke the next morning to a cacophony of magpies cawing in the distance and howler monkeys seemingly laughing at the arrival of a new day. In a state of grogginess, Shanna thought that she even heard a lion roaring in the surrounding hills.

Erich got up to take a shower, and Shanna checked on McKenna. The little girl was awake but lying quietly in a beautiful mahogany crib. Shanna took her into the main house to find Sabu and inquire about breakfast. She was starving and was sure that Erich and her daughter were too. As she wandered into the dining room, Sabu was waiting patiently beside an elegantly set table with the most extravagant breakfast she had ever seen.

The cook had prepared kippers and eggs, meats, fresh fruit, smoked salmon, and an endless selection of breads and cheeses. There was also a variety of fruit juices in crystal pitchers and exotic blends of teas and coffees steaming in their pots. Shanna couldn't believe her eyes and thanked Sabu again for his thoughtfulness in preparing such an early morning feast. She informed him that her husband would be in shortly and that she would return as soon as she had fed and bathed the baby and showered herself. He nodded sweetly as she collected some milk and cereal for McKenna and retreated to their room.

After they finished their fabulous breakfast, Erich and Shanna decided it was time to tour their temporary home and the grounds. The owner of the plantation was out of the country, so they had the estate to themselves except for the servants. His father's friend had left them in good hands, for Sabu was a loyal and dutiful worker. The cook was a renowned French chef. The maid Matilda kept the home immaculate, and the owner had even been so kind as to hire an English nanny named Miriam to take care of the baby. Shanna and Erich felt very fortunate to have been left in such capable hands and knew that their stay in Kenya was going to be one that they would never forget.

Erich started work on his architectural project one week later while Shanna and McKenna stayed at the plantation to explore and learn about African culture from Sabu. Shanna arose early each morning with her husband, had breakfast with him, then saw him off in his chopper that carried him to his site. She would then sit on the porch listening to the wildlife, sipping tea, and writing. The property was no longer a working plantation; however, the natives who had once been employed there still came around often to see if there was any work to be had.

Shanna employed as many of them as possible to do yard work, polish silver, and do other odd jobs around the main house that really didn't need doing; yet she felt sorry for them and wanted to help them feel useful. Sabu was touched by Shanna's kindness and grew quite fond of her. They became close friends, and she questioned him endlessly about his tribe and the culture of the people around her. In his broken English, he graciously answered all her questions on a daily basis and delighted in her beauty and her company.

Erich came home each evening at dusk and was met by his loving wife, a beautiful little girl, and a meal fit for a king. After dinner, he and Shanna would usually take long walks as the antelope that had wandered onto the property scattered all around them. They would return to the house and soak in the hot tub until it was time to retire to their elaborate bedroom. For both of them, their perfect existence in Africa ended each day after saying good night to their daughter and then slipping into bed together where they made love for hours.

Their six months in Kenya were the happiest times Erich and Shanna had ever spent with each other. They had grown closer than they had ever been and had enjoyed their daughter to the fullest.

When it came time to depart, Shanna was brokenhearted to leave what she now felt was her home. Her time there had been so special, peaceful, and spiritual. Africa was now a part of her soul, and its people had become her people.

On the morning of their departure, Sabu predictably had all their bags immaculately packed and waiting on the front verandah. Erich said his good-byes to the staff, tipped them handsomely, and carried his daughter to the awaiting Hummer that would transport them back to the airport. He knew Shanna had developed a deep friendship with the African houseman and allowed her time to say farewell to him.

Sabu stood stoically by as Shanna tried to collect herself so as not to get hysterical in saying good-bye to her loyal servant and now dear friend. She finally pulled herself together and turned to face him. "I really don't know how I can ever thank you for the kindness you have shown to me and my family."

Sabu remained silent but looked at her tenderly.

Shanna continued, "I will never forget you, and I hope that we can stay in touch and always be friends."

Sabu took her hands in his and looked sweetly into her eyes. "We will, Shon non," he responded softly in broken English.

She raised his hands to her lips and kissed them gently. "So long, my friend." Shanna eventually pulled away from him and headed toward the car. She looked back once to wave, and then she was gone. Sabu remained on the porch standing still as he watched their vehicle disappear into the distance. Only after it had vanished from his view did tears spill slowly down his cheeks as a distant red sunset burned in the sky behind him.

# CHAPTER 32

The Shandons were riding high on life when they returned to New York after their trip to Kenya.

Their new penthouse was spectacular and had been well worth the two-year period of time of getting it renovated and decorated to perfection. Their decorator, Phoebe Belford, was waiting for them; and when Erich and Shanna first stepped foot into their new home, they couldn't believe its grandeur and beauty.

One entered immediately into the ballroom laid with black and white marbled flooring, opulent crystal chandeliers hanging overhead, two magnificent staircases sweeping upward to more floors held together by ebony railings, and, above, a forty-foot-high ceiling with intricate carvings and gilded crown molding.

Exquisite artwork and priceless sculptures were placed in appropriate settings, and antique furniture imported mostly from Europe was strategically planted to perfectly enhance the entire ambiance. And the grandiosity continued as the young couple toured their new home, which had been created for the most part in their absence; but so far, it was perfect.

On the main floor, aside from the ballroom, was the kitchen equipped with all state-of-the-art appliances and shrouded with a beautiful golden-colored Italian marble on the floor and countertops.

Still, on the main level were two guest bedrooms, the nursery, a gymnasium, four baths, and the library, which held over five thousand books. An elevator to the second floor opened into a charming sunroom decorated with chintzes and bright colors, overlooking the city. Also, on the second level was a bar, recreated in the style of an old English pub, equipped with pool table, dartboards, wide-screened television, and a movie screen. It also came with an impressively stocked wine cellar, a cigar humidor—a room any man would deem heaven on earth.

Erich and Shanna could not wait to see their bedroom as their decorator was proudly showing them around. The master suite was her pride and joy, and she eagerly awaited their reaction when they saw their room. As they swung open the door, the couple immediately caught their breath because the room was indescribable. Phoebe had undoubtedly created a masterpiece. The entire suite was done in varied shades of deep blues, which was both masculine and feminine. The walls were painted in a color called Mediterranean Sea, with thick drapes just a shade lighter embracing the bay window that looked out over the stunning New

York skyline. The bed linens complimented the room beautifully as did the antique chairs and overstuffed love seats and chaise lounge.

The marvel of the room continued as Shanna and Erich took in all the other features of their new bedroom, such as the beautiful cherry bookcase and bar, an entertainment center equipped with all the latest technology, huge walk-in closets for each of them, and, of course, a bathroom that would rival all bathrooms, done entirely in blue Spanish tiles and marble to keep with the peace and tranquility of the "blue" theme that Phoebe had created throughout the rest of the suite.

The rest of their tour paled after viewing their quarters; however, they were still very pleased with the rest of their home. On the second level where their bedroom was were three other guest rooms, laundry facilities, and three baths. On the top floor were the servants' quarters that were also accessible by a private elevator.

All in all, the young couple couldn't have been more pleased with their new abode and the work that Phoebe Belford had done for them over the past two years. She had made everything perfect. She kissed them both as Erich gladly wrote her an astronomical check for her services, and she promised to keep them on her guest list for every party thrown in the city that was worth attending. Erich and Shanna found it very easy to settle into their new home, and McKenna loved her nursery. Erich resumed working in his father's office as the entire staff at Shandon Incorporated made plans for Alexander's retirement. The senior partners were all very pleased with the work Erich had done on the African project and felt at ease with him taking over his father's position as head of the company.

Shanna was also very happy to be back in New York and grew to love the penthouse more than the Beverly Hills estate. She had hoped to return to modeling; however, her days were filled with society functions, lunches with other wives in Erich's company, and chairing a number of philanthropic foundations that her husband strongly encouraged her involvement in. Shanna had very little time to spend with her daughter, and when she arrived home late in the day in hopes of seeing McKenna, there was usually a message from Erich saying they were expected at a dinner party that evening.

When Shanna wasn't attending charity meetings, she attended fashion shows where she spent thousands of dollars on designer gowns, sitting among the social elite, such as Ivana Trump, Denise Rich, and Leona Helmsley. She also was privileged to be introduced to Carolyn and Jackie Kennedy; Diana, Princess of Wales; and Duchess Sarah Ferguson. Although they were considered to rank at the top of the world socially, Shanna found the royals to be the warmest and most gracious of anyone she met in the elite realm where she now existed.

What Shanna really longed for was to be back upon the stage wearing the clothes and accessories these snobs, including herself, were spending a fortune on, which benefited nothing except their bottomless purses and endless egos. She was not happy in their world and longed to return to the existence where she felt more comfortable and mingle with people whom she could actually relate to. Although

she reigned supreme at the top of the world of fashion, at least in that sphere, she knew where she stood. While on the catwalk, she could look down on the ostentatious crowd below her and be thankful she was not a part of them.

Upon their return to the Big Apple, Erich and Shanna became an overnight sensation as the richest and most sought-after young couple in town. They were invited to a minimum of two parties a night, not to mention dinners, cocktail gatherings, and jaunts to the Hamptons, Palm Beach, Beverly Hills, and Europe.

Shanna grew more and more restless in her new position whereas this lifestyle flowed naturally through her husband's blood. Erich thrived on the social acclaim and accepted nearly every invitation that the couple received. They began to argue constantly about whether or not they would attend an event until eventually, they were both so stressed with their relationship that the pressure began to take its toll once again.

# CHAPTER 33

Phoebe Belford was the most noted decorator in New York City, and her creation of Erich and Shanna's penthouse did not go unnoticed by nearly every home décor and architectural magazine in the country. All of the city was abuzz about "the Young Shandons" and their magnificent home above Madison Avenue. Phoebe decided to throw a dinner party to introduce her new rich young couple to everyone who was anyone that she had worked for previously.

Phoebe had also decorated homes in Beverly Hills, Palm Beach, and Aspen. It was in Colorado where she had met an oil baron who had persuaded her to decorate his country estate in Boulder. His name was Joe Stephenson, and he was the wealthiest man for his age in the business. Joe was the most handsome, polite, and honest man Phoebe had ever met. He was all business, yet he came across as a gentleman and truly genuine. So when Phoebe learned that he was in New York the week of her party, she tracked him down at the Plaza and delivered an invitation to him by messenger.

When Joe received his invitation to Phoebe's party, he immediately chuckled and threw it down on the desk in his suite, knowing he would not attend. Soirees weren't really his style, and he knew just the kind of crowd that would be in attendance—people he did not care for nor choose to mingle with. Joe was not a person who was impressed with the upper class whatsoever, considering them to be too flashy for his tastes. Joe preferred mingling with people who *knew* how to live without the worry of social status. Rich snobs held little interest for him.

Joe Stephenson was still part of a wild breed of man. He often thought about and sometimes longed for the days when owning an oil company was only a vision in his head. In those days, he had been a young buck laboring in the oil fields of Texas with his equally wild buddies. They were a raucous bunch back then, drinking excessively, screwing Mexican whores, and tanning hides of leather as their tequila-tainted sweat poured into the dry Texas earth. He still missed those guys, and if it hadn't been for his aunt Caroline becoming a wealthy widow and backing his dream, he would probably still be in the fields or working in an offshore oil rig somewhere. In either case, he wondered if he wouldn't have been happier.

The phone rang suddenly, jolting Joe from his memories and causing him to spill his whiskey.

He answered, shaking the brown liquid from his hand but smiled when he heard his decorator's voice.

"Hello, daahling," Phoebe crooned, "did you get my invitation?"

Joe continued smiling and answered, "Yes, I got it but—"

Phoebe blurted in, "Oh, but, daahling, you simply *must* come. The Shandons are just the most divine couple and the hottest duo in the city! Oh, please say you'll come. They are your age, and you will just love them!"

Phoebe was so excited that Joe could not refuse her, so he agreed to see her at 7:00 p.m. When he hung up the phone, Joe poured himself another whiskey and water and sat dreading the moment when he would have to meet the newest and richest snobs who had invaded Manhattan.

The cocktails were in full swing as Joe was ushered into Phoebe Belford's living room overlooking Rockefeller Center. The butler took his coat, and he was promptly offered a drink that he gladly accepted. Phoebe spotted him immediately and went rushing to his side to welcome him. Joe didn't really know why he tolerated her; but somehow, the older woman amused him, and he found it hard to say no to her. He graciously kissed her cheek; and once again, she complimented him on being a gentleman. She led him quickly into the crowd looking for her guests of honor.

Erich was in the library smoking cigars and drinking brandy with some of his former Harvard alums, but Phoebe spotted Shanna across the room chatting with a small group. Joe saw her too and was instantly captivated by her beauty. He recognized her from her ads and marveled at how much more incredibly beautiful she was in person. She was wearing a dark blue evening dress with a plunging neckline and open back. Her dark brown hair was swept up on the sides but hung almost to her waist, and when she turned to look at them as they approached, Joe noticed that her eyes were the color of dark blue pools.

As Phoebe enthusiastically introduced Joe and Shanna, she waved the rest of the small group away and told them dinner would be served soon. She wanted to give the two new acquaintances a few moments to chat before the butler summoned them in to enjoy the elaborate meal that awaited. Although Joe was spellbound by Shanna's beauty, he found her easy to talk to and unbelievably down-to-earth. In conversing with her, however, Joe sensed something that suggested an insecurity despite her poise and popularity.

They chatted until the butler called everyone into Phoebe's elaborate dining room for dinner and were sad that their conversation would have to end for the moment. To their surprise, their place cards were directly across from each other at the dining table, and Joe never took his eyes off her for the entire meal. Erich, seated beside Shanna, was so wrapped up in his conversations with his old friends that he failed to notice the connection forming between his wife and the oil baron.

After dinner, the crowd dispersed back into the living room for cognacs and conversation. A string quartet began to play in the entry hall, and the guests gradually migrated toward the music. Erich returned to the library, and Shanna ventured back into the living room where she inadvertently slipped out onto the balcony overlooking the skyline. She wanted to be alone and escape from the crowd if just for a few moments.

Joe had never taken his eyes off Shanna and witnessed her retreat onto Phoebe's patio. He hesitated but eventually decided to follow her, for he needed an escape as well. She was standing with her back to the building, looking out into the night. He approached her slowly as she leaned against the railing of the balcony. She didn't appear startled but glad to see him. He joined her at the railing and said, "I see you feel the same about these types of events as I do. I'm more comfortable under the stars."

Shanna smiled and answered, "I suppose so. I just feel so out of place with these people, and I'm supposed to be the guest of honor, well, my husband and I are."

Joe responded, "Your husband seems to be in perfect company."

Shanna looked sad and replied, "He is; this is his world, not mine."

Joe felt sorry for her and moved closer to the railing where she stood.

The moon was full and hanging directly overhead as Joe looked at the beautiful woman standing beside him. Feeling his gaze on her, she turned, and their eyes met.

Joe said softly, "Shanna, I know we've just met; however, you are the most incredible woman I've ever encountered, and I hope we can keep in touch."

Shanna didn't pull back from him but looked directly back at him and said softly, "I want to keep in contact with you too, Joe; you seem to be a wonderful man, and I hope we can be friends."

Joe then took her hands in his and held them until Shanna started to act nervous. He gently released her fingers and suggested they go back inside.

When they returned to the living room, Joe asked Shanna to dance with him, so they meandered into the marbled entry foyer and moved magically together to the music. Joe had never felt so alive before in his life as he felt holding this magnificent creature in his arms, taking in the aroma of her hair, and feeling the delicate softness of her skin. She clung to him too, making him feel like her protector against whatever it was that frightened her.

For a brief segment of time, they were lost within one another in motion and music. Their stolen moments were halted, however, when suddenly Erich jerked Shanna roughly by the arm away from Joe.

She gasped at the unexpected interruption but stood silently by, wondering what her husband planned to do. Joe didn't say a word either but stood ready to take anything that Erich Shandon had to dish out.

Erich continued to hold Shanna firmly by the arm as his gaze never left the man whom he now considered to be his latest competition where his wife was concerned. Erich was drunk, and the other guests were aware, so they began to disperse in order to avoid getting caught up in any unpleasant altercations. Shanna hated the fact that the evening had succumbed to so much disappointment and longed to escape from the situation. She pulled herself free from Erich's grasp and told him it was time to go home.

By then, Phoebe had arrived on the scene and was mortified that a disturbance such as the one before her had broken out at her elegant affair. She agreed with

Shanna that it was time to get Erich home, for she had seen him earlier in her library and had felt then that he was imbibing too much.

Phoebe waved for her butler and instructed him to summon the Shandons' limousine. She and Shanna tried to calm Erich to the best of their ability; however, he continued to mouth obscenities toward Joe as they lead him to the entry hall. Shanna was terribly embarrassed and felt like crying, but she managed to maintain her dignity as she left the shocked crowd that had gathered to watch them leave. Before finally exiting the door, Shanna turned to apologize once more to Phoebe and saw Joe gazing at her longingly from across the room. Tears were in her eyes as she stared briefly at him; then she turned and was gone.

After the Shandons departed, the rest of the group began to disperse quickly. Joe also prepared to leave and had one more drink while he waited for the crowd to thin. He wanted to speak with Phoebe for a moment. He inwardly seethed over what he had witnessed in the behavior of Erich Shandon and wondered how any man could treat such a wonderful woman that way. Joe had developed a deep hatred for the man and also an undying painful desire for his wife.

When he finally was able to say good night to Phoebe out of earshot of the few remaining guests, he asked her how he could contact Shanna since he didn't get to say a proper farewell. Phoebe smiled, sensing instantly the handsome young's man attraction to the gorgeous model. Joe wasn't in the mood to be teased; so not wanting to irritate him further, she gave him the address to the Madison Avenue penthouse. Phoebe also warned her rugged friend that his new love was married to an insanely jealous man, who was part of a very rich and powerful family. Joe simply kissed her cheek, pulled on his coat, and strode out of the foyer saying, "I'm not afraid of Erich Shandon."

# CHAPTER 34

After the incident at Phoebe Belford's, Shanna and Erich began to drift apart in their relationship. Shanna had been humiliated by her husband's drunken behavior, and he was furious with her for showing an obvious attraction for another man at a social function. Although Shanna had tried numerous times to explain to her husband that she was only trying to be cordial, he had innately been aware of the attraction between Shanna and Joe Stephenson, and he was not pleased.

Erich began to travel more and take on projects for his father who was due to retire within the year. With Erich gone most of the time, Shanna decided to forego most of her philanthropic endeavors and resume her modeling and recording career, at least on a part-time basis. Her nanny Tracy was most competent, so Shanna felt her little girl was in good hands at all times, and she did not worry.

Tony was thrilled that his sister was removing herself from the elite limelight, at last, and returning to the world of music where she belonged. Although he had always stood behind her in her modeling career, it was in the concert arena where he felt like her true talents lay. She had always been gifted musically; however, it had been Tony who had coached and guided her into the successful artist she had become.

With Erich gone, Shanna spent more and more time with her brother and thrived on the success they achieved onstage and from their album sales. Tony and Shanna frequented the trendiest clubs in Manhattan on a nightly basis and partied with their celebrity friends. The VIP sections of the hot spots were always reserved for the famous siblings, and the ever-present cocaine that accompanied them went unnoticed by the management.

One evening, while Erich was in London, Tony and Shanna went to Studio 54 after a show. They were immediately ushered in and placed in their private room along with their accompanying friends.

Their entrance to the club created quite a stir as fans recognized them and tried to press closer to the popular duo. Joe Stephenson happened to be in town, meeting with his attorneys when he heard the ruckus in the crowded club. When the waiter returned to his table, Joe asked what the mayhem was all about, and the server informed him that Tony Masterson and Shanna Somers had just arrived and were being taken to the private rooms upstairs.

Joe couldn't believe that Shanna was in the same club and was determined to see her again. He wasn't sure she would even remember him, but he decided to try his

luck and approach her. Joe pushed his way through the crowd and upstairs to the VIP lounge. When he reached the top of the stairs, a bouncer barred his way and told him only privileged guests were allowed. Joe handed him a one-hundred-dollar bill and begged him to inform Ms. Somers that he was there. The large black man grunted an "okay," then disappeared behind the doors to the private area.

Within moments, Shanna appeared in front of him, and he was speechless when he saw her. She was more beautiful than he remembered; and tonight, she was wearing a tight animal-print short dress, and her hair was wild and carefree. Shanna took his hands in hers, kissed his cheek, and said, "My god, Joe, how good it is to see you!" She led him inside where her brother and the others were drinking expensive champagne and snorting massive amounts of cocaine. Shanna led Joe over to where Tony sat between two gorgeous models with white powder on his nose looking extremely high. She proudly introduced Joe to her famous rock star brother; and although Tony was incredibly inebriated, he could tell that his sister was very fond of this man. Shanna served Joe a glass of Dom Perignon and poured herself another one as well. She then led him to one of the plush sofas in the suite and invited him to sit beside her.

Joe was instantly uncomfortable in these surroundings, but his attraction for Shanna allowed him to overcome his anxieties for the moment. The night he had met her at Phoebe's, she had looked elegant in a midnight blue evening gown and pearls; but tonight, she was a wild vixen in a leopard dress, and her long hair was blowing wild. She had a mild buzz going as well and was flirting with him shamelessly.

Joe finally took her hands in his and said, "Honey, let's get out of here and go back to my hotel."

Shanna giggled from the champagne and teased him about wanting to take advantage of her. He reassured her in all seriousness that he needed to leave, and he wanted her to accompany him. Sensing his sincerity, Shanna agreed to go with him but stated that she must find her brother first. Tony was still wedged between the two models but had long since passed out. She instructed their friends to make sure he would be transported home all right, and they all assured her that they would see to his safety.

Joe escorted Shanna from Studio 54 with the aid of bodyguards into an awaiting taxi that carried them back to the Plaza. The stress of the crowd at the club had left Joe's nerves in a frenzy, and he was eager to relax in the Oak Room and order a strong scotch and water. He pulled Shanna down beside him into one of the legendary red leather booths of the restaurant and instructed the waiter to bring her a glass of their best white wine.

The establishment had been closed for several hours; however, when the night manager learned that Mr. Stephenson and the famous Ms. Somers requested late night cocktails, he had instructed a member of his late-night staff to reopen the bar for as long as they desired. They sat together in the bar until Joe courteously suggested they retreat to his suite so that the night server could close and go home.

Shanna hesitated at first; however, she was getting tired but enjoying Joe's company very much.

When they arrived in Joe's room, it was nearly 4:00 a.m. in the morning. Neither one of them wanted the night to end but were apprehensive about where to go from there. Joe had fallen desperately in love with Shanna, and she had developed deep feelings for him too. He sensed her nervousness and, being the gentleman that he was, did not make any demands on her.

She quickly retreated into the bathroom and emerged wearing one of the Plaza's luxurious robes.

"I hope you don't mind," she said quietly. "My dress was becoming a little uncomfortable."

Joe looked at her adoringly and simply replied, "No, I don't mind in the least." He then poured them each some wine, and then he excused himself as well to change into something more comfortable.

Shanna sat and sipped her wine while she waited for Joe to return. He came out soon wearing white cotton pajama bottoms and no shirt. She caught her breath at the sight of him, for his body was hard and chiseled, and she knew it would be impossible to resist him if he made physical moves on her.

Shanna sat quietly on the sofa in Joe's suite as he approached and sat down beside her. He could tell she was uneasy, so he took her face in his hands and said, "Sweetheart, you don't have to be afraid of me. I will never hurt you."

Shanna looked straight into his eyes and responded, "Joe, it's not you that scares me; it's the consequences that will erupt from loving you that I'm afraid of."

Joe put his arms around her and pulled her close. He knew she was tired and could tell that she was close to falling asleep, yet he wanted her to hear what he was saying. "Listen, sweetheart, I realize that you are in a difficult marriage; however, I want you to know that I love you and will wait for you always."

Shanna sighed and put her hand on his face, pulling his mouth toward hers. He couldn't resist the urge to kiss her and willingly gave in to her temptation.

As they kissed, Joe succumbed to passion and eagerly swept Shanna from the sofa to the voluminous bed in his suite. He had never wanted any woman more in his life and eagerly striped the robe from her as she continued to kiss him as he hovered above her. At last, they lay together naked and ready to give into nature's purest form of love when Shanna, suddenly in tears, stopped him. Joe was poised above her, ready to enter her, and was shocked when she begged him to stop.

He lay down beside her and held her tenderly and asked, "Baby, what's wrong?"

Shanna just sobbed in his arms and replied, "No, sweetie, you haven't done anything wrong. I'm just not ready right now."

Joe didn't say a word but held her gently until she stopped crying. She finally fell asleep in his arms, and he languished in being able to hold her close for the rest of the night. At 8:00 a.m. later that morning, Joe helped Shanna into a cab that would carry her back to her Madison Avenue penthouse.

# CHAPTER 35

When Shanna arrived back at her apartment, she was exhausted. She quietly made her way up the sweeping staircase to the master bedroom so as not to awake the servants; however, her butler and the cook witnessed her retreat up to her room. Shanna locked the door behind her and looked beside the phone for any messages that were always left by her maid. No notes were present, so Shanna breathed a sigh of relief.

The night she had spent with Joe Stephenson had been magical; however, she was confused by her feelings and uncertain about what to do next. She had promised she would call him as soon as she arrived home, so she picked up the phone and dialed his room at the Plaza.

Joe was eagerly awaiting Shanna's call and picked up the phone on the first ring. "Hello," he said quietly.

"I made it home just fine," she whispered.

Joe smiled just hearing her voice again and replied, "No swarms of paparazzi then?"

She giggled at him. "Not too many, just a few hundred photographers," she replied.

Joe laughed as well, not used to life in a fishbowl, and replied, "Knowing you, my dear, that is entirely possible!"

In all actuality, several photojournalists had snapped their picture not only leaving Studio 54 but entering the Plaza as well.

Shanna turned their conversation to a more serious note and said, "Joe, I'm sorry about what happened earlier. I hope I didn't disappoint you too much."

Joe held the phone in his hand and, shaking his head, replied, "Sweetheart, you couldn't disappoint me if you tried. You are the most incredible woman I have ever met, and nothing you could do will shake my faith in you."

Shanna smiled on her end with tears in her eyes and said, "I think you are a very special man too, Joe; and as much as I want you, I am married and have a daughter to think about. However, as you know, my marriage is not a happy one, and I will consider moving on, only if I know you'll be there for me."

Joe was beside himself with emotion over hearing her words and eagerly responded, "Oh, I'll be there, sweetheart. I'll be there."

After they bid each other good night, Shanna curled up in her bed underneath a luxurious comforter and had beautiful thoughts about the wonderful man she

now had in her life. She couldn't believe how intensely she had fallen for him. Shanna also pondered her life with Erich and wondered if he really loved her or just considered her a possession. She felt a deep emotion for him but also wondered if her feelings stemmed from a sense of dependence or obligation. Her thoughts reeled as exhaustion quickly overcame her; and as she drifted off to sleep, she dreamed of two men calling to her in a distant fog.

# CHAPTER 36

Joe and Shanna were not able to see each other again before he had to return to his company in Denver, just two days later. She was busier than ever with her modeling career and was somewhat grateful that her brother had taken some time off from their concert venues to write music at his manor in upstate New York called Montclair. The estate, a castlelike setting in the mountains, was the perfect retreat in which to escape to and find peace and tranquility. Shanna and Joe only spoke briefly in the rare intervals when they were able to steal a few moments for a phone call between their hectic schedules.

Erich returned from Europe grumpy and irritable; the project his father had put him in charge of in London had not gone well. Their clients were not satisfied with the plans he had drawn up for a new banking complex in the financial district and would not give their approval in order for his firm to begin construction. Alexander Shandon would not be pleased with his son, and Erich dreaded informing him that a new proposal would have to be drawn up.

As he deplaned the 747 that had carried him from Heathrow to LaGuardia, he looked impatiently for his driver in the gate area. Erich didn't see him yet; and looking at his watch, he realized that he had arrived a few minutes early, so he took a seat while he waited. He was exhausted, and his eyes were on fire; however, he hated to close them for fear he would fall asleep in his seat. Instead, he decided to keep his mind occupied on anything other than work, so he looked around for something to read.

Erich glanced around the preboarding area until he spotted the *New York Daily News* a few seats away, so he reached over and grabbed it. He quickly scanned the front page searching for any earth-shattering news, but his eyes burned so much that he didn't want to focus on anything too detailed. He instead decided to glance at the headlines from each section of the paper when suddenly, he saw his wife's name mentioned under the section that centered around celebrity gossip.

Erich quickly flipped to the page directing readers to the story about her; and to his horror, there was a picture of Shanna leaving a club, arm in arm with a very handsome man, both looking extremely happy and somewhat drunk. There was another picture of the couple at the bottom of the page entering the Plaza Hotel, still holding each other and looking as though they might kiss.

Erich was sure that he recognized the man pictured with Shanna; however, in his tired state, he couldn't place him. The report read that "Shanna Somers, supermodel

and recording artist, was seen partying at Studio 54 with her brother, Tony Masterson, and several other high-profile individuals in the club's VIP lounge and that Ms. Somers had obviously decided to continue a private party in the arms of a handsome stranger from out of town, at the Plaza."

Erich closed the paper in utter shock. She had done it to him again! For the second time in their marriage, he had returned from a miserable trip only to find out reports of his wife's vulgar and elicit behavior during his absence. Erich was initially brokenhearted; however, his emotions quickly turned to humiliation and rage. He threw the paper to the floor, grabbed his briefcase, and decided to head toward the ground transportation area on his own to hail a taxi and get home. He was only a few steps away from the gate when he heard James, his chauffeur, call his name. Erich never changed his stride but veered toward the older man and said, "What the fuck took you so long?"

As they made their way quickly to the awaiting limousine, James followed behind him and meekly answered, "I'm sorry, sir."

When Erich arrived home, Shanna was in the penthouse returning phone calls and answering invitations to society functions in the library. She loved spending time there because of the manly feel of the room. Although it was Erich's sanctuary, Shanna often ventured inside to be surrounded by the huge animal heads adorning the mahogany walls, the wild colors of the striped tiger and zebra rugs on the hardwood floor, and the heady aroma of leather that permeated the entire interior. To her, it was like escaping into a scene from "Out of Africa"; and on occasion, when she awoke in the middle of the night fighting sleep, she would sneak down to partake of Erich's expensive brandy that was part of his private collection.

Erich entered their massive entry hall and, in a very loud voice, demanded to know his wife's whereabouts. No one was around with the exception of their Hispanic maid who spoke little English, and she was busy polishing the brass banister. However, she understood her employer enough to point him in the direction of the library. He tried to recall her name in order to thank her; however, Erich could never remember any of their names except for his long and trusted valet, Bentson, and his Japanese chef, Benvoi.

When he arrived at the library, the massive wooden door was closed, and he took a deep breath before he pushed it open. Shanna was seated behind his enormous desk and gasped when she saw her husband. Neither of them spoke as he entered the room and closed the door behind him. Finally, Shanna said quietly, "You surprised me."

Erich didn't reply but moved slowly toward the desk and, reaching it, sat on the end. He never took his eyes off her as he replied, "Well, my dear, you never cease in amazing me."

Getting a little nervous, Shanna responded, "What do you mean?"

Without hesitation, Erich moved upon her rapidly, pulling her from the chair and forcing her to look at him. His eyes were like daggers, piercing into her soul,

as he moved closer to her face and said, "I saw the reports of your disgusting behavior with your lover; now I want to know who he is, and I demand to know now." He tightened his grip on her arms and continued to press her. "Who is he, Shanna? I recognize him from somewhere, and I want you to tell me his name, damn it!"

Shanna remained quiet for a few moments then she answered. "We met him at Phoebe Belford's party, and we are just friends. Please understand that, Erich," she pleaded.

Erich didn't understand; and thus, fueled by jealousy, he pulled his wife to him and kissed her roughly, bruising her lips. Shanna whimpered at his abruptness and tried to push him away to no avail.

Erich was enraged that his wife had indulged in yet another affair; however, somehow he knew that this one was different. He remembered the oil man from Colorado and the attraction he had sensed between the two of them weeks before was undeniable.

Erich continued to hold her tightly in his arms and moved his aggressive kisses down to her neck where they turned more into bites that caused her pain. She begged him to stop, but her protests seemed to anger him more. He then began to tear at her clothes; and as she struggled, he easily pulled her to the floor. The silk skirt and blouse that she wore were ripped apart as Erich continued his quest to debase his wife.

Shanna struggled with Erich, but he was too strong for her; and before she could stop him, he had removed her panties and was tugging at her bra. "Erich, please!" she pleaded. "Don't do this!"

Erich sneered at her and slapped her across the face saying, "You cheating bitch, this is what you deserve."

With that, he proceeded to remove his own clothing while holding her down. But Shanna was so stunned by his blow that she lay helpless under him while bleeding badly from her mouth.

When Erich was completely naked, he straddled his helpless wife and looked into her frightened eyes and whispered evilly, "Was he worth it, my dear?"

She only looked back at him in desperation and pleaded, "Erich, I explained to you that we were just friends and nothing more. Please understand that."

Erich only shook his head and looked at her with an accusing stare. "Oh, honey, if I only thought you were friends, I wouldn't be behaving this way."

With that said, Erich pulled her face to his again and kissed her hard. He then moved his mouth down to her breasts where he suckled them and bit her nipples. She screamed in desperation; however, none of their servants came to her rescue. Shanna tried desperately to push him away; however, Erich was too strong and powerful for her to fight. She continued to struggle, but he hit her again. Shanna knew then that there was no hope and that she would have to succumb to him for now, but in time, she would get even.

Erich looked down at his wife who now lay helpless and bleeding before him, and he felt a sense of power that he had never known before. She was his, and God help the man who was trying to take her away from him. Shanna realized that it was hopeless to struggle against him, for he was now in complete control. He straddled her, then suddenly began to stroke himself; and with the emotions he was experiencing, he became harder than ever. Again, he looked at his wife and smirked; then he spread her legs and plunged himself eagerly inside of her. Shanna gasped as she felt his hardness moving rapidly against her, yet she didn't dare scream, for fear that the servants would see her in such a compromising position. Erich kept holding her down as he continued to rape her, yet she didn't utter a word. She couldn't; he was in charge, and she was his victim.

Erich finally climaxed and collapsed on top of his wife. Shanna lay motionless underneath him awaiting his next move. Her lip was already crusted over from the blood, and she was in pain. Tears sprang from her eyes knowing what her husband had just done to her. It broke her heart. She would never love him in the same way again.

Erich remained on top of Shanna for a few more minutes; then he rolled over and collapsed beside of her. "So where do we go from here?" he asked.

Shanna responded quietly, "Well, I don't know where you're going, but I'm leaving you, you bastard!" Saying that, she pushed him away, pulled her torn clothes around herself and retreated upstairs to their bedroom to pack a suitcase.

# CHAPTER 37

Shanna had never felt so disgraced and humiliated in her life, and she didn't know where to turn next. She had experienced some low points in her life; however, being raped by one's own husband was despicable. As Shanna gathered her things together, Erich entered their bedroom and quietly sat down on the bed. He had a drink in his hand. Shanna supposed it was his usual scotch and water. He sipped from his glass and eventually asked her, "Where are you going, baby?"

She simply stared at him sarcastically and responded, "As far away from you as I can possibly get, you bastard."

When Shanna had finished packing, Erich was still sitting on the bed sipping his scotch and watching her intently. In frustration, she retreated into their bath to bathe and collect her toiletries and some wee bit of privacy. The steam from the hot tub she was running began to fill the room when she turned and felt him behind her. Startled, Shanna jumped at his presence, but she didn't move for fear she would anger him further, and he would hurt her again.

Erich set his drink down on the sink and put his arms around Shanna's waist. She kept her back to him as tears filled her eyes as he started to kiss her neck. Shanna then turned to face him with her eyes brimming over like tidal pools. They stared at each other in silence for a few moments; then Erich spoke, "I'm sorry, honey. You know how I get crazy sometimes where you're concerned, and when I think of you with another man, I lose control. I'm sorry if I hurt you."

He reached up and gently touched her bruised, swollen lips with his fingertips; and she winced. She pulled away from him and drew her robe around her tightly. Wiping her eyes, she said quietly and angrily, "Well, you did hurt me not only physically but you have hurt me deep down, and I don't know if I'll ever get over this." With that, Shanna's emotions got the best of her, and she gave into the tears that she had been fighting back and started sobbing uncontrollably. Erich went to her and held her tightly, hating himself for causing his wife so much pain and heartbreak.

Finally, her crying subsided, and she pushed him away saying, "I'm leaving you for a while, Erich. Please understand. I will be at my brother's home upstate, and I want you to leave me alone so that I can sort out where we stand. I want you to bring McKenna to visit often. I would take her with me, but I don't think I will be in a good emotional state for quite some time, and I don't want her upset. Now, if you'll excuse me, I would like to finish my bath."

Erich nodded and replied, "I do understand, sweetheart. Take all the time you need to, but promise me that you aren't thinking about divorce or anything."

Shanna looked back at him in disgust and said, "I can promise you nothing at this point in time, Erich. But I will guarantee you that if you ever lay a hand on me again, I will not only divorce you but I'll have your ass thrown in jail!"

Understanding how she felt, Erich picked up his drink and left the room.

# CHAPTER 38

Tony's estate in the Finger Lake Region of upstate New York was beautiful. It was a large rustic manor nestled in the mountains with panoramic views of the water from every room. The home had once been owned by an older couple, the Montclairs, who were tragically killed in a plane crash. After their deaths, their children quickly auctioned off the property, and Tony purchased it as a reward to himself for successfully completing a nine-month drug and alcohol rehabilitation program.

Montclair, as it came to be known, provided the perfect setting for a major star in the music industry. There was adequate security and privacy, not to mention a cozy guest cottage that Tony immediately turned into a recording studio. The wooded surroundings also were the perfect backdrop for someone in recovery. The serene setting inspired Tony to create more balladlike lyrics that he couldn't wait to present to his sister. Even though his new style of music would be a diversion from the pop rock genre that he was known for, he felt that his new material would be a hit with the public and his devoted fans.

Before purchasing Montclair and before his treatment, Tony's life had nearly spiraled out of control. His addiction to alcohol, cocaine, and, occasionally, heroin had become so powerful that he was unable to function on any level, much less maintain the life of a highly successful and popular recording artist. Tony's reputation suffered. He missed shows. Concert tours had to be postponed, and he was arrested frequently for public drunkenness.

Ultimately, Tony's band walked out on him during a performance in Toronto, when he was so high that he proceeded to expose himself, urinate on the front row of the audience, then pass out face first on the floor of the stage. After spending three days in a detoxification unit and then three days in jail, his manager finally approached him and told Tony that his career and possibly his life would be over soon if he didn't seek help for his dependency problems.

Devastated, weak, and humiliated, Tony put his head in his hands and cried like a baby in his jail cell. He realized that he had allowed drugs and alcohol to take control of his life; and the guilt and shame of what he had done to his band members, his fans, and himself was almost overwhelming. But Tony knew he needed to do something to regain the helm of his existence, so with a tear-soaked hand, he reached out to his manager and said, "Tell me what I need to do, man."

Within a matter of days, Tony was admitted to the Santa Riatta Treatment Facility in New Mexico. He had called his sister from Canada and told her of his plans to

enter treatment. Although Shanna was extremely proud of her brother for making such a commitment to change his life, she was ashamed of herself for not realizing that his addiction had gotten so severe. She knew that he did drugs and drank excessively, for she had partied with him on several occasions, yet only recently had she heard reports of his outlandish behavior. Shanna cried when she realized that she could have lost him forever like she had her sweet brother, Todd, whose death she had never completely gotten over.

Shanna met Tony in Santa Fe, and she was amazed to see him looking so pale and thin. Again, she berated herself for not being a better sister and for being so self-absorbed in her own life that she had not seen the downward path that her brother's life was taking. They held each other for a long time and cried in each other's arms.

Finally, Shanna looked into his eyes and said, "I just want you to know, dear brother, that of all the accomplishments you've made, not the Grammy's nor the songwriter awards or any of the accolades that you have received, none of them will be as rewarding as what you are about to face, and I am behind you all the way."

Hearing that, Tony pulled her to him again and kissed her hair, and they held each other briefly until a nurse came to take Tony to his quarters. "I love you," he said as he walked slowly away from her and eventually disappeared down a long corridor.

"I love you too," Shanna whispered; then she sadly left the facility and looked around outside in the bright New Mexico sunshine for her driver.

# CHAPTER 39

After Shanna left her brother at the treatment facility, sadness overcame her. She hated leaving him there; however, for his own good, it was the best solution. Hopefully after nine months at Santa Riatta, he could reclaim his life and career and look forward to a brighter future. As Shanna sat quietly in the back of the limousine, her driver sensed her melancholy and cheerfully asked her if she would like to take a drive to view the breathtaking scenery before going to the airport. She smiled at his kindness, and since her plane didn't depart for another two hours, she agreed.

Shanna was truly amazed with the spectacular views that could be seen in every direction. Her driver was eager to point out the various canyons, mountains, and landmarks that held a special significance. Shanna fell in love with the landscape and also the climate, so it was by sheer luck that they happened to drive by a pair of massive black iron gates that guarded the entrance to a ranch set off the main road where a For Sale sign hung. Shanna spotted it immediately and ordered the driver to stop.

She got out and peered through the iron bars; however, the home was situated far down the drive and difficult to see. She looked up above the gates and saw the name, Blue Diamond Ranch, and smiled.

Shanna asked the driver if she could use his mobile phone; and soon, she had the realtor on the phone and scheduled a time to view the property. The realtor agreed to be there within the hour, so Shanna called and cancelled her flight back to New York and booked a room at a hotel in town. The Blue Diamond Ranch was everything Shanna had hoped it would be. It was two hundred acres of beautiful property, and the main house had over four thousand square feet of living space and was decorated in the typical Southwestern style. There was also a guest house, a pool with adjoining cottage, a splendid horse barn with a show arena, and separate living quarters for hired hands.

The price was fair, so Shanna made an offer on the ranch as soon as they finished their tour. The realtor called it in, and the owners accepted immediately. Shanna was thrilled. She knew that Erich would be furious by her making such a sporadic purchase; however, she had always loved horses and dogs, and this way, she could have as many as she wanted and be near her brother at the same time. It was ideal, and she wished that she could call Tony immediately; however, they had told her at the facility that he would be incommunicado for several days, so when she arrived at her hotel, the first thing she did was write to him.

Months went by, and Tony made great progress with his treatment at Santa Riatta. Shanna visited him often, and he was glad to see that she was totally consumed with her new ranch and that her life in general seemed to be going smoothly. Since Tony's band had broken up, Shanna had continued to model and spend time with her daughter.

Upon his graduation from treatment, Shanna and McKenna attended the ceremony then they went to Blue Diamond Ranch to celebrate and spend a few days in quiet relaxation. Tony was impressed with the magnificence of the estate and was very proud of the improvements Shanna had made to her new home. She had already purchased several Arabians from Poland, and they enjoyed racing into the sunset atop the spirited beasts nearly every evening.

McKenna enjoyed the ranch too; at five years old, she already loved animals and the outdoors as much as her mother did and was thrilled when Shanna surprised her with a collie puppy. They named him Lance, and McKenna cried when they had to leave him to return to New York; however, Shanna assured her daughter that they would return to see him often and that Josh, their hired hand, would take excellent care of the little dog.

When they returned to New York, Tony moved into the penthouse with Shanna. Erich was none too pleased, for he had never really cared for his brother-in-law and didn't want a junkie living around his daughter. He was also not happy about Shanna spending so much time in New Mexico, and he complained that they all smelled like livestock when they returned. Shanna ignored him for the most part, for she wanted to get her brother settled in and make sure he was adapting to his new lifestyle. Tony seemed on edge to her and nervous about being back in "the real world," but the counselors at the treatment facility had told her to expect this type of behavior.

Since their arrival from New Mexico, McKenna had not stopped talking about the ranch, the horses, and her new puppy. Erich grew tired of hearing his daughter go on and on about her trip. He hated any existence outside of urban living, and the thoughts of his little girl traipsing around in horse shit, cow dung, and hanging out with a Lassie-want-to-be sickened him. McKenna was a Shandon; she was supposed to be attending charm schools and elegant tea parties at the Ritz-Carlton.

One afternoon, while Shanna was at a modeling shoot, Erich decided to take the afternoon off from work and spend time with his daughter. He had resolved that he would not be outdone by his wife, so he had the nanny dress McKenna in a white lace dress, and they headed out into the city for a father-daughter day together. Erich took her to FAO Schwartz, where he spent a fortune, then to lunch at the Plaza; then before they returned home, they stopped at a pet store, where he bought his daughter a white Standard Poodle and a Yorkshire Terrier puppy.

When Erich and McKenna arrived back at the penthouse, Shanna was upstairs in the bedroom resting from a hard day's work in the photography studio. Her daughter entered through the front door and ran screaming through the ballroom

in excitement for her mother as she carried her Yorkie and lead her new Poodle by a diamond-encrusted leash. Shanna heard her and hurried out of her room and looked down from the stair railing above to see her beautiful little girl looking like a dog handler from the circus.

"Hi, sweetheart, what on earth have you got there?" Shanna smiled. The maid had told her that Mr. Shandon had taken the little missus out for the afternoon; and although Shanna was glad they were spending time together, she never expected this.

McKenna made her way awkwardly up the stairs with her two new pooches. The little girl was grinning from ear to ear when she reached her mother; and after kissing her on the cheek, she exploded with happiness and said, "Mommy, look what Daddy bought me today. These are my city dogs that I can have here. Of course, I still love Lance that we have in New Mexico, but now I can have my dogs wherever we are, can't I?"

Shanna's eyes filled with tears by seeing her young daughter's joy and responded, "Of course, you can, my darling."

The standard poodle began to lick the tears from Shanna's face that reminded her of a poodle that she owned many years ago that gave her the same loving affection. "Look, Mommy," McKenna pointed out, "my new dog loves you already."

Shanna looked at her daughter lovingly and replied, "And I love him too, sweetie."

McKenna asked her mother if she could go and introduce her new pets to her nanny, and of course, Shanna agreed.

As her daughter ran down the hall to her room, Shanna called after her and asked, "What are you going to name them, honey?"

McKenna turned and answered her, "Oh, Daddy's already named them. The little one is Napoleon, and the big one is Pierre."

Shanna simply shook her head and whispered to herself, *Oh, I see.*

Erich eventually made his way up to their bedroom after stopping in his office to check his messages and pour himself a drink. The many toys he had purchased earlier were being carried up to his daughter's room as he climbed the stairway. He hoped that McKenna had informed his wife of the many wonderful things he had bought her; however, his young daughter seemed far more interested in the living creatures that had come home with them. Erich never ceased to be amazed at the similarities between his wife and daughter. There was a something to them that he didn't quite understand, a genuine quality that he had never been exposed to before, an innate happiness for the simplicities of life that left him perplexed.

When he entered their bedroom, Shanna was reclining on a chaise lounge with a glass of white wine in her hand. Erich greeted her when he entered the room, but she immediately rose and approached him front and center. "I hope you enjoyed yourself today, you bastard," she exploded. "How dare you try and outdo me with our own daughter; I know what you are up to, and you've got some nerve!"

Erich downed his drink and moved to the bar to pour another one. "I'll be damned if I let you turn our daughter into some hillbilly from the sticks of Tennessee, my dear," he sneered.

Shanna responded, furious, "And I refuse to let you turn her into some rich snob like you and the rest of your family."

Neither of them said anything for a few moments; then Erich finally turned to her and said, "Baby, I'm sorry that was cruel of me to say, and maybe I am a rich snob, but that's all I know how to be, believe it or not. I'm jealous of the values that you have and obviously are inflicting upon our daughter. I suppose that I selfishly wanted her to myself today to love her in the only way I know how, and that is to indulge and spoil her."

Shanna sat down beside him on their bed and took his hands in hers. "That's not what we need, Erich; your daughter and I only want your love and affection, not the world on a silver platter."

Erich took his wife's head between his hands, moved his mouth upon hers, and kissed her tenderly. "We don't do this enough," he whispered.

"You're right," she said.

Erich pulled her down beside him and removed the silk robe she was wearing that revealed her slender body. "My god," he remarked, "you're still as beautiful as the day I met you."

She didn't speak but gently began to pull him into her, and before long, they were making love like they had not experienced since their trip to Africa.

# CHAPTER 40

Shanna and Erich still maintained a turbulent relationship with brief moments of respite during a storm. They frequently argued over how to raise their daughter, his jealous tendencies still flared on occasion, and they argued over Tony's presence in their household. Shanna wanted her brother there under her watchful eye; however, Erich had always been jealous of their relationship.

Tony had remained sober for several weeks into his recovery, but the constant bickering between Shanna and Erich caused him stress; and before long, he felt the urge to use again. He didn't tell his sister about his cravings and called his sponsor on several occasions. When he felt the desire was about to overcome him, he luckily found out about an estate in upstate New York and purchased the property sight unseen. The wooded environment and tranquil setting sounded perfect to him and his manager agreed.

Two days before Tony was about to leave for his new home in the mountains, some old friends learned of his whereabouts and contacted him at Shanna's. They invited him out for an evening of dinner and drinks, and before he knew what he was saying, Tony accepted. Before long, Tony had found himself back in the club scene, and the alcohol and cocaine invaded his system again. He called Shanna after reaching Studio 54, and although she was disappointed to hear of his relapse, she agreed to join him.

Erich had left town again for Europe, and she was bored with dinner engagements and society functions, so she was ready for a night out. She knew of the real estate purchase Tony had made in the Finger Lakes and told him she would only agree to play with him one last time if he would promise to resume sobriety and retreat there very soon. Tony assured her that he would, so she dressed for a night out and met him a few hours later.

When Shanna arrived at the club she was immediately surrounded by ardent fans and persistent photographers; thankfully she had her faithful bodyguards to protect her. As usual, there was a line of eager patrons waiting along the street to get in, however Shanna and her entourage entered effortlessly and were quickly ushered upstairs to where Tony and his friends were partying.

Shanna was disappointed yet not surprised to see her brother, a couple of his band members and several groupies already surrounded by empty liquor bottles and dwindling mounds of cocaine. Tony's face lit up when he noticed that Shanna

had entered the room. He still harbored an undying love for his sister, so he arose and unsteadily moved towards her. Tony took her in his arms and held her tight. Smelling the sweetness of her perfume, he kissed her cheek, then led her over to where his friends were seated.

Shanna greeted the group as a tuxedo-clad waiter quickly poured her a glass of Champaign. Tony rejoined his two blondes on the sofa and instructed their server to bring up more booze. The others resumed their slurred conversations so Shanna moved to the glass wall sheltering them from the crowd below. She sat on an ottoman next to the window overlooking the dance floor. Shanna felt depressed, partly because Tony had resurrected his bad habits and ignited his addiction once again and partly because she was miserable in her marriage and longed to be with the man she truly loved.

The club was still jumping and was filled to capacity. Shanna watched the people below her and sadly wondered what it would be like to be a "normal person" for once. As she sat and stared at the chaos on the dance floor she thought of Joe and longed for him. Shanna reminisced over their last time together, when they had accidentally bumped into each other at 54, then ended up at his hotel room at The Plaza. Shanna had berated herself over and over for not making love with him that night. As she rethought the episode, she deduced that she must have been nervous, confused and overwhelmed by his kindness and understanding nature.

Her mind then drifted to a dark thought; the price she had paid with Erich over her dalliance with Joe. Erich had brutally raped her and subjected her to a level of shame that she had never known before. She hated herself for allowing him to treat her like an animal, and she despised herself for giving her body to him willingly before he left for Europe. Tears began to spill down her cheeks as she watched the frenzied dancers below in a bleary haze.

Joe must have been reading Shanna's thoughts that night, for he was back in New York on business and after completing the evening meetings, he had abandoned his corporate colleagues to walk the streets and think of 'her'. Joe stopped into several bars as he meandered the avenues of Manhattan, and when he finally stumbled upon Studio 54, he wondered if fate had caused him to walk that way, or if he had just done so on purpose? He muttered, "What the hell," and after paying the expensive cover charge at the VIP Entrance, he entered and seated himself at the first bar he came to.

It was after 4 AM, yet the crowd was still hopping. He looked around miserably at the seemingly happy people pairing up with one another and he thought briefly about picking up someone and fucking her brains out, just to try and get Shanna out of his mind. Before the thought had barely left his mind, a young girl around twenty rubbed up against him and asked him to buy her a drink. She was young enough to be his daughter, yet she was attractive. Her name was Brandy. She had long auburn hair, hazel eyes and big boobs, barely concealed by a black halter top. Her legs were long and they were plunged into thigh-high leather boots that led to the short leopard-print skirt that clung to her tight little ass.

Joe looked her up and down, and whereas most men would have jumped on her advance in a heartbeat . . . he did not. He did buy her a cocktail in order to be polite, but being the gentleman that he was, Joe felt sick at his stomach at just being in such a predicament. He downed his Scotch and explained to Brandy that he had an early morning appointment and that he must leave. As he rose to go, she instinctively pressed her breasts into his face. "Oh please don't leave," she whined into his ear, "I've already been turned away by my idol in the VIP lounge tonight and it broke my heart," she pouted.

Joe pushed her away and replied in an uninterested way, "And just who is your idol?" Brandy moved back and put her hands to her cheeks, Oh my God! Tony Masterson of course!" Joe looked at her in disbelief. "Who did you say?" he asked. Brandy swayed a little, being intoxicated, and said again, "Oh my God, everybody's king . . . 'The' Tony Masterson and his band!" Joe continued to stare at the bimbo in front of him and asked in an urgent voice, "Is Shanna Somers with them?" "Oh yea," Brandy giggled, "They're all up there." Joe pushed her aside in an instant and bolted towards the stairway that led to the private lounge upstairs. Brandy pleaded for him not to leave her, but Joe ignored the girl completely to go and find the woman he truly loved.

The bouncer at the VIP Club halted Joe immediately as he tried eagerly to push his way inside. The bouncer won the altercation and explained that only celebrities were allowed into the private area; he demanded to know Joe's reason for wanting to enter. In frustration, Joe blurted out that he was a dear friend of Shanna Somers and that he *must* speak to her! The muscular guard eyed Joe with a modicum of sympathy, sensing his desperation and eagerness. He told Joe that he would go inside the lounge and inform Ms. Somers that she had a 'special' visitor. Joe nodded frantically and agreed to wait.

It seemed like an hour before the bouncer returned as Joe nervously looked around. Then he saw her; Shanna stood shyly in the large man's shadow, expecting to greet a smitten fan. When she spotted Joe, her mouth flew open and she stopped in her tracks. As Joe moved slowly towards her the bouncer held out his arms protectively. Shanna assured him that *this* visitor was all right, so he went back to his duties of guarding the door.

Joe finally stood in front of Shanna. He took her hands in his as she looked tenderly into his eyes while tears rolled slowly down her cheeks. "I can't believe this," he said smiling. She continued to cry but managed to say, "Neither can I." Joe pulled her into his arms and even he started to sob into her hair. They held each other tightly for a few moments, then he whispered, "Let's get the hell out of here!" She readily agreed, but first she said that she had to go and inform her brother that she was leaving. Joe followed her into the VIP room, although Shanna hesitated at first; she did not want him to see Tony in his 'messed-up' state.

Tony was still 'messed-up', but he was able to stand and stagger over when Shanna motioned for him. She introduced him to Joe and explained that he was taking her

home. Tony eyed the man who was leaving with his sister. Even in his inebriated shape, he could sense that Joe was a decent man, and someone whom he instinctively liked. He weakly shook Joe's hand and warned him to take good care of Shanna. Joe assured Tony that he indeed would, and told him to take care of himself. Shanna kissed her brother good-bye, then turned to happily leave with the man of her dreams.

Without hesitation, Joe took Shanna back to The Plaza where it had all started for them. Ironically, Joe was staying in the same suite that he had had before. When they entered the lobby it was after 5 AM and thankfully there were no paparazzi in sight. As they passed the concierge, Joe instructed him to have a bottle of the hotel's finest Champaign sent to his room. Despite the early hour, the man did not hesitate and assured Mr. Stephenson that it would be there post haste.

Once inside his suite, Joe and Shanna just stared at one another in disbelief that they were finally back together again. The stars had willed them into union at last, and they were determined not to let anyone or anything pull them apart ever again. Finally, they could stand it no longer and before either of them knew what was happening they were in each other's arms, kissing and undressing each other in wild abandon. Shanna and Joe fell into bed and made love over and over. They never heard the bellman tapping at the door with their chilled bucket of Cuvee' Dom Perignon.

Joe did finally sneak quietly out of bed while Shanna was dozing, rescued their Champaign and ordered breakfast to be delivered to them around noon. He crawled back underneath the covers with Shanna as she sighed softly at his touch. Joe was beside himself with happiness and he made love to the woman he so adored once again while she was still half asleep.

When the bellman once again knocked at their entrance with brunch, Joe got up and answered the door. He tipped the man handsomely and motioned silently that he would wheel it in by himself. Joe parked the cart near the bed, then went to wake Shanna. She was already stirring from the smell of eggs benedict. They both ate ravenously since they were starving from an evening of heavy love making. After breakfast they took a long, hot bubble bath in the Jacuzzi tub and enjoyed rubbing each other with the luxurious bath soaps provided by the hotel. They laughed and kissed and never wanted the day to end.

Eventually, their day did have to end; Shanna had to return to the penthouse to check on McKenna and of course there was the high probability that Erich would call from Europe. Shanna really didn't care anymore, for she had decided to divorce him so that she could live her life with Joe. She loved him beyond belief and she had made up her mind that there was nothing that Erich could do to stop her.

They spent glorious times together over the next three days until Erich returned from London. Joe and Shanna reluctantly left each other at The Plaza. Joe was hesitant to leave for Colorado, but Shanna assured him that she would be all right, and that she was determined to stand her ground when she asked her husband for

a divorce. She promised to call Joe at his oil company as soon as she had delivered the news.

Erich was in a jovial mood when he arrived in New York; his business meetings had gone well and he looked forward to picking up where he had left off with Shanna. He had replayed their last sexual encounter repeatedly in his mind, and he couldn't wait to get his wife into his bed once again.

When his chauffeur delivered him to the Madison Avenue building, Erich raced up to the penthouse in the elevator that opened directly into their massive ballroom. McKenna was playing with her dogs in the middle of the very formal black and white marbled room. She squealed when she saw her father, and ran to him with her dogs in tow. Erich scooped her up and kissed her on both cheeks. He twirled her around in the air and told her how much he had missed her and how much he loved her. He then set her down and sent her off to the kitchen with one of the maids for some milk and cookies. The driver was entering the foyer with the luggage and Erich instructed him to take it up to his bedroom later.

As he was heading up the winding staircase to their master suite, Erich heard a quiet voice call his name. It was Shanna. She knew better than to wait for him in their bedroom . . . it made it too easy for him to barricade her inside and abuse her. Instead, she was waiting on the patio overlooking Manhattan. When she broke the news to him about Joe he might throw her over the balcony, she thought, but at least all of the servants could see them through the glass.

Erich bolted towards the balcony with a broad grin on his face. Shanna looked lovely in a long white silk dress and her dark hair hung loose around her. A soft breeze was blowing and it tousled her long tresses around her ever so softly. She looked very fetching and Erich was instantly aroused by her. Andrew, the butler had left a silver tray with a pitcher of martinis awaiting. Shanna was already sipping one and looking very serious.

Erich approached his wife and took her into his arms, slightly spilling her drink. She was very stiff as he held her, until he finally pushed her gently back and looked into her eyes. They were dark and foreboding. "What is it sweetheart?" he asked cautiously. Shanna pulled away from him and turned to look out over the city.

Erich watched her as she stared . . . silently, sipping on the martini. He asked her again, in a more demanding voice, "Shanna, God damn it . . . what is the matter!" She finally turned to look at him and with all of the courage she could muster she replied, "I'm leaving you Erich." He looked at her in anger and disbelief and responded, "What did you say?" Shaking somewhat, she said again, "I want a divorce Erich, there is someone else and I just can't do *this* anymore. He moved to her and pulled her roughly to face him. Shanna was still shaking a little, but she wasn't afraid, for she had expected this behavior from him; she had experienced it all before.

She stared bravely into his eyes as he asked her in a soft, yet evil voice, "Are you insane?" Shanna's look never wavered as she answered, "Only for staying with a

madman like you for all of these years." Erich was stunned at her answer, for she had never acted so defiant with him before. Her response also enraged him, so he slapped her hard across the face. She hardly flinched, which maddened him all the more. He hit her again from the other side. She faltered somewhat, but still held her ground and did not try to defend herself.

Erich stared at her in outraged disbelief and yelled, "Are you crazy bitch?" Shanna narrowed her eyes and answered him again, "Only for staying with you, you bastard." His next blow sent her crashing into the side of the balcony. The city swirled below her and she thought briefly about throwing herself into the traffic below, however her love for life, her daughter and Joe, made her hang on. She was *not* going to end it all like her mother!

Andrew was making his way from the kitchen with more martinis when he saw his beloved mistress bleeding and hanging onto the railing of the balcony. In a panic he raced towards the sliding glass door but not before Erich leveled Shanna with another punch, sending her sprawling onto the floor of the tiled patio. Andrew screamed for one of the other servants to call the police as he rushed to Shanna's side. He had never interfered before, but it had pained him greatly to know that the woman whom he cherished and worked for had been punished for so long. He would stand for it no longer.

Erich ordered Andrew to leave, but the devoted butler stood his ground. "I will not sir," he replied in his very British accent. He turned his attentions to Shanna; she was conscious, but dizzy and her mouth was bleeding profusely. Erich was incensed and started to advance upon them as the police entered the front door. The other servants ushered the officers quickly to the balcony, for their concern was as great as Andrew's.

Erich was livid when he realized that the police were actually in *his* home and coming to arrest him! He went into a complete fit of unbridled rage as two officers held him by his arms. Never in his life had he been succumbed to such humiliation and he blamed it all on his wife. One of the deputies knelt beside Shanna and asked her if she was going to be all right. She nodded weakly and told him that Andrew would take care of her. The captain who was holding Erich then asked her the all important question of whether or not she wanted to press charges.

Shanna looked at the policeman and then at her husband. She pleaded for Andrew to please help her up. Her loyal servant raised her to her feet with the help of the deputy. She stood and spoke directly to the arresting officer. "I cannot press charges; it would leak to the press and would hurt my daughter. Please take him to a hotel, I do not want him here tonight." All of the policemen agreed. Shanna then looked at her husband in hatred, her lips still bleeding from his abuse. "I hate you Erich and I *am* leaving you! I will be gone in the morning."

As the New York City Police Department escorted the infamous Erich Shandon to The Plaza, his wife watched as her husband was led away from their home like a

common criminal. Shanna was extremely glad that McKenna was asleep and that she had never witnessed any of her father's violent outbursts. As Andrew assisted Shanna up the staircase to her bedroom he inquired about her plans. She informed him to instruct her maid to pack her bags, for she was leaving in the morning to stay with her brother in Upstate New York.

# CHAPTER 41

Tony did continue his quest for sober living and moved to his new home in the mountains soon after the episode with his old friends and his sister at the nightclub in New York. Although he was disappointed in the fact that he had succumbed to the temptation of drugs and alcohol again, he now realized that he never wanted to experience those feelings of physical sickness and self begrudging ever again.

He was excited to hear his sister's voice on the phone when she called and alerted him of her visit. Although he detected something in her voice that didn't sound quite right to him, he knew they could make anything better by just being together. When Shanna arrived at Montclair, she looked worse than Tony had ever seen her. She had lost a lot of weight, and she still had traces of the bruises on her face where Erich had slapped her.

When Tony saw his sister, he ran toward her in alarm and instantly demanded to know what had happened. The last time he had seen her was when she had left Studio 54 with the man from Colorado, so Tony's first thoughts were that she had experienced a violent attack from him. Shanna fell into his arms crying as he held her, but he still begged her to explain what was wrong. She was embarrassed to tell him; however, she finally blurted out, "He raped me, Tony," as she continued to sob.

Tony was mortified as he still held his baby sister and answered softly, "Who did, sweetheart? The man from the club? Did he do this to you?"

Shanna looked at her brother in surprise and responded, "No, it was Erich. He beat me and forced himself on me when he saw the tabloid reports of us leaving the club." She continued to cry as Tony led her into the house.

When they were seated comfortably in his living room, he still held her close on the sofa. The maid brought them some hot tea and cookies on a silver tray; however, it remained untouched. Shanna was inconsolable, and Tony was furious over what Erich had done to her. When she finally stopped crying, he looked at her seriously and insisted that she press charges against her husband for his abusive actions. Shanna refused, fearing the scandal it would cause and the damaging publicity that would undoubtedly harm her career and hurt her daughter.

Tony agreed to keep silent as far as the press was concerned; however, he vowed to kill his brother-in-law if he ever laid a hand on his beloved sister again.

Shanna stayed at Montclair for several weeks, and eventually, she started to recover from the devastating treatment she had received from her husband. Tony remained

very supportive towards her and managed to shield her from the majority of Erich's phone calls except for the ones when McKenna was on the other end. Shanna always loved hearing from her daughter, and Tony delighted in the joy that his niece brought to his sister.

Despite the privacy and seclusion of Tony's estate, the paparazzi eventually located them, and the news of Shanna's whereabouts reached Joe. He had longed to see her ever since they had spent time together in New York and had been worried when he had not heard from her. By pulling strings, Joe was able to get the number to Tony's estate, so he phoned Shanna immediately.

She was thrilled to get his call and begged him to come to Montclair for a visit. Joe was somewhat hesitant at first; however, he really wanted to see her again despite the fact that she was married and had a child. He remembered all to well her reasons for not engaging in an affair with him earlier, and he asked to know now why the circumstances had changed. Shanna regrettably admitted to him what had happened between her and Erich, and immediately, Joe's heart went out to her. With no delay, he booked a flight from Denver to Ithaca and was by her side in a matter of hours.

Joe arrived at Tony's estate and was overjoyed to see Shanna again. She was undeniably the most beautiful woman he had ever met, as well as the most intelligent and intriguing individual he had ever encountered. She was excited to see him again as well and led him quickly to her bedroom so that he could unpack his things. Joe wasn't as eager to unpack his clothes as he was to hold the woman of his dreams in his arms and make love to her. As soon as they closed the heavy oak door behind them, she was his. Joe pulled Shanna to him and kissed her hungrily, and soon, he showed her how a man can truly love a woman. The time Joe and Shanna spent together at Montclair was idyllic. They walked through the wooded hillsides hand in hand, enjoyed cozy evenings by the fire, and overindulged in the fabulous meals prepared by Tony's cook.

Gretchen was an older woman who was a local in the area, and almost everything she created was native to the upstate region. She and her husband still resided in a cozy cottage that was nestled in the heart of beautiful vineyard once owned by his ancestors. The land had long since been bought up by a huge winery, but as part of the purchase, Gretchen and her husband were allowed to keep their home and live out the rest of their lives there.

Every day, she brought scrumptious treats to Montclair, such as cheeses, wines, homemade scones, fresh produce, and free-range meats. Shanna, Joe, and Tony eagerly awaited her arrival every day to see what she would make for their next meal. Shanna began to complain that she had put on a few pounds during her stay at Montclair and jokingly stated that if she kept eating Gretchen's food, she would be released from her modeling contract.

Joe and Tony had also noticed a change in Shanna's appearance; she had put on some weight; however, she also looked pale and seemed to tire easily. One morning,

Joe awoke at dawn and reached for Shanna. He loved holding her, and they both enjoyed their early rousing sessions of sex, only this morning, she wasn't by his side. Concerned, he sat up and looked around the room. Possibly, she had gone outside to sit on the balcony, only the French doors were closed and the drapes still pulled. Then as he looked around the room, he saw a glimmer of light coming from underneath the bathroom door.

Joe rose and walked toward the light and put his head next to the door. There was no sound coming from the other side, but then he thought he heard a soft moan and crying. "Shanna," he called out to her, "are you all right, sweetheart?" She still didn't answer him, so he slowly opened the door; and there she sat on the marbled floor, leaning against the bathroom wall beside the toilet. She looked positively green, and there were dark circles underneath her eyes. Joe rushed to her and knelt down beside her saying, "Oh my god, baby, what is the matter?"

Shanna looked up at him sadly and answered, "I'm not sure, but if I had to guess, I would say that I'm probably pregnant." Joe looked at her in shock and realized immediately that the baby couldn't possibly be his; they had only been together for less than a month.

He helped Shanna to her feet and walked her slowly back into the bedroom. Her silk nightgown was stained from where she had been sick, so he gently pulled it from her and helped her into bed. Shanna looked at Joe miserably and watched him pace around the room.

Finally, he turned to Shanna as he ran his fingers nervously through his hair and asked, "If you are pregnant, did this happen when that monster you're married to raped you?"

Hesitantly, Shanna responded, "I guess so."

Joe continued to pace and uttered, "Goddamn him! I'm going to kill that bastard!"

Shanna reached out her hand to him and motioned for him to come and sit beside her. Joe moved to the bed and took her hand in his. "We don't know for sure, honey, that I am pregnant; maybe it was something I ate that didn't agree with me," she said, trying to comfort him. But they both knew that the chances of that were slim since everything Gretchen served them was healthy and very natural.

Joe pulled her fingers to his lips and kissed them; then he replied, "Maybe, darling, but we need to get you to a doctor and find out for sure."

Later in the morning, when Shanna felt better and was able to keep down some dry toast, Joe phoned the one and only physician in town and made an appointment. By lunchtime, they received the results, and Shanna's prediction had been true. She was indeed expecting a baby. The elderly doctor that had examined her could tell immediately that she was pregnant and announced that she was approximately eight weeks along.

Shanna cried all the way back to Tony's house, and Joe simply held her hand and remained quiet. She didn't know how this news would affect their relationship, for

she had made a decision while at Montclair that she was definitely going to ask Erich for a divorce since she was desperately in love with Joe. When they arrived home, Gretchen placed Shanna back in bed with a tray of hot soup and crackers while Joe went for a walk in the woods to think.

Tony knew something was wrong, and he was worried about his sister. When he saw Joe leave the house, he chased after him and caught up with him on the wooded path. After catching his breath, Tony asked him nervously, "Hey, man, what is going on? I know Shanna isn't feeling well, and you look like hell. So what gives?"

Joe sat down on a rock and motioned for Tony to sit down beside him. "Shanna's pregnant, and she conceived when that jerk she's married to raped her," Joe said sadly.

Tony put his arm around his new friend and said loudly, "That fucking asshole! I can't believe this has happened; we ought to go to New York and beat the living shit out of him!"

Despite himself, Joe couldn't help but smile at Tony's remark and responded, "Yea, I'd like to, but that would probably just land both of us in jail."

The two men sat together for several moments quietly until Tony broke the silence and said, "So what are you two going to do?"

Joe shook his head and answered, "I don't think either one of us has thought that far yet; we just found out this morning." He looked straight at the man who he also considered a friend and some day hoped would be his brother-in-law and said, "I love her, Tony, more than you'll ever know. I don't think I can bear to lose her if she goes back to that bastard."

Tony patted Joe on the back and responded softly, "I know she loves you too, and God willing, it will all work out."

Shanna remained queasy and weak for a couple of days, and Joe waited until she started to feel better to approach her about discussing their future. They were seated on the winding front porch watching the sun set behind the mountains when Joe took her in his arms and turned her to face him. He looked into those beautiful eyes of hers that reminded him of the blue skies of Texas and quietly asked her, "Baby, I need to know what we're going to do . . . about this 'situation,' about us, about our future, about everything."

Shanna looked back at him in all tenderness and responded, "I have considered a lot of things since we've been here, Joe. When I first arrived, I was devastated emotionally; then you found me, and I feel like I've been born again. I had planned to return to New York and file for divorce against Erich, but now that I'm carrying his child, he will never let me go. In the past few days, I've considered abortion as well, but his act of violence is not this innocent baby's fault. I just don't have it in me to do that."

Joe interrupted her, saying, "And I would never have let you destroy that sweet life that you've got inside you, Shanna. I already love this baby as if it were my own."

Shanna looked at the man sitting beside her with more love than she'd ever known, hating to break his heart by saying what she had to say. "I have to tell Erich,

Joe, and I am going to have to stay married for the time being. Maybe, after the baby is born, I can discuss divorce with him, but I know he will never give me my freedom knowing that he's going to be a father again. Please understand."

Joe did understand, but he was brokenhearted, nonetheless. He put his arm around her and held her close. "I respect you for your loyalty, sweetheart, but I want you to promise me that we can still see each other from time to time and that if that son of a bitch ever lays a hand on you again, you will leave him. If you don't, I will kill him."

Shanna knew that he meant what he said, and she believed him.

# CHAPTER 42

Whew Shanna returned to New York, she was happy to see her daughter but apprehensive about reuniting with Erich. He had been out of town a lot and had respected her wishes to be left alone while visiting her brother. Erich had no idea that she had been with Joe for nearly a month nor that she was desperately in love with the man.

Her first night back was peaceful; the staff was glad to have her back, and her maid had ordered fresh flowers to be placed throughout the penthouse. Erich had advised his chef to prepare an extra special meal for them, and after they put McKenna to bed, they dined on a feast of rack of lamb, steamed vegetables, scalloped potatoes, and fresh bread, accompanied by a bottle of expensive red wine from Erich's private collection.

Shanna barely sipped her wine that Erich found strange, for she loved rare vintages and usually enjoyed them heartily. But she had been very quiet and reserved since her return, and Erich suspected she was still very angry with him for the way he had treated her. After dinner and dessert, he invited her out onto the balcony that boasted the most spectacular view of the city. Their butler delivered after dinner drinks on a sterling tray, and although Erich eagerly accepted a cognac, Shanna turned it down. She walked over to the railing and looked out at the twinkling lights of Manhattan.

Erich sensed something was desperately wrong and went over to her. He stood behind her and put his arms around her waist, letting the sweet smell of her hair intoxicate him more than the brandy.

"What's wrong, sweetheart?" he finally asked.

Shanna turned to face him and said softly without hesitation, "I'm pregnant, Erich. We're going to have another baby."

Erich looked at her in disbelief then pulled her tightly into his arms, spilling his drink.

He hugged her as hard as he could and said excitedly, "You have made me the happiest man on earth, Shanna. I can't believe this!"

She didn't respond at first, then said, "I'm glad you're happy, Erich."

He pushed back from her and asked, "And you're not?"

Shanna looked at him sadly and responded, "I think I would have been happier if the child hadn't been conceived when you raped me."

Erich pushed her away then and poured himself another drink. "Oh, here we go again. I suppose you are going to hold that episode against me for the rest of our

lives? Look what has happened, we're now expecting a miracle; and hopefully, it will be a boy."

Shanna just stared back at him and said quietly, "Hopefully, it will be, Erich." With that, she bid him good night and retreated to their bedroom.

Erich stayed out on the patio and continued to drink for hours to celebrate the magnificent news his wife had just delivered to him. He honestly wished she was happier about another child. But *Fuck her,* he thought. He had just made love to her a little roughly for once, and look at the good that had come out of it. Erich eventually passed out on the terrace, but his loyal valet, Bentson, managed to move him inside to one of the downstairs guestrooms.

Shanna had an easy pregnancy, and although physically she was fine, emotionally she was a wreck. After leaving Joe at Montclair, she had spoken to him infrequently because she was terrified that Erich would catch her in a conversation with him. And knowing her husband's jealous nature, she feared he would get aggressive with her again and harm the baby. Little did she know that since they learned that the child was a boy, Erich would never have laid a finger on her, even if he caught her in the act. He was concerned that Shanna wasn't more enthusiastic about their baby; in fact, she seemed very depressed about something, and he could not get her to talk to him.

Shanna was depressed. She missed Joe terribly and began to take it out on Erich. She inwardly blamed him for separating her from the man she truly loved and hoped that she wouldn't resent her little boy for the way he was conceived. As Shanna's delivery date grew closer, she became more and more withdrawn until Erich finally consulted her obstetrician about her behavior. The doctor assured him that Shanna was one of the healthiest patients he had ever treated and that she was probably just experiencing hormonal mood swings, which were entirely normal.

The day that she delivered their son was the happiest moment of Erich's life. He totally adored his wife for giving him an heir and promised to be the best husband she could possibly hope for and give her everything she could ever desire. As Shanna lay in her hospital bed thinking about all she had been through, she had to admit that giving birth to her two children was the greatest achievement she had ever accomplished in her life. McKenna was the light of her life, and now she looked forward to many happy times with her new son.

They named him Alexander, after his grandfather, and with his impressive heritage, he had the potential to become anything he wanted to be. Shanna had no doubt that her son would achieve greatness in his lifetime, and although she planned to encourage him, she also hoped to instill in him the more unpretentious ways of life. She knew that this would not be an easy task with Erich and his family so eager to mold her son into the successor he was destined to be.

Erich was elated with the birth of his prominent son and ever grateful to Shanna for delivering him the ultimate gift anyone could have ever given him. He showered his wife with affection and bought her an outrageously expensive sapphire and

diamond necklace to celebrate the occasion. Shanna was thrilled with the birth of her son as well and recuperated quickly after childbirth. She planned to return soon to her work schedule when Alex was a little older, for she had definitely decided that there would be no more children in her future. And she felt now that Erich had his male heir, he would be satisfied and might someday allow her the freedom she so desperately longed for.

Shanna's beautiful body resumed its natural slim, tight figure; and she soon hit the runways again and graced the covers of the major fashion magazines. Erich resumed his work in his father's company and began traveling again not long after Alex's arrival. Shanna was almost relieved when her husband left on his business trip to Tokyo, for although he had been wonderful to her throughout her pregnancy, his doting nature was annoying her. She knew that he would never have been this caring toward her if she had not produced the next heir to the Shandon empire.

After Erich's departure, Shanna was eager to contact Joe and share with him the events surrounding her son's birth. She longed to reconnect with him and tell him about the pain, excitement, and joy of delivering a human being from one's own body. Shanna and Joe had spoken only a few times in many months, and they had not seen each other since the time they had spent at Tony's estate in the Finger Lakes.

When Alex was barely a month old, Shanna finally summoned up the courage to call Joe at his office in Denver. She was apprehensive over how he would react to her, in that she had somewhat ignored him in recent months and she knew how much he wished that the baby were his. He longed for nothing else than for them to have a life together and for them to have children of their own to create the future he so desperately longed for.

With Erich gone, Shanna languished in her privacy and the special moments she shared with her children. She had been breast-feeding Alex successfully, which she had not been able to do with McKenna. There was something strangely sensual and wonderfully tender about the experience that left her feeling peaceful and very maternal. Erich found it disgusting and refused to watch, but she innately knew that Joe would see the tenderness of it.

After the children were in bed, Shanna went to her room; and curling up in the middle of her massive bed, she phoned the love of her life. Joe had poured himself into his work since his separation from Shanna and answered his office phone on the first ring. He was working late into the evening and had long since sent his secretary home. His voice was abrupt upon answering the phone, but when he heard her soft voice on the other end, he melted.

Shanna spoke hesitantly to him at first then dove into an excited conversation about her son. Joe smiled on his end, thinking how much he wanted her to have his own child. Oh, how he longed for a future with this woman. She was the only woman he had ever loved, and he would always love her no matter what. It was heaven for him to hear her voice, and he apologized quickly for not calling her at the hospital.

"I didn't want to intrude on a tender family moment," he said somewhat sarcastically. "In truth, I just couldn't take it."

"I understand," she said softly. "It's all right. You must know that even though Erich and I haven't had a husband-and-wife relationship in a very long time, that this little boy is truly a wonderful gift from God."

Joe was silent for a few moments; then he finally said, "Well, I'm sure if he is anything like his mother, then he must be absolutely breathtaking."

They talked for a long while about the times they had spent together and finally about their future. Joe eagerly wanted to know when he could see her again, and she surprised him by saying, "How about tomorrow? I could book a flight out in the morning and be in your arms by lunchtime!"

Joe was beside himself with excitement and replied, "Well, I can't think of a tastier morsel than you, my dear!"

Teasingly, she responded, "And you're pretty damn delicious yourself, mister!"

They were like two giggling teenagers as they made plans to reunite. Joe was thrilled at the thought of seeing her so soon and knew he wouldn't sleep a wink until he held her again. She warned him that her trip would have to be a short one, in lieu of the fact that Alex was so young and Erich would be back in a few days. Joe frowned at that thought, but he was beside himself over seeing Shanna and meeting her infant son.

Shanna had Mike, her secretary, charter a private jet to fly her to Colorado. She left New York in the wee hours of the morning after tiptoeing into her daughter's room and kissing the little girl good-bye. The nanny promised her that McKenna would be fine and handed her Alex, along with an overstuffed diaper bag and suitcase containing his little duds. Carrying her precious dark-haired little son in her arms, Shanna flew toward the Rocky Mountains as the sun rose behind her to be with the man that she so desperately loved.

When she landed in Denver, Joe was eagerly awaiting at the private airplane terminal with a black limo and chauffeur patiently ready to transport them back to his ranch in the mountains. Shanna exited the plane wearing a tight light blue cotton dress with matching sandals, and the way that it clung to her body nearly took his breath away. It was impossible to think that she had just delivered a baby a month ago. Her long dark hair hung loose and blew freely in the wind. Joe couldn't wait to take her into his arms and bury his face into those luxurious thick locks.

Joe stood behind the security checkpoint as Shanna made her way to him holding her baby in his carrier. When she reached him, he kissed her gently and then looked down to see her child. Alex was the most beautiful baby Joe had ever seen, and he wished desperately that the child was his. One day, he vowed, *Shanna will carry my child, and we will have a son of our own.*

He helped Shanna to the car with the baby as the driver placed the luggage in the trunk. They stopped in town and had lunch at a trendy restaurant called Zeneth, before making the two-hour drive to his home in the mountains. Shanna loved Joe's

ranch overlooking the Colorado Rockies because it was a truly magical place to be. It was rustic and bold, just like him, but, at the same time, had a romantic and sensitive essence to it that was indescribable.

When they arrived, his housekeeper Juanita greeted them immediately and was overjoyed to welcome a baby into the household. She had always hoped that Joe would someday find a wife and settle down with a family. She took the carrier from Shanna, and after settling the baby into an antique crib that had been in Joe's family for generations, she fed the young couple a spicy meal of traditional Mexican food that was a specialty of hers.

After dinner, Shanna sat by a roaring fire and breast-fed her son as Joe looked on in wonderment. He had never seen anything so moving in his life as watching the woman of his dreams hold her newborn child in her arms and his little fingers push tenderly at her breast as he suckled her light pink nipple. Tears filled his eyes as he took in the magnificence of nature and all that it beheld.

After Shanna finished nursing her son and Alex was soundly asleep, Joe suggested they go for a walk in the moonlight up a wooded path that led to a secluded clearing where they had picnicked before.

It was in a secluded grove of cedar trees where the aroma took ones breath away and the gentle carpet of fallen needles underneath seemed to almost welcome two lovers to lie upon them.

As they left the house, Joe grabbed a bottle of wine and an old handmade quilt that had been his grandmother's; and together, hand in hand, they strolled off out into the night hiking upward into the upper hills of his property. The elevation led to a shortness of breath that made Shanna have to stop frequently to rest. Joe laughed at her and called her a city slicker; however, she retaliated by saying that he wouldn't last too long in New York City without her by his side. He was inclined to agree, for he hated Manhattan and only traveled there for business emergencies.

They finally reached the top of the ridge that Joe wanted to show her. Both of them were breathless but happy to be alone in such a beautiful setting. Joe spread out the old quilt and quickly pulled Shanna down beside him. They lay there for a few moments admiring the remote setting of the small clearing yet still able to view the twinkling lights of a tiny village far down below them. The sky was black, and the stars blinked brightly above them providing a perfect overhead blanket sheltering them from the rest of the world.

Joe turned on his side and looked at her. Shanna lay on her back gazing up at the sky hoping to witness a shooting star. As luck would have it, she did see one and squealed to Joe in delight that this was a sign for them and that their life was being blessed by something divine. He laughed at her zany cosmic beliefs but loved her for them anyway. He leaned over her and looked into those eyes that mesmerized him in so many ways and said, "I want you know that I have never loved anyone more than I have you and I would give my life for you, Shanna. You are in my soul now, and I don't want us to ever be apart again."

She didn't respond at first, then reached up, and touched his cheek, looked lovingly into his eyes and said, "Joe, believe me, my darling, that I am yours now, and I am prepared to prove that to you tonight." With that, she pulled his mouth to hers and kissed him hungrily. He responded with a vengeance as she started to remove his shirt from him while running her fingers over his furry chest. He easily came out of his top and crushed her to him with as much force as he could, without fear of hurting her. She moaned as he pulled her into him while removing her own clothing with smooth expertise as his lips moved over every inch of her face, lips, and neck.

Joe expertly had her undressed in minutes, and when he finally laid her back on the quilt, he lost his breath just staring at her naked beauty underneath the glowing moonlight. She was like a vision before him, and he couldn't believe he was in the presence of such a goddess. He quickly stripped out of his jeans and moved to her immediately. She reached up to him and pulled his mouth to hers and started to kiss him again, gently yet fervently, as she remembered how much he enjoyed her tongue flickering in and out of his mouth and how much she loved it too. His taste fed her, and his body nourished her unlike any man she had ever known.

After completely shedding his clothes, Joe was on top of her, and all their old feelings for each other returned in a rare passion that most couples never find in an entire lifetime. As he looked down at her, she reached up and, with her fingers, traced the outline of his face, taking in every line of him, every scar, everything that defined the man she so desperately loved. Shanna put her fingers in his mouth, and he suckled them gently, sending a tingling sensation through every inch of her. She began to feel his hands move along her body, and she was shaking with anticipation for his touch was like hot brands as he stroked every inch of her.

Joe took her head between his hands and lowered his mouth to hers, kissing her long and hard.

Shanna turned away from him finally, panting, and whispered, "I can hardly catch my breath!"

"Good," he responded in muffled tones. "Oh, baby, you don't know how much I've missed you!" He moaned softly as he moved his kisses down to her neck and then down to her swollen breasts. Shanna gasped with pleasure; and then suddenly, realizing what would happen, she pulled away from him in horror.

Startled, Joe looked at her in surprise as she looked down at her chest and took her breasts in her hands. Warm milk began to ooze from them as she was still nursing, and with her being away from the baby for a while and the manipulation, they had started to flow. Shanna began to cry, "Oh my god, this is so embarrassing. I can't believe that happened. I'm so sorry."

Joe smiled tenderly at her with tears in his eyes. "Don't be, baby, you sweet thing. I love this about you, and I'm very aroused by it. You shouldn't be ashamed by the way your body reacts to pregnancy, and being a mother, it's completely natural. I think it is a beautiful thing and part of what makes you a woman."

Shanna looked at him lovingly and replied, "You are one special man, Joe Stephenson, and I'm so very lucky to have your love."

He placed his fingers over her lips, silencing her while his other hand continued to caress her, causing her breasts to continue to spew warm milk, making them very slippery and very inviting. "Don't worry about it," Joe whispered as he continued to stroke and kiss her wet chest. She eventually gave into the sublime sensation he was arousing within her and allowed him to do as he wished. As he kept stroking and suckling her nipples, she succumbed to the pleasurable feeling as millions of tiny darts of ecstasy shot through her body, causing her to heighten to orgasm.

"Oh my god!" she screamed, and she panted breathlessly. His tongue continued to massage her nipples for a few more seconds until she lay back and relaxed in his arms. Shanna looked up at him tenderly, and he looked down at her with more love in his eyes than she could ever imagine. "What did it taste like?" she asked.

"What?" he answered.

"My milk."

Joe bent down and nuzzled her neck and said, "Warm and sweet, just like you!"

She just smiled and, putting her arms around him, pulled him down to her.

Shanna began to run her hands along his body, taking in every curve and muscle. He was so defined, his chest furry and muscular, and his arms hard as steel from the days when he labored long and hard in the Texas oil fields. She could feel his ribs and hipbones and marveled over his flattened stomach with the little trail of hair leading to his belly button. Her hand followed the hairy trail down farther until it collided with his hardened penis. Joe rolled over, and she leaned over and took him in her mouth. She licked ever so softly as Joe began to moan.

As her tongue stroked him, her mind began to think of the many differences between this man and the man she was married to. How diametrical they were. Erich would never touch her with her breasts full of milk nor would he like fucking on a hill in northern Colorado. Joe, on the other hand, was rugged and all male; yet he coddled her, kept her warm, and loved her like no man had ever loved her before.

Shanna continued her licking and stroking and concentrated mostly on the end of his penis and moved her tongue round and round causing Joe to escalate into a frenzy of desire. He began to move his hips up and down in anticipation until he could stand it no longer. He took Shanna by the shoulders and rolled her onto her back. She sensed his excitement and lay still, waiting for his next move. Joe opened her thighs and looked down between her legs. "God, you're beautiful," he breathed. He looked at her longingly and remembered how much he enjoyed oral sex with her and how much she enjoyed receiving.

He knelt down as Shanna whimpered in anticipation, for she remembered how much this man could excite her. Joe moved between her legs as his tongue softly began to caress soft folds of her womanhood and then moved slowly in circular motions. Shanna began to breathe heavily as he continued to explore and venture farther inside of her, inspecting the deep folds of her moistness. Joe wished he had

more than just the moonlight to showcase the glory of her female beauty; however, he was enjoying the woman beyond his wildest imagination, and he didn't care how he attained her.

Shanna felt very vulnerable and utterly naked as he propped her legs up over his shoulders and concentrated completely on the glorious sight before him. She moaned in almost unconscious satisfaction and felt completely loved and desired by this man who would go to such great lengths to pleasure her and make her happy.

His tongue continued to move in slow circles then faster; then it moved along toward the base of her spine, causing her body to react in sporadic movements out of her control. He returned his attentions to the center of her and plunged his tongue deep within her causing her to scream in utter abandon. She began to move her hips naturally until she eventually felt his fingers move to where his mouth had been.

Joe moved his mouth up to hers and kissed her as she tasted herself within him. He kissed her neck, her face, and breasts. He held her with one arm while with his other hand he took hold her buttocks, and before she knew what was happening, a lone finger had made it's way to her anus, where he caressed slowly yet hesitantly.

Joe whispered to her, "Is this all right, sweetheart?"

Shanna was too aroused to answer; she just moaned deeply with the new sensation he caused. Joe continued to stroke her from behind gently until he felt her body began to tense up with another orgasm. She came with a vengeance and uttered a cry that would challenge that of any wildcat in the vicinity. Her reverberating climax was so intense that Joe began to feel his own desire come alive, and he felt himself grow harder than he ever had been.

He moved back between her legs and lowered himself down and entered her slowly. Shanna whispered his name as he plunged deeper within, making them one. Joe lifted his face to look at hers and said, "I love you," then he turned his gaze to where they were joined, and all politeness disappeared. His body began to thrust up and down in fast, rapid jerks as Shanna joined him in the rhythmic movement.

Joe slowed down somewhat but continued to thrust deeper and deeper as he hovered above her beautiful face while occasionally glancing down to where they were connected. Suddenly, he looked directly into her dark eyes and said, "Kiss me." Shanna looked at him quizzically but didn't speak. Joe repeated, "Kiss me. I want you to kiss me when I come." He lowered his wet mouth to hers and kissed her hard. Shanna kissed his back and accepted his tongue eagerly. She could still taste herself on him. Joe gave a couple more deep thrusts within her; then raising his head, he too emitted a sound resembling that of a wild animal. Shanna smiled in deep satisfaction and contentment, for she could feel his love flooding through her.

Their lovemaking seemed to go on forever. When they both finally realized that they could go on no longer, they collapsed in utter exhaustion. Their bodies could take it no more, but their love would now last throughout eternity. Joe eventually

leaned upon one elbow and looked down at her. Her body glistened in the silvery light of the moon above them. Shanna looked at him tenderly and reached her hand up and touched his cheek. He turned and kissed her fingers and laced them within his own. He said softly, "I want you to marry me, Shanna."

She looked back at him with tears rolling down her cheeks and replied, "I will, my darling. I will."

# CHAPTER 43

Reluctantly, Shanna returned to New York after her euphoric time spent with Joe. He had been wonderful to her, and their love for one another was now deeper than ever. She was thrilled over his proposal; however, she was terrified to tell Erich about her relationship with Joe and equally as terrified to ask him for a divorce. Shanna was afraid of how he would react and of what he might do to her. His violent reactions in years past to things that did not please him were all to present in her mind, so she waited nervously until she could find the appropriate time to break the news to him.

Erich arrived home from Bangkok just hours after Shanna returned from Denver. She had cut it very close and had almost been caught. He had only called twice during the week that he was gone, and the servants simply told him that Mrs. Shandon was out. Erich knew that his wife was an active woman, and he suspected that after several months of being cooped up and pregnant, she was out visiting friends and catching up on the latest happenings in their social circle. He didn't fault her for that. Little did he know that Shanna despised the people in their social realm and couldn't wait to escape the confines of their presence to be with her lover in the mountains of Colorado.

As Shanna put off telling her husband about her affair and her plans for a divorce, she became more and more nervous and distracted. Erich noticed her behavior after a while and became irritated with her for rebuffing him and frustrated with her lack of enthusiasm about the birth of their new baby. Shanna had indeed been ignoring her children. She kept to herself in their bedroom pacing and drinking and thinking of a way to explain to her powerful spouse that she wanted to leave him and marry another man—a man he despised.

When Erich had finally had enough, he decided to confront his wife about her inexcusable behavior of neglecting their children and avoiding him. In the past several days, when he had retired to their bedroom, Shanna had already passed out from too much alcohol and, he suspected, sleeping pills. Tonight, he was determined to catch her awake and coherent enough to talk some sense into her and force her to act responsibly where her family was concerned.

Shanna was actually awake when he entered their room; she was relaxing in a whirlpool bath with bubbles up to her chin and a glass of chilled champagne at her fingertips. Erich threw open the bathroom door and startled her from the obvious daydream she was in. Shanna was indeed daydreaming; she was reminiscing about

her night on the mountaintop with Joe. Her eyes flew open, and she gasped when Erich entered the room; then she relaxed back into her bubbles and ignored him.

Erich walked over to the tub and knelt down. "Shanna, we need to talk," he said.

She looked at him pensively and responded softly, "About what?"

Erich pulled a towel from a heated rack and sat down on it so as not to get his clothes wet. He looked at his wife intently as she stared back at him with concern in her eyes. "I'm worried about you, Shanna, and somewhat pissed at the way you're behaving lately. You stay locked up in here all day drinking, and besides that, you are ignoring your children and your husband. And I want to know what has brought this on?"

Shanna looked away from him and responded, "I don't want to talk about this now."

Erich was starting to grow irritated with her petulance. He reached over and roughly took her chin in his hand and jerked her head toward him and said, "Well, you will talk about it now or else!"

Shanna pulled away from him, downed her drink, and rose from the water. She stood before him glistening as suds clung to her beautiful wet body. Erich just stared at her and marveled at how sexy his wife was, and lust grew within him. He reached out to touch her, but she stepped over him, dripping all over the clothes he had so desperately tried to keep dry.

Shanna wrapped one towel around her body and another around her head, then padded into their massive bedroom. She poured herself another glass of champagne from the chilled bottle resting in a silver ice bucket, then settled comfortably on her chaise lounge. Erich exited the bathroom in his water-stained clothes and watched her attempting to towel dry her long dark hair. She had her head hung over, and her tresses almost touched the floor. The towel around her body had slipped, and her breasts were exposed. Erich again felt desire began to mount within him as he watched her.

Shanna finally threw her head back and noticed Erich gazing at her, so she secured the towel tightly around her chest again and went to her closet to get a robe. His eyes followed her until she disappeared.

*I have to keep it together,* he thought, *I can't let her get to me. I have to find out what's bothering her.*

Shanna returned from the closet wearing a yellow silk nightgown and matching robe. She retrieved her glass, then went to stand before her husband. "All right, Erich, let's talk. It is time," Shanna said in a serious tone.

"Sit down then," Erich suggested.

She resumed her seat on the chaise lounge, and he remained on the edge of the bed. There were several moments of silence between them until finally, Shanna spoke, "Erich, I really don't know where to begin, except to just be honest with you. I want a divorce," she said meekly.

Erich just stared at her and didn't respond. Shanna looked at him nervously, fearing his reaction. He still continued to stare. "Did you hear me?" she asked.

"I heard you," he said evenly.

Shanna began to fidget; he was making her extremely nervous.

Finally, he spoke again, "Can I ask what has brought this on?"

Shaking, she answered him, "We haven't been happy for some time, Erich; we have grown apart, and that's not how a marriage is supposed to be."

Erich looked at her hardly and said loudly, "That's bullshit!" He rose and began to pace around angrily. "You must be crazy. We have everything, you bitch! We have a beautiful home, two beautiful children, fame and fortune, notable friends, and all the material possessions anyone could ever want! How can you possibly say we aren't happy?" he yelled.

Shanna looked at him sadly and replied softly, "None of the things you mentioned, Erich, with the exception of our children, make a person happy. Love is what makes people happy; it's all that matters."

Erich looked at her steadily and said quietly, "You're wrong, my dear; love doesn't get you very far in this life. It is wealth and power that get you through this existence. But for what it's worth, I still love you."

Shanna looked down at her hands for several minutes before she spoke. Finally, she looked at him and painfully admitted to her husband that there was someone else. Erich looked at her in shock, not believing what she was saying to him. "I want a divorce," she repeated. "I need my freedom, Erich."

He was still looking at her with an astounded look on his face then he rose and moved toward her. Shanna's heart beat faster as he approached her and pulled her up to face him. "What did you say?" he asked.

"Erich, please," she whispered as she tried to turn away.

He jerked her back roughly and asked her again, "I said, what did you say to me?"

Shanna squirmed, but he held her tight. "I'm trying to tell you as gently as I can that I'm in love with someone else, and I want to be with him."

Erich pushed her roughly to the bed and proceeded to pace around the room again as he yelled at her. "Who the bloody hell is it?" he demanded. Shanna raised herself from the bed and moved toward her champagne bottle. Erich intercepted it and, grabbing it from the cooler, whirled it across the room as it crashed against the wall and shattered.

Frightened, Shanna headed for the door, but Erich blocked her path and grabbed her by the shoulders. He looked directly into her eyes and, in an icy tone, said, "You tell me who it is or I do to you what I just did to the fucking champagne bottle."

Shanna looked at him with tears forming in her eyes and quietly replied, "It's Joe Stephenson."

Erich stared at her with a look that could have melted an iceberg, and she quivered in his arms. "You're fucking kidding me," he said. Shanna didn't answer him; she just nodded.

Erich shook his wife violently until she screamed for him to stop. One of their servants heard the noise and rapped softly on the door. Erich ordered whoever it

was on the other side of the door to go away, and the rapping ceased. He stopped shaking Shanna and looked viciously at her. "How long has this torrid affair been going on, my dear?" he asked.

Shanna looked at him with tears streaming down her face and answered, "Not long. We were only together at Tony's estate, and then I didn't see him again for months. We only just reconnected since Alex's birth."

Erich continued to stare at her with evil in his eyes. "What does that mean reconnected?" he inquired.

Shanna squirmed in his arms, but he kept a tight hold on her. "Answer me! Goddamn it!" he yelled.

She looked at him with all the courage she could muster and replied, "I only just returned from Denver this morning. We've been together all week. He wants to marry me."

Erich finally released her and walked to the French doors and looked out at the city below. Shanna panicked for a moment and wondered if he planned to throw her from their balcony; then she reassured herself that he wouldn't act that crazy, or would he? She thought about making a run for the door; then pride stopped her. Why should she always act terrified of him? *Because he was a madman at times,* she reminded herself.

Shanna stood in silence watching him until he finally turned to face her with a devastated look on his face. "Do you love him?" he asked.

Shanna looked at him squarely and answered quietly, "Yes, I do, very much." Erich then began to walk toward her, and she expected the worse. When he was close enough to touch her, he took her chin in his hands and said, "Get out." Shanna looked at him in puzzlement. "You heard me," he repeated, "I said, get out."

She continued to stare at him in disbelief and asked, "What do you mean?"

Erich sneered, "I mean, my dear, that you can pack your things and get out of this apartment tonight. If you don't, I won't be held responsible for what I might do to you."

Shanna pulled away from him and, in anger, said, "You can't be serious! Where would I go tonight?"

Erich moved to the bar and poured a straight scotch. "There are a million hotels in New York. Pick one," he offered as he downed his drink and poured another one.

Shanna continued to protest that she couldn't leave at that time of night and that she needed to be there for her children.

Reacting to her comment, Erich was on her in two seconds and grabbed her again by the shoulders. He looked squarely into her eyes with a dark stare that bore a hole right through to her very soul and said, "Venom runs through your veins, my dear, and you'll only emit poison to any man who tries to love you. And as for our children, you haven't been here for them in days, so I don't know why you should start now. Now, for the last time, get out!"

With that, he threw her to the floor, strode to the wall speaker, and rang for a servant. When a maid arrived, he told her to pack an overnight bag for Mrs. Shandon

and then to summon their chauffeur to drive her to the Plaza. Shanna still sat in the floor crying heavily. Erich went to her, picked her up, and threw her into the closet, ordering her to get dressed. When Shanna emerged, she was wearing jeans, a white sweater, and brown boots; Erich was nowhere to be seen.

The maid helped Shanna down the stairs with her suitcase and makeup bag, then went to check on the car and driver. Shanna stood in the marbled ballroom looking around in dismay. She wanted to check in on McKenna and Alex, but she was afraid Erich would catch her and cause a scene, and she didn't want them to wake up to his ranting. Shanna decided she would wait and call her children in the morning.

When the maid returned, she informed Shanna that the chauffeur was waiting at the entrance of the building to take her to the hotel. Shanna looked at the woman sadly. She didn't even know her name. She was recently hired by Veronica, their head housekeeper, before she left on vacation. Ronni, as Shanna called her, was wonderful; and Shanna loved her dearly. She reminded her of the black woman who had practically raised her, growing up as a child. Shanna smiled when she thought of Fanny; then tears slowly began to roll down her face when she thought of how much she missed that old woman and how much she could have used her guidance now.

Shanna slowly began to make her way to the entry foyer as the maid waited impatiently by the door. She wanted to get back to her room since Erich had summoned for her after she had already retired. Shanna hesitated and asked the girl if she should maybe go and speak with Mr. Shandon before she left.

The young woman shook her head violently and stated that he had specifically ordered her not to let Mrs. Shandon interrupt him in his den. Shanna started to cry again feeling desperate and shunned at being turned out of her own home.

She wept all the way to the Plaza as the driver watched her from the front seat. He didn't speak to her whatsoever, for he had worked for Erich for a number of years and was completely loyal to him.

When they arrived at the hotel, just a few blocks away, he helped her to the curb and then turned the rest over to the doorman. Shanna thanked him; but he simply nodded, returned to the limousine, and drove away.

The doorman beckoned for a valet, and within minutes, Shanna was ushered to a suite on the top floor with only herself, her luggage, and her thoughts. Before the valet left, she tipped him handsomely and asked him to send up someone from room service with a bottle of their best champagne. He nodded and said that he would make sure that it was delivered immediately. In the meantime, Shanna slipped out of her clothes and into the luxurious robe that the Plaza always provided to their guests.

After the champagne arrived, Shanna poured a glass and downed it quickly. She filled another glass, then settled on the bed, picked up the phone, and called Joe at his ranch in Colorado. His housekeeper answered and said that Mr. Stephenson was in the city attending a charity function and that he had mentioned staying the

night at his place in town. Shanna then dialed his number to his penthouse on Pennsylvania Avenue, in downtown Denver, and there was no answer there. Depressed and lonely, she sat in bed drinking and trying Joe over and over. Finally, she passed out drunk, crying, and wishing she were dead.

In the morning, Shanna awoke with a throbbing headache that was only compounded by the ringing of the telephone. She was still half asleep and somewhat inebriated; so when she reached for the receiver, the whole phone crashed to the floor. *Shit,* she moaned, then reached over, gathered it up, and managed to get it reassembled and back upon the nightstand. The phone rang again immediately, scaring Shanna nearly to death. *Goddamn it!* she screamed and then answered on the second ring. It was Joe. He had called his ranch house and was told by the housekeeper that Shanna had been trying to reach him.

"What is it, baby?" he asked worriedly.

Shanna started to cry when she heard his voice and didn't answer him. "Shanna, you're scaring me. What is it?" Joe demanded.

Shanna finally managed to stop crying long enough to respond. "He threw me out."

Joe was silent for a few seconds; then he asked, "What are you talking about, honey?"

Shanna sniffed and told him again, "Erich forced me out of the penthouse because I told him about us."

Joe sighed on his end and wished desperately that he was with her so that he could hold and comfort her.

"Everything is going to be all right, sweetheart. I will get there as soon as I can. Where are you staying?" Joe asked.

Shanna started to feel better just knowing that he was coming to be with her. "I'm at the Plaza, room 1040. When can you be here?" she begged.

"I'll catch the next flight out, baby. Don't worry. Just stay calm, and I'll be there as soon as I can," he promised. "I love you, Shanna," Joe said softly as he hung up.

"I love you too," Shanna whispered as tears filled her eyes again.

Knowing Joe was on his way gave Shanna the will to get out of bed and summon the strength to get bathed and dressed. She crawled out from under the covers and stumbled across the room to the minibar. She mixed a screwdriver and then went to run a bath. As the water ran, Shanna decided to call her children. She picked up the phone and dialed the penthouse.

Erich's valet answered immediately; and Shanna instructed him to put her through to the nanny so that she could speak with her children. He didn't say anything, so Shanna said again, "Bentson, ring me through to Tracy so that I can talk to McKenna and Alex." The old butler was completely loyal to Erich; and therefore, he informed Shanna that he had been instructed to hang up if she should call, which he did promptly. "If only Andrew would have answered," she thought . . . "he would have helped me."

Shanna sat staring at the receiver in her hand after Bentson had slammed the phone down in her face. She couldn't believe that he could be so heartless as to not let her at least hear her children's voices.

She felt like crying again, but she had to get ready for Joe's arrival; he would help her with the mess she was in and solve everything. Shanna knew that with Joe by her side, she would find the determination to fight for her children, her future, and a chance at happiness. With a glimmer of hope, Shanna rose, mixed another drink, and sank into a hot bubble bath.

# CHAPTER 44

When Joe arrived at the Plaza, he hurried to an elevator and rode upward to the tenth floor. He found Shanna's room without any trouble and knocked eagerly at the door. There was no answer, so he rapped louder, thinking she might be in the shower or asleep. When she still didn't come to the door, he started to panic, thinking the worst. Finally, he began to call her name loudly and banged on the door with such a vengeance that the other guests began to peer out of their rooms. Joe apologized to them and tried to decide what he should do. At last, just when he was about to go and alert security, the door opened, and Shanna peeked out.

Joe was immensely relieved and pushed the door open with such a force that it knocked Shanna down onto the floor. He rushed to her and tried to help her up, but she could barely stand on her feet. Joe looked at her carefully. She was still wearing the hotel's robe. Her hair was matted from where she had passed out with it, wet. There were dark circles surrounding her puffy red eyes, and she reeked of alcohol.

"My Jesus, baby! You're drunk!" he said in surprise. Shanna didn't respond. She just clung to him tightly with her face buried in his neck. Joe pushed her back so that he could look at her closely and asked her softly, "Sweetheart, how much have you had to drink?" She still didn't speak, but she didn't have to. He looked around the room and saw the empty champagne bottle and miniature vodka bottles scattered everywhere.

"Oh my god, honey, why did you do this?"

Shanna looked at him and replied, "I don't know, Joe. I was just so upset about everything that I just couldn't deal with it. I had to numb the pain."

Joe pulled her close to him and held her tight. "Oh, sweetheart, I'm here now. Everything is going to be all right." She clung to him like he was her only buoy in the sea of life and begged him not to leave her.

Joe promised her that he was not going anywhere, but that first, he needed to get her sobered up and rested. He searched through her luggage until he found the silk nightgown ensemble that her maid had packed the night before. He helped her change out of the hotel robe that had become almost like a second skin to her; in fact, she had already decided that she must purchase one upon checkout.

After she was comfortably dressed, Joe slipped her under the thick coverlet and called room service to order some hot tea. He then propped Shanna up against some pillows and proceeded to brush out her long brown hair. She yelped as he

plowed through the thick mats that had formed while she lay passed out. Joe eventually worked out all the tangles and continued to stroke her hair until a waiter delivered the tea. Joe poured Shanna a steaming cup, squeezed a lemon into it, and handed it to her, ordering her to drink. She did as she was told and sipped slowly while she watched Joe drink a beer.

After Shanna finished her second cup of tea, she announced that she was feeling better but that she was still extremely exhausted. Joe removed her bed tray holding the empty tea cup and then helped her settle comfortably under the covers.

Shanna was asleep almost immediately, and Joe just sat watching her as he finished his beer.

She was the most beautiful woman he had ever seen, and she looked so peaceful and innocent lying there in the middle of the huge bed. He had never seen her so drunk before, and it worried him. But she had been through a lot, and he guessed that the alcohol had helped her to dull all the pain she felt. Things would be different now though; he was determined that they would never be separated again, and he would see to it that Erich Shandon would pay dearly for what he had done. Joe was tired too. The trip and the anxiety over the whole ordeal had left him physically and emotionally drained. He threw the empty beer bottle in the trash, stripped out of his clothes, and climbed into bed with Shanna. Joe held her as close to him as he possibly could and thought about how deeply he loved her and could never live without her.

# CHAPTER 45

Shanna quickly climbed out of her depression with Joe back in New York and by her side. Although she was still reeling after being thrown out of the penthouse and heartbroken over being separated from Alex and McKenna, Joe's presence gave her the strength and determination to take on her powerful spouse and fight for the right to be near her children. Joe helped Shanna retain a divorce attorney with an excellent reputation who also specialized in child custody cases. His name was Reuben Stein, and although his fee was the most expensive in the city, he assured Shanna and Joe that he had no fear in going up against the mighty Shandon family.

Erich had also retained a powerful legal mind and was prepared to bring in an entire team of attorneys, if necessary, to gain sole custody of his children and take down Shanna at the same time. He was intent on ruining her financially, socially, and personally to pay her back for the many times that she had hurt him. Erich's parents, Elise and Alexander, backed him totally, for they had never approved of Shanna as his wife, and the countless tabloid coverage of her had made their lives unbearable within their social circle.

Joe was livid that Erich was being such a ruthless bastard and making Shanna's life miserable. He did everything possible to keep her mind off the situation by keeping her constantly entertained with the many activities available in New York City. They went to Broadway plays, art galleries, the opera, and the ballet. Shanna loved spending time with Joe and was so thankful to him for coming to be by her side when she needed him the most.

They went shopping on Fifth Avenue, ice-skating in Rockefeller Center, took handsome cab rides through Central Park, and dined at only the finest restaurants. One evening, Joe and Shanna returned to her suite at the Plaza, after having dinner at Le Perigord. At the end of their meal, the waiter had delivered a small silver-covered dish to their table, which Joe encouraged her to open. Thinking it was a special dessert, Shanna giggled and lifted the lid. To her amazement, there was an emerald and diamond ring the size of an almond, resting on a heart-shaped sugar cookie that read, "Will You Marry Me?" Shanna cried in joy and assured him that she would, without a moment's hesitation. It had been the happiest night of Shanna's life, and she clung to Joe lovingly as they entered their room.

Joe pulled his bride-to-be down onto the bed and leaned over to kiss her. He happened to see the red light on the phone blinking rapidly, indicating that there

was a message waiting to be retrieved. Shanna followed his gaze to the phone as well and immediately panicked, thinking that something could be wrong with the children. She asked Joe to contact the front desk to find out who had called, and he did so while she waited anxiously.

When he hung up the phone, Joe had a worried look on his face. Shanna looked at him in concern and asked, "Honey, what is it?"

Joe looked at her solemnly and replied, "Sable phoned, and she asked that you call her at once. There has been an accident."

Shanna couldn't imagine what could possible have happened, so she took the phone from Joe and dialed her aunt immediately. Sable's butler, Benjamin, answered on the first ring in a somber voice, which wasn't uncommon, for Old Ben, as Shanna called him, had always sounded depressing. She asked to speak to her aunt, and within seconds, Sable was on the phone.

Shanna was so nervous that she could barely speak, but she managed to ask in a shaky voice, "Jesus, Sable, what has happened?"

Her aunt was silent for a moment, and then she replied, "It's your mother, sweetheart. She's had an accident."

Shanna signed in exasperation and said in irritation, "Now what has she done? What the hell has happened?"

Sable began to cry on her end but managed to sadly say, "She's gone, honey. Jackie has committed suicide. She jumped from my balcony earlier this evening."

Shanna was speechless for several seconds; then she managed to find her voice. "My god," she finally sighed and sank to the bed.

Joe rushed to her side and asked anxiously, "What is it, babe?"

Shanna looked at him in shock and replied, "It's my mother; she's committed suicide."

Joe pulled her to him and took the phone. He spoke quietly to Sable and told her they would be right over. Shanna sat in silence beside him staring straight ahead. After Joe hung up the phone, he called down to the concierge and asked for the hotel's limousine to be brought around immediately.

The ride to Sable's penthouse was a short one, for she lived on Fifth Avenue, only a few blocks from the Plaza. When Joe and Shanna arrived, Sable was waiting in the salon, calming herself with a pot of tea. Shanna rushed to her when she entered, and Sable rose to greet her. The two women embraced, and Sable began to cry again as her niece held her close.

They finally sat down together on an antique love seat as Sable explained the dreadful situation to them. Joe took a seat opposite them as Benjamin served him a scotch and water, which he gratefully accepted. Sable instructed him to bring her a brandy, and Shanna asked for a straight vodka on the rocks. Joe gave her a concerned look, but she ignored him.

After Benjamin delivered their cocktails, Sable tearfully told them all she knew about what had happened to her sister. She began by saying that Jackie had seemed

very depressed for days and that she had been drinking excessively, even more than she normally did. Sable had observed countless pill bottles in Jackie's bathroom and suspected that she had been abusing those as well. Apparently, something had been building within the woman for quite some time until she could take it no more and, in her inebriated state, had climbed atop the railing of the balcony and flung herself some thirty floors into the traffic below. At least that is what several witnesses had reported.

Sable had returned from a dinner party to find numerous fire trucks, police cars, and paramedics outside her building, along with dozens of curious onlookers. Officers were frantically trying to disband the crowd when Sable passed by the scene and hurried inside. It wasn't until she entered her apartment and found the authorities waiting for her did she start to piece together that something was desperately wrong. It was then that she learned that her sister was dead.

Joe and Shanna sat listening intently to Sable's account of the situation, and they both had tears in their eyes, wondering how another human being could sink to such misery, that they could end their life in such a tragic manner. They were all silent for several moments after Sable finished speaking. The body had been transported to the morgue and would remain there until the family had made arrangements. Sable was prepared to take charge of everything, knowing her niece had already experienced too much pain in her life, and dealing with this tragedy might prove to be too much for her to bear.

But despite all the losses she had encountered, as well as the emotional turmoil in her personal life, Shanna was a strong woman in her own right and one not to be underestimated. She finally spoke and told her aunt that she would help her arrange a memorial service for Jackie and that she would go and find her father and tell him of the news. Holding Joe's hand, she said softly, "My mother obviously experienced a dark night of the soul and chose to go into blackness instead of toward the light. Her memory will not fade into the oblivion though; I will see to it that her final farewell to this world paints a brighter picture of her than the dismal gray canvas that was her existence." Both Joe and Sable nodded in agreement and remained silent.

# CHAPTER 46

During the years of Shanna's rise to fame and fortune, her mother's life had continued to spiral downward. The Mastersons' marriage ended after Jackson left Jackie to be with his mistress. Jack and Jackie's relationship had deteriorated rapidly over the years, and the affection they once shared for one another had turned to hatred. Neither of them could ever say that they had exactly been "in love" with one another, which was something they both had learned to accept. However, they had shared an intense passion and desire together, but that too dissolved into violence, fueled by Jackie's constant abuse of alcohol and prescription drugs.

Jack was forced to resign from his political post after being charged with illegal fund-raising actions. His legal practice quickly dwindled away, and eventually, his law partners had no other choice but to let him go. A handsome salary, the opulent lifestyle, and his popularity all vanished quickly, so Jack saw no other option but to relocate to another city and start over. He scraped together what was left of his savings; and he and his girlfriend, Lois, moved to Chicago where Jack opened a small practice downtown.

Jackie also decided to leave Nashville after Jack divorced her, and the political scandal ensued. She received a decent settlement from Jackson and reaped half the proceeds from the sale of their stately home. With her own money and a chance to start over, she chose New York City. Jackie only hoped that her sister would be decent and forgiving enough to take her in and allow her to begin a new life.

Sable was an honorable woman and an understanding one as well. Despite all the ugliness between her and her sister over the years, she was only too willing to take Jackie in and help her rebuild the shattered remnants of her existence. Shanna was not as willing to neither overlook the past nor pardon her mother for all the pain she had caused. In her eyes, Jackie was a selfish, vengeful, and cruel woman; and she wanted nothing to do with her whatsoever.

Shanna begged her aunt not to allow Jackie to take up residence with her, but Sable was determined to do what was right as far as family was concerned. Markus had taught her that family was everything; and no matter what horrible things a relative may have done, anyone could change, and everyone deserved a second chance. She was adamant about the matter, so Shanna finally relented and agreed to attempt to be cordial to her mother and try to put their differences of long ago to rest.

Jackie was ecstatic about being in Manhattan. The lights and energy of the city gave her a new vitality and, for once, a positive lease on life. She loved the clubs and

frequented them nightly. Sable's chauffeur had never been worked so hard in his life as he was driving Jackie around all over the city and at all hours of the night. Timothy eventually complained to Sable about the situation, so she quickly put an end to her sister's inconsiderate demands on the older man and instructed her to take a cab in the future.

Jackie not only abused the driver but the maids, the cook, and Sable's elderly butler Benjamin. She was constantly ordering them all around in a disrespectful manner, commanding the entire staff to cater to her every need. Old Ben finally took his mistress aside and told her very firmly that if Jackie did not stop acting like the queen of England, they were all going to resign and seek employment elsewhere.

Sable apologized profusely to the servants and gave them all a handsome bonus. She promised them that there would be no more demands made of them other than their normal duties. She also took Jackie aside and explained to her very plainly that if she did not stop tormenting "the help," she would personally escort her to a hotel. Jackie halfheartedly apologized and agreed to abide by Sable's wishes.

Months went by, and as much as Sable had hoped that a deeper bond would develop between her and her sister, the fates did not permit it. Jackie was the most self-centered, narcissistic, and uncaring person Sable had ever encountered. It pained her to think of her own flesh and blood as being someone of such an evil nature, and it broke Sable's heart to think of the miserable existence Shanna must have endured in growing up with such a woman. She was ever so thankful that she had been able to invite her niece to come and live with her and only regretted that Shanna couldn't have moved in with her sooner.

Sable finally decided to throw a party, in hopes that if Jackie could meet some new friends, she might be a more pleasant person. Sable always sought to find the good in people, and she accredited her sister's nastiness to recovering from a bitter divorce and adjusting to a new way of life. So with any luck, Sable hoped that a social gathering in her home might help matters a great deal.

Over one hundred invitations were mailed to Sable's acquaintances on the Upper East Side and to a few of her dear friends in Greenwich, Connecticut. The event was black tie, and Sable hired only the finest caterer and the most acclaimed party planner in the city to assist her with the affair. She naturally invited Joe and Shanna; however, Shanna refused to go. She knew how her mother would most likely behave, and she didn't want to be embarrassed in front of the crème de la crème of New York society. Shanna hated her mother and had never forgiven her for the way she had treated her over the years.

Jackie, in her daughter's eyes, was a heartless bitch, and she wanted nothing to do with her. Joe hated to see the woman he loved harbor such bitterness against the person who had given birth to her. He begged Shanna to make peace with Jackie if only to find peace within herself and to make her aunt happy.

Shanna explained to Joe that he would never understand the pain that her mother had caused her over the years; however, in order to please him, she agreed to attend the party.

Joe's best friend, Dexter Davis, happened to be in town the week of Sable's party, so Joe invited him to join him and Shanna as their guest. Dex and Joe had worked together in the oil fields of Texas back in the days of the big petroleum boom. They had worked their asses off and had often felt as if they would die of heat exhaustion and dehydration, but they both agreed that those days had been the happiest times of their lives. The two men had remained close, and Dex had even moved to Denver as well and was president of a chemical engineering firm.

He was thrilled to see Joe again and most impressed to meet Shanna, the famous and beautiful model that he had seen on countless magazine covers and never dreamed of meeting in person. Dex found her to be sweet, charming, and very down-to-earth. She was perfect for Joe, and he was very glad that his friend had found such a wonderful woman. Shanna liked Dex too; he was so much like Joe that she teased them about being long lost brothers.

They were all excited about attending Sable's soiree; even Shanna had overcome her reluctance over not going now that Dex would be accompanying them. She enjoyed his company and was excited about introducing him to members of New York City's elite. The threesome arrived promptly, and the party was already in full swing. A string quartet played in the grand entry foyer as finely dressed couples waltzed to the beautiful music. There was a festive air in the room, and everyone seemed to be having a wonderful time.

As they made their way through to the main salon, Joe heard someone shriek his name and looked up just in time to see Phoebe Belford hurrying toward them with her arms spread wide open.

Phoebe was responsible for his meeting Shanna at her gathering, for what seemed now, very long ago. So much had happened since that night, but Joe would be forever grateful to her for introducing him to the woman of his dreams.

Phoebe finally reached Joe and planted a kiss on both cheeks, leaving ruby red lip imprints on each side of his face. He graciously accepted her display of affection and smiled at her grandiosity. Phoebe then turned to Shanna and hugged her gently saying how happy she was to see the two of them together. Shanna introduced the older woman to Dex and asked her to help make him welcome. Phoebe was delighted to be given an assignment that allowed her to escort a handsome eligible young man, especially to be given the opportunity to present him to all of her well-to-do friends.

Shanna giggled as Phoebe eagerly led Dex away and into the crowd. She turned to Joe and put her arms around his waste and pulled him close. He laughed and embraced her as well, asking her what she was up to. Shanna looked up at him and said sweetly, "I just wanted to have you all to myself for a few moments before we get sucked into this mass of rich snobs!"

Joe smiled and looked down at her saying, "Must I remind you, my dear, that we too are rich?"

She nodded and replied, "Yes, but we still remember what matters most in life, and that is having someone to love." Joe didn't respond but reached down and kissed her gently on the mouth.

In the distance, they heard someone calling their names, and when they looked up, Sable was motioning for them to join her in the other room. They looked at each other lovingly and headed in her direction. As a waiter passed by them, Shanna grabbed a napkin and a club soda from his tray. Before they took another step, she turned Joe to face her, and dabbing her napkin in the soda, she then touched it to his face and wiped Phoebe's red lips from his cheeks.

Sable's party was a success, and everyone had a splendid time. Jackie felt she had died and gone to heaven in that she was surrounded by the crème de la crème of society, and she had been the guest of honor. She had looked beautiful in a gray-sequined evening gown, which set off her silvery-frosted hair that she wore swept up in an elegant French twist. For once, Jackie had behaved in a sophisticated fashion and drank very moderately. Everyone who met her that evening found her to be elegant, witty, charming, and worthy of being Sable Chandler's sister.

Jackie had danced with almost every man in attendance, but she had focused most of her attentions on Joe's friend, Dexter Davis. He was the most striking young man Jackie had ever seen; with his broad shoulders, lean frame, handsome face, and dark features, she couldn't take her eyes off him. She flirted with him relentlessly, and she enticed him to move with her to the music many times throughout the evening. When the evening came to a close and everyone started to leave, Dex stayed behind and urged Joe and Shanna to go on without him.

Shanna protested, for she had seen her mother and Dex together, and she already had surmised her mother's intentions toward Joe's friend and assumed that Jackie had invited him to stay longer. Dex assured them that he just wanted to remain a little longer to chat with Sable briefly since he hadn't been able to speak with her in the presence of her guests. He also wanted to get to know Jackie a little better and possibly invite her out for a drink, but he sensed Shanna's apprehension and didn't want to upset her.

There was an intensity between the two women, and Dex picked up on the visual daggers Shanna had thrown Jackie's way all evening. He hoped to someday learn the reasons behind their animosity, but for now, his interests lay in unveiling the new woman he had met.

# CHAPTER 47

Dexter Davis became smitten with Jackie Masterson. After meeting her at Sable's party, he had taken her out for drinks, then later delayed his return to Colorado in order to stay in New York and develop a relationship with the mysterious, challenging, and alluring new woman he had met. Dex took Jackie out to dinner every night for a week, and then the couple would dance away the evenings at the trendiest nightclubs in the city. Soon, they were a regular item and on their way to becoming a steady couple.

Shanna was furious over the fact that her mother was dating Joe's best friend and vehemently opposed their relationship. She voiced her objections to her fiancé over and over until Joe could take it no longer and agreed to speak with Dex about Jackie. Although he strongly believed in staying out of other people's personal affairs, he felt he owed it to Shanna to intervene in the situation, and he somehow too innately felt that Jackie was not what his friend needed in a woman.

Joe took Dex out for dinner and drinks at the Harvard Club and talked to him man-to-man about Jackie. He explained in all sincerity and honesty that in his opinion, perhaps Jackie was not the best woman for him. Joe told Dex all that Shanna had confided to him about her past relationship with her mother and all the turmoil that had erupted between them due to Jackie's selfish nature and abusive personality. Dex smiled at his friend, ordered another round of scotch, and assured him that all mothers and daughters had conflicts and that he found his new love to be charming, sophisticated, and very sexy. To Joe's surprise, Dex announced to him that he planned to propose to Jackie and take her back to Denver with him as soon as possible.

On the ride back to the Plaza, Joe dreaded telling Shanna about his meeting with Dex. He knew that she would be devastated to learn that not only had he failed in convincing his friend to stop seeing Jackie but that an upcoming marriage loomed in the very near future. Joe was right, of course, for Shanna was horrified and in shock to hear the news that he delivered to her. She vowed to put a stop to Dex's plans even if she had to throw her mother in front of a taxicab to stop the engagement. Joe managed to calm her down, but not without several glasses of white wine.

Shanna called Sable immediately the following morning and begged her aunt to do something about the dreadful event that was about to take place between her mother and Dexter Davis. Sable sadly explained to her niece that Dex had proposed

to Jackie that morning during a champagne brunch on her balcony. He had ordered an elaborate breakfast prepared by a renowned French chef, and that a five-carat diamond ring had been hidden in one of the freshly baked croissants. Sable went on to say that Jackie had been overjoyed and accepted Dex's proposal without a second thought.

Shanna almost dropped the phone over her aunt's news. Her face grew pale, and Joe rushed to her side to find out what was the matter. "My mother is getting married," she said solemnly. Shanna said good-bye to her aunt and hung up the phone. She then rose and proceeded to the hotel minibar where she mixed a vodka and grapefruit juice.

Joe looked at her sadly and asked, "Do you think that a drink is going to help matters, sweetheart?"

Shanna stared back at him and replied, "It can't bloody fucking hurt."

Jackie and Dexter were married at Sable's Copper Island estate. The wedding took place outdoors with the Canadian coastline in the background. Jackie looked stunning in a slim-fitting ecru gown with long gloves and her hair swept up on top of her head, held in place by an antique crown. The reception was held in the master hall of the majestic castle that had been Sable's home during her ideal marriage to her beloved husband Markus.

Only a small crowd was in attendance; however, the affair was elegant and in extreme good taste. Everything Sable accomplished was a classy and well-organized event, and her sister's ceremony had been no different. It would be a day that Jackie would always remember as one of the happiest days she had ever experienced. She had overcome many years of personal struggles to finally secure the love and affection of a very handsome and successful young man. She couldn't wait to write to her friends back in Tennessee and gloat over her new status in life and also to brag over the fact that she still had the ability to snare a sexy husband, many years her junior.

Shanna and Joe attended the wedding; however, they did not feel that the event was cause for celebration. They both felt that the union only posed impending disaster, but for now, there was nothing that either of them could do about the matter, so they decided to wallow in their own happiness and love for one another. Shanna suggested that since they were on the West Coast, they fly over to Hawaii and spend a few days in tropical bliss. Joe agreed with her, and before nightfall, they were on their way to a Pacific paradise.

# CHAPTER 48

Shanna and Joe returned from Hawaii rested and tanned from the two weeks that they spent in Honolulu. Their time there had proved to be a rejuvenation period and had provided the peace and tranquility that the couple needed to somewhat recuperate from all the pressures that life had dealt them of late.

Jackie and Dex returned from a brief honeymoon in San Francisco and began their new life in Colorado. Jackie was disappointed that their trip was so short and not spent in a more exotic location; however, Dex had to report back to his company and catch up on all the work that had been neglected since he had been away in New York, pursuing Jackie Somers.

Sable had given her sister and her new husband their honeymoon as their wedding present. She had spared no expense and arranged for them to stay at the Mark Hopkins Hotel, in the honeymoon suite, provided orchestra-level seats to the opera, and gave them ten thousand dollars in travelers' checks to spend as they desired. In every way, it was the most generous gift from Sable, yet Jackie still felt as if her sister owed her more.

Dex pointed out to his new wife that her sister had been very giving in offering up her home for their wedding and, in addition, giving them a wonderful honeymoon trip that they could remember for the rest of their lives. Jackie, unfortunately, still felt as if she had been shortchanged in not getting a trip around the world or something to compensate for all the pain she had been through. She felt that at the very least, her rich celebrity daughter should have coughed up enough money to send her mother away in grand style.

Jackie Somers always felt as if she had received the short end of the stick where life was concerned. She assumed that around every corner in life, something better was waiting for her. The only problem was she wasn't willing to do anything to achieve it. Jackie felt that the world *owed* her and that it was only a matter of time before she made her mark on society and made it profoundly.

Dexter Davis, however, was a simple kind of man. He was decent, kind, and good. The collection of traits that made him a man was not unlike those of Joe Stephenson. That was why the two men had remained friends for so many years and had stayed loyal to one another. Dex never knew how much he would come to cherish his friendship with Joe after marrying Shanna's mother.

Jackie became impossible. She made life unbearable for her new husband. Nothing he did seemed to please her. Her true nature surfaced and, along with it,

the demons of addiction that were her constant companions. Her bitterness and selfish nature become all too apparent to Dex within weeks of their marriage. He sought out the comfort of Joe and Shanna, which infuriated his wife all the more.

Finally, Dex encouraged Jackie to go and visit Shanna and Sable in New York, explaining to her that he had weeks of endless meetings with his board members and he didn't want her to feel neglected. He urged her to go and spend as much money as she wanted to at fashion shows, attend Broadway shows, and possibly find them an apartment to rent when they visited the city. Jackie agreed to go to Manhattan but only to appease her husband. She innately felt as if Dex were trying to deceive her in some way, and in fact, he was.

Jackie had a good time in New York. She enjoyed shopping and visiting with the few friends she had made during the short time she had lived there. Sable invited her to stay at her apartment again but quickly questioned her judgment in allowing her sister to move in with her, even if it were for only a short while. Sable was a very patient, kind, and understanding woman; however, Jackie's behavior became so intolerable that Sable finally asked her to move into a hotel. Since her arrival, Jackie had done nothing except drink, smoke, and pop pills. She would return from her shopping sprees and lunches so intoxicated that she would strew her packages all over the apartment, curse at the servants, and make endless long-distance phone calls bragging about her new husband.

Predictably, Jackie was livid when her sister asked her to move out of her apartment. In her drunken state, she screamed obscenities and threw a Ming vase through Sable's drawing room, sending it crashing against a priceless painting. Sable finally was forced to call the police; however, Jackie quickly gathered her things and fled from the building before they arrived.

She hailed a cab and ordered the driver to take her straight to Kennedy Airport. When she arrived at the terminal, Jackie purchased a one-way ticket to Denver and then went to the bar where she ordered a vodka martini. Jackie continued to drink as she sat comfortably in her leather seat in first class. She decided to call her husband and tell him she was on her way back to him; however, Dex was not home. She rang his office next, but the receptionist informed her that Mr. Davis had left hours ago to meet with his attorney. Jackie didn't consider it odd that her husband was meeting with a lawyer; after all, he held a prominent position in a large firm, and she was sure he had frequent meetings with attorneys. So she settled a back in her seat and passed out for the remainder of the flight.

The plane landed with a mighty thud, waking Jackie from a sound sleep. She cursed loudly as the vibration jolted her, causing the other passengers to look her way in annoyance. When the captain alerted the passengers that it was clear to disembark, the flight attendant helped Jackie out of her seat and assisted her out the door.

The Denver airport was bustling with people as Jackie slowly made her way through the terminal and searched for a pay phone. She was hungover and groggy

from drinking so much, but she decided to try and call Dex once more before she headed for the bar. Jackie hoped that if she reached him, he would offer to come and retrieve her, which would give her time to down a few drinks in order to quell her pounding head and still her shaking hands.

She made her way to a phone and clumsily fumbled through her purse for her calling card. Her hands were trembling so that she could barely hold her wallet, much less open it to find anything. Finally, cursing loudly, she threw her bag down onto the floor, roughly pulled the receiver from its hook, and yelled into it for an operator. After several tries, she was eventually patched through to her house; and at last, Dex answered the phone. He had expected her call, for Sable had phoned him earlier to forewarn him of Jackie's arrival.

When he heard her voice, Dex could tell that his wife had been drinking, and drinking heavily. He wasn't surprised, and dreaded seeing her in that condition, especially when he knew that the news he had to deliver to her would do nothing except devastate her and inevitably enrage her to heights of fury he had yet to experience. During their brief marriage, Dex had encountered several of Jackie's violent drunken outbursts and, at times, had feared for his own safety. But he had had enough of her outrageous behavior and selfish nature, and although he hated the episode he would soon face, Dex wanted his life back and needed his freedom from the impossible woman he had become entangled with.

Jackie begged Dex to come and collect her from the airport; however, he explained to her very calmly that he was awaiting an oversees call from Singapore but that he would send a car and driver for her right away. This appeased her somewhat, for that would give her time to send a porter to gather her luggage and allow her at least half an hour to spend in the cocktail lounge. She tipped an attendant generously and instructed him to locate her bags, then wait in front of the ground transportation area, and have her paged when her car arrived. With those arrangements made, Jackie hurried to the nearest bar stool and ordered a double vodka on the rocks and uttered a contented sigh of relief as the Russian liquor streamed down her parched throat.

The sounding of her name over the loud intercom came all too soon for Jackie, but she downed her third cocktail quickly and made her way out of the building to locate the car that would take her home.

She was feeling much better, now that she had a few shots of courage under her belt and excitement filled her as thoughts of seeing her sexy young husband entered her mind. As she settled comfortably into the supple leather of the limousine, she sipped on a glass of champagne and fantasized about ripping the shirt from Dex's defined, furry chest and driving him into a frenzy with her mouth and eager hands.

Jackie continued to daydream and have sexual thoughts about her young man that would undoubtedly be anticipating her return, and she planned to pleasure

him in ways he never thought imaginable. Little did she realize that Dex had no intention of ever touching his wife in a sexual manner again, much less continue any sort of relationship with her.

When the sleek black limo dropped Jackie off at their house, Dex was waiting for her. He helped the driver carry her baggage into their entry hall and tipped the man heavily, knowing that he had probably been through hell in transporting his wife. Jackie stumbled into the living room, threw down her purse, and proceeded to the liquor cabinet to mix herself another drink.

Dex set her luggage at the base of the stairway in the hall and walked hesitantly into the living room as well. He frowned when he saw that Jackie was already mixing a cocktail and instantly voiced his disapproval to her. She smirked at him, and after stirring her drink with her finger, she told him plainly to get over it and leave her alone. Dex began to lose his patience with her and was growing very nervous just being in her presence and dreaded approaching her with what he had to say.

Jackie moved to a plush sofa and plopped down into its enveloping pillows, kicking off her shoes. She slowly sipped on her cocktail, enjoying the warm familiar flow of the alcohol trickling down her throat.

Dex finally moved closer and sat on the coffee table in front of her and said softly, "Jackie, we have to talk."

She swirled the ice around in her glass with her finger and answered him, "About what?"

Dex cleared his throat and looked down at the floor, fidgeting with his hands. He looked at her seriously and said, "We can't go on like this, Jackie; I am not happy with our relationship and quite frankly . . . I want out." Dex waited hesitantly for some sort of response; however, Jackie just sat there looking smug, sipping on her drink. "Did you hear me?" he asked softly.

She continued to stare at him with a gleam in her eyes and finally said, "I heard you, you son of a bitch. So just what are you saying to me?"

Dex squirmed uneasily again and replied, "I'm saying that I want a divorce."

In an instant, Jackie was on her feet and hurled her glass across the room, sending it shattering into the fireplace. Dex jumped at her sudden move and ducked just in case she felt like throwing another object. Instead, she turned on him and began hitting him brutally with her fists, demanding to know what or who had put this insane thought into his head. Suddenly, she grew still, and with a look of pure evil on her face, she turned to Dex and whispered, "Shanna did this, didn't she? That little bitch got to you, I'll bet."

Jackie began circling him like a cat cornering a trapped mouse and screamed loudly, "What did you do, my dear, fuck her?! Tell me!" she demanded.

Dex's mouth dropped open with her accusation, for he couldn't believe that any one person could be that vicious, especially against their own daughter.

He shook his head as she continued to rail at him. "Answer me, you goddamn prick!" she yelled again.

Dex finally gathered his thoughts and was trying hard to control his anger, but the mad woman in front of him was pushing him to the limit.

Jackie reached out to slap Dex again, but this time, he grabbed her wrist and roughly twisted it against her chest. He looked deep into her eyes, his own turning dark as his temper raged and said, "Now you listen to me, you crazy bitch. Shanna has been nothing except a very dear friend to me, and she always will be. Your selfish nature and disgusting sense of values are what have destroyed this relationship. Not to mention the fact that you're drunk and abusive, ninety percent of the time!"

With that, Dex maneuvered her roughly back through the entry hall and toward the front door.

Jackie squirmed in his hold and resisted him in every way that she could, only she was not strong enough to break free of him. "Let me go, you ass!" she protested.

Dex continued to force her out of his house as she couldn't believe what was happening. He finally managed to push her out of the front door where she tripped and fell hard onto the bricked porch, tearing her slacks and cutting her hand.

Dex felt a momentary wave of sympathy for her; however, it didn't last long. Jackie had meant nothing to him except heartache and pain, and their entire relationship had been a huge disappointment for him. Even in a compromising position, Jackie continued to scream obscenities at her husband while she struggled to pull herself to her feet. When she managed to regain her balance and stand, Dex threw her valise past her onto the lawn and slammed the front door in her face.

Jackie felt as if she were in the worst nightmare of her life. She looked in bewilderment at her suitcase in the yard, the disarray of her clothes, and her hand that was now dripping blood. It was only a matter of moments before her fury rose again, and she began pounding on the door and throwing rocks at the windows. Her tantrum was interrupted, however, by the sounds of sirens blaring along the driveway to their home. Dex had phoned the police, and within minutes, they had Jackie subdued and confined to a squad car.

Instead of taking her to jail, she was driven to the Denver airport, escorted to an awaiting private jet, and told that she was never allowed to set foot on Mr. Davis's property again. Jackie sat in silence with tears rolling down her cheeks as Dex's company plane whisked her back to New York City.

# CHAPTER 49

Sable was seated at her writing desk when she got the call. Her maid knocked softly on her bedroom door and announced that Mrs. Davis was on the phone. Sable was taken aback for a moment or two, not readily remembering who "Mrs. Davis" was. Quickly, she realized that Jackie was calling, and she hesitated about whether or not to pick up the receiver; however, something within Sable's decency summoned to her to reach out to her sister.

Jackie was calling from the airport and begged her sister to send a driver to pick her up. Sable could tell immediately that Jackie was drunk and dreaded already the inevitable episode that would undoubtedly transpire once her sister showed up. But still, Sable revered her kin and assured Jackie that she would send Timothy to collect her as soon as possible. Once Jackie arrived at Sable's, she said very little and retired to her room. She stayed there for two days drinking and popping pills to dull her misery.

Sable was worried about her sister, yet she stayed out of Jackie's way and respected her privacy.

Dex called and spoke with Sable at length once he knew his wife had arrived in New York. He sadly explained to his sister-in-law that he could not continue an existence with a self-indulged, totally selfish woman, such as Jackie. She had made his life miserable, and he had seen no other alternative but to terminate their marriage and send her packing. It was not in his nature to throw her out on such an aggressive note; however, her actions had driven him to behave in a manner he never thought possible.

Sable understood and didn't blame Dex in the least for the way he had treated her sister. She knew Jackie was impossible, and there was only unending sympathy for any man that had the nerve to tolerate her. She told Dex that she hoped that they could remain friends, and he readily agreed.

Jackie eventually emerged from her bedroom looking haggard and weary. She had taken her husband's rejection hard, and her fragile ego had been shattered as a result. Sable was out shopping when Jackie ventured out to request a new supply of liquor and snacks, yet there were no servants to be found. She wandered about the penthouse alone until a plan began to form in her mind. Jackie stole back to her room, cleaned herself up, and then picked up the phone and called her son-in-law, Erich Shandon.

Jackie's intense hatred for her only daughter often pushed her to limits that even she found surprising. When yet again, life had forwarded her a cruel blow, her

only recourse was to blame her downfall on Shanna. When the telephone rang at Erich's Madison Avenue penthouse, he was most surprised to hear his mother-in-law's voice on the other end. She begged him to allow her a visit with her grandchildren, explaining that she was only going to be in town for a short while.

Erich had been at a loss ever since he had forced Shanna from their home, and although he longed to have her back, he definitely wanted to avoid having anything to do with her mother. However, offering Jackie an audience might somehow improve his chances of getting closer to his wife. Shanna was in Paris for a few days where she had been assigned a last-minute magazine layout. Joe thought the change of scenery might do her good, and he could use the time to fly back to Denver to check on matters with his company. So Jackie had purposely seized the opportunity to pay a visit to her son-in-law while Shanna was away.

A meeting date was set for Jackie to come to Erich's apartment to see McKenna and Alex. She arrived early; and despite her broken heart and shattered self-esteem, she looked attractive in a sleek black pantsuit and, for once, she was relatively sober. As the butler led her through the massive ballroom, Jackie marveled at the magnificence and splendor of the penthouse, and once again, envy engulfed her as she considered her daughter's good fortune. *She'll get hers someday,* Jackie muttered softly to herself, *and that day may be today.*

Jackie was invited to take a seat on a beautiful antique sofa in the formal living room, and again, she was in awe over the fineness of the furnishings. She accepted a glass of Chardonnay from the butler and waited quietly for Erich and the children to appear. Soft music played throughout the room, and for the first time in several days, she felt a unique sense of peace.

Soon, Erich entered the room with Alex and McKenna walking quietly beside him. They were dressed impeccably in stylish clothes and looked every bit the offspring of the blue bloods of society. The children didn't know the woman who sat before them, for Shanna had never allowed visits with her family other than her brother. She felt as if her parents had done enough damage raising her, and she didn't want either one of them passing along their evil influence. Jackson and Jackie had visited the hospital briefly when McKenna was born but had never laid eyes on their grandson.

The children were nervous about meeting the strange woman who sat in their home. The only grandmother they had ever known was Erich's mother Elise, and they adored her, for she spoiled them rotten. Jackie didn't reach out to the children; however, she spoke quietly and said, "Hello, children."

They clung shyly to their father until he finally pushed them forward and encouraged them to speak to their grandmother. They visited for only a brief while, for Alex and McKenna were clearly restless in the presence of the stranger, and Jackie was plainly uncomfortable in being with them. So Erich finally excused them to their rooms to play with their nanny.

Erich poured himself a whiskey and water and waited for Jackie to make a move to leave, now that she had seen her grandchildren. But Jackie didn't make a move.

She sat where she was and eyed Erich steadily. He squirmed, not knowing what to do, so he drained his drink and quickly mixed another one. Finally, not being able to stand the silence and the intensity of the atmosphere any longer, he said, "Jackie, was there something else you wanted while you were here?"

Jackie looked at him seductively as she ran her tongue along the outer rim of her glass and nodded. Erich fidgeted anxiously as he watched her until she finally spoke, "As a matter of fact, there was something else I wanted."

Erich stared back at her suspiciously and answered, "What?"

Jackie didn't answer right away but rose and sauntered over to him as she unbuttoned her blazer and let it fall to the floor. She moved in front of him in just her black bra and slacks and looked squarely into his eyes and replied, "You."

Erich looked at her in disbelief and chuckled, "You're fucking kidding me, right, Jackie? I mean, this is a joke, isn't it?"

She inched closer to his face and whispered, "Hardly, I *want* you, Erich. I can make love to you so good that you won't even think twice about my daughter ever again."

Erich couldn't believe what he was hearing as his anger began to rise. Jackie moved her lips to his, but to her surprise, he roughly pushed her away. "You must be out of your goddamn mind, you crazy bitch, to think I would ever go to bed with you, much else ever forget Shanna!" With that, he pushed her aside, reached down, and grabbed her jacket and shoved it into her arms. "Get out of my house," Erich commanded, "and don't ever show your face here again!" He then yelled for his butler and instructed the elderly gentleman to escort Mrs. Davis to the door.

Jackie awkwardly gathered her things and made her way back through the ballroom and to the foyer. Before she entered the private elevator that would carry her down from Erich's penthouse, she turned back and looked once more at her son-in-law. Erich stood holding his drink, watching her in disgust. Jackie felt his hatred and contempt for her, which made her crumble inwardly. Her last attempt at attaining attention from a man and seeking some sort of revenge on her daughter had failed, leaving her feeling that all was lost for her and that there was no hope.

Jackie hailed a cab back to Sable's apartment and walked sadly through the lobby. The doorman recognized her as Mrs. Chandler's sister and noticed that she was terribly troubled. Yet he did not speak to her, for she had always been extremely rude and nasty to him, and he had been forced to help her on more than one occasion when she had come in drunk. He watched her walk to the elevator with her head down, and she appeared to be crying.

When Jackie entered the penthouse, it was dark and quiet, and there was no one in sight. She guessed that it must be the servants' day off and figured that her sister was attending some sort of charity event or fashion show. She didn't care though, for she wanted to be alone to carry through a plan that she had set into motion earlier that day.

Jackie made her way to her room but not before stopping by Sable's bar and mixing a very strong martini. She took a bottle of Stolichnaya with her, then went to

her bathroom, and ran a hot bubble bath, full of expensive bath salts. She swallowed a couple of Xanex and plopped down into the marbled tub. As she bathed, Jackie thought about all that life had dealt her. It seemed that she had always struggled to achieve happiness, yet it always evaded her. Just when it appeared that things would start to flourish, someone would inevitably knock her back down and block her pathway to success.

She was tired of living that way. No one appreciated her. No one respected her, and no one believed in her, she thought. *Well, I'll show them,* she whispered to herself. After her bath, Jackie dressed in her best negligee and applied her makeup artfully. She brushed her silky frosted hair until it looked like spun silver, then swept it up onto her head in an elegant fashion. After she inspected her looks in the mirror and decided that she looked more beautiful than she had ever looked, she made her way back out into Sable's drawing room, carrying her bottle of vodka with her.

Jackie sat staring at the view of the Manhattan skyline and sadly wondered why she had never been the toast of the city the way her daughter had. As she continued to drink and reflect over the past, the more depressed she became. Her husband Jack had left her for a younger woman. Dexter had dumped her because Shanna had poisoned his mind, and now Erich had found her sexually detestable, which had been the ultimate blow.

Tears ran down Jackie's face when she thought about what a despicable existence she had led. Even her own grandchildren abhorred her. Depression and desperation overcame her, and not even the liquor seemed to help anymore. Jackie gulped down the last drop of vodka and then sent the Stoli bottle hurling across the room, where it shattered against the mantle into a million pieces.

She rose unsteadily to her feet as the pills combined with the alcohol altered her balance and blurred her vision. She moved slowly and carefully toward a large antique mirror, holding on to the furniture to try and avoid falling. When Jackie looked at her reflection, she stared miserably at a woman that she inwardly hated. She admitted that the outside package was striking indeed; however, what lay on the inside was a creation made of pure evil, bitterness, and self-destruction. Before she turned to go out onto the balcony, she turned to examine herself once more. She wiped the mascara stains from underneath her eyes and straightened the wisps of hair that had gone astray. When satisfied with her appearance, she opened the sliding door and proceeded outside.

The twinkling lights nearly blinded her, yet she was able to make her way to the railing and pull herself up to where she was sitting on the edge. With shaking arms, she maneuvered herself around until her legs hung over the side and dangled freely above the ground far below. The car horns sounded endlessly as Jackie teetered precariously above them. She took one last look at the city that had never accepted her, and without another second of hesitation, Jackie Somers Masterson Davis opened her arms wide, pushed off with her feet, and flung herself into eternity.

# CHAPTER 50

The day after her mother's death, Shanna set about helping Sable make arrangements for Jackie's funeral. She didn't know what to feel about what had happened. Although she and her mother had hated each other from the very beginning, Shanna found it horribly sad that the woman who had given her life had been disturbed enough to want to destroy herself. It was an obvious fact that Jackie had been slowly killing herself for years with substance abuse, but no one would have guessed that she would have sunk to a level of desperation that would have caused her to suddenly take her own life. Jackie Somers had been a very vain woman, and everyone was shocked that she had caused her own demise.

Sable was more upset than anyone, for she felt that she had not given her sister the support she had needed and had not sympathized more over Jackie's total breakdown over losing Dex. But Sable was a strong and dignified woman, and she diligently went about organizing the memorial service and taking care of every detail. She definitely did not want the press to make a heyday of the event; however, she knew it would be impossible to elude them altogether. Sable arranged for the ceremony to be held in a small chapel in Midtown and hoped that the paparazzi would not find out the whereabouts until after it was all over.

Shanna was instructed by her aunt to call the two ladies that had been Jackie's closest friends since she had been in New York. She also told Shanna to try to contact the few people in Nashville that had been acquaintances of her parents and inform them of the terrible news. Shanna did as she was asked; however, sadly, none of the people she spoke with in Tennessee acted as if they cared, and the two women in Manhattan agreed to come, yet they didn't seem overly sympathetic.

Shanna called her brother at Cherokee Studios in Los Angeles, where he was recording a new album. Tony had practically moved to the West Coast after he took a hiatus from touring with his band to write and produce new songs. He had a whole new set of friends, and with his constantly being on the road and pushing himself to greater heights of stardom in the music world, he had begun to use drugs again.

When Shanna heard his voice on the other end of the phone, she could tell immediately that he was drunk and high. Although she was greatly upset to hear him that way, she was not surprised, for Shanna had suspected that her brother was using again, in that he rarely contacted her anymore. She tearfully broke the news to him about Jackie, and even though he was inebriated, he understood what she told him and promised to catch a flight out to New York the first thing in the morning.

Even though the phone call with Tony disturbed her to no end, she knew that she couldn't dwell on his problem; for now, she had to deal with the situation at hand. After she hung up from speaking with her brother, Shanna knew that she must try and locate her father. The last she had heard was that Jack had moved to Chicago to live with his new girlfriend Lois, but that was all she knew. She tried to get his number from information, but the operator told her that there was no listing for a Jackson Masterson.

Shanna had no idea what the Lois woman's last name was, so she finally phoned the one man in Nashville who had stood by her father and remained his friend. Louis Kincaid had remained loyal, even when Jack was found guilty of illegal fund-raising efforts for his campaign and after the law firm dismissed him.

Shanna phoned Mr. Kincaid, and he had indeed stayed in touch with her father. He gladly gave her Jack's number and address in Chicago and was especially sorry to hear of the news about Jackie. Shanna thanked him, and upon hanging up, she instantly called her father. There was no answer at their residence; however, Shanna decided to go ahead and test her luck at finding him in person since there was no time to waste. Her mother's funeral was two days away, and she was determined to locate him to inform him of his former wife's horrible death.

Shanna booked a flight on United Airlines and immediately regretted going commercial, for the press hounded her from the moment she left Sable's apartment until she boarded the Boeing 727 to Chicago. She tried to rest on the plane, but it was hopeless. Shanna felt uncomfortable about seeing her father again, and she especially dreaded meeting this woman named Lois who had stolen Jack away. She desperately wanted a drink on the plane but declined, knowing that she needed her wits about her to take care of matters once she landed at O'Hare Airport.

The cab ride to Drake Street was bleak and dismal. The weather was frigid, and sleet beat angrily against the windshield. Shanna shivered as the wind blew in mighty gusts, causing the taxi to sway to and fro as it moved steadily through the streets of Chicago.

At last, the driver stopped the car in front of a shabby, run-down building in the heart of the lower-rent district of town. Shanna gasped as she viewed the depressing condition of the neighborhood. She couldn't believe that her father, a once very noted and distinguished attorney, living in such squalor. But here she was, and obviously, here he was—existing with some cheap woman in the slums. Shanna gathered her fur coat tightly around her and prepared to exit the cab and step out into the icy weather. She instructed the driver to wait for her. The old man agreed and wondered why such a pretty and sophisticated lady would venture into this part of the city on such a miserable night.

Shanna made her way carefully down the slick sidewalk and looked for apartment 2E. She finally found the right door, but it had been hard, for the complex was dimly lit with rusted lanterns on poles aligning the sidewalks. She slid once or twice but finally made it to the apartment supposedly housing her father and knocked eagerly at the door.

She heard shuffling inside the abode; however, no one appeared. Shanna rapped ever harder until eventually, a raspy woman's voice from the other side yelled, "Yea, what is it?"

Shanna pressed her cheek to the door and responded, "Yes, I'm looking for a Mr. Jackson Masterson. Is he there?"

There was silence for a moment; then the woman bellowed in a slurred voice, "Who the hell wants to know?"

Shanna sighed loudly as her breath came out of her mouth like white smoke, but she responded, "Tell him his daughter is here."

There was no sound from the inside; however, suddenly, the door creaked open just enough for the hoarse creature she'd been conversing with to check her out. Shanna stood still as the wind whipped through her hair until finally the woman opened the door and motioned for her to come in. She stepped inside to a room so thick with smoke that she choked before she walked two feet. The room also reeked of burnt coffee and beer, which made Shanna almost gag on the odor.

She stood motionless once inside, for the room was poorly lit; and with the swirling clouds of smoke, she couldn't see a thing. When her eyes finally adjusted, she began to look around the cluttered interior; and what she saw disgusted her to no end. There were empty beer cans, liquor bottles, dirty clothes, and ashtrays full of cigarette butts everywhere.

In the corner of the room under a rusted floor lamp sat a haggard-looking man in a tattered orange lounge chair. In one hand, he held a Camel and, in the other hand, a glass of Jack Daniel's. Shanna approached him slowly and said, "Father? Is that you?"

The man in the chair took a long drag on his cigarette and then a drink of his whiskey and replied, "Hello, my dear."

Shanna couldn't believe that this bedraggled human being had once been one of the most prominent attorneys in Nashville and a front-runner for political office.

He motioned for her to sit down, so she took a seat on the ottoman in front of him. Lois stood quietly in the corner of the room smoking and watching them intently. Shanna looked at her father sadly and said quietly, "Daddy, I guess you're wondering why I've come." Jack looked at his daughter with bloodshot eyes and nodded. She didn't know any other way to tell him except to blurt it out and get it over with so that she could leave this depressing place and return to New York.

Shanna reached over and took his hand in hers and noticed that it was dry, chapped, and wrinkled and his fingernails were filthy. Tears filled her eyes as she looked directly into his and whispered, "Daddy, Mother's dead. She committed suicide last night in New York."

Jack looked at her wearily and replied, "I'm sorry to hear that." Shanna started to cry as she lowered her head down and leaned her forehead on her father's knee. She wept soundly until Jack put his other hand on her head and stroked her hair

tenderly. Lois remained in the background and watched them, still inhaling on her cigarette.

Shanna finally lifted her eyes and looked at her father tearfully. "You will come back with me for the funeral, won't you, Daddy?"

Jack took another drag and answered tiredly, "I don't think so, sweetie."

She looked at him in surprise and replied in irritation, "Why the hell not?"

He stared back at her and then went into a fit of violent coughs. When he could catch his breath, he answered her in a raspy voice, "I don't have the strength, Shanna. And even if I did, your mother and I had nothing left between each other, and besides, she never really loved me; she just loved the kind of lifestyle I gave her. So I don't feel like I owe her anything."

Shanna realized that what he said was true, but she was still upset that he cared so little that he wouldn't even attend the memorial service for the woman he had been married to for over twenty years. She was even more hurt that he didn't even feel enough love for her to support her in the most difficult and emotional time, but she knew that trying to convince him of that would be useless.

Shanna finally realized that coming to Chicago had been a mistake and the trip managed to make her more depressed than she already was. She rose slowly and looked down in pity at the man she had once admired and revered as her hero. Now, he was nothing more than a withered, tired, and broken-down old drunk. As she turned to go, Shanna knew that she would probably never see her father alive again. She said good-bye and walked out of the paint-chipped door. Once outside again, the bone-chilling wind seemed almost a welcomed atmosphere than what she had experienced in the dingy room.

Shanna leaned against the door and let the wet snow hit her full in the face. As she looked up into the dark sky, the flakes fell like flour being shaken through a sifter. Staring into the heavens, she sent up a little prayer and asked God to help her get through the next couple of days and also to give her peace in accepting her mother's death and the inevitable end that would soon come to her father.

The taxi driver had seen her exit the building, so he blared loudly on the horn. The blast startled Shanna and jerked her back into reality. As the wind swirled around her, she gathered her fur coat tightly around herself and walked carefully through the ice to the car. Shanna stared sadly out the window into the blizzard as the cab sped away, carrying her back to the airport.

It seemed to Shanna that the cold Chicago weather followed her back to New York, for the next day, the wind blew harshly through the streets of the city, and it was bitter cold. Only a handful of people ventured out to attend Jackie's funeral, which only added to the dismal aura of the whole ordeal.

Joe stood stoically beside Shanna, and although she looked extremely tired and pale, she was holding up very well. The trip to Chicago had been depressing for her, but Joe admired her for having the fortitude to seek out her father and do her best to urge him to have the decency to attend her mother's funeral. But even till the

end, both of her parents had remained true to their selfish nature—her mother, in taking the coward's way out, and her father, in refusing to stand by her when she needed him the most.

*Well, to hell with both of them,* Joe thought as he surveyed the sparse number of floral arrangements around Jackie's coffin. *Shanna has me now, and I will never let her down.*

Sable maintained her usual calm and sophisticated demeanor throughout the entire episode exemplifying the strength of an aristocrat that her beloved husband had instilled within her. Erich and the children were also in attendance; however, they sat near the rear of the chapel, and Erich saw to it that they remained separated from their mother. He was determined to make Shanna suffer as much as possible for leaving him for another man and making him appear a fool in front of the entire country. As far as he was concerned, he would not rest until he brought her down and brought her down hard.

# CHAPTER 51

$A$fter the horrible event of Jackie's death, Joe and Shanna began to focus on brighter things, such as building their life together and planning a wedding. Both of them wanted to get married as soon as possible; however, Erich had other plans. He was absolutely furious that Shanna had left him and was even more devastated that she was in love with Joe Stephenson. Erich made a vow to himself that he would do everything humanly possible to destroy their relationship or he would die trying.

Joe and Shanna maintained a suite at the Plaza while Shanna continued to model and occasionally perform with her brother's band. Tony was at the height of his success in the music industry, but sadly, his popularity and the strain of the constant exposure caused him to lapse back into the world of heavy drug and alcohol abuse. Shanna worried about him constantly; however, there was little she could do except urge him to quit or at least cut back. But Tony was always able to convince her that "his problem" wasn't really that bad and that he needed the booze to cope with his hectic schedule.

Joe stayed with Shanna as much as possible and commuted back and forth to Denver frequently to check on his oil company. She missed him terribly when he was away and felt totally alone, especially since Erich forbade her to see her children. Not only would he not let her visit them but he banned her from their penthouse and instructed his servants to ignore her phone calls. Shanna thought she would go out of her mind if she wasn't able to see Alex and McKenna soon, and she expressed her desperation to her husband when she called him at his office.

Erich seemed to wallow in some sort of sadistic pleasure in making Shanna suffer. He even went so far as to report to the newspaper and the tabloids that she was an unfit mother, a drunk, and an adulteress. The press had a heyday with the story, and it appeared in every media venue from the *New York Daily News* to the *National Enquirer*. Most of the papers also showed photos of Shanna looking very strained and weathered, and all the reports mentioned her former involvement with Ricardo Belicci and many supposed affairs with other notable men. Other rumors suggested that she had appeared drunk on several occasions in public and on modeling jobs.

Needless to say, Shanna was mortified and humiliated over the hideous accusations; however, Erich continued to feed the press more lies about his wife's unsatisfactory behavior. As a result, her modeling jobs began to diminish, and the companies for which she was a spokeswoman started to question her ability to remain

a positive role model for the public. Although her agent, Liz Lyndale, argued desperately in Shanna's defense to salvage her reputation, millions of dollars in earnings slowly began to slip away.

Things continued to worsen when Shanna received a court order to stay away from her children and a notice to appear before a judge to determine whether she would lose custody and visitation rights forever. She tried over and over to reach Erich and try and talk some sense into him, but he refused her phone calls and shredded every letter that she sent to him unread.

Shanna thought that she would go out of her mind over what her husband was putting her through, and although Joe tried to comfort her as much as possible, he too was at a loss as to what to do about the situation. He went to Erich's office to try and talk some sense into him; however, the security guards were promptly alerted and instructed to throw him out onto the street. Erich found that he actually enjoyed the misery and heartache that he was causing both of them and literally laughed out loud as he imagined Joe stumbling on the curb and the media hounds capturing another embarrassing moment.

Eventually, Shanna decided to go and pay a visit to her evil husband on her own and risk his abuse in person. She arrived at his building on Madison Avenue amid a throng of hungry photographers and almost tripped on the curb as she hurried to get away from them. The doorman finally took sympathy upon her and assisted her through the revolving doors and instructed the guards in the lobby to bar the press from entering. The kindly older man also permitted Shanna to take the elevator up to Erich's floor unannounced.

When she arrived in front of Erich's office, fortunately, his secretary was away from her desk that Shanna considered a lucky break, for the dreadful woman who had worked for him for years hated Shanna and would never have let her inside. Shanna stood in front of the huge mahogany doors, and her hand shook as she reached for the knob to let herself in.

Erich was standing quietly beside the window scanning over a file when Shanna entered the office. He looked up when he heard the door open and stood looking at her in silent consternation.

Shanna stood where she was by the door and didn't move. Finally, Erich laid down the folder and said, "Well, well, look what the cat has drug in."

Shanna rolled her eyes at his comment and approached him saying, "Erich, what in the hell are you trying to do to me? You are ruining my life with your evil lies and rumors to the press!"

He smirked at her and responded, "That was my intention, my dear." Shanna shrieked in aggravation and, with her hand, violently pushed all the papers from his desk, sending them flying across the room. Even though she didn't know what good that action would do, it somehow made her feel better.

Erich just laughed at her and added to her frustration; and although she had been determined to remain strong, his taunting eventually got the best of her, and

she started to cry. She leaned against his desk and wiped her eyes, knowing that she'd been beaten. He had won; there was no way that she could ever compete against him and win, for Erich was far too powerful, and he had the backing of his parents, whose wealth and influence could bring down anyone they desired.

Erich walked over to his wife and handed her a handkerchief. She took it and looked up at him with tear-filled eyes. "What do you want, Erich?"

He stared back at her for a few moments before he spoke, "I want you back, Shanna. I want you to come home, live respectably as my wife, and be a decent mother to our children."

Shanna looked at him wearily and answered, "I will always be a good mother to my children; but you must understand, Erich, I just don't love you anymore. And besides, I just cannot and will not put up with your abusiveness toward me. I shouldn't have to live like that!"

He stared at her, his eyes darkening. "So that is your decision?"

"Yes," she answered meekly.

Erich turned and walked to his desk and pulled out the top drawer. Shanna watched him curiously, wondering what he was doing. He pulled out a letter and opened it. Then he turned to Shanna and asked, "Do you know what this is?"

She looked at him in puzzlement, "No. How would I know what you have there?"

Erich moved back in front of her and looked at her sternly and said, "It's a letter from your mother." Shanna felt her knees grow weak and knew she would have surely crumpled had the desk not been holding her up. Erich continued, "Jackie gave this to me the night that she came to my house and tried to seduce me." Shanna grew weaker as nausea began to overtake her.

*There was no telling what was in the letter,* she thought.

"She told me not to read it until the following day; now I know why," he stated. Shanna still didn't speak as Erich watched her intently. "Do you want to know what it says?" he asked.

She looked at him bitterly and whispered, "Do I have a choice?"

Erich grinned evilly and responded, "No, I guess you don't." Shanna tried to prepare herself for the worst; however, nothing she could have ever done to brace herself could have prepared her for the shocking revelation in her mother's note.

He began reading:

> My dear son-in-law,
>
> Although we never really got to know each other very well, I thought there was something you should know about your beloved wife. It is no secret that Shanna and I have never been close; however, please know that what I tell you here and now is the God's honest truth, and DO NOT ever let her make you believe that what I am saying is a lie.
>
> As you know, there has always been an unexplainable bond between Shanna and Tony, one that for many years, I myself could not fathom.

One night many years ago, I happened to witness the two of them having sex in front of the fireplace in our family's library. They were only young teens at the time, but they definitely knew what they were doing. At first, I didn't believe it myself; yet it did happen and was proven a few months later.

So I tell you this because I know how much you think that you love my daughter, but now maybe you will see her for the common and incestuous slut that she really is and know that the only love and desire that she will ever have for any man is for her brother.

All my love,
Jackie

When Erich finished reading, he folded the letter up and looked at his wife. Shanna was absolutely ashen and looked as if she might faint. Tears streamed down her face as she just stared out the window at the sun setting behind the skyline.

Finally, she looked at her husband helplessly and asked, "Why did you feel obligated to read that to me? You know that my mother was vicious and would say anything to destroy me with something that is totally untrue."

Erich glared back at her in irritation and replied, "I'm no fool, Shanna, and I have a funny way of knowing when something is so or not, and I tend to believe that what Jackie wrote is the absolute truth. In fact, this answers many questions and suspicions that I've harbored for years. It explains a lot."

Shanna couldn't find it in herself to answer him, for she knew that everything was now out in the open about her former illicit relationship with her brother, and there was no denying it.

Humiliated and embarrassed, she finally lifted her eyes to his and asked, "So what are you going to do with your newfound information, Erich? Torture me forever?"

Erich laughed smugly as he threw the letter onto his desk and then turned to his wife. He took her roughly by the shoulders and gazed steadily into her now-reddened eyes. "I'll tell you what I'm going to do, my dear; unless you give up your lover and come back to me, I will have your nasty little secret on the cover of every magazine and newspaper in the country! Do you understand?"

Shanna pushed him away suddenly and grabbed her mouth, but it was too late. She involuntarily vomited all over his priceless antique rug. Erich jumped back in disgust and brushed himself off, just in case his expensive suit had been hit.

Shanna attempted to make her way across the office to his private bathroom, but she collapsed on a sofa before she fell. Erich poured a glass of water and took it to her. She accepted it gratefully and drank slowly. He sat down beside her and said quietly, "What's it going to be, sweetheart?"

Sadly, Shanna looked back at him and replied, "I'll come back to you, but know this, Erich, I will hate and despise you until the day I die. And one day, yes, someday, I will get even with you." With that, she rose and stumbled across the room and out

the door. Erich stared after her for a moment, then went to the bar, poured himself a scotch, and stared out at Manhattan, feeling like he owned the world.

When Shanna arrived back at her hotel room, Joe was waiting anxiously for her. She looked terrible and was still crying hysterically as she entered their suite and fell down face first onto the bed.

Joe rushed to her, worried beyond belief as to what would have caused her to be so upset. He pulled her into his arms as she sobbed uncontrollably. Joe felt helpless as he asked, "Baby, what is it?"

Shanna continued to cry heavily, but she managed to answer, "I can't do this anymore, Joe. Erich has won. I have to go back to him."

Joe looked at her in confusion as she continued, "He is going to ruin my life if I don't do as he says and live with him as his wife. He's going to destroy me, Joe, my career, my reputation, and my relationship with my children."

Joe held her close and tried to comfort her. "Now, baby, it's going to be all right; there is nothing that Erich can do that we can't overcome," he assured her.

Shanna pulled away from him, looked at him somberly, and said, "Yes, he can. Erich knows something about me and my past that he will hold over me for all eternity. And he has threatened to leak my secret to the world if I don't come back to him. So you see, Joe, even though I love you with all my heart, I cannot continue our relationship and risk forever destroying my reputation and losing the respect of my children."

Joe stared at her in disbelief. "You can't mean that," he said.

She simply stared at him tearfully and nodded, "Yes, my love. It's over."

Joe started to pace frantically around the room, running his fingers through his hair in frustration. He went to the bar, filled a glass with whiskey, and slung it back. Some of the dark liquid dripped down his chin and onto his white shirt. He looked at Shanna with panic in his eyes and asked, "What in the hell is it that that bastard has on you, sweetheart? It can't be that bad!"

Shanna looked at him helplessly and responded, "Yes, it is, and it's something that you can never know about or you will hate me too."

Joe eyed her in confusion, not knowing what could possibly so hideous that she wouldn't confide in him. "Why won't you tell me?" he begged.

Shanna sternly shook her head and said flatly, "I can't."

She rose and started packing her things in her valise as Joe frantically watched her. He filled another glass with whiskey and drank it greedily. He approached her and yelled, "What the fuck are you doing?"

Shanna continued folding her clothes and answered, "I'm packing. I'm going back to the penthouse tonight."

Joe was now hysterical and grabbed her, turning her around to face him. "Shanna, if you do this, we are through. Is that what you want? Are you going to let that son of a bitch ruin our happiness and bury any hopes we had of a future together?"

Shanna faced him, and with every ounce of strength that she could muster, she responded, "I have to, Joe; please understand that. I want you to leave, now."

He looked at her with defeat in his eyes. Joe was absolutely devastated that the woman he adored was ending their relationship and going back to live with a man who dominated, controlled, and abused her. He pushed her roughly away as his emotions began to overtake him. Tears started to pour from his eyes as he grabbed his coat and headed for the door. He looked back at her and in a choked voice said, "I will always love you, Shanna; no one will ever care for you the way I do. Please know that I will never get over this." With that, he walked out of the suite and was gone.

Shanna watched the ornately carved door slam behind him. For a moment, she was so stunned that she couldn't move. The shock of everything that had happened that evening was too much. Her past had come back to haunt her, and now her life would never be the same. Erich would always shame her for the relationship with Tony and so would the rest of the world—a relationship that, at the time, seemed the only way to find comfort within a terribly dysfunctional family. Her brother had provided the love and nurturing that her parents had never offered. Now, her sinister mother had arisen from the grave to prove to her daughter just how much she had hated her.

It was almost too much to bear. Shanna couldn't believe that Jackie had despised her so much that she would set out to ruin her life forever. But now, her life would be unbearable, living with a man whom she didn't love and who would always taunt her for the childish mistake she had made. Pondering her future, and the dreadful blows that life had dealt her, Shanna walked to the bar, picked up a bottle of vodka and drank until the dark web of alcohol overtook her; and she passed out, face first onto the floor.

# CHAPTER 52

A distant ringing tore through Shanna's consciousness like the reverberating gongs that rang out from the Tower of London at high noon. Her head felt as if it were concealed by a thick fog, and her eyes were so bleary from alcohol that she couldn't seem to see past the visual blockade that drunkenness provided.

She moaned as the loud, piercing sound invaded her blackout state and prayed that if there was a god, he would make it go away. But the ringing continued, and Shanna eventually had no choice but to answer the phone and put an end to the incessant irritation that the caller seemed destined to bestow upon her.

Shanna prayed that it would be Joe, calling to beg her to reconsider their relationship, and although she longed to be with him and hear his voice, she knew Erich's newfound information about her past would forever prohibit a fulfilling life with the man she truly loved.

She had long since buried the affair with her brother, deep within her subconscious, and Erich's revelation of her mother's letter had launched the entire former relationship back into the present. The realization devastated Shanna, and she didn't know how she would ever recover emotionally and be able to continue on with her life. But she had no choice; she had to put the past behind and move forward, just as she had always had to do with the tragedies that had come her way.

The phone continued to ring until she crawled clumsily to it and picked up the receiver. In a hoarse, muffled voice, she answered and then strained to hear what the caller on the other end was saying to her. She heard a man's voice, yet it was overpowered by the sound of sirens in the distance. She immediately panicked, thinking that something had happened to one of her children; then terror gripped her as she envisioned Joe being in an accident. The blaring noise drowning out the caller ceased, and the man informed her that he was Sergeant Mahoney, calling from the New York City Police Department.

Shanna's heart stopped, for she now was certain that something horrible had happened to someone she loved. It just wasn't apparent who. She weakly pulled herself upon the bed and waited for the policeman to deliver the bad news to her. The officer explained to her in a forceful voice that a man's body had been found bearing the identification of her brother and that she needed to proceed to the city morgue to identify the corpse.

For a few seconds, Shanna's world stood still. Her heart froze, and her body went limp. She felt as if she might faint but then managed to regain her senses enough to

ask the sergeant in a shaky voice where she needed to go. Mahoney gave her the address to the morgue and then, in a softer tone, offered his condolences. Shanna thanked him quietly and assured him that she would be down as soon as possible.

After she hung up, Shanna sat where she was for a few moments, trying to digest the terrible news and wondering how she would ever accomplish the despicable task he had asked her to perform. How on earth, she thought, would she find the courage to venture downtown to the city morgue in the middle of the night alone to identify the body of her beloved brother Tony? It was almost too much to bear, yet she had to somehow summon an inner strength to do the unavoidable. And Shanna knew that she had to do it alone, for now, she had no one.

She had tried to contact her aunt Sable; however, the maid informed her that Sable was in the south of France for the winter and would not be back until May. So with Joe gone and her aunt out of the country, Shanna somehow bravely found the courage to pull herself together enough to venture out into the cold New York night to carry out a task that would have conquered even the strongest person on the planet.

Shanna called the front desk and asked them to summon a cab for her. It was 3:00 a.m., and the night manager expressed his concern. She reluctantly explained what had happened and begged him not to leak the news to the press. The kindly gentleman was used to celebrities visiting the hotel and had been trained to provide the utmost in discretion where they were concerned. He insisted that she allow their night guard on duty to accompany her, and Shanna readily agreed.

Her head still throbbed from all the alcohol she had consumed earlier, but she somehow managed to pull on a pair of designer jeans, a turtleneck, and some suede boots. On the way out of the door, she grabbed her full-length mink coat and hurried to the elevator. When she arrived in the lobby, the guard was waiting for her and so was a taxi. Within minutes, they were on their way to the city morgue as a light snow fell in the dark night.

The morgue was the most dismal and ominous place Shanna had ever seen. The building was cold and gray, just like the bodies it held within. The driver let her out at the front door, and the guard from the hotel was kind enough to volunteer to escort her inside. She more than welcomed his company, for she did not know how she was going to get through the ordeal without fainting or getting sick. The thought of seeing her brother's body was more than she could bear to think about, and she feared that without someone by her side, she would totally collapse.

Once inside, the policeman on duty led Shanna and her guard down to the lower level where he instructed them that they would have to wait for the coroner since it had been a busy night. The first floor of the building was dark and cold, and the waiting area where they were instructed to sit had only hard metal chairs with broken backs. The hotel guard, who finally introduced himself as Vinney, helped Shanna to a chair and sat quietly beside her. She apologized for not asking his name and thanked him for being by her side.

Time passed, and still the coroner on duty did not appear. Shanna was weary, frightened, and anxious; and she didn't know how much longer she could hang on without passing out. Vinney remained close and even invited her to lean against him for warmth and lay her head on his shoulder. Shanna tried to relax against him; however, her nerves were shattered, and she eventually begged him to go and check with the officer to see what was taking so long. Vinney obeyed and assured her that he would hurry back as soon as he could. Shanna looked at him gratefully as he left; then she sat alone shivering, her mink coat providing little warmth in the chilly room.

Joe sat alone in the bar at John F. Kennedy Airport. He was heartbroken that Shanna had ended their relationship, and he was totally bewildered over why she had chosen to shatter their dreams and plans for the future. It was 3:00 a.m., and the airport had been closed for hours because of the snowy weather. But Joe had opted to wait there until the morning and drown his sorrows, and the bartender had only been too willing to serve him, especially since Joe poured out money almost faster than he could pour out drinks.

All Joe could think about was how much he loved Shanna and how much he despised Erich Shandon for whatever it was he had threatened her with. The more he thought about the situation, the madder he became. He and Shanna had been through too much to give up now, and he knew that she loved him as much as he loved her. They were meant to be together, and by God, he thought he was not going to let her throw away their chance for happiness.

Joe downed his drink, threw a one-hundred-dollar bill on the counter, and raced through the airport. Outside, he looked frantically for a cab; however, due to the bad weather, there were none to be found. He felt desperate, yet he was determined to get back to the woman he loved that night and tell her how much he worshipped her. Just when he was about to go inside and call a taxi service, a gentleman yelled at him from across the median dividing the airport from the parking area. "Hey, mister," the man shouted, "if you're needing a ride downtown, I can take you there." As it turned out, the driver was supposed to transport a foreign dignitary into the city, but the storm had caused all flights to be cancelled. So he now had a vacant limousine and no passenger. Joe leapt at the chance, jumped into the awaiting car, and headed determined back to the Plaza.

When he returned to the hotel, Joe paid the kind limo driver handsomely and raced into the historic building almost falling as he slipped on the icy sidewalk. He ran through the lobby toward the elevator, only to be stopped by the night manager. The man somberly informed Joe about the horrible news that Shanna had received that evening and that she had gone to the city morgue with his night watchman. Joe could not believe what he was hearing; and before he even thought about thanking the manager, he was off and out the door again, searching desperately for a cab. Luckily, a taxi just happened by, so Joe flagged it down and was on his way to the morgue within a matter of minutes.

Shanna still sat shivering in the downstairs' waiting area of the stone building, even though Vinney had been kind enough to bring her some hot coffee. She couldn't imagine what was keeping the coroner, and she felt that if he didn't come soon, she would go out of her mind! Finally, behind them, a door creaked open; and just when Shanna expected the county mortician to enter, in walked Joe. Tears spilled from her eyes as she jumped up, spilling her coffee. She ran to him and fell into his arms crying harder than she had ever cried before. Joe held her close, whispering into her hair.

Finally, the coroner entered the room accompanied by a guard and announced in a formal tone that he was ready for them to proceed to the next room. Shanna still clung to Joe as he attempted to lead her into the direction that the men were indicating for them to go. She pulled away from him and hysterically wailed, "I can't do this, Joe . . . Please help me . . . I can't do this!"

Joe pulled her to him again and told her in a comforting voice that he would go and identify the body and that she should just wait for him. Shanna nodded tearfully but did not speak. As he turned to go, she said in a soft voice, "Wait, Joe, I need to go too; after all, he is *my* brother."

Together, they followed the two men into a room with bright lights and a bleached white floor. Shanna and Joe were almost blinded by the brightness after being in such a dimly lit area. The coroner walked nonchalantly over to a gurney holding a body concealed underneath a crisp white sheet.

With his arm around her, Joe led Shanna over to the stretcher supporting the body of her dead brother. Together, they held their breath as the mortician slowly pulled the shroud from the corpse, and both of them simultaneously gasped out loud. Shanna suddenly screamed, "It's not him! Joe, that is not my brother! Tony's alive!"

Joe pulled her to him as tears rolled down his face too. "I know, baby. I know!"

Joe and Shanna left the morgue feeling like an anchor had been lifted from their shoulders, knowing that Tony was still alive. "But where could he be?" Shanna asked as they climbed into an awaiting cab that Vinney had summoned for them.

"I don't know, sweetheart," Joe replied, "but we'll find him."

They arrived back at the Plaza, and Joe had to practically carry Shanna up to their room, for the weight of exhaustion had finally overtaken her. He placed her gently in the bed and tucked the luxurious down comforter over her. She fell asleep immediately; and as Joe watched her, he knew that his love for her ran deep within his very soul, and he was so grateful to whatever higher force that had urged him to come back to her. The weight of the events of the evening began to affect him as well; however, he was way too restless to sleep. Joe poured himself a drink, turned off the light, and went to sit beside the woman he adored. As he sipped on his scotch, he watched Shanna doze peacefully in the moonlight.

# CHAPTER 53

When Shanna finally located her brother, it turned out that Tony had been partying with friends, had gotten extremely drunk and high on heroin; and unfortunately, someone had stolen his wallet when he left it at a bar to go home with a model. Although Shanna was immensely relieved that her brother was alive, she was also very concerned about his heavy drug and alcohol use. It terrified her that the next phone call she received from the authorities might be one informing her that he had overdosed. When she tried to broach Tony about his addiction, he told her quite frankly that he had everything under control.

Joe urged Shanna to restart the planning of their wedding; yet she remained hesitant, terrified of what Erich would do if she didn't go back to him. She tried to explain to Joe that she just needed more time to sort things out where her marriage was concerned; however, he was eager for them to get married and curious over what was worrying her so.

Joe was certain that Erich was behind Shanna's hesitation in marrying him, and his fears were confirmed when she accepted an invitation to go away with him and the children to the Shandon estate in Connecticut. She tried to convince Joe that it was strictly a retreat to allow her to spend lost time with McKenna and Alex and that she would have nothing to do with her husband. Joe was understandably miserable knowing that she would be at the mercy of the evil man she was married to, but there was nothing that he felt that he could do without fear of losing her forever.

Erich, Shanna, and their children arrived at his parents' house, and they all were extended a warm welcome except for Shanna. Alexander and Elise Shandon despised their daughter-in-law and had only agreed to tolerate her for the weekend for their grandchildren's sake. None of them could understand why McKenna and Alex had such an undying affection for their mother, but their love for her was undeniable, for they lit up like Christmas trees when Erich told them that they could see her again.

Their first night in the mansion was strained, and Shanna slept in the children's room in order to avoid any contact with her husband. Alex and McKenna were delighted to have their mother spend the night with them, and they stayed up much later than they should have listening to the bedtime stories that she told.

The next morning, everyone sat down to a wonderful breakfast in the main dining room. Erich's parents were cold yet cordial to Shanna for the sake of propriety.

After the morning meal, Elise drove her grandchildren into town for a shopping spree. Erich pulled Shanna aside after they had left and told her that they were going for a walk on the grounds. She hesitated; however, he insisted. So as to avoid a scene, she relented and went with him.

They strolled in silence for a while, and then Erich finally spoke, "So have you thought about our little discussion that we had in my office?"

Shanna hesitated for a few seconds and then replied, "Yes, I have."

Erich kept walking and said, "And what have you decided to do?"

Shanna stopped at the entrance to the gardens and turned to face him. "I ended my relationship with Joe, if that's what you're inquiring about," she said sadly.

Erich smiled cruelly at her and asked, "So when are you moving back to the penthouse?" Tears welled up in her eyes as she looked at the ground in despair. "I asked you a question," he repeated, "when are you moving back in with the children and me?"

Shanna still didn't reply but began to cry openly as her husband continued to press her. Finally, he jerked her roughly around by the shoulders and looked straight into her eyes demanding, "Answer me!"

Shanna finally managed to respond although she choked on her words saying, "I'll move back in on Monday, Erich; you win."

He stared at her intently and then pulled her close to his face. "I always do, my dear. I always do." With that, he kissed her hungrily, then pushed her backward onto the hedge causing her to fall.

As Erich strode back to his parents' house, Shanna pulled herself out of the bushes and then sat down on the plush lawn and wept bitterly. All she could think about was Joe and how much this was going to crush him and ruin their chance of obtaining happiness forever. Eventually, she pulled herself together enough to start walking back to the mansion. She knew that she must call Joe and end things with him once and for all, and that was one phone call that she would have rather died than make.

Joe was waiting miserably back at the Plaza worrying about the woman he loved so deeply and wondering if she was surviving in the midst of her dreadful in-laws and her evil husband. He was overjoyed when she finally called him; however, he sensed immediately that something was wrong by the sound of her voice. He could tell she had been crying, and he demanded to know what was wrong or if anything had happened to one of the children.

Shanna assured him that McKenna and Alex were fine and were enjoying their visit with their grandparents and that she was thrilled to be spending time with them again. But Joe could still tell that there was something in the tone of her voice that worried him, but he was in no way braced for the news that she finally blurted out to him amid a downpour of tears. Shanna lied to him by saying that she and Erich had reached an understanding in their relationship and that she had to move home for the sake of their children.

Joe was dizzy from frustration on his end as he shouted into the phone, "What in the hell is that supposed to mean, Shanna? What is this *new understanding* that you and that bastard have supposedly reached?" Joe was frantic and demanded to have his suspicions and questions answered.

Shanna was shaking so on the other end that she almost dropped the receiver onto the parquet floor of her in-laws' library. Joe continued to press her, but she refused to give him a reasonable explanation as to why she was abandoning their relationship yet again to return to a miserable and abusive marriage.

She finally told him that she had to go, which sent Joe into a frenzy. He begged her relentlessly to reconsider her decision until he himself was almost in tears. Shanna knew that if she didn't end their conversation quickly, she would either break down completely or give in to him, which would mean forsaking her children and her reputation, which she undoubtedly could never do.

Shanna finally said good-bye to the man she loved beyond measure, and as she did, she collapsed into an enveloping leather chair and cried uncontrollably. On his end, Joe sat staring into space, holding a now-buzzing receiver in his hand. He could not fathom that the fairy-tale life he had come to know with a woman he considered to be his princess was now over. When he could take the irritating noise reverberating from the receiver any longer, he hurled the entire phone across the room, sending it crashing against the hotel wall.

Joe sat alone in the suite for hours, drinking and aching to the core of his soul over the fact that Shanna had left him. Something had to be desperately wrong for her to suddenly end things so abruptly between them. And he knew that Erich must have been behind her rash decision and was probably threatening her somehow, most likely causing her a lot of hurt. That he would not stand for, not while he had a breath left in his body.

As soon as the light of day broke the next morning, Joe showered and checked out of the Plaza. He had never slept the night before, and while he drank the hours away, he decided that he must go to Shanna and force her to admit to him face-to-face why she was destroying their life together.

When Joe arrived the next morning at the imposing entry gate of the Shandon estate, he was anything but intimidated, for his determination was set on seeing Shanna and forcing her to tell him why she was so intent on ending their relationship. With all that they had been through, he would not let their love be extinguished by the inflamed ranting of her controlling husband.

Joe stopped his rented Jaguar at the turn of the circular driveway when he saw a hired man loading bags into a Rolls Royce parked in front of the stately home. Shanna and her children were standing together on the front verandah watching their suitcases being placed securely into the car. They heard Joe's car spin to an abrupt stop on the pavement and were staring in wonderment as to who would be arriving just as they were departing.

As Joe stepped out of the Jag, Shanna recognized him immediately, and her heart instantly leapt to her throat. *Oh god*, she thought, *why has he come here, and what on earth will happen when Erich learns that he's here?* Shanna told McKenna and Alex to stay where they were; then she steadily made her way down the stairs of the porch and walked toward him.

Joe stood stoically beside the car as he watched her approach. When she reached him, Shanna asked softly, "Why did you come here?"

Joe leaned tiredly against the car and sighed, "I had to see you, Shanna. I had to know why you are throwing our love away."

Shanna stared down at the ground as she felt her resolve starting to collapse. She looked up at him; however, she couldn't find the strength within herself to respond. Joe was growing so frustrated with her that he could no longer take the fact that she was being so evasive with him. Finally, he grabbed her by the shoulders and pulled her close, forcing her to look him straight in the eyes. Before he could speak, Erich came up behind them and shouted, "Take your goddamn hands off my wife, you asshole!"

Shanna pushed away from Joe and turned to face her husband in abject terror. Erich advanced toward them and pulled Shanna to him and asked her forcefully, "What in the hell is he doing here?"

She looked back and forth between her husband and the man that she loved and finally said softly, "I don't know."

Erich looked at her in frustration and demanded that she give him a better answer. Shanna could not respond, for she was too upset with the whole situation.

Erich was livid with her silence, which caused him to grab her and shake her violently saying, "Say something, you cheating bitch!"

Joe exploded with anger over the way Shanna was being treated, and he leapt to her defense. He pulled Erich away from her with such force that Erich lost his balance and fell awkwardly to the ground. He scrambled quickly back to his feet only to be knocked down again by a heavy punch to the face from Joe. Shanna screamed as she saw blood fly from her husband's nose, and Joe stood where he was as they watched Erich writhe around on the grass moaning in pain.

Joe finally turned to Shanna and said, "Are you all right, sweetheart?"

She simply nodded and stared at him tearfully.

Alex and McKenna had viewed the scuffle from the landing of their grandparents' home, and when they saw their father fall, they ran inside to get help. Elise Shandon made her way quickly across the lawn, accompanied by the butler, after instructing the children to stay inside. She was understandably alarmed at seeing her son covered in blood, and she was furious with her daughter-in-law for once again inviting havoc into their midst.

When they had helped Erich to his feet, Elise ordered Jacobs, the servant, to escort her son back to the house and to phone the police once they arrived inside. As Erich was being led away, he turned and said in a vicious tone, "Shanna, you had

better end this now or you will regret it for the rest of your life! And I promise you this, you whore, you will never see the children again." With that, he turned and left with the butler.

Shanna and Joe stood quietly where they were until Elise broke the silence. She turned to face them both and said, "Well, Shanna, you have disgraced this family again. What my son sees in you, I cannot understand. But I warn you right here and now, do not hurt him or ever embarrass this family again!" She looked at them both in disgust, then started to walk away.

Shanna blurted out in a teary voice, "Elise, please do not summon the police here. I'll take care of this. Joe is leaving."

The older woman simply huffed in irritation and kept walking.

Joe finally turned to Shanna after Elise left them and asked her again. "Are you all right?"

Shanna turned to look at him with an exasperated look on her face, ignoring his question. "Why did you come here, Joe? You have caused nothing but trouble by this visit. I thought I made it clear to you in New York that we were through. Now please leave and let me get back to my life with my husband and children."

She then turned to go, but Joe grabbed her, forcing her to look at him. He looked at her with a look so intense that she felt as if his gaze bore right into her very soul.

He continued to stare at her with doubt and despair in his eyes. "Why are you doing this, baby?" he begged sadly. "I know that you still love me, so I just don't understand why you are deserting me."

Shanna looked back at him with a loving expression as tears ran down her face. "I can't do this now, Joe. It's not the right time for us. Even though I care deeply for you, I have to go back to my family."

Joe felt his heart breaking, for he knew that he was losing her for reasons that he could not fathom.

As she turned to go once again, he put his arms around her, pulled her face to his, and kissed her long and hard. She gave in to his kiss for the moment; then she pulled away abruptly and started walking toward the mansion. Joe yelled after her, "I love you, Shanna. I will always love you!"

Hearing his words, Shanna turned to look at his sweet face one last time; then she ran across the lawn as fast as she could with the wind blowing her hair wildly around her.

Joe watched the woman he adored run away from him and the life they had hoped to build together. He saw her climb the steps to the verandah and collapse on one of the white wicker chaise lounges adorning the lanai. He longed to go to her, but he knew that she was now lost to him forever. Feeling beaten and totally devastated, Joe climbed back into his fancy rented Jaguar and sped out of the driveway, throwing stray gravel in all directions.

# CHAPTER 54

Shanna's marriage to Erich remained just a marriage, in name only. There was no passion, no caring, and, namely, no love. They coexisted in the same world and were there for their children. Erich felt a sense of victory over having his wife back, yet it was a hollow victory in that there was nothing left between the two of them. They stayed together but led separate lives.

Erich immersed himself in his work in his father's company, of which he was now the president.

Shanna dove back into the world of fashion and music, spending the majority of her time at the recording studio that she owned with her brother in Nashville. She never confided in Tony over the fact that she was still in an abusive relationship and that she was heartbroken over losing Joe.

Tony innately knew that his sister was sad, and her misery fueled his own unhappiness in his own existence. At this point in his life, his own career was soaring, and he was one of the most popular musicians in the world. His concert tour schedule was grueling; then there were the endless photo shoots for every music magazine in the world, and when he wasn't allowing personal interviews and giving public press conferences, he was holed up in his studio listening to songs and composing new music. Tragically, Tony's explosion of fame overwhelmed him with endless pressure, which caused him to cushion his stressful emotions once again with drugs and alcohol.

After his successful period of abstinence, the fast-paced, high-living style of a rock star won out, and Tony succumbed to the familiar peace that addiction temporarily provided. Although his mainstay was alcohol, he used cocaine to get through the day, then found his greatest euphoria in heroin. All his pressures seem to melt away with the slight prick of a needle, then the sweet warmth of a dirty brown liquid that coursed through his veins carrying a heated dizziness that offered him momentary peace. The only problem was that his temporary tranquility would only last until the drug wore off. Thus, he became the addict, always clinging to that next high.

Shanna spent more and more time with her brother in order to avoid going home to New York and having to deal with Erich. She explained to her husband that her music career was booming right along with Tony and that she needed to remain in Nashville to assist in the production of their next album. In typical fashion, Erich was not happy with her spending time with her brother and even angrier that she

was once again abandoning their marriage and ignoring their children. He called and berated her constantly for being a horrible mother, which only made her feel worse and much more determined to put distance between them. She longed to be near her children; however, life with Erich was hell, and she preferred not being burned.

Understandably, the time Shanna spent with Tony exposed her to his maddening lifestyle, and the ever-present drugs and alcohol began to take their toll on her as well. She fell into the pattern of partying all night with the band, then passing out drunk as the sun rose every morning. By midafternoon, the white powder seemed to help them all recover from their massive hangovers and spur them on to create and produce and perform. Shanna stuck primarily to drinking although she did inhale her fair share of lines just to keep going and somewhat counter the effect of the alcohol. Only once, did she allow her brother to inject her with a minimum amount of heroin, and to everyone's horror, she fell face first onto the floor and stayed unconscious for hours. Tony was so terrified that he had killed his sister that he vowed never to have the stuff in her presence again and threatened to murder anyone that ever offered it to her.

Shanna and Tony only sank further into an abysmal sea of substance abuse. The unending party pulled them down so low that they stopped working on their music, cancelled concert dates, and did nothing but lay around and get high with their friends. Shanna would go for days on end, forgetting to call home to check in with her husband and speak with her children. When Erich finally did reach her at Hounds Run, she sounded strange and incoherent; thus, he could tell immediately that something was dreadfully wrong with her.

At last, after three weeks had passed, Erich decided to go and see about his wife and to see for himself just why she was avoiding them and what was making her sound so sick. He landed in Nashville and hired a driver to take him straight to the estate. As the big black car carried him from the airport, he felt a sinking feeling come over him that began to arouse his familiar instinct of jealousy. Erich started to believe that Shanna's evasive behavior could only mean that she was holed up with another man, and most likely that man was Joe Stephenson.

As the limousine pulled into the long tree-lined driveway of Shanna's huge pink-colored mansion, Erich's rage had risen to the point of where he would definitely kill someone if he found that his wife was being unfaithful to him again. But as he pounded on the massive door, nothing could have prepared him for the sight that he was soon to behold.

The servants at Hounds Run had abandoned the manor weeks ago, for they were disgusted with cleaning up after a drunken, drugged-out group. They all walked out together, including Shanna's butler, who had been working for her for years. As a result, after their departure, the interior developed into a virtual pig sty, and the grounds became an overgrown landscaping nightmare.

Erich got no response as he knocked loudly at the front door. Frustrated, he circled around to the rear of the home, tripping over fallen branches as he walked.

The grass and weeds were even higher in the backyard; and Erich was grateful, for his wife's sake, that the massive walls surrounding the property protected the unkempt sight from the public's view. He surveyed the rest of the yard and noticed that the once beautiful sea blue swimming pool water was now a moss green color with dirty brown leaves floating on the top.

As Erich approached the back entrance of the house, he suddenly began to feel a little frightened and wondered if something dreadful had happened to the inhabitants of Hounds Run estate. He rapped heavily on the door and was surprised when it opened easily and was unlocked. He stepped into the kitchen and almost tripped as an empty vodka bottle spun across the tiled floor and crashed into the opposite wall. Erich regained his footing by grabbing onto the counter; and as he did, a beer can, still half full, tipped over, spilling the foamy liquid onto his hand and down his pants. *Shit!* Erich muttered loudly.

Shaking the beer from his fingertips, he looked around the kitchen in search of a dish towel, and in surveying the room, he could not believe the sight his eyes were taking in. Empty liquor bottles were everywhere; crusted-over dirty plates sat piled high in the kitchen sink, and collapsed pizza boxes lay strewn around with particles of toppings still clinging to the cardboard. Most horrifying of all, used syringes with droplets of brown fluid clinging to the sides were scattered all around, and uneven lines of white powder lay waiting to be consumed through one of the many rolled-up bills lying around.

Erich looked at the entire scene in dismay. He couldn't imagine what had been going on in the place during the past several weeks. Suddenly, he heard voices coming from another room, so he made his way quietly out of the kitchen and down through the hallway. He smelled cigarette smoke coming from the den and slowly continued to walk toward what he heard and the scent that he followed.

When he arrived at the doorway of the library, Erich backed against the wall and peered cautiously around the corner. There, lounging around the dark room was Tony and his four band members. They were all seated haphazardly on leather chairs, and Tony was perched behind his desk with his feet propped up downing Jack Daniels and inhaling on a joint. The others all had drinks in their hands too, and Erich noticed that there was also a considerable amount of cocaine piled onto a mirror at the corner of the desk.

As he looked around from where he stood, Erich had a hard time seeing much else, for the room was incredibly smoky, and his eyes were starting to burn. He wondered where Shanna could be, and just when he turned to go and search the rest of the house for her, he noticed that someone was passed out on the leather sofa in the corner of the room and that someone looked to be his wife.

Erich entered the room abruptly and walked to the sofa where the motionless figure lay. He knelt down and gently turned her over, and it was indeed Shanna. She was in a deep sleep and one probably induced by alcohol, and God knows what else, he thought.

Tony rose from where he sat behind the desk and moved awkwardly toward Erich yelling, "You get your bloody hands off of her, you bastard!" As he staggered forward, he tripped over a chair and fell face first onto the hardwood of the library floor. He lay there moaning with his face to the floor as blood streamed out of his nose and trickled like a stream, reaching the edge of an oriental rug. Tony's friends went to his side, and Erich returned his attentions to his wife.

Shanna stirred as he propped her up against a pillow and examined her closely. She was deathly pale and appeared to have lost an extreme amount of weight. Erich looked at her in shock in dismay at the shape she was in. Her eyes finally flickered open, and as she stared at him in puzzlement, he noticed that there were dark circles outlining her bottom row of lashes. And the bright blue eyes he had once admired now looked like two faded pools, surrounded by streaks of red.

As she continued to stare at him, Erich began to grow frustrated and angry. "Good god, Shanna, what the hell is the matter with you?" he commanded. She looked at him now in full recognition as tears welled up in her eyes. "I asked you a question!" he said again. She looked down helplessly and began to cry. "Stop it!" he ordered as he began to shake her violently.

Tony's friends had managed to set him up, but he remained on the floor, covered in blood. "Leave her alone," he said helplessly.

Erich ignored him and finally softened his voice and demeanor and repeated, "Shanna, please tell me what is wrong with you. You have obviously been drinking, but please tell me that you haven't been doing drugs with this crowd too."

Shanna raised her head and sadly looked at her husband. She eventually mustered enough strength to answer him and replied, "It's gotten out of control, Erich," she sniffed. "I can't control it anymore."

Erich looked at her, more concerned now, and asked, "What's gotten out of control, honey?"

She gazed at him in a completely beaten fashion and responded, "Everything! Everything has gotten out of control! The drugs, the alcohol, life, you name it. Everything is out of control!" With that, she dropped her head into her hands and sobbed harder than Erich had ever seen anyone sob before.

Erich knew what had to be done, so he picked her up in his arms and proceeded to carry her up the magnificent staircase of the manor to her room. Tony struggled to get up, but his friends stopped him. He just sat on the den floor helplessly and yelled, "Don't you hurt her, you motherfucker, or I'll kill your fucking ass!"

Erich ignored him as he continued on up the stairs, holding Shanna tenderly in his arms. He found her bedroom, which overlooked the once-verdant front lawn. Laying her on the bed, he then went and opened the French doors to the balcony to let some fresh air in.

Shanna lay where she was, still crying softly and shaking. Erich watched her and wondered if she was suffering from the DTs that he had heard that alcoholics do when coming off a drinking binge.

Suddenly, he grew worried, for he had also read that delirium tremens could often lead to a seizure. Frightened, Erich raced out of the room and down the stairs in search of a maid, the butler, or some member of the household staff who would help him. Finding no one, he ran back up the steps to try and decide what to do. He was afraid that if he called an ambulance, they would detect what was her obvious drug use and would also find illegal substances in the house, which would most likely land them all in jail. So Erich decided to help her himself.

Shanna had stopped crying but still lay on the bed looking positively green. She felt as if she were going to be sick, so she raised herself to try and make it to the bathroom. Unfortunately, she was so weak that she could only lean over the side of her bed and vomit onto the floor. Erich watched her in disgust and pity, but he realized that getting mad at her at this point would be useless, so he became determined to get her well enough so that he could locate professional help for her.

Shanna wretched until she was completely empty of fluids; then she lay back on her bed, breathing heavily. Erich went to her and helped her out of her clothes that were wrinkled and smelly. He wondered how long it had been since she had bathed, so he offered to run a tub for her. Shanna nodded weakly and sat completely naked with her arms around her knees, rocking back and forth as her husband disappeared into the bathroom.

Erich carried his wife to the bathtub and lowered her gently into the sudsy water. He sat near her. As she slowly washed herself, Shanna stared straight ahead thinking about her behavior over the past couple of weeks. She and her brother, and their friends from the band, had had one continuous alcohol and drug binge, resulting in very little progress being made on their upcoming album, not to mention the numerous concert appearances that had been cancelled, due to the group being too stoned to perform.

Tears began to fall down her cheeks again as she thought about all the wasted hours and the sadness that had filled the time, veiled by the happy shroud that the drugs temporarily provided. Erich watched her and empathized over the pain that she felt. He blamed everything on her demented brother, and the sooner he rescued her from Tony's evil influence, the better off she would be.

Erich reached over and helped Shanna finish washing her back and then helped her to her feet. He dried her off, wrapped her in a towel, and carried her back to her bed. She slid under the thick comforter and shivered violently. Erich was still worried that she might still be in danger of slipping into a seizure or becoming very ill from withdrawals.

He knelt down beside the bed and whispered to her that he was going to go in search of something for her to eat and possibly some hot tea for her stomach. Erich also made a mental note to phone a doctor friend of his in New York, whom he had gone to Harvard with, for advice on what to do in this situation.

Shanna begged him not to leave; however, he promised her that he would only be gone for a few moments.

Erich ventured back downstairs and noticed that the group in the library had gone, probably fleeing in fear that he would call the police, he thought. He was correct in his thinking, for the band members had grown tired of the constant partying several days ago but had only hung around because their leader, Tony, had begged them to stay. With Erich's arrival, they figured that the party was over and that they had better leave while they still could.

When Erich entered the kitchen, he found Tony hung over the sink, washing his bloody face in running water. Erich ignored him and proceeded to search for anything edible that he could take to Shanna. Tony rose up and looked at his brother-in-law in hatred and said, "Get the fuck out of my house, man." Erich ignored him and continued to look through the cabinets. Tony repeated himself, "I said, get out of my fucking house!" as he started to stagger forward.

When Erich had had enough of his brother-in-law's ranting, he turned and advanced upon Tony, slamming him backward into the countertop. Erich held him down and looked viciously into his eyes saying, "Now, you listen to me, you goddamn loser, you can kill yourself if you want to with all this shit, but I'll be damn if I'll let you kill my wife and the mother of my children!" With that, Erich threw Tony across the room, sending him crashing headfirst into the heavy leg of the kitchen table. Gathering together the crackers and club soda that he had found, Erich strode back upstairs to Shanna's room, not even taking the time to glance twice at Tony, who was now lying completely unconscious on the kitchen floor.

When Erich arrived back in the bedroom, Shanna was still huddled under the covers shaking, but she managed to rise up and nibble on the crackers that Erich delivered to her. She downed the club soda in gulps, for she was very dehydrated and terribly thirsty. While she ate, Erich prowled through the upstairs' bathrooms until he located a bottle of Tylenol PM capsules, which he hoped would make Shanna stop shaking and help her to get some sleep. He went to her bedside and offered his sick wife the pills, accompanied by a large glass of water.

Shanna accepted the medication Erich offered and felt almost immediate ease within her system. She settled back under the enveloping comforter of her bed and fell asleep within minutes. Erich sat beside Shanna's bed for several moments, watching her. She was so beautiful, sweet, and vulnerable; and his heart went out to her. After everything that they had been through, he still loved her.

It had been a long day, and his concern for her had exhausted him. Erich rose, stripped out of his clothes, and locked the door to Shanna's room. Climbing in bed beside her, he pulled her close to him, removing the towel that encircled her body. As they lay close together, Erich held Shanna close to him, loving her in his own special way and worrying that her addiction might ultimately kill her. That was a worry that he would not tolerate.

# CHAPTER 55

Erich stayed at Hounds Run with Shanna until she recovered from the weeks of alcohol and drug abuse she had put herself through. When she felt stronger and got her color back, Erich approached his wife about entering a rehabilitation center for substance abuse. He felt that her behavior over the past few weeks exemplified that of an addict, and he wanted her to get well—for her sake and for the sake of their children.

Shanna resisted Erich's suggestion of going into treatment and begged him to allow her a period of rest and relaxation at her ranch in New Mexico. He argued with her over the situation, but she won out, convincing him that going to a treatment facility would make media headlines and cause their family and his parents a lot of shame with making her addiction problems public. Erich eventually agreed because he wanted to spare his parents any more scandal than they had already experienced. He did, however, warn his wife that if she ever lapsed into the form of behavior that he had just witnessed, he would commit her into the Betty Ford Center without a second thought.

Shanna promised that he would never find her in that shape again and agreed to go into treatment if she could not overcome her problem after a lengthy stay at her ranch. She insisted that Tony go with her to New Mexico, for she was terribly worried and wanted to take care of him to repay him for the many years of protection he had provided to her. Erich rebelled at first, fearing that they might resume their old relationship; however, Shanna scolded him for digging up old memories and reassured her husband that her only mission was to heal herself and help her beloved brother get well. Erich finally gave in, for he had never really believed Jackie's insane letter; and even if it were true, he honestly believed that Shanna and Tony's relationship had only been that of two curious teens, playing around with mild petting.

So Tony and Shanna went to Blue Diamond Ranch and spent six months there—writing music, riding horses, and walking in the desert with the sun setting into the mountains. They hired a live-in alcohol and drug counselor, a nutritionist, a fitness instructor, as well a guru to enlighten them in the more spiritual practices, such as meditation, yoga, and many Eastern practices of self-healing. After six months of healing, Shanna and her brother were ready to face the real world again and take it on with a vengeance.

Shanna returned to New York to her husband and her children. The world of modeling still wanted her; however, she only committed to projects that would allow

her a lot of rest and free time with her family. Tony went back to Los Angeles and formed a new band, but he altered his heavy touring schedule in order to nurture his recovery and make way for a new way of living that he so desperately sought for himself and his sister.

Even though Shanna had agreed to reconcile with Erich, and recommit herself to their marriage, she never stopped thinking about Joe and how much she loved him. It pained her greatly to think of how much she had hurt him and what he must be going through, knowing that she was back living as Erich's wife.

In the weeks after their breakup, when Shanna had hidden out at Hounds Run in an effort to avoid her husband, her heartache and despair over losing Joe had caused her to sink to levels she never would have thought possible. Remembering the rush of the cocaine as it raced like fire through her nostrils, and the orgasmic feeling that came over her, as the heroine coursed through her veins made her shudder now. Suicide had almost seemed a better solution than coming down off the drugs that had become a mainstay in her life. But Shanna's inner strength and her devotion to her children had given her a burning desire to live and conquer her addictive demons.

On a flight to Los Angeles, where Shanna had landed a small acting role, she began to pine for Joe. Tears streamed down her cheeks as she watched the silvery clouds float by as the Shandon Incorporated private jet carried her through the sky. Erich had insisted that she take the company plane so that she could fly to Hollywood at daybreak, complete her work in a couple of days, and hurry back to him and the children.

Shanna knew that his reasoning was insane and that quick of a trip would be exhausting for her; however, he owned her now and had complete control over everything that she did. She felt relieved though to at least have a couple of days of freedom from him to enjoy her role in a popular soap opera.

As Shanna continued to reminisce over the man that she loved, her sadness overcame her to the point where she decided to call him. Hesitantly, she picked up the phone on the jet and dialed Joe's number in Colorado, desperately hoping that the call would not be traceable. On the first ring, a recording came on that told her that his number had been disconnected. Confused, she tried his office number and was shocked when they informed her that he had moved out of the country.

Growing worried, Shanna began to wonder if Joe had completely lost his mind or had succumbed to a nervous breakdown over their breakup. She was being foolish and vain, she thought, to think that he would totally fall apart on her account, but nonetheless, she was disturbed that he would suddenly flee to a foreign land. *And where was he?* she thought. As she grew more and more puzzled, Shanna decided to contact Joe's aunt Caroline in Wyoming to see if she knew anything about his whereabouts. She and Joe had once visited his wealthy widowed aunt, at the Double WW Ranch, just south of Cheyenne.

When Caroline Wagner heard Shanna's voice on the line, she was thrilled to hear from the younger woman. She had always loved Shanna and had sincerely hoped that Shanna and Joe would someday be married and find the happiness that they so desperately deserved. Unfortunately, the older woman had sad yet shocking news. Joe was now married, living in Central America, and he and his new wife were expecting a baby.

Caroline hated having to be the one to deliver the bad news, but Joe's marriage had received major media focus. However, during her isolation at the ranch, Shanna had not followed current events or any society gossip. The coverage had all revolved around her mainly and the fact that the former fiancé of Shanna Somers, world-famous model, had been drowning in depression, only to be saved by an unknown woman he had met on the ski slopes of Colorado.

Shanna couldn't believe what she was hearing, and Caroline was amazed that Shanna had not seen the numerous reports broadcasting the event. Shanna explained tearfully to Joe's aunt that she had fallen victim to the vise of alcohol and drugs, which had almost killed her, and that she had been recuperating for months in New Mexico. Caroline was shocked and saddened to hear of Shanna's addiction, but she was genuinely glad that the younger woman had battled her demons and won. The two women said tender good-byes to one another, and when they hung up, both of them gave in to tears.

Shanna completed her acting job in California but felt that she delivered a horrible performance in that she was so upset over Joe's marriage, she couldn't concentrate on her lines, causing her to stumble through the script. After her assignment was completed, Shanna went out on the town, and she and her new friends from the show partied through the night at the swankiest bars in Beverly Hills. The next morning, Shanna awoke in her suite at the Four Seasons with a tremendous hangover and wishing that she would die.

She phoned her brother and begged him to go back to New Mexico with her in that she needed to spend more time in the peace and tranquility of the ranch to heal her broken heart and continue to fight her addiction. Tony readily promised his sister that he would join her at Blue Diamond and that they would stay as long as it took for her to get better physically and recover emotionally. He knew how much Shanna and Joe loved each other, and he couldn't imagine what had possessed Joe to marry someone else and to leave his business and the country. But whatever the reason, Tony was determined to stay with the sister that he loved so much and see to it that she was safe.

Shanna stayed at Blue Diamond Ranch for another month with her brother watching over her. They rode horses, wrote music, and helped each other heal. The two siblings recovered through the support of each other, and for the first time in either of their lives, they both finally felt that they could face the future with new hope and focus.

# CHAPTER 56

After the day at the Shandon estate, when Shanna went running back to her in-laws' house, Joe left in a wild rush, convinced that his relationship with the woman of his dreams was over and her love for him dead. He raced back to the city and caught the first plane headed for Denver. He vowed to himself that he would forget her and get on with his future. She had hurt him for the last time. But he couldn't forget her; he loved her with all his heart, and she would always be a part of his soul.

Joe knew that he had to somehow rebuild his life, so he hired an oil executive to run his company and escaped to the slopes of Aspen for a month of relaxation and rejuvenation. He felt that the cold mountain air would help lift his spirits and clear his head, so he skied every day for hours until he was so tired that all he could do at the end of the day was retire to his room with a brandy and a hearty meal.

One evening, when the snow was falling steadily, Joe decided to leave his hotel suite and venture down to the lounge. There, he met a lovely girl named Jenny Drake, who was there vacationing with her sister. Jenny had just completed her doctoral studies at Vanderbilt University in anthropology and was heading to Guatemala in one month to begin a research project in Mayan archaeology. Joe found her fascinating and intelligent. Jenny was also pretty but in an earthy sort of way.

They stayed in the bar until it closed, then returned to Joe's suite where they spent the night together. The next morning, Joe awoke with a splitting headache and found himself in bed with the young woman he'd been drinking with all night. He groaned, knowing that he had slept with Jenny out of loneliness and despair, not to mention drunkenness, and he felt instantly ashamed of himself for taking advantage of her. Jenny, on the other hand, did not feel used in the least when he apologized and explained the reasons behind his unchivalrous behavior. She fell head over hills in love for Joe Stephenson, finding him to be the most gentlemanly and kindly man she had ever met, not to mention, the most sophisticated and the richest.

Jenny wasn't about to let a man like Joe slip away, so she stuck to him like glue during the rest of her stay in Aspen. Joe knew that he was sinking into a relationship that he wasn't ready for, yet he was too polite to end it with Jenny, for he knew that she had fallen for him, and he didn't have the heart to hurt her. Joe was greatly relieved when it came time for her to go and felt guilty for his feelings as she sobbed in his arms at the airport. Jenny promised to keep in touch with him, even though she

innately knew that he didn't have feelings for her and that their brief encounter had only been a rebound fling for him.

When Joe returned to Denver, he decided to return to his oil business and bury himself in his work. Without Shanna, he had no interest in other women and still greatly regretted getting involved with Jenny, praying that he had not hurt her too greatly. He avoided her frequent phone calls, feeling guilty every time that he instructed his secretary to tell her that he wasn't available. Finally, Jenny got through to him with a telegram, demanding that he call her. She ended her note by saying that it was urgent. Joe folded the wire and stuffed it in his pocket; he would call her that evening from home.

It was snowing heavily when Joe left his office, so he opted to stay at his penthouse in town, instead of driving the two hours back to his estate in the mountains. He rode in the clear elevator that carried him up to his apartment on top of the building and marveled at the huge flakes that clung to the glass. He threw his keys on the entry table in his foyer and fumbled in his pocket for Jenny's telegram.

Before he sat down to call her, he poured himself a stiff drink and then pulled off his jacket. As Joe sank into his leather chair in his den, he reached for the phone and dialed the number on the card.

Jenny answered on the first ring as Joe nervously said hello and asked her how she was. She immediately screamed at him for ignoring her since their trip and railed at him for avoiding her calls. Joe tried to interject his apologies, but she continued to scold him. He finally managed to shush her and was able to muster enough strength to explain as calmly as he could that their affair had been a mistake and that he was sorry if he had lead her on in any way.

Jenny was hysterical on her end and screamed loudly at him, "I'm pregnant!"

Joe was dumbfounded, for he couldn't imagine any worse news than what she had just delivered. She informed him that she was definitely keeping the baby and that she expected him to live up to his duty and marry her.

Being the honorable man that he was, Joe assured her that he would do the right thing. After their conversation, Joe picked up a bottle of whiskey, walked out onto his balcony overlooking the lights of the city, and drank as the Denver snow fell all around him.

# Chapter 57

Joe and Jenny married at a small ceremony in her hometown of Springfield, Illinois. Soon after their wedding, Jenny had to report to her assignment in Central America, and despite her pregnancy, she intended to continue on with her project and work up until time for the baby to be born. Joe existed in a daze through it all for the lack of anything else going on in his life. Joe was an honorable man; so therefore, because of his sense of duty, he abandoned his business for a while in an attempt to sort things out in his life and in his mind.

He phoned his aunt Caroline to announce to her, unenthusiastically, that he was married, moving out of the country, and expecting a baby. Caroline was in shock, to say the least, and felt on her end the pain that her beloved nephew was going through. She had always loved Joe like a son, for she had taken him in when his parents forsook him to pursue a life of reckless abandon in a commune nestled high in the mountains. His aunt sympathized over the dilemma that Joe had stumbled into knowing all too well that his heart was still with the woman of his dreams, Shanna. Joe assured Caroline that he would call her as soon as they reached Guatemala. She hung up on her end, feeling blue and wishing that she could have done more to ensure his future with the woman who had captured his heart.

Joe and Jenny arrived in Guatemala City and immediately set up housekeeping in a small dormitory-like dwelling that the school had provided for all the doctoral students. Jenny assured her husband that their stay there would only be temporary until she could arrange for more suitable accommodations through the university. Joe was so miserable over being in Central America and just his life in general that the inadequate lodging was the last thing on his mind.

True to his word, however, he called his aunt to inform her of their safe arrival. Caroline was relieved to know that he had arrived without incident but still dismayed that her beloved nephew was so distraught over his predicament. She wanted more than anything for Joe to be happy, but she knew that his life would never be complete without Shanna.

During their conversation, Joe asked his aunt if she had heard anything about Shanna, and he was thrilled to hear that she had called, inquiring about him. Caroline was hesitant to inform him of Shanna's intense involvement with drugs, but she felt that he needed to know. Joe was horrified to learn that the woman whom he loved beyond all measure had sunk to almost killing herself with alcohol and cocaine. He

begged to know where Shanna was, and against her better judgment, Caroline confided to her nephew that she was hiding out at the ranch, recuperating and avoiding the press.

After hearing the news of Shanna's addiction, Joe quickly ended the conversation with his aunt and began to sort out in his mind how he should go about contacting her and what to say to his wife in order to go back to the States for a while. He decided that he had better go before the baby was born; otherwise, he might never find the chance to get away.

Joe explained to his wife that a huge oil well acquisition in Texas had gone awry without his control and that he needed to fly to Houston in order to straighten out the mess. Jenny was livid that he was leaving her, yet he promised that he would return as soon as he could. So only one week after his arrival in the Yucatan, Joe boarded a plane and headed for New Mexico.

When he landed in Santa Fe, Joe rented a Jeep and headed straight for Blue Diamond Ranch. Pulling up to the huge arched black iron gate that graced the driveway, he stopped for a moment to collect his thoughts. What would he say to her? How should he approach her about her drug use? When could he explain about his marriage to Jenny? All these questions raced through Joe's head until he shook it violently to clear it for a better path of reasoning. He decided just to approach her head on, tell her that he still loved her beyond reality, and that he would do anything to have her back in his life.

Joe meandered his vehicle along the long winding road that led to the main house. There was no one around, except for the ranch hand John, who was working an Arabian in a paddock area by the barn. Joe made his way on up to the front porch and rang the doorbell that seemed to chime throughout the entire canyon. There was no answer, so he pounded loudly on the heavy wooden door. He waited a few seconds; however, there was still no answer. Finally, he decided to turn the brass knob, and to his amazement, it opened.

As he entered and quietly made his way into the huge vaulted living room, he called out, "Hello?" but received no response. Joe ventured into the kitchen where he found a note on the counter, left by the Spanish maid, Carlota, informing "Mizzus Somers" that she had gone into town to the market. Joe left the note where it was and continued his search throughout the rest of the house. As he looked around, he decided that Shanna must have gone out for a ride on one of her stallions. Suddenly, his eyes rested on a slight figure on the leather sofa, nestled snugly in a ball, covered by finely woven Indian blanket.

Joe walked over to the couch and knelt down beside the sleeping figure. Gently, he pulled the coverlet back and found Shanna sleeping peacefully underneath. He smiled as tears spilled out of his eyes; just seeing her lying there so innocently and sweetly warmed his heart and reminded him of just how much he had missed her. He reached down and stroked her cheek with the back of his fingers, causing her to jump in fright at his touch.

Joe reassured her that she was safe and then took her in his arms, holding her close. Still in shock, she embraced him too, crying into his neck. Suddenly, she pulled away in anger and said, "What are you doing here? I heard that you had gotten married and are expecting a baby! Am I supposed to believe that what I was told is all a lie? Tell me, Joe, why have you come here and what do you mean to accomplish with this unexpected visit?" With that, Shanna rose from the sofa in insolence, wrapped the blanket around her shoulders, and went to stand in front of the crackling fire.

Joe jumped to his feet and went to stand before her. "Please, sweetheart, I want you to know that I am extremely remorseful over what has happened with Jenny; however, I feel that I have to do what is right by honoring her and this child that I am responsible for. You must understand that!"

Shanna looked at him in irritation and replied, "Oh, give me a break, Joe; remorse is for naughty children and priests, and the last time I checked, you are neither one of those!"

Joe bowed his head in regret as she pulled away from him and returned to sit on the couch. Joe quickly joined her and spoke to her in a calming voice. He explained the entire fiasco in meeting Jenny in Aspen and their drunken escapade, which resulted in her getting pregnant. He admitted that it had been a stupid and childish thing to do; however, he had been so devastated by the breakup that he had behaved like a fool, and now his life was in a shambles.

Shanna felt for him, and before she could stop herself, she had pulled him into her arms—holding him, kissing him, and loving him. Joe returned her kisses, and before either of them knew what was happening, their desire for one another overpowered them and gave way to the most intense passion either of them had ever known. They made love on the sofa and lay together for hours kissing, embracing, and reassuring themselves that their actions had not been wrong; they had just been apart for far too long.

Carlota returned from the market to find her employer and Senor Stephenson entangled underneath the Indian blanket. The Mexican housekeeper was discrete and respectively kept her distance from the great room until she heard the two lovers moving around. Only then did she cautiously enter the huge den to inquire about dinner. Shanna giggled sheepishly as she tried to wrap the throw around her naked body and instructed her to prepare whatever she pleased, for they were starved. Carlota backed out of the room in embarrassment and announced in Spanish that she would be serving chili con carne in one hour. Shanna then led Joe upstairs to the enormous master bedroom, and they made love again before showering and returning downstairs for dinner.

Joe and Shanna spent three blissful days together at the ranch renewing their love for each other and deceiving their spouses as to why they weren't coming home. Joe felt terrible about lying to Jenny in her condition, fearing that his upsetting her would somehow endanger the pregnancy. Shanna didn't feel guilty in the least

about avoiding her husband; she simply told him that she needed a few more days to fully recuperate and that she would be home by the end of the week. Fortunately, Erich was agreeable, for he wanted his wife back; but he wanted her back drug-free and healthy. When they both finally admitted that they had to return to their respective relationships and responsibilities, Joe and Shanna made a pact that they would see each other as often as they could and that they would merely exist in their unbearable marriages until the time was right for them to be together.

# CHAPTER 58

Shanna returned to New York in high spirits after rekindling her love for Joe. For the first time in a long time, she felt rejuvenated and sensed a new beginning for her future. Upon her arrival at the Madison Avenue penthouse, her reunion with her children was a happy one, and they were thrilled to see their mother again. Erich watched them from the staircase overlooking their massive ballroom and shook his head in confusion over the unexplainable bond that his daughter and son still had for a mother whom they hardly ever saw. It amazed him that despite the nanny and the governess who cared for his children, they still preferred the company of their mommy. Erich finally came to the conclusion that perhaps a part-time mother was better than no mother at all.

Soon after Shanna's return, she insisted on moving into one of the guest suites in their large apartment, explaining to her husband that she needed time to herself in order to regroup after the serious soul-searching she had done in New Mexico. Erich, being no fool, immediately suspected that she had other reasons for distancing herself and refusing to sleep in his bed. When he broached her on the matter, Shanna surprisingly admitted to him her reinvolvement with Joe and told him quite frankly that if he tried to stop her from seeing him, she would leave, forever. Erich relented temporarily, vowing silently to eventually destroy his wife's adulterous relationship. He slowly began to develop a plan to permanently rid himself, and the world, of Joe Stephenson.

Although life was still not perfect for Shanna, for the first time in many years, she was happy. She and Erich had come to a civil agreement to stay married. She felt that if she can have Joe in her life, keep her husband at bay, and still be near her beautiful children, she could conquer almost anything. Shanna dove headfirst back into the world of fashion that had missed her. Magazine publishers and designers were ecstatic to have her back, gracing their covers and parading down runways. Modeling jobs began flooding in, and she was finally offered a long-awaited movie role. She wrote her autobiography, titling it *Somer Time,* and it immediately became a best-seller. Between book tours, fashion shoots, and shows, Shanna worked with Tony, recording in their Nashville studio and performing in concerts with the band when she could find the time.

Shanna and Erich remained distant with one another, but they occasionally appeared together at social functions. Coincidentally, they encountered Joe and Jenny at a charity benefit in Dallas. Both couples felt uncomfortable in the situation,

yet they all remained civil and appeared gracious. Erich seethed when he thought of Shanna and Joe together, and his mental visions of their making love nearly drove him to madness. But he was willing to tolerate their fling temporarily until his plan was completed to destroy the adulterous relationship for good.

Jenny also harbored her suspicions about her husband and the world-famous model. Ever since Joe had left Guatemala to supposedly return to the States to check on his company, she had innately felt that his story wasn't true. Her mistrust was compounded when she could never locate him at any of the hotel rooms he claimed to have occupied. She held her fears to herself, however, because confronting Joe might anger him; and she was terrified of losing him.

Joe and Jenny welcomed the birth of their daughter, whom they named India. She was a beautiful baby with dark hair and eyes the color of the Indian Ocean, thus resulting in her name. Joe was ecstatic about having a child; his only regret was that he wished the baby would have been shared between him and Shanna. He had desperately wanted her to get pregnant as a result of their many intense lovemaking sessions, but sadly, the fates had ruled in the favor of Erich fathering her children.

It seemed to Joe that the fates had always been on Erich's side, for he had always lost when it came down to choices where Shanna was concerned. She always chose her husband, or so it seemed, no matter how much it appeared that she loved him. So Joe became resigned to stay focused on his wife and child and let Shanna get on with her life. He would put their pact to still see each other on hold, at least for the time being, or until he heard from her. His heart would have a hole in it, but at least he could forever cherish the times that they did spend together and the brief moment in time when he truly felt that he had experienced nirvana.

Joe sent Shanna an announcement, telling her about the birth of India. He wrote also that he felt that they should abandon their plan to seek stolen moments together, for something deep within him had changed. The birth of his child stirred his soul and awakened his sense of obligation, stopping him from doing anything that would jeopardize him loosing his daughter.

When Shanna received his note, she felt both elated and heartbroken at the same time. She knew just how much Joe had always wanted a child and admired his devotion in wanting to keep his family together. She was devastated, however, that their relationship would be on hold for a while, and perhaps indefinitely. It was up to Joe now, and without him, she would have to find ways to occupy her time so as not to think about how much her heart was aching without him in her life.

Without Joe in her life, Shanna continued to pour herself into her career and revived her career as a singer, soaring to new heights with her brother's band. They toured nonstop, and the pace was grueling for both of them, but the siblings found strength in each other and managed to avoid the pitfalls of addiction that they had succumbed to in the past. On a trip to Europe, the group played to sold-out audiences in nine countries. Shanna was gone for two months, causing her children to feel neglected and her husband outraged.

Erich was furious that his wife was once again abandoning their marriage. Even if they didn't live in the typical existence of a husband and wife, he still felt that she had a responsibility to her children and him, to be with them at least some of the time. Erich knew that he would probably never be able to tame Shanna into being the perfect wife and living the exemplary role he envisioned, but he would never give up. That was mostly the reason that he loved her. Erich loved a challenge, and Shanna Somers was beyond any challenge he had ever come across. She was like the female version of Mount Everest; she was magnificent and mysterious yet challenging at the same time. Eventually, Erich was sure he would conquer her, and once he did, no other man would ever have the nerve to approach her again.

One week before Shanna was to return home from Europe, a letter addressed to her and marked Urgent and Personal appeared in the mail at the apartment on Madison Avenue. The butler handed the letters and packages to Erich when he arrived home from the office and he retired to his den to look through his correspondence in private.

He poured himself a scotch, the way he always did after a long day at his company. In shuffling through the envelopes, he noticed the one marked international, postmarked from Central America. Seeing the words "personal" and "urgent" addressed to his wife, he surmised instantly that the letter must be from her lover.

Slugging back his drink, Erich tore open the envelope and quickly read the obviously distressed handwriting of the person composing the letter. The note was indeed from Joe, and it stated sadly that his wife and daughter had been killed tragically in a freak car accident in Guatemala. The letter went on to say that Jenny was taking their baby to meet her colleagues at their digging sight on the side of the mountain and the winding road gave way, causing the car to careen down the hill, plunging into the ground below and bursting into flames. The mother and baby were killed instantly. There was more to Joe's writing expressing his love for Shanna and how much he needed her now, more than ever.

Erich stopped reading the note at that point. He folded the letter and stuffed it back into its envelope. *My god,* he whispered aloud as he poured himself another scotch. He almost felt sorry for poor Joe. Erich couldn't imagine bearing the pain of what a man would feel over losing his wife and child simultaneously. *The poor bastard must really be suffering,* he muttered to himself again.

Erich sat in his library as the sky turned dark outside and the stars shown outside his window overlooking New York City. He drank a lot as he thought of Joe's plight and what his wife would do once she found out that the love of her life was in such pain and now available and vulnerable. Erich knew exactly what she would do. She would forsake her life with him and run to the man she truly wanted, even if it meant losing her children and destroying her reputation. Erich would not let that happen; he was in control. Shanna was his wife and the mother of his children. Nothing was going to change that. He downed what was left of his drink and threw Joe's letter into the fireplace. He watched until the last bits of the paper had crumpled in the flames; then he turned off the lights and staggered up the winding staircase to his bedroom.

# CHAPTER 59

Two years passed, and Tony's career also flourished. His production company did extremely well, and nearly every album he recorded soared to the top of the record charts. He also discovered and promoted an up-and-coming artist named Joshua Sands, who became an overnight success and got nominated for a Grammy after his first solo hit. Shanna remained in the band, and her vocal collaborations with her brother and Josh became so popular that their days of just being "stars" were forever gone. They evolved into the realm of superstardom, to the limit of where their very existence drowned amid a sea of ardent fans and persistent paparazzi.

On a tour to Honolulu, the band performed to a sold-out crowd at the Aloha Auditorium. Shanna caught a midnight flight back to Los Angeles with plans to continue on to New York the next morning. She too was feeling guilty over not spending more time with her children, and since the band was heading on to Japan after their Hawaiian tour, Shanna really felt that she should return to New York and check on her children. Tony stayed on in Oahu and finally met a woman who could take his mind off his undying love for his sister. Her name was Lanna.

Lanna Holahai was the most exotic women Tony had ever seen. She was a native to the island, dark-skinned, with hair the color of coal that hung to her waste. He met her in a bar one night after his band's last performance. Lanna was working as a cocktail waitress trying to support her elderly mother. She had been working in the Mona Loi Bar for two years while she maintained a position as a travel agent during the day.

Upon seeing her, Tony felt he had to speak to her and invite her to his table for a drink. She declined at first, saying that she didn't get off for another half hour. Tony promised that he would wait, for she was someone he definitely wanted to get to know in more detail. He moved to a barstool after the other band members left and sat and watched Lanna work until her shift was over.

After they left the lounge, Tony and Lanna walked along the beach, and she told him about her childhood, growing up on the island. Although she had heard of the Tony Masterson Band, she had no idea that the man she had met was one of the most famous performers in the world. Most of her life had been spent taking care of her siblings after her father was killed in a farming accident. Lanna's mother went to work as a housekeeper for the owners of the pineapple plantation, leaving the two younger children in her older daughter's care. After her brother and sister grew up

and went out on their own, Lanna's mother took ill, leaving Lanna no choice but to forsake a life of her own in order to take care of her ailing parent.

For the past twelve years, Lanna had worked two jobs in order to support her mother and pay for the exorbitant medical costs necessary for the older woman's care. Tony listened sympathetically as he listened to Lanna's depressing life story. He admired her loyalty and devotion to her mother and was amazed that this beautiful woman had never experienced a serious relationship with a man. Lanna explained to him bashfully that there had been countless suitors who had begged for her affections, but there was no way that she could have abandoned her mother to pursue her own happiness.

Tony begged her to spend some time with him for the remainder of his stay in Honolulu, and she promised that she would take the following night off so that they might spend some time together. They walked back to Mona Loi together, and fortunately, another waitress was leaving the now-closed bar and offered Lanna a ride home. She gave Tony her phone number at the travel agency and kissed him delicately on the cheek before she got into her friend's car. Tony watched longingly after her as they pulled away and drove into the night. He walked for a while in the direction of his hotel, thinking of the exotic beauty he had encountered. Finally, he hailed a cab, and on the ride down Pacific Avenue, he began counting the hours until he would see Lanna again.

Tony was due in Tokyo in three days, and before he left, he wanted to try and spend as much time as possible with the Hawaiian beauty he was now so crazy about. They spent the next seventy-two hours together amid a flurry of publicity hounds and crazed fans. The press couldn't get enough of the popular rock musician and his new love interest. Tony was used to the paparazzi, but their constant presence frightened Lanna and upset her terribly. He increased his staff of bodyguards and promised her that she would not be bothered after he left and continued on his tour to Japan, but he couldn't have been more wrong.

After Tony left Hawaii, the reporters and photographers continued to hound Lanna at her workplace, in the bar, and at the small home she shared with her mother. The constant attention was terrifying, and she cried hysterically when Tony phoned her from the Orient. Tony felt helpless in not being able to protect her, so he cancelled the rest of his sold-out concerts in order to return to Honolulu and rescue the woman he had grown to love.

Understandably, Tony's band members were furious with his decision to cancel their Eastern tour, but there was nothing they could do without their lead singer and the star of the show. Tony flew back to Lanna and promised to take her away from the madness for a while, assuring her that the media interest would die down after a while.

He decided that they would flee to Tahiti for a few weeks and get to know one another better and to let their relationship become "old news" in the tabloids. Lanna protested at first, afraid to leave her mother and her jobs, but Tony assured

her that he would take care of everything financially and that he would hire her mother the best nurse on the island. She finally agreed, so Tony chartered a private plane, and the next morning, they took off at sunrise, headed toward the South Pacific.

While in Papeete, Tony and Lanna enjoyed a time of being together and relaxing in the tropical sunshine. It was the first time in a long time that either of them had been able to take a break from their busy lives and just enjoy being with another person without a care in the world. For Lanna, the trip was the only occasion she had ever been away from her mother or off the island of Hawaii for that matter. For Tony, it was a chance for him to regroup, after a year of a grueling tour schedule and band rehearsals. He too enjoyed a period of respite from being hunted and stalked by the paparazzi, and for the first time in ages, he didn't feel the urge to drink or abuse drugs. Maybe, he thought, Lanna was a gift from God sent to give him peace and a sense of spiritual tranquility.

The Polynesian people were very gracious to the young couple, so obviously in love, and the natives were overjoyed when Tony and Lanna invited them to witness their wedding, held at the base of the Moorea mountains. The entire trip was the most magical time of Lanna's life. She adored her new husband and vowed never to let him out of her sight.

Upon their return to Hawaii, Tony purchased a beautiful beachfront home for his wife, equipped with a separate living quarters for her mother. The sprawling estate cost over $5 million dollars and was completely surrounded by a high wall to ensure their privacy from the press and Tony's adoring fans. Lanna's happiness and security meant everything to Tony, and he did everything within his power to please her.

Sadly, Lanna was not content in her new life. She hated being in the public's eye; she complained every time Tony mentioned going back out on the road with his band, and she even argued that her mother was not happy being in a strange place. Tony constantly tried to make it obvious to her that her life was significantly better now than it had been before, but she continued to be perpetually unhappy.

Tony was growing increasingly restless himself, and his band members were rapidly losing patience with him. They were also losing money, and their popularity was dwindling. Finally, his four fellow musicians issued him an alternative—tour again or break up. Tony's lifelong dream had been to be a rock star and now that he had reached that pinnacle, he wasn't about to let his stardom slip through his fingers and allow his entire career to disappear. He desperately tried to explain to Lanna how dire it was that he return to work; however, she hit him with some news that sent him reeling. She announced to him that she was going to have a baby and that if he even dared try and leave her, she would pack up her mother and forbid him to ever see her or their child.

Tony couldn't believe that the happy existence he had almost obtained for himself was falling apart. He felt as if he were caught between the woman he was

married to, his band who depended on him, and the people around the world who had followed and supported him for so many years. He wanted to please them all, but that would be an impossible accomplishment.

Reluctantly, Tony phoned his manager and told him that he wouldn't be back and that the group would have to somehow exist without him. He knew Shanna would survive. She had so many other venues in which to parlay her talent; in fact, Tony always felt that his little sister had only participated in his musical ambitions to make him happy. In fact, everything that Shanna seemed to do was in an effort to make him happy. Just thinking about her made Tony smile; he missed his sister and felt very guilty about being out of touch with her for so long.

Shanna had only spoken to her brother a few times over the past several months. She knew about the new woman in his life and the hasty marriage. Although she was concerned that he was moving into the relationship too quickly, it was his life, and she wanted more than anything for him to be happy.

The pressures of his marriage, the baby, losing his band, and annihilating his career finally got the best of Tony; so he turned to the only solace he knew, and that was drugs. Tony found a supplier on the island and began using heroin, pills, and alcohol with more vigilance than ever before. He wanted out of his current situation, and if he couldn't do it physically, then he would do it mentally.

Tony was barely coherent during the entire length of Lanna's pregnancy. He was so messed up when it was time to deliver the baby that he couldn't even be present at the birthing. They had a son, whom Lanna named Noah. As a child, she had always loved the biblical story of Noah and the Ark, so she chose that name for her firstborn child.

Tony cleaned up during the first few days of his son's life. After spending time with Noah, he began to feel a deep sense of remorse over his actions and decided then and there to get his life back on a straight path, if for no other reason than for his only child. He called his sister and excitedly told her about the birth of his son. Shanna was very happy for Tony, albeit a little shocked that her brother had gone from being the most popular rock star and the lust of every woman in America to becoming a recently married man with a new baby. In just a little over a year, his career had gone from skyrocketing to forgotten.

After a while, Tony's manager finally got through to him. He insisted that they meet and discuss the disintegration of the Tony Masterson Band and the crumbling of Tony's popularity and, eventually, his financial empire. Max Harrison had managed Tony and the other members since their beginning, and he finally convinced Tony that if he did not return to work, there would be numerous lawsuits to face due to cancelled concerts and unfinished albums.

Tony saw reason and agreed to resume touring. He really didn't want his career and fame to be over, and he felt ashamed for disappointing his fans and walking out on his fellow band members. They had been like brothers for almost twenty years, and he had let them down. He assured Harrison that he would return to LA in one

week and that he would produce a new album in record time and tour his ass off to make it a hit. His manager was pleased and promised to inform the rest of the band and start immediately alerting the media about his return.

Tony began making plans to leave Hawaii that greatly upset his wife. Lanna was irate and hysterical that her husband would even consider leaving her and their new baby to return to a life of rock and roll and crazed groupies. Tony tried to assure her that he had to go back to his band or else his world would most likely collapse into bankruptcy as a result of lawsuits and lost record sales. Lanna refused to support him, for she did not understand the music industry and had no idea what he would be giving up if he left his band.

She screamed at him and cried for the entire week leading up to his departure. By the time he boarded the plane for California, he was so rattled and shaken that he drank all the way to LAX. A limo awaited Tony at the airport, and all three of his bodyguards who accompanied him had to practically carry him to the car. He was so drunk that it took two days before he recuperated enough to go into the studio to begin work on his new album. His band members were understanding, for they knew what he had been through, but they confided in Harrison that they would not tolerate Tony's drunken behavior for very long.

Tony did recover and dove back into his music with his old enthusiasm. He realized that he had missed his work and the public attention that came with it. He enjoyed being back in the limelight again and having hordes of women throw themselves at him as he and his friends frequented the Hollywood clubs. Their latest tour was about to take off, and the publicity surrounding the band was at an all-time high. Tony realized that he had missed the limelight of being in the public eye, but most of all, he had missed performing with his sister and seeing her every day.

Being away from his baby boy was going to be hard, but Tony planned to fly Lanna and Noah to Los Angeles as soon as he found them a new place to live. At least his family would all be in the contiguous states while he toured. His new record deal stated that he would only perform within the United States for the next two years. That way, at least, he would be around most of the time to see his son frequently through infancy and as a toddler.

Lanna continued to be incensed over her husband returning to his band and abandoning their family. Her mother harped at her constantly over marrying a deadbeat hippie who had just gotten her pregnant and then taken off. Lanna defended Tony at first; then as her hysteria grew, she too began to agree with her mother. She phoned her husband several times a day, interrupting his recording sessions and causing him to be jumpy and agitated. He was worried about her and their son; however, there was nothing he could do on his end except to try and bring them all together again as soon as possible.

Tony purchased a beach house in Malibu, hoping that his wife would acclimate better to her new surroundings if she were around water. Lanna arrived reluctantly, not wanting to leave Hawaii or her mother. She had only been in Los Angeles a few

days when Tony announced that he had to leave for Phoenix to play the first show in their new concert tour. Predictably, Lanna was furious over her husband leaving again, but her ranting seemed to do no good, for he left again anyway.

As time went on, Lanna's behavior turned psychotic, causing Tony to worry about the safety of his child and wonder about the harm his wife might do to herself. He was forced to cancel a couple of show dates; and reluctantly, his band covered for him and performed anyway although they were not pleased. The stress of the situation caused Tony to again relapse into heavy drug use, and he was arrested one night while venturing out to buy cocaine. A few nights in jail, a media frenzy, and the threat of a possible prison sentence shook him into the realization that things had to change or else his life would be over.

Tony forced Lanna to return to Honolulu with their son. Although he hated like hell to say good-bye to Noah, his relief over putting his wife on a plane was immense. She had almost driven him to madness and almost cost him his career. Although he hated to hurt her, Tony decided that after his legal problems were resolved, he would file for divorce and sue for custody of their child.

Luckily, due to his celebrity status, Tony's high-priced attorneys were able to get his drug possession charge dropped and his sentenced reduced to probation and a brief stint of community service.

During this period, Shanna was beside herself with worry over her brother; however, her work schedule had her buried, and he forbade her to come to him anyway. She surmised that he was involved with drugs again and that he was probably too ashamed to see her and admit his failure with sobriety yet again. Shanna agreed to stay away but assured him that she would always be around when he needed her.

After Lanna arrived back in Hawaii, her mental health continued to deteriorate. She pined for her husband and was devastated that he had chosen his career over her and their baby. She felt like a total failure for not being able to keep him at her side; so one evening, after she put Noah in his crib and fed her mother, Lanna locked herself in the bathroom and slit her wrists.

The police and paramedics arrived a few hours later, after Lanna's mother had heard the baby crying and maneuvered her wheelchair down the hallway to check on him. She saw blood flowing from underneath the bathroom floor and managed to push the alarm button to summon help. The emergency crew swiftly transported Lanna to the local hospital where she survived, but just barely.

Two days later, word finally reached Tony in Dallas that his wife had attempted suicide. He was frantic with worry for his wife and his son. He immediately informed his manager and his band that he was returning to Hawaii, so he chartered a plane and flew nonstop to Honolulu. Unfortunately, the jet experienced mechanical difficulties and had to land abruptly in San Francisco and was grounded for another eight hours. Tony was nearly out of his mind with frustration, especially when he learned that there was not another private jet to be found, and every commercial flight was booked.

When he finally reached the island over twenty hours later, the news he received upon arriving at the palatial beachfront home was dismal. Lanna had survived her bloody episode with a razor blade; however, after her return home from the hospital, she sneaked from her bedroom away from the private nurse who accompanied her from the psychiatric wing and completed the task she had set out to do earlier. With steadfast determination, Lanna Holahai Masterson left her room and headed slowly across their property and into the Pacific Ocean. She walked and walked until the waves engulfed her, pulling her into their mysterious depths, taking her away from the confines of her existence.

Upon the realization of learning that his wife had committed suicide, Tony felt a great sense of remorse yet a somewhat subtle sense of relief over the fact that he was finally free of her possessive ways and jealous nature. He knew that he should be hurting more over her loss; however, being released of the confines of their captive marriage was like being released from the doldrums of a dark prison. Tony knew that he loved Lanna in the beginning; but somehow, somewhere, something had gone strangely amiss in their relationship.

The memorial service took place in a small chapel in a remote village on the island, where Lanna's mother had grown up. There were few mourners present, and Tony was very touched that his sister made the trip and attended his wife's funeral. Erich came with her, of course, and surprisingly, he too was very sympathetic over his brother-in-law's loss.

After the tragedy was over, and everyone returned to their everyday lives, Tony was left totally bewildered over what to do with his own existence. His career had suffered terribly since his involvement with Lanna; but now that his son was here, and Tony was his only guardian, life had a whole new meaning. Thus, he chose to leave his band once and for all and pursue a career as a solo artist, which would allow him a life with his son and he wanted to venture into it with a clean and sober attitude.

Tony decided to return to his roots and go back to the place where life maintained some semblance of belonging and refuge, and that was at Hounds Run. When he returned to his southern estate, Tony hired an experienced child-care worker to care for his son, then set out to create a collection of music that would set the world on fire.

Shanna went to visit her brother shortly after his return to their home in Tennessee, and she was encouraged that he was doing so well in his bereavement. She brought her children with her and was very happy that McKenna and Alex befriended their cousin so well. The children got along splendidly, and both Shanna and Tony were overjoyed that they all regarded each other as siblings.

# CHAPTER 60

After Shanna returned to the States following Lanna's funeral, she watched over her brother carefully for a few months. After convincing herself that Tony would survive his grief, she returned to her career, which offered a bright new future for her in the arena of motion pictures. Tony's only solution following his catastrophic marriage to Lanna was to return to Nashville and seek refuge in the recording studio. He wanted to pour his soul into new creations that he hoped would eventually place him back into the musical limelight again and someday return him to the status of a superstar he had previously known.

Tony's new music and his new sound quickly landed him back at the top of the charts, and within months, his career as a solo artist was considered to be one of the most incredible comebacks in musical history. He relished in returning to his life as a rock star, but now his focus lay in not only protecting his artistry but also his son and his sobriety. Tony in no way wanted to slip back into the snare that alcohol and drugs had laid for him. He felt that God had given him a second chance with everything and everyone that mattered to him and by no means did he intend to allow his happiness to slip away.

Shanna was proud of her brother's overnight comeback and was thrilled by his commitment to staying sober and being a devoted father. She invited Tony out to her home in California, and while dining on her patio overlooking Los Angeles, she excitedly told him about the fabulous role she had been offered in a movie. "Finally," she exclaimed happily, "I'm going to experience what I've always dreamed of, starring in a major motion picture!"

Shanna rambled on and on about her part in the picture. She was to play an American journalist who follows her lover, a soldier fighting in the Middle East. The movie was to start filming in two weeks, and Shanna was scheduled to fly to Israel and report to the set as soon as she arrived. Her leading man was one of the most sought-after young actors in Hollywood, and the director Sonny Horizon had won two Oscars. Shanna was so excited that Tony laughed, amused by his sister's enthusiasm. She had wanted to be a movie star for so long, and he was happy that she had finally landed a leading role. Tony had always great faith in his sister, and finally, he thought, she would receive accolades for another one of her many talents.

Erich was, as expected, adamant that his wife should not venture into a part of the world where there was still so much unrest; however, Shanna was determined to

tackle and succeed in a medium that she had yet to conquer. She was so emphatic over the matter that her husband finally relented and allowed her to go.

Shanna flew to Jerusalem and arrived at the set of her new movie, eager and ready to tackle the project. The male costar, Rex Seaton, eagerly awaited her arrival and was thrilled to meet the famous model he had been infatuated with for years. Shanna and Rex got along splendidly, and they worked together brilliantly to the delight of their director.

After they had completed their third week of production, Shanna started feeling tired and lethargic. She was barely able to complete her scenes due to utter exhaustion, and finally, Sonny Horizon insisted that she see a physician. The local doctor examined Shanna thoroughly, and although he could not accurately diagnose her condition, he guessed that she had succumbed to an infection. He could only guess that she had come in contact with a rare bacteria that attacked her system.

Shanna fell into an unconscious state, following her doctor's prognosis and lay helpless in the Dahani Hospital, leaving her fellow costars and director in a state of powerlessness and helplessness over what to do in her behalf. They all paced around aimlessly, wondering what to do and who they should contact first about her sudden illness and steady decline.

Sonny called Erich and sadly informed him of Shanna's condition. It was hard to deliver such news and even more devastating when it involved such a promising young starlet who only had great performances to offer the public. Erich was stunned to hear the news of his wife's illness and booked a flight immediately to be by her side. Before he left New York, he felt obligated to call Tony and let him know about Shanna's condition. Tony was horrified to learn that his sister was in a semi-coma and possibly at death's door. He too booked a ticket to Israel but not before phoning his best friend and Shanna's great love, Joe.

When Joe got the call about Shanna, he was frantic and terrified over losing the woman that he so cherished. He had all but given up on their relationship and had been crushed when she hadn't even called or written her condolences over his tragic loss of Jenny and his baby daughter. He told Tony that he would meet him in New York, and together, they would fly across the world to be near the woman that they both so desperately loved.

Ironically, Erich, Tony, and Joe all arrived at the hospital around the same time; and their interaction with one another was not pleasant. Erich was furious with Tony for calling Joe and inviting him to come along and visit Shanna. When Tony and Joe entered the waiting area at the hospital, Erich leapt at Tony and viciously shook him saying, "Man, are you fucking crazy? What is that jerk doing here?" he said, motioning toward Joe.

Tony pushed his brother-in-law away and calmly replied, "Look, Erich, my sister may be dying, and Joe is probably the only man who can touch her enough and possibly make a difference in her waking up. She loves him, and he loves her, and I guess you're just going to have to get used to it!" With that, Tony shoved Erich to the side and led Joe toward Shanna's room.

Once inside, the two men looked at the beautiful woman whom they both adored and cried when they saw her lying in a vegetative state. Tony ran to her at once and stroked her hair while he kissed her cheeks. He sobbed loudly as he held her and only made a move when Joe touched his shoulder and asked him to let him be near her. Tony reluctantly scooted aside as Joe went to the bed and sat beside her.

Joe took her hand in his and spoke softly to her. Tony watched from the other side of the room while Erich stood outside and looked desperately through the small glass window in the door as his wife's lover touched her, willing her back to consciousness.

As Joe whispered to her, Shanna started to respond. Within minutes, she opened her eyes and clutched his hand tightly with her own. Tears spilled down Joe's face as he looked into the eyes of the woman he so desperately loved and uttered softly to her, "Welcome back, sweetheart." Shanna looked around the room, bewildered by the surroundings that she was now in. She saw her brother standing impatiently in the corner, and she smiled at him but was confused over where she was.

Joe continued to hold her hand and spoke again to her, asking, "How do you feel?"

Shanna looked into his eyes and focused her attention directly on him. She responded in a shaky voice, "I guess I feel fine, but where am I and what had happened to me?"

Both Joe and Tony broke down with laughter through their tears and simultaneously responded, "You're alive! That is what's happened to you."

Upon witnessing her return to consciousness, Erich burst through the door and advanced upon his adversaries. He violently pushed Joe from the bed and proceeded to take Shanna by the shoulders and ask her repeatedly if she was all right. Shanna looked at him confused and fearful until Tony moved toward him and begged him to give her some space. Erich reluctantly obeyed and moved away so as not to scare her. His feelings were crushed; however, he wanted his wife to get better, and if it meant staying away from her for a while, then he would. But he wanted Joe Stephenson out of the way, once and for all.

Erich exited Shanna's room, led by Tony, but told her that he would be back very soon and that he wanted her lover gone when he returned. Joe returned to Shanna's bedside and held her hand again. She asked him about Jenny and the baby, and he looked at her with shock and remorse. "Don't you remember, sweetheart, I wrote to you that they were both killed in a tragic car accident?" he asked.

Tears welled up in Shanna's eyes as she responded, "Oh my god, Joe, I am so sorry. I never received your letter informing me of the accident, or I would have called immediately. You know that!"

Joe pulled her to him and cried into her hair. They held each other close for a few moments; then he said, "It was a horrible situation, baby, but maybe it was God's way of paving the road for us to be together. Jenny was a sweet and wonderful girl, but it just wasn't meant to be."

Shanna looked at him sadly, not really knowing how to respond. Finally, she said, "No matter how overwhelmed we become by the endless flood of information in our

day-to-day lives, death forces us to recognize the meaning that certain individuals contribute into our everyday world. I know that Jenny was a passing presence in your life, Joe, but she did have meaning, and her existence had influence."

He held her to him for a few minutes longer; then he asked, "So where does that leave us? I know that Jenny's life and death had meaning, but her untimely passing and the loss of our child must be a sign that you and I were destined to be."

Shanna looked at him intently and again, tears sprang up in her eyes; then she replied, "I can't, Joe. I cannot leave Erich and forsake our marriage because he will totally destroy me in every possible way. As much as I love you, I cannot risk my reputation and the respect of my children if I embark on a new life with you."

Joe sat and stared at the woman of his dreams in utter disbelief. "You're going to let him dominate you until the end of time?" He blared.

"I don't have a choice," Shanna responded.

He rose from the bed in aggravation and nervously paced the room. "This is it!" he shouted. "If I leave today, then we are over. You will never see me again!" he promised.

Shanna looked at him unhappily and answered, "I do love you, Joe, with all my heart. But as long as Erich is alive, he will never let me go, and he will never give up in ruining me."

Joe looked at her in dismay and finally said, "Then it's good-bye then. I can't do this anymore, Shanna. I would give up my world for you, but you won't take it. As much as I love you, I can't go on like this any longer." With that, he waved and left the room.

Shanna just stared after him in silent dismay. The love of her life had just walked out, and there was nothing she could do about it. As the door slammed behind him, Shanna dropped her head into her hands and wept bitterly.

Erich saw Joe rush by him in the waiting room on his way to leave the hospital. Erich rose and went to his wife's room. Shanna still sat in her bed crying, so he went to her. He took her into his arms and uttered softly to her, "You know that I still love you, sweetheart, and I want us to be together. After you are discharged, I want us to return to Vanilla Island and rekindle our love for one another."

Shanna looked at her husband tenderly. Some part of her being loved him, yet she couldn't deny her undying passion for Joe. She felt that she owed Erich her loyalty and devotion as a wife and mother, but she knew that she could never be emotionally dedicated to him for as long as she truly loved another man. For now, Shanna decided to forsake the love of her life and focus directly on her husband and family. She accepted Erich's invitation of returning to the Caribbean and promised him that she would do her best in being a good wife to him and an excellent mother to their children.

When Shanna's doctor gave her the clearance to leave the hospital, her fellow crew members from the movie came to see her off. Unfortunately, she was not strong enough to resume filming, which distressed her greatly. Her greatest dream had been to become a success in the motion picture industry, but yet again, her hopes had been extinguished.

Erich hired a private jet and crew to jet him and his wife back to the United States. They stopped over in New York and saw their children; then they flew on to Vanilla Island for their tropical rekindling.

Shanna was not quite ready to resume lovemaking with her husband, and for once, Erich was compassionate and understanding. He knew that his wife's heart belonged to another man, yet he was determined that they would stay together and was adamant that he would keep her solely to himself.

Their time on the island was relaxing, and Shanna had an opportunity to recuperate and heal—emotionally and physically. The loss of Joe had been devastating for her, yet she appreciated her husband's attempts at keeping their relationship in tact.

After only five days into their stay, Erich got an emergency phone call from his office, stating that he needed to return and handle a delicate situation that occurred at one of their operations overseas. Since he had been the one to build the company's ties to the Orient, it was essential that Erich rectify the mishap.

Regrettably, Erich flew back to Manhattan and worried about leaving Shanna. She assured him that she would be fine and that she wanted to stay on Vanilla Island a little longer to regain her strength.

After her husband's departure, Shanna languished in her time alone and the opportunity to stroll along the beach to collect her thoughts and repair her emotions.

One evening at dusk, after she had finished her dinner on the verandah, Shanna decided to take a stroll along the shore. The sun was setting into the ocean, and the glimmering beach appeared very inviting. She thanked Hattie for an excellent meal, then strode off into the sunset with a lilt in her step. Hattie watched her go and worried inwardly that the young woman was hurting and hoped desperately that she would someday find the happiness that she so surely deserved.

As she walked along the beach, Shanna reminisced over her life and the many trials, tribulations, and successes that had been handed her way. Truly, she thought, as she reflected over the past, her life had been somewhat of a dichotomy of events. It was amazing to her that her existence had been forced to endure so many losses yet experience so many triumphs at the same time. *Of human misery*, she thought, *can only come self-gratification in the end.*

# CHAPTER 61

The sun finally sank in the blue depths of the ocean as Shanna started her return to the beach house. She was only a few yards away from the villa when a strange man appeared from behind a coconut tree and grabbed her arm. Shanna screamed in fear until the man spoke to her in a comforting voice, reminding her that they had already met. When the light shifted in the clouds, and the moon was overhead, Shanna recognized the dark stranger to be none other than Ricardo, from Italy.

"What on earth are you doing here?" she asked forcefully and accusingly.

Ricardo put her hand to his lips and replied, "I'm here on vacation, mi bella. My father has a lovely cottage here on the island. He is one of the co-owners."

Shanna pulled away from him in shock and reproached him for jumping out at her, scaring her out of her wits. Ricardo soothed her instantly, telling her how beautiful she was and laboring over how much he had missed her.

Shanna accepted his compliments in stride, for she had been very depressed lately over losing Joe, missing her chance at movie stardom, and having to exist in a marriage with a man with whom she felt trapped. Ricardo's embellishments uplifted her, so Shanna invited him back to the villa for a drink.

They sat on the deck for hours, enjoying expensive cognacs until finally, Ricardo carried Shanna to her bedroom and made love to her. She was so intoxicated that she wasn't fully aware of what was happening; however, deep within, she loved the attention but feared the outcome.

Hattie had watched her employer's wife take her lover into their bedroom, and she was not pleased with Shanna's behavior in the least. She intended to speak with Erich regarding the matter.

The next morning, Ricardo awoke, ready and willing to make love to Shanna again. She opened her eyes and moaned over the pain she felt from a night of heavy drinking. Ricardo teased her and accused her of being a lightweight, but she brushed him off and ordered him to leave. "Get out of here now," she demanded. "You almost ruined my life once, but by God, you're not going to do it again!"

He admonished her gently and assured her that he would go.

After Ricardo's departure, Shanna was more depressed than ever. She knew that she shouldn't have scolded Ricardo the way that she did because she had been the one to invite him over for cocktails. Secondly, she regretted the fact that she had given in to his charms and unwittingly had sex with him out of sadness and loneliness.

She figured, however, that she had made the unconscious decision to sleep with the man, and now she would just have to face the consequences.

Shanna packed her bags and returned to New York City. She and Hattie never spoke about her indecent actions with the Italian, yet Shanna knew that the old Haitian woman was unhappy with her and, if given the opportunity, would inform Erich with the indiscretion she had witnessed. Shanna decided to leave the matter a closed subject and hoped that it never resurrected itself again.

Her return to the city gave Shanna new inspiration. She approached a new medium in which she had yet to succeed, the theatre. She auditioned for several parts and finally managed to land a role in a new rendition of *The King and I*. Her performance of "I Could Have Danced All Night" amazed the producer and the director, and she landed the part immediately.

Production on the new musical started three weeks later, and Shanna appeared on time, the first day of scheduling. She was working onstage when dizziness and nausea overtook her and caused her to faint.

The directors and crew rushed to her side and helped her to her dressing room. They called Erich immediately, and he hurried from his office to come and collect her.

Shanna was awake but groggy when her husband arrived at the theatre. He was desperately worried and knew that something from her previous illness had to be the cause of her collapse, for she had looked extremely pale for several days. Shanna refused to go to a doctor just yet, so Erich took her home and forced her to lie down. She assured him that she was only tired from the rehearsal and just needed some rest.

When her exhaustion and queasiness continued, Shanna became worried herself and decided to call her physician. Her obstetrician, Dr. Latham, cleared his schedule on the spot when his office manager informed him that Mrs. Erich Shandon requested an appointment. After only a brief examination, Shanna's doctor happily announced to her that she was pregnant.

Shanna was stunned and terrified over her physician's prognosis. She knew that the only sexual encounter that she had been in was with Ricardo and that he had to be the father of her baby. Panic over took her, and she had no idea what to do about the unfortunate predicament. Crestfallen, Shanna considered abortion but devised a plan to possibly rectify the dreadful situation that had befallen her. She decided to attempt to try to convince her husband that the baby was his, so she created an alternative escape. Knowing that Erich would ruin her life if he learned of her condition, she vowed to come up with a strategy that would keep her marriage in tact and still ensure her status as a supermodel and public celebrity.

Shanna decided that her only way out of her predicament was to have sex with her husband as much as possible, and then when the time was right, she would announce to him that she was pregnant. He would be overjoyed and never know that the baby wasn't his. She knew her plan was farfetched, yet she did not know what else to do. There was no one whom she could confide in except Tony, and he would be furious with her for sleeping with "the sleazy Italian," the phrase he used to describe

Ricardo, so Shanna decided to keep her decision to herself. Her only fear was that she knew that Hattie, their housekeeper at the villa on the island, held the key to unlocking the door of disaster, but Shanna just had to pray that the elderly Haitian woman would never release her suspicions about the father of the baby.

Shanna tried several times to seduce Erich, but he was always too tired after coming home from a stressful day at the office. He tried to make love to her a couple of times, but his exhaustion and stress level left him unable to perform his husbandly duties. Shanna was distressed and at the point of growing frantic over the situation. She knew her time was running out.

One Friday morning, she approached Erich before he left their suite to go down to breakfast. Shanna begged him to come home early, adding that she wanted them to spend a romantic evening together. She informed him that she was going to spend the day shopping for a sexy dress, shoes, and possibly some new jewelry. She also said that she was going to pamper herself at a day spa so that she would be beautiful for him when he came home.

Erich smiled at her, for he wanted his wife to behave in this manner for as long as they had been married. He wanted a socialite wife, who shopped all day, spoiled herself at expensive spas, and waited patiently for him to come home in the evenings. He kissed Shanna long and hard and promised her that he would indeed take off early and hire a limousine to chauffeur them to the best restaurant in the city. He assured her that he would have his secretary make reservations and that this would be an evening to remember.

Erich left the penthouse on a happy note that morning, eager to be done with the day and return to his gorgeous wife. Shanna spent the day just as she had promised that she would. She bought a classy but alluring dress at Bloomingdale's with shoes to match; then she strolled on down to Cartier and purchased a sparkling yellow diamond tennis bracelet and matching earrings. She then took a cab to the most expensive day spa on the Upper East Side called Evan's, where she received the deluxe treatment, which pampered her from head to toe. She too was lighthearted when she left the spa and headed back to their apartment on Madison Avenue. She noticed that a couple of photographers had snapped pictures of her during the day, but she didn't care. This was going to be a great night.

When Erich arrived, Shanna was ready and waiting for him in their bedroom. She was seated on a chaise lounge, sipping a martini and watching the hustle and bustle of life below her in the streets of New York City. She didn't hear Erich enter and was startled when she realized he was standing next to her. He simply stared at her in awe, for she looked more beautiful that he had ever seen her. She smiled and rose to greet him with a kiss, but he pushed her back just to look at her. The dress she wore was pale yellow with tiny sequins and clung to her body like magic. It was long, tapered at the bosom with a slit in the back that plunged down to her waist. Her dark hair hung loose, and the yellow diamond earrings and bracelet made the most elegant statement.

"My god, Shanna!" he exclaimed. "You look spectacular!"

She giggled and put her arms around him. He held her for a few moments, and for the first time in a long time, he was aroused. He could have taken her right then and there and said to hell with going out. But he knew that she had her heart set on an evening out on the town, and he was not going to disappoint her. Little did he know that she would have much rather opted for his first notion and completed her plan. Erich pulled her from him again and told her that he would take a shower and be ready in no time. As he headed for their bathroom, Shanna returned to her chase and finished her martini.

They dined at Le Cote Basque, and Erich ordered the most expensive champagne the house had to offer to celebrate what he called "a reunion with my wife," as a toast. Shanna raised her glass to his, and they both smiled as the crystal glasses came together and made a loud clink. Everyone in the restaurant recognized the well-known couple and marveled at how happy and beautiful they looked together. After they had fully enjoyed their dinner accompanied by the finest wine and finally followed by the chef's specialty, chocolate mousse, Shanna told Erich that she felt absolutely enormous after consuming so much food, but he just kissed her and told her she looked beautiful as they left hand in hand.

They decided to go for a ride in a handsome cab through Central Park, but before they did, Shanna told her husband that she wanted to walk off a little of the food they had eaten. Erich agreed, so they began to stroll leisurely down Fifth Avenue. It was a breezy night in May, and there was still a slight chill in the air. Erich put his arm around his wife and held her close. It had been a happy night for him, the happiest he could remember in a long time.

They walked a few more blocks, then decided to cross over and head back toward the park.

Shanna was feeling a little groggy from the rich meal and red wine, so when Erich mentioned crossing the street, she immediately stepped off the curb onto the side of the street. She didn't see the cab that came racing by, missing her by inches. Erich screamed her name and jerked her roughly by the arm and out of the way of the speeding taxi.

With the mighty jerk by her husband that most definitely saved her life, Shanna lost her footing and fell backward with a heavy thud onto the sidewalk. As her back crashed into the pavement, her neck snapped, causing her head to hit hard as well. The passersby all screamed as they watched the lovely young woman nearly be mowed down, who was now unconscious on Fifth Avenue.

Erich yelled for someone to call an ambulance as he held his wife's head in his hands and watched her frantically. The paramedics finally arrived, and after examining her briefly to make sure there were no back injuries, they whisked her off to the hospital in a wail of blaring sirens and red flashing lights. Erich rode beside his wife and watched as the medical crew took her blood pressure and examined her head. He could see that there was blood in her hair, and he

was terrified that her skull might be cracked or that she might have a serious concussion.

As they wheeled her into the emergency room, Erich was told to wait outside until the doctors had time to examine her to determine if Shanna might need surgery or not. Erich paced around the waiting room, worried sick about his wife, as the night slowly turned into daybreak. After what seemed like an eternity, a nurse motioned for Erich to follow her as she led him down a long corridor, pointing him toward a door labeled E2, which he took to mean Emergency Room 2. As he entered, Erich heard the steady bleep of a noise coming from a machine that was hooked up to his wife, monitoring her every move. He rushed toward her, only the nurse held him back, telling him not to disturb her but to just sit quietly beside her, and the doctor would be in momentarily.

Erich walked softly and slowly to his wife's bed and sat down in a chair beside her as he reached for her hand. She moaned gently when she felt his touch, but she did not stir. Erich watched her intently as tears streamed down his face. "My God," he whispered, "if I lose her now, I will kill myself!" He put his head down against the sheet and wept bitterly. He was crying so hard that he didn't hear the doctor when he entered the room.

"Mr. Shandon," he began rather coldly, "I'm Dr. Sloan. I've been assigned to your wife's treatment."

As the doctor looked over Shanna's chart, Erich stood, wiped his eyes on his sleeve, and approached the man. "Hello, Dr. Sloan. I'm Erich Shandon."

The doctor looked at him a little more kindly then and replied, "I know, son. Your father serves on our board."

Erich sniffed, ignored Dr. Sloan's comment about his father, and asked, "How is my wife?"

The doctor then looked back at his chart and answered Erich without even looking up, "I'm happy to say that Mrs. Shandon does not have a serious head injury, just a bad concussion." The doctor continued, "And I can promise you that she'll have a mighty nasty headache."

Erich breathed a sigh of relief, but it was short-lived as Dr. Sloan spoke again. The old doctor cleared his throat and looked straight at Erich. "I am sorry to say though, son, that she did lose the baby."

Erich stared blankly back at him. "What did you say?" he asked.

"I said," Dr. Sloan repeated, "that your wife miscarried. The fall terminated the fetus, but she was only eight weeks along, so there will not be any permanent damage." With that, he explained to Erich that they would keep Shanna overnight for observation and that she should be able to go home in the morning. Dr. Sloan bade the young man a good-bye and good luck, then went to check on his other patients.

After he left, Erich walked back to his wife's bedside in complete shock. He looked at her as she breathed steadily. She had cheated on him yet again; he knew that the baby she had lost was not his.

Shanna must have sensed his presence, for she opened her eyes slowly and stared up at him. She tried to smile at him, which caused pain to race through her head. She winced and closed her eyes again.

Erich continued to look down at her in emotional agony, but he felt he had to speak. "I know about the baby, Shanna."

Hearing his words, she opened her eyes suddenly and looked at him in terror. She didn't say anything at first; then she began to cry. Even though her sobs caused her head to throb, she couldn't help herself. She looked up at him again and saw a pained look in his eyes and the depressed look on his face. Tearfully, she began to try and explain about the pregnancy, but Erich stopped her abruptly.

"Oh, just stop it, Shanna!" he yelled. "Cut the goddamn crap! You cheated on me again! Whose was it? Joe's? Or was it your dear brother's?" he said cruelly.

Shanna wept bitterly as he shouted accusations at her. Erich continued to rant and rave around the room until a nurse entered and ordered him to be quiet or she would have him removed from the hospital. He quieted down as the nurse went to Shanna, checked her vital signs, and asked her if she was all right. Shanna managed to sniff out an "I'm okay," enough to appease the woman to leave.

Erich just stood over his wife and stared sadly at her. She couldn't bring herself to look into his eyes again, so she just turned away and watched a bird on a limb outside her window. The thought of her carrying another man's child had ultimately crushed him. Erich had to finally admit to himself that she just did not love him anymore.

He pulled the chair beside her bed again and sat down, taking her hand. She turned to look at him.

"I'm sorry, Erich," she said softly.

He put her fingers to his lips and kissed them gently, closing his eyes. Tears streamed out of them as Shanna watched him, devastated that she had hurt him so badly. Erich finally spoke as he wiped the moisture from his face with the corner of the sheet. "You win, sweetheart. I can't take this anymore. I'll give you a divorce if that is what you want."

Shanna just stared at him in amazement, not knowing what to say.

As Erich rose to leave, Shanna begged him to reconsider their relationship, saying that she had just made a stupid mistake in having an affair. He just shook his head, raised his hand, and told her that it was too late. While Shanna wept and kept pleading for him not to abandon her, he again told her that that was *not* going to happen. "Just tell me one thing," he said in a ragged voice, "whose was it?"

She put her head in her hands and said, "Oh, Erich, please don't ask me that!"

"I want to know," he said solemnly.

Shanna raised her eyes to his and said honestly, "Ricardo."

Erich couldn't find the will within himself to even respond to the name she had just spoken. He simply nodded, turned, and silently left her hospital room.

After he vanished down the hall, Shanna lay back in her bed, put her face into the pillow, and wept harder than she had ever wept in her life.

Back at the penthouse, when Erich entered, all the servants rushed at him wanting to know how Mrs. Shandon was feeling; they had all heard of her fall on the news. He brushed them all away angrily and went to his library. There, he grabbed a decanter of brandy, sank down into a luxurious leather chair, and began to pour drink after drink. He intended on getting drunk, very drunk.

# CHAPTER 62

They experienced a very civil yet somber divorce. Erich was very generous in dividing property with his wife, for he had loved her dearly and wanted her to have everything she needed to be happy and comfortable. He regretted all the things he had done to turn her against him, but she had driven him to madness on so many occasions, causing him to act in ways he never would have thought possible.

They shared custody of the children with Erich keeping them at the penthouse during the week and Shanna taking them on the weekends. She had not yet decided on where she would live; most definitely, she would have to take a place in New York to be near McKenna and Alex, but she also wanted to spend some time at Hounds Run and at her ranch in New Mexico. Healing was what she needed at this point in time, and depression loomed ever nearer.

By fall of that year, Shanna found herself a single woman, and she longed to get away and collect her thoughts. She weighed a variety of emotions—feeling relief yet saddened over the final end to a long-lived and tumultuous marriage. She really didn't know how to act as a single woman, for she had always had the comfort of a man to help handle the problems in her life, save the one period of time when Tony had been overseas during the horrible pregnancy and birth that forced her to face the choice of adoption.

To escape from it all, Shanna phoned her aunt Sable in Canada and asked her if she could come to Copper Island to recuperate from all the pressure she had been under lately. Sable readily agreed and, in fact, was overjoyed to have her beloved niece come to stay with her for a while. Shanna left the children with Erich's parents. Elise and Alexander were always complaining about not spending time with the children, so they were thrilled to get their grandchildren for at least a couple of weeks. After the nanny called and affirmed their arrival at the Shandon estate in Greenwich, Shanna hopped a flight to Seattle and then chartered a sea plane to carry her on into Victoria. From there, a boat would meet her and transfer her to her aunt's castle on Copper Island.

Sable was ecstatic with the arrival of her niece, whom she revered as a daughter. After all, she had taken Shanna in long ago, and an everlasting bond had formed between them. So in anticipation of Shanna's arrival, Sable had instructed Jerome, her butler, to tidy the place and make it most welcome.

Shanna's plane landed in an atmosphere of mist and fog, but the accomplished pilots she hired effortlessly carried her to safety. Sable met her at the local yacht

club, and the two women were delighted to see each other once again. Shanna told her aunt about her divorce from Erich, which had been in every newspaper around the world. Sable was sympathetic; however, she was inwardly glad that the marriage had come to an end, for her niece's sake.

While on Copper Island, Shanna and Sable mostly sat and talked beside a roaring fire, drinking hot apple cider prepared by the ever-capable Jerome. Shanna's mood continued to remain in the dungeon, so Sable opted to revive her niece's spirits. Sable phoned an old friend of her husband's and invited a young woman to visit.

Natalie was a beautiful blond widow who had been married to a Canadian prime minister who was close friends with Markus Chandler. She and Sable had met at a political dinner and had gotten along famously and had formed a lifelong friendship. Natalie Chamberlain was a lovely young woman and was also experiencing a bout of depression, mourning her lost husband. Sable had been a rock for her, which made her ever indebted to the woman.

Shanna and Natalie found that they had a lot in common. Shanna was thrilled to co-invest in Natalie's lifelong dream of restoring old hotels. The two women developed an endearing relationship as well as a business partnership, and Shanna promised to always stay in touch with her newfound friend.

When Shanna returned to New York, she called her ex-in-laws to tell them that she had returned and would be coming to collect the children. After she hung up the phone at LaGuardia, she located her driver who transported her to Connecticut in silence. She dreaded visiting Erich's parents, for they still despised her and were predictably joyous over the divorce. Thus, she dreaded the confrontation of seeing them again. When she arrived at the Shandon estate in Greenwich, she was greeted by their ever-stodgy butler Clarence, after the limousine carried her through the massive iron gates to the front entrance. Shanna giggled at the pageantry that awaited her arrival but scoffed at why it was all necessary.

Alex and McKenna were happy to see their mother when she arrived. They had missed her but innately knew that she was under a lot of pressure and could not be the mother that they truly wanted her to be. The anticipated reception she received at her in-laws' home was exactly what Shanna expected. They were cold to her and tried their best to persuade her to transfer custody of the children to Erich, thinking that his influence would carry them further in life.

Shanna tolerated her mother-in-law's badgering as long as she could, but after a while, she had to get away from the insufferable older woman. When Elise went to check with the cook about their evening meal, Shanna bolted and ran to the stables. She felt that a nice ride in the snowy woods would help clear her head and put her in a better mood. Shanna loved horses and was an accomplished rider, so she instructed the stableman to saddle up their most spirited stallion, for today she felt like racing into the wind and hopefully never coming back. Patrick, the stable hand, excitedly agreed to saddle their prize horse, Conundrum, a chestnut stallion who was a descendent of the great thoroughbred Man O' War.

While her horse was being prepared, Shanna wandered through the luxurious barn greeting the other horses that were residing in their ever so lavish stalls. She laughed and muttered, *Some people don't even live this good!* Suddenly, she felt a presence beside her and turned to look into the face of her now ex-husband, Erich.

"What are you doing here?" she said nervously.

Erich moved closer to her, pinning her against a stall, and replied, "There's no law against visiting someone's parents and children . . . now is there?" he smirked.

Shanna smelled whiskey on his breath and knew that he had been drinking, and fairly heavily, if she was any judge.

Erich continued to press himself against her and slur accusations toward her about who she had been sleeping with now that she was a single woman. He lowered his mouth to hers and kissed her savagely, biting her lip.

Shanna was terrified and furious at how he was treating her; so with every ounce of her strength, she pushed him away, causing him to fall against the opposite stable. The horses all neighed at the disturbance as Shanna raced back to the opening of the stable. Patrick had Conundrum ready, so without a word, Shanna leapt onto the handsome stallion's back and raced out into the night across the Shandon property.

A steady mist of snow and ice had begun to fall in Connecticut. Shanna continued to ride into the precipitation in full force to escape her current situation. Conundrum carried his rider eagerly, for he was excited to be out of his stall and allowed to run freely by his mistress atop, whom he could sense was a horsewoman, and would allow him his freedom in a controlled manner.

As Shanna and her horse raced into the night, the visibility grew exceedingly worse. Carelessly, she reined Conundrum into a thicket of woods where a protruding branch on an old oak tree stuck her full in the face, knocking her from the horse's back.

Conundrum paced nervously around his fallen mistress. The intelligent horse somehow felt responsible for causing her harm, yet there was nothing he could do. He pranced around for nearly an hour, then headed back toward the stable.

# CHAPTER 63

Nickolai Tarkonovitch hated the holidays. He had been joyfully married to Angelic, a beautiful French woman for seventeen years. They had experienced the idyllic life. He was of Russian nobility; she was from the French court of Charlemagne, and their love for one another was endless. Sadly, two years prior, Angelic had been out riding. The horse attempted to jump a log, enviably throwing his rider to the side. The fall unfortunately broke Angelic's neck and fractured her skull so badly that the doctors gave her a very grim outlook. Nickolai agonized over the decision to cease her life support but, in the end, saw no other alternative. Since her death, he had predictably remained in a trancelike state, not relating to anyone or seeing to any of his business matters. Out for his nightly ride, he too was looking for a way to somehow clear his mind and lighten his thoughts of depression.

The snow continued to fall as Nickolai and his horse made their way through the woods. The Tarkonovitch property backed up the Shandon estate, but being as elusive as he was, Nickolai had never ventured out to meet the influential couple.

The horse whinnied as they approached a clearing in the forest. Nickolai noticed an unconscious figure lying in the snow in his path. He immediately bolted from his horse and knelt by the hurt figure in the snow. As he turned her over, Nickolai noticed that she was very beautiful, and his mind instantly reverted back to his beloved wife who had been killed in a similar accident. This woman had obviously crashed into a tree limb and needed immediate care. Nickolai mounted his horse and placed his rescued victim in front of him and raced back to his castle with her in his arms.

The Tarkonovitch Castle was named Winterhill. The family had owned the property since World War II, when so many of the Russian immigrants fled to America. Nickolai's father had been a pioneer in many industries, leaving his offspring a hefty settlement of many millions when he passed on.

Nickolai had enjoyed his life of privilege, yet it had come with a lot of sacrifices. When he met Angelic, he thought that her presence in his life would bring him great joy for the rest of his years, yet her sudden death had delivered him great anguish. So when he laid eyes on the mysterious maiden lying in the snow on his property, he felt as if the gods had handed him back happiness on a silver platter.

Shanna awoke with a pounding headache three days later and looked into the eyes of the most amazing man she had ever seen. A dark-haired gentleman with a whiskered face loomed above her as she battled awareness as to where she was.

Nickolai had never left her side. He had monitored her continuously for seventy-two hours, ignoring his all-too-intrusive housekeeper who was also his former mother-in-law. She kept insisting that he report the situation to the authorities.

Nickolai finally snapped as a result of Helga's badgering and threatened her viciously that if she so much as revealed one tiny word to anyone, he would throw her out of the castle and cut her off from his financial support forever. Helga reluctantly agreed; however, she was furious that he could forget her daughter so easily, and she was terrified at the thought of being stranded in the United States with no funds to return to Europe. So she kept her silence and watched her son-in-law nurse the beautiful stranger who lay helpless in his bed.

Shanna continued to stare into the dark eyes of the man who loomed over her.

He smiled and gently stroked her forehead, which still pounded from the fall. Nickolai spoke softly to her and said, "How are you, my princess?"

Shanna looked at him bewildered and replied, "Who are you?"

Nickolai laughed, reached down for her hand, placed it against his lips with a soft kiss, and responded, "I'm your knight in shining armor."

She still continued to gaze at him in puzzlement and asked, "Where am I?" With that, she tried weakly to sit up, but her head throbbed so that she had to lay back again on the enveloping pillow.

Nickolai calmly told her to stay still and that he would get something to make her feel better.

Helga had been hovering in a dark corner of the room watching angrily, but she leapt to his side when he called her name.

"Go and retrieve some aspirin and prepare some hot tea and warm soup for our wounded visitor and be quick about it," he ordered. He was growing tired of the old woman's insolence, and Helga could tell by the roughness of his voice that he meant business. So she hastened to the kitchen to prepare some chicken broth.

Upon her rush downstairs, Helga forgot about the pain relievers, so Nickolai went and found them himself. He sighed in irritation again but quickly returned to Shanna's bedside. "Here you go, my sweet," he said tenderly.

She reached out and took the pills from him and quickly downed them with a cold glass of water that he handed her. Shanna did manage to sit up then as he helped her puff up the pillows behind her back. He took her hand again and just stared at her. She asked him again with more persistence, "Who are you?"

He smiled his brilliant smile again and announced, "I am Nickolai Tarkonovitch, from Russia, and you are in my castle called Winterhill."

Shanna looked at him blankly and said, "How did I get here?"

He explained about how he had found her lying helpless in the woods and that she had obviously fallen from her horse, for he had seen the hoofprints in the snow. She continued to stare at him but did not speak. "Do you remember your accident, my dear?"

Tears slowly began to roll down her face as she replied, "No, I can't recall anything at all."

Nickolai took her into his arms and told her not to worry, that he would take care of her, and that she was going to be all right. She put her arms around his neck, thankful for his comforting hug. He pushed her back gently and said, "Now, can I ask you something?"

"What?" she sniffed.

He touched her nose tenderly with his handkerchief and inquired, "What is your name?"

She looked at him in bewilderment as fear ran through her. "I do not know!" she exclaimed; then she began to cry.

Nickolai pulled her quickly into his embrace again and whispered gently into her hair, "It's all right, baby. Everything will be okay." He continued to rock her back and forth until Helga entered the room carrying a tray and cleared her throat in a rude manner.

Nickolai turned and looked at her in irritation as she said bluntly in broken English, "I've brought the food." She placed the large silver platter on a stand and abruptly left the room.

He helped Shanna get situated in her bed with the heavy tray and offered to help her with the broth.

She laughed and said, "I think I'm strong enough to feed myself!"

Nickolai grinned at her and started to pull a chair closer to the bed when he heard the heavy chimes ring through the castle, indicating that someone was at the door. He couldn't imagine who would be calling on him, for he knew no one in the area, and the property was securely sealed off by an iron fence that was strong enough to keep out Hitler's army. He decided that the gardener must have left the gates open when he arrived early that morning to tend the grounds. And, he concluded, the stable boy must have kenneled the Dobermans that guarded the property like Cerebus guarded hell's gates. Nonetheless, whoever it was, he wanted to get down to the door before Helga had a chance to open it.

Nickolai raced down the winding staircase and just barely beat the housekeeper to the entryway. He told her that he would answer the door and ordered her back to the kitchen. He opened the massive portal slightly and saw two police officers standing outside. The light snow had speckled their dark blue uniforms. "Yes?"

The two gentlemen looked at him in curiosity, for everyone in the community had wondered about the elusive stranger who resided in the dark rock castle on the hill. Finally, one of the officers spoke and said, "We're sorry to bother you, Mr. Tarkonovitch; however, a young woman disappeared a few days ago while out riding in this area, and she hasn't been seen since. Her horse ran back to the Shandon estate on the other side of the woods without a rider, and there has been no trace of her at all. We wondered if you might know anything about her disappearance."

Nickolai stared at them solemnly, yet fear was churning inside of him. He stared at the two men intensely for a few moments, then replied, "No, I know nothing of a

young woman. You see, I get out very seldom and do not watch television, so I have heard no reports."

The two policemen looked at each other, a little intimidated by Nickolai's gruff response. The second man spoke then and said, "But Mr. Tarkonovitch, her disappearance has been on the cover of every major newspaper. Surely, you must have seen the reports."

Nickolai began to grow very impatient with their persistence and said loudly, "Look, gentlemen, I have companies all over the world, and I stay very focused on my businesses. I told you that I know nothing about this young woman, so please get off of my doorstep and leave my property!" With that, he slammed the heavy oak door in their face.

Reluctantly, they turned to leave until they heard the door swing open again. As they continued to make their way down the icy walkway, they heard Nickolai yell, "And that's Count Tarkonovitch!"

Nickolai's brush with the lawmen bothered him greatly and made him terribly afraid that the authorities would not give up their search and that they would return to question him again. He refused to lose his new love, so he made up his mind to escape with her to Europe. He raced back up the stairs and found Shanna sitting up straighter in her bed and looking much better. She had managed to set the heavy tray on the floor, and he noticed that she had finished every bite of the soup and toast that Helga had prepared.

He quickly moved and sat beside her on the bed. He took her hands in his and said in an urgent voice, "Listen, my dear, I know a doctor in London who specializes in head injuries. I want to take you there to see if you are all right and see if he can help you regain your memory."

She looked at him quizzically saying, "But Nickolai, there must be a doctor here who can help me, wherever *here* is."

He nervously watched her and replied, "I know, my dear, but this man is excellent, and I think we should take you to the best physician in the world for your type of injury." He knew time was of the essence, and he didn't want to risk losing her; he had to persuade her to go to Europe or else. Shanna finally agreed to fly to London with Nickolai, for she was helpless, she trusted him, and she didn't know what else to do. Hell, she thought, she didn't even know who she was or where she had come from.

Nickolai had a helicopter come to Winterhill and fly them to the small airport where he kept his private jet. He had phoned ahead and hired a pilot, who would carry them across the Atlantic. Shanna was still very weak, but she was able to sit up and enjoy the view as they sailed through the air in Nickolai's luxurious plane.

They landed at Heathrow at a section restricted to privately owned airplanes. From there, a limousine whisked them away to Nickolai's flat in the heart of London, overlooking the Thames River.

After sitting for so long on the flight over, Shanna assured him that she was strong enough to walk inside.

The interior of the dwelling was beautifully decorated yet very inviting and comfortable. The butler had built a fire in the fireplace, and the maid had already prepared a light lunch for them. Although they were so exhausted from the trip, they did not eat very much.

Nickolai carried Shanna upstairs to his bedroom and put her into bed. He assured her that he would return momentarily, but there was a phone call that he needed to make first. After he left the room, the maid knocked lightly on the door, then entered shyly. She informed the missus that Count Tarkonovitch had called ahead and instructed her to purchase a variety of essentials that "my lady" might need.

Shanna watched as the woman entered a huge closet and reappeared with an elegant silk nightgown with matching robe and slippers. She laid them on the bed, and with a curtsey, she was gone. Shanna managed to slip out of bed and into the delicate lingerie that Nickolai had purchased for her. *Who is this kind and mysterious man?* she thought. With that, she crawled back under the covers and was asleep within seconds.

Nickolai had indeed gone to his study to make a phone call. He spoke with the doctor he had told Shanna about, and his old friend assured him that he would visit her in the morning. Nickolai felt sure that she was all right; however, he would feel more relieved after a physician looked at her. But, he decided, he didn't care if she ever regained her memory.

The next morning, Shanna awoke to find Nickolai asleep on an antique sofa in the corner of the room. He was lying there so peacefully, yet he looked awfully scrunched up and uncomfortable. She got out of bed and walked over to him. He didn't stir, so she knelt down and began to study his features. He was very handsome, with dark features, a broad muscular build, but had a narrow waist and hips; and she marveled at his height. He was well over six feet tall, yet he was curled up on the love seat like a small boy.

She was still surveying him as he opened his eyes and saw her looking him over. He reached out and pulled her to him, and before he could help himself, he was kissing her eagerly and hungrily. She kissed him back, letting her emotions overtake her. Nickolai rose from the sofa and swooped her into his arms. He carried her to the bed, and before either of them knew what was happening, they were entwined in each other's arms and kissing madly. Nickolai feverishly pulled her nightgown from her body, and the beauty of her figure took his breath away. He quickly stripped out of his wrinkled clothes and was instantly back with her as their bodies melted together.

Nickolai stopped for a moment and looked down at her. He spoke in a husky voice filled with lust, "Do we want to go all the way with this?"

Shanna looked back at him eagerly and whispered, "Yes!"

With joy in his heart, Nickolai pulled her under him and entered her with full force. She gasped as he penetrated her, and joy filled her too as she felt this wonderful

and powerful man holding her, kissing her, and loving her with his entire body and soul. When it was over, they both lay entwined in utter satisfaction and happiness, breathing heavily as they enjoyed the pleasure they had both felt. Nickolai pulled her lips to his and kissed her. Then he asked, "By what name shall I call you, my love?"

She thought for a moment, then said, "I like the name Anna; just call me Anna."

Nickolai grinned and replied, "It sounds Russian; I like it too!"

Later that morning, the doctor came and examined Shanna thoroughly. He found her to be fine; she had just suffered a slight concussion. As for her memory loss, he explained to them both that there was nothing that could be done except to give it time. Nickolai thanked his friend and offered to walk him to the door. He assured Shanna that he would return shortly after he paid the doctor and arranged for their lunch.

As he left to go downstairs, Shanna noticed that there was a television in the room, so she walked over and turned it on. She couldn't even remember when she had seen or heard about anything that was happening in the world and thought that she would watch a little news until Nickolai returned.

Shanna flipped through the channels, smiling at the British shows that she passed by. At last, she found a London news station and stopped there. After the stories about the unrest and hunger around the world, a celebrity report caught her attention. Suddenly, she saw her own face on the screen and scenes of her modeling and acting days. The broadcaster also talked about her frantic husband and two devastated children and grief-stricken brother.

Shanna sat transfixed, aghast at the sight she was seeing in front of her. In an instant, her memory came flooding back as she realized that she was the woman in the newscast and that she was being held captive by a Russian count. *He had to have known*, she thought, *after all, he is an international businessman who kept his ear to news reports almost twenty-four hours a day*. Hearing Nickolai at the door, Shanna flicked off the TV and waited for him to enter.

He stepped into the bedroom and looked at her and smiled. "The doctor says you're going to be just fine in a few days," he announced.

Shanna just glared at him, not saying a word.

"What is it, sweetie?" he asked, moving toward her.

"Stay away from me, you kidnapping bastard!"

Shocked at her outburst, Nickolai stood where he was, instinctively knowing why she had snapped at him. He looked down and saw the remote lying by her side. He started toward her again and said, "Sweetheart, let me explain."

"There's nothing to explain!" she screamed. "You kept me hidden from the world and hidden from my own identity. How could you do that?"

Nickolai leapt to her side, but she turned away from him and began to cry. She wept bitterly until he finally pulled her to him and said over and over again how sorry he was. He told her the story of Angelic and how tragically she had died. He

begged her to forgive him and to understand why he had felt the need to shelter her and keep her as his own. "I love you, Anna, with all my heart and soul. I did what I did initially to heal my pain, but now I have fallen for you with all of my being," he said sincerely.

Shanna looked at him and noticed that tears were rolling down his face. "My name is Shanna," she whispered.

"I know," he replied.

They looked at each other for several minutes, neither of them saying a word. Finally, Shanna spoke softly, "I've been falling in love with you too, Nickolai, especially after this morning. You truly are a good man, and you saved my life. What you did, however, was wrong, but I love you anyway."

Overjoyed, Nickolai pulled her to him and held her so tight she thought she would break. "You're squashing me," she giggled. "And one more thing," she asked, "can I call you Nicki?"

He smiled his broadest grin ever and answered, "Only if you want me to come running, sweetheart!" With that, Nicki pulled Shanna to him, and they made love until dinnertime.

# CHAPTER 64

Nickolai Tarkonovitch and Shanna Somers Shandon were married at a basilica in Rome as the world looked on. When Shanna resurfaced after a month since her disappearance, the media went wild with the news of her reappearance. Reporters across the globe were in a frenzy over the Russian nobleman wedding the American starlet. Nickolai was extremely uncomfortable with the constant intrusion from the press and much more upset by the ever-present photographers who captured their every move. Shanna, who was used to living life in a fishbowl, tried to comfort her new husband and assured him that the hubbub would end soon. "Rest assured," she promised, "our wedding will be old news by next week."

Nickolai realized that there was nothing he could do about the press except to hire security guards to surround them until they left for their honeymoon. He had arranged for his jet to fly them to Hawaii, where they would continue on to Fiji, Tahiti, and, finally, to Australia, where they would vacation for a month. Shanna was overwhelmed at where her life had finally taken her. Throughout all the trials, tribulations, and heartbreaks, the fates had finally seen fit to honor her. This was going to be the happiest time of her life. She and Nicki stopped in New York where she said hello and then good-bye to her children before they left for their long honeymoon. They met their mother in a private club at the airport, accompanied by a nanny. McKenna and Alex really didn't know what to say to her and stood quietly as she hugged and kissed them. At last, the private flight attendant Nicki had hired summoned them, saying that the pilot was ready to take off. Shanna bid one last farewell to her children, then left to board the luxurious plane. As the jet took off into the air, the children and their nanny waved upward toward the sky. Shanna laid her head on Nicki's shoulder as they soared through the clouds, and she realized happily that all the human misery she had experienced in her life had finally come to an end.

# EPILOGUE

Erich Shandon awoke in his bedroom lying diagonally across the bed, still wearing his clothes from the night before. There was an empty bottle of scotch beside him, and he reeked of liquor from head to toe. The room was spinning, and his head throbbed uncontrollably. He moaned and rolled over, feeling a lump beneath him. The empty bottle rolled onto the floor as Erich reached behind his back and found the remote control. Out of sheer misery, he turned on the television to take his mind off his pain.

Suddenly, it all came back to him. Shanna had gotten married yesterday. He flipped through the channels until he found CNN. The news was nonstop about her marriage to Count Nickolai Tarkonovitch.

Erich watched as they exited the Italian basilica amid a shower of rose petals and a cacophony of white doves. His heart sank as he realized that the only woman he had ever loved now belonged to another man.

Erich continued to scroll through the channels, wanting to forget the whole event. Unfortunately, nearly every station was broadcasting the extravaganza. Finally, in frustration, he turned off the television and threw the remote across the room. He closed his eyes, yet the wedding scenes kept playing over and over in his mind. Suddenly, Erich began to feel sick, his stomach churning. Unsteadily, he rose to his feet and stumbled to the bathroom. He closed the door, turned to the toilet, and vomited violently.

**the end**

*Other Novels by*
*Tammy Andrews*

*The Sea Of Faith*
*Love, Let Us Be True*
*Of The Night Wind*
*The Moon Lies Fair*
*The Cliffs Of England*
*The Tide Is Full*
*The Sea Is Calm*
*In The Tranquil Bay*
*A Land Of Dreams*